M000170158

DEATH BY
THE THAMES

An absolutely gripping crime mystery full of twists

GRETTA MULROONEY

Tyrone Swift Book 9

Joffe Books, London
www.joffebooks.com

First published in Great Britain in 2021

© Gretta Mulrooney 2021

Cover art by Nick Castle

ISBN: 978-1-80405-027-9

For Fleur, a port in the storm

CHAPTER 1

She picked up the card that her parents had sent with a cheque inside for £5,000 and smiled at their distrust of online banking. They couldn't make the wedding because of her father's ill health. He'd recently had a heart scare and wasn't allowed to fly. The card was hand-embroidered by her mother and featured doves perched on the branches of a lime-green tree, carrying little crimson hearts in their beaks. Inside, her mother had written in her tiny, elegant hand,

Darling Toni, We'll be thinking of you and Sam on your special day. Remember the saying, "Marry in September's shrine, your living will be rich and fine."

'Rich and fine.' She laughed to herself in the bedroom mirror. 'Rich and fine.' She doubted that she and Sam would ever be rich and neither of them had such aspirations. But she would look pretty fine today, if she said so herself.

She'd wanted to be on her own to prepare for her wedding. No fuss, bother or friends flitting around. Keep everything simple. She'd learned from her first marriage to Alec. Maybe she should have noted the old adage about a March wedding, *If you wed when March winds blow, joy and sorrow both you'll know*. The joy had lasted just months.

1

She'd been twenty-two, riding high on the glow and promise of love. Alec was a hedge fund manager. She'd never really understood what that meant, except that he was wealthy, swimming in money. His mother had wanted them to have a big, showy wedding, so that was what they'd had. Such a grand affair wasn't her kind of thing at all, but she'd taken the path of least resistance and gone along with it. It had taken months of planning and it was huge and expensive. Her dress alone, bought by Alec, had cost thousands. It had been a frothy, lacy affair with fiddly buttons, a voluminous skirt, a tulle veil and a long train. Inside it, she'd felt packaged and restricted. The lace was so fine, she'd worried that she'd tear it before she got to the church. She'd resembled a throwback to Princess Di and when she was struggling into it, assisted by Alec's sisters, she'd felt like a medieval monarch preparing for their public.

There'd been pageboys and flower girls throwing rose petals from wicker baskets. The masses of blossoms, bursts of red and yellow, had made it seem as if whole Dutch bulb fields had been harvested. The ceremony was held in the fifteenth-century church at the heart of the Suffolk village where Alec had grown up. Next was a lavish, four-course lunch for 200 guests in the orangery of a five-star hotel, with crates of Dom Pérignon and a live band, followed by a honeymoon in Fiji and then back to a house in Highgate.

Afterwards, she couldn't remember much about it. It had seemed like a dream. Eight months later, she'd had a miscarriage and two weeks after that, Alec had left her for a woman he'd met at his tennis club.

So — this wedding was modest and low key, jointly planned by her and Sam. He'd been married before too, with what he referred to as 'all the fireworks'. This time, there'd be no bridesmaids, flower girls, pageboys or best man. Just twenty friends at a register office and lunch in a local bistro. She was going to be *in* the day and recall every minute of it. She didn't want to tempt fate.

She'd risen at eight, had peppermint tea with a croissant and raspberry jam followed by a lovely long shower. She dried and smoothed her hair and twisted it up on top of her head, then slipped on the knee-length, ivory silk shift dress that she'd bought from Oxfam's online shop for £70. Next, she fixed a thin circlet of gold baby's breath flowers into her hair. Cream satin ballet shoes completed the picture.

She had half an hour before Conor was due to take her to the register office. He'd be driving his vintage red-and-yellow motorbike and sidecar. He and Sam shared a passion for motorbikes. They'd met attending a classic show. Sam's was a burgundy 1956 Norton, also with a sidecar. She'd accepted Conor's offer of transport after a few too many glasses of wine. His Lambretta had a habit of breaking down, so she was keeping her fingers crossed. It would be a great way to arrive, though.

The photos will be amazing, Conor's wife Lucy had said with a smile. She and Conor had married in Dorset and she'd travelled to the church in a pony and trap. *At least a motorbike won't deposit a pile of steaming manure outside the register office,* she'd told Toni. *I had to be careful where I stepped in all my finery.*

Toni was amazed that she was getting married again. When she'd reached thirty, the decent straight men had all seemed to be taken, leaving the weirdos, the shy and the frankly repulsive on the market. It hadn't bothered her much. She hadn't even been sure that she wanted another marriage, after that first misstep. She had a job she liked, her own little flat in Archway above a chemist, a circle of friends. Then Sam was sitting there in Conor's garden with merry eyes and a shy smile and life altered course. She was in no doubt that she wanted to marry and spend the rest of her life with him.

Her phone rang.

'Hi, Toni. Just checking in. Everything okay?'

'Hey, Lexie. Everything's fine.'

'Butterflies?'

'Slightly, but pleasant ones.'

'Not having any doubts?'

Lexie would be all ears if she said she was. She couldn't understand why Toni wanted to marry again, having helped to pick up the pieces when Alec bolted.

'None at all,' Toni replied firmly.

'Was Sam having a wild night out last night?' Lexie teased. She had a running joke that he was the Tom Hanks of the finance world. The go-to man for reliability and decency. On Lexie's lips, these qualities sounded undesirable.

'Hardly. He rang me and said he was going to put his feet up and have a takeaway and a bottle of beer. I have to tell you, I'm gorgeous — he's got no reason to go out anymore.'

'Course you are. Remind me, what's Sam wearing?'

'Blue chinos, deep pink shirt, and a tweedy pink-and-blue-flecked waistcoat that he got in Lucy's charity shop.'

'An upcycled wedding, then. Well, if you must get hitched again, I'll be keeping an eagle eye on Sam and making sure that he behaves himself. See you there, very soon.'

It was a mild, sunny morning with tiny puffs of high white cloud. A lovely, temperate day for a wedding. Now that she was ready, she was restless. She wandered into her living room and stood at the window that overlooked the street. She hadn't spent much on the flat, but she'd had triple glazing installed. It meant that it was a surprising oasis of calm above the north London bustle. She opened the window and took deep breaths of warm city air, tasting diesel, dust and something metallic. She loved it, even if it was poisoning her lungs. The street seemed cleaner and quieter than usual, but maybe that was her mood.

The parade of shops opposite had been her view for the last eight years: the greengrocer with stacks of fruit and vegetables, the mini-mart with post office, the betting shop, the craft emporium, the DIY shop that was so tiny it could only allow two customers at a time, and the wine cellar. Beside that was the charity shop that had changed hands with dazzling speed, and was now called *Go Kids Boutique* and run by Lucy. Just past the shops was Meadow House, a low-rise block of upmarket, assisted living apartments for older people. Toni managed it and nine others around north London. Every evening, in every season, seventy-two-year-old Dora Melides came on to her first-floor balcony around eight o'clock and sang '*O Sole Mio*'. She'd appeared in operas all over the world, but she only ever chose that song. Some locals came regularly to listen and threw flowers to her.

She'd miss Dora's nightly performance and her little home perched above the street. She'd sanded the floorboards and painted the walls the palest of greens, but it was too small for a couple. She'd finally sold it after a couple of buyers had messed her around. Everything was now ticking along with solicitors. She and Sam were having a honeymoon in the Scilly Isles at the beginning of October, so completion was timetabled for later that month. Once she'd handed the keys over, she'd live in Sam's terraced house in Belsize Park.

A police car wavered into her line of vision, stopping at the zebra crossing to let a man and three children cross. It accelerated slowly and pulled in by the kerb. She saw a uniformed woman lower the passenger window and peer out, then up. The woman met Toni's gaze and ducked back into the car. Toni shut the window and went to the kitchen for a drink of water. She'd have a final pee, a last check in the mirror and apply a dash of lip gloss.

She was puckering her lips when the doorbell sounded. *Conor's early*, she thought. He was more nervous than she was about today. He'd introduced her and Sam and he took his responsibilities seriously.

She ran down the stairs to the door, lip gloss still in her hand. Two police constables, a man and a woman were standing there. The sun was in the woman's eyes and she raised a hand to shield them, giving the odd impression that she was about to salute.

'Are you Ms Toni Sheringham?'

'That's right.'

'May we come in? We have some difficult news.'

'What news? Is it about work? Has one of the residents had an accident?' She didn't move. She didn't want these two barging into her morning.

'It would be best to talk inside.'

She saw Conor behind them, pulling up on his bike. Passers-by turned to stare and smile. It had that effect on people, probably because it resembled a large toy. She waved to him and he waved back, removing his helmet. 'This is my lift to my wedding,' she told them.

Then Conor was there, saying her name, and the police were talking about Sam, and she seemed to have frozen. The traffic noise increased. Brakes screeched by the crossing. A horn blared.

Conor helped her up the stairs.

She sat on the sofa, gripping her lip gloss and listened to the officers say ridiculous, unbelievable things. Glancing down, she saw that one of her cream pumps had a dirty mark on the toe. She slipped it off.

'Look,' she said to the female police officer. 'Isn't that just typical? Scuffed already.'

'Ms Sheringham — Toni — have you heard what we've said?'

'Yes,' she said, 'but I don't understand. I don't understand any of it.'

CHAPTER 2

'Ruth really isn't being fair. Marcel doesn't have any children. Let *him* uproot — he'd get a job in London. If Ruth wants to live with him, marry him, then she should set up home with him here, so that you can still see Branna. Guernsey is hardly on the doorstep. It might as well be Australia, as far as Branna is concerned. She'll realise she's a long way from you.' Simone crossed her elegant legs and waved a slender hand. 'You should fight your corner, Ty.'

Tyrone Swift said nothing and gritted his teeth.

Mary Adair, Swift's cousin, poured more coffee and said in her light, even voice, 'It's complex, of course. Whatever happens, all you can do is make it as easy as possible for Branna.'

Simone shook her long curls. 'Always the diplomat, Mary. We'll never split up, but if we did, and you met someone else and proposed moving to another country with Louis, I'd pursue you through the courts like a hellhound. *No one* would separate me from my child.'

They'd eaten a wonderful lunch, cooked by Simone: pasta with salmon and roast vegetables, a huge green salad and a fruit fool. Now they were having coffee and homemade chocolate truffles. Swift wanted to tell Simone to mind her own business, especially as his daughter Branna was playing with Louis nearby on the balcony. The sliding glass door was closed, and Branna had impaired hearing but even so. 'It's a painful subject,' he said. 'I'd rather leave it. These chocolates are wonderful.'

Simone smiled. 'Thanks, I tried a new recipe. Louis and Branna can have one each when they come in.'

Swift watched his daughter. It was an unusually warm day for February and her face was glowing in the sun. 'I'm amazed that Branna hasn't spotted them through the glass. Her chocolate radar is usually unerring. You'll be lucky if you limit her to one.'

'Louis understands that sweets aren't negotiable and the health reasons for keeping sugar to a minimum,' Simone said in a prissy tone. 'It's so important to explain these things to children, and to have ground rules and abide by them.'

Implying that he was too lax with Branna. True, probably, and one of the difficulties of the part-time parenting arrangement he had with Ruth. There was a desire to make up for the absences. The guilt factor that made him overcompensate. But Simone did like to harp on.

Louis was carefully sorting and completing a jigsaw. He'd taken his little folding table out to the balcony and was sitting on his bright red chair, head bent, his neat hair parted to one side, like a mini chairman of the board. He was a chunky, stolid boy and looked as immaculate as he had at the start of lunch, dressed as usual in a 1950s type outfit. Today's was a blue striped shirt over navy chinos and a knitted grey checked tank top. Branna was in green leggings and a polka dot sweatshirt, which was spattered liberally with shreds of food and marked with felt-tip pen. She refused to have her hair cut at the moment and it was shaggy and wild. It could also have done with a wash. She'd been staying with him for a couple of days and standards had slipped. There'd have to be a smartening up before she returned to her mother. She danced up and down the balcony, blowing bubbles through a huge wand and watching them float. Swift could hear her shouting in her loud, gruff voice, 'Fly away! Fly away!'

Simone was, as always, a dog with a bone. 'I do hope you're consulting a solicitor, Ty. I'm sure Ruth will. You need to make sure you've got proper legal support, all the i's dotted and t's crossed. There are so many angles to be considered — financial, emotional, and psychological.'

'How is Branna doing since the operation?' Mary asked, aware of his annoyance. 'She seems on sparkling form.'

'So far, so good, everything going to plan. She's adapted remarkably well and post-op, she seemed more concerned that she'd had patches of hair shaved away than about the implants. She's thrilled not to have to wear hearing aids.' Branna had had cochlear implants, with the hope of boosting her hearing and confidence. There'd been a chance that she could lose any remaining hearing if they didn't work well, so it had been a hard decision for him and Ruth to make. His heart had been in his mouth for days before and after the operation.

Simone's phone rang and she left the room to take the call.

'Sorry about Simone going on,' Mary murmured.

'It's okay,' he lied. 'I'm used to her. I can forgive a lot for these chocolates.'

He helped himself to another and bit into the orange centre. He'd accepted some time ago that he had to put up with Simone's opinionated pronouncements. Mary had married her and he loved his cousin dearly. He'd have tolerated Lucrezia Borgia for Mary's sake, and Simone was generous with her time and knowledge. Her expertise as a forensic pathologist had come in handy on some of his cases. He regarded Mary's strong face and warm eyes. They'd been close since childhood and he couldn't imagine life without her.

She took a chocolate. 'Simone does have a point though, Ty. Don't just roll over. Ruth has a habit of getting what she wants. She has a tremendous sense of entitlement, as if she always has a right to come out smelling of roses.'

Mary said he had poor judgement where women were concerned. Ruth had broken their engagement because she'd

9

met and then married Emlyn Taylor. Afterwards, Mary had acknowledged that she'd never liked Ruth. *Too aware of her own beauty*, she'd said. She told him that Ruth had led him a merry dance and still was. But his ex had had her own struggles. Her marriage to Emlyn had gone badly wrong, hardly helped by her getting pregnant after a one-off night together with Swift. Emlyn had developed MS and had become angry and vengeful. Ruth had sunk into depression after Branna was born and the divorce from Emlyn had been painful.

'Mary, what can I do, realistically? If I try to obstruct Ruth's move to Guernsey, it will make things very difficult. She's happy with Marcel, wants to marry him, live by the sea at Fermain Bay and have more babies. Am I going to deny her that? Branna will get to live by a beautiful beach instead of in a London street and she'll have siblings, which is a good thing.'

'She might not like them,' Mary pointed out. Then she relented. 'Okay, I hear what you're saying.'

'When Branna's older, she'll be able to come and go independently. Until then, we'll just have to work out the best arrangement we can.'

It was going to be tricky. Branna's life, based elsewhere, would inevitably separate from his. He wasn't a man who cried easily but he had wept once, in the small hours, anticipating the rift to come.

'When is Ruth getting married?'

'End of April. Branna is building up to it, making big plans. If Ruth's not careful, she'll be overshadowed on the day.'

Mary laughed. 'Well, give me a heads-up if I can help.' She selected a chocolate. 'Regarding the workaday world, does Swift Investigations have any interesting stuff on at the moment?' She was an Assistant Commissioner in the Met and liked to hear about the cases he took as a private detective.

'Something's just come in. I'm going to visit a woman about her drowned fiancé. Tell you more when I've seen her.'

'Sounds harrowing.' She leaned across and ruffled his wayward dark curls. 'No offence, but you and Branna could both do with a visit to a hairdresser. You look like you're raising her in a hippie commune.'

Before he could reply, Branna burst through the door, slopping bubble liquid and pointing her wand imperiously at the table.

'Chocolates! Yes! I having *lots*!'

* * *

Swift stopped to examine the bay window of Camberley chemist and read the white labels on the rows of blue glass jars: *Oxymel Scillae, Syr. Sennae, Syr. Auranti, Aqua Rosae, Tinct. Aromat, Acet Acid*. In front of them was a display of aspirin, paracetamol, cotton wool, plasters, bandages, cough syrups and laxatives. To the right of the shop was a dark green door set in a black-and-white tiled porch, where someone had thrown an empty condom box. The label declared, *Extra Safe*. Any condom should surely offer that certainty. Had someone had sex in Toni Sheringham's doorway? He hated litter, so picked it up, pressed the yellow centre of the flower-shaped cast iron bell and waited.

The woman who answered the door was wearing a paint-spattered shirt and worn jeans. On her feet were brown clogs, no socks. Her hair was covered by a pink beanie hat and she had a streak of golden paint on her pointed chin.

'Toni Sheringham? I'm Tyrone Swift.'

'Are you early?'

'No. Two thirty, as agreed.'

'Oh. I must have lost track.' She saw the empty box in his hand. 'One of the hazards of living above a chemist. I found a couple having a knee-trembler against the door when I came home a while ago. Sometimes there are used condoms on the ground. Sam used to joke that maybe I featured in an alternative London guide. *Come to Toni Sheringham's sheltered porch in Archway beside a handy chemist if you want an outdoor grope.*'

She gave a wry ghost of a smile and stared past him.

'I'll put it in your bin,' he said.

Toni didn't move. She stood, stroking her folded arms. Her nails were bitten down.

'Your bin?' he prompted.

'Oh yes. Sorry. I'm upstairs.'

He followed her up. There was a smell of fresh paint and also something else, like ripe mango or kiwi fruit.

All the furniture had been moved into the middle of the living room, and the edges of the pale honey floorboards were covered with newspaper. A tray with a paintbrush stood on a set of folding steps. One wall was half pale green, half deep gold.

She didn't apologise for the mess. 'I decided to have a colour change, brighten things up. I'm not at all sure about the gold now. What do you think?'

He wasn't sure either. 'It's bold.'

'Oh well, it's just a distraction. I was supposed to be selling this flat and moving in with Sam, but I had to pull out of the deal. Never imagined I'd be redecorating.'

'Maybe just making a change is good.'

'Maybe. Have you come far?' She bit her lip. 'I sound like the Queen. Isn't that what she says?'

'Allegedly. From Hammersmith, where I live.'

She had hooded almond-brown eyes that were full of misery. An interesting face, not conventionally pretty but attractive. 'Near the river?' she said sadly.

She'd be remembering how her fiancé had died. 'That's right. I can smell the Thames from my house and easily take my boat out.'

'Nice. I grew up in Richmond, so I spent a lot of time by the river. Now it's become part of my life in a way I could never have imagined.' She dabbed the paint brush, clearing off excess emulsion and stood it in a jar. 'I thought you'd be older. You sounded older on the phone. I'd pictured you crinkly, grey-haired and stocky, for some reason.'

'Are you disappointed?'

'Oh . . . no.'

There was nowhere to sit because books, magazines, boxes of tissues, candles, jumpers and various other bits and bobs were piled on all the chairs. Toni took an unsteady breath and leaned against a wall. She was thin and wiry, with a boy's body, flat and narrow. When she kicked her clogs off, he saw that her feet were bony, a paler olive than her face and arms. The middle toes on her right foot were strapped together.

'I've suddenly realised, I'm very hungry. I forget to eat. Is it okay if we sit in the kitchen and I make toast?'

'Of course.'

The kitchen was a good size and tidy. It teemed with plants. A lush ivy hung above the large sash window, trailing elegant leaves. The shelves and window ledge held aloe vera, spider plants, basil, a snake plant, oregano and an aspidistra. She switched the kettle on, sliced bread and put it in the toaster. She pulsated with weary tension.

'Would you like a slice?'

'Please.' He wasn't hungry, but it might help her if they ate together.

Toni removed her beanie. Her hair was long and bushy, the same raven black as his, but without the silver streaks. She took an elastic band from her pocket and tied it back.

'My gran always wore her hat in the house,' she said. 'She'd tell me it was to keep her brain warm. I suppose a lot of hat manufacturers went out of business when women stopped wearing them routinely. Cheese, peanut butter, honey or jam for your toast?'

'Jam, thanks.'

She put a tray with a cafetière, mugs, milk, toast, butter and a pot of cherry jam on the table. The coffee slopped slightly, but she didn't notice.

'Breakfast in the afternoon,' she said, blinking rapidly and surveying the tray. 'I'm quite proud of managing to get this on the table. I do a lot of that thing that's supposed to overtake older people — walking into a room and wondering, what did I come in here for?'

'That's grief and stress making you absent-minded. It will pass.' When Ruth had left him, he'd kept losing things.

He'd filled his car with diesel instead of petrol, left shopping in the supermarket, put laundry in the washing machine and forgot to switch it on.

Toni said, with the ghost of a smile, 'At least I manage to remember my own name.' She spread a thick layer of butter on her toast and spooned a small blob of jam on it.

He ate his toast and sipped coffee. She cut her slice into small pieces and ate several quickly, then seemed to lose interest. The light outside was starting to fade and they sat in a warm twilight. The dishwasher beeped three times.

'I'm not right in the head,' she told him, licking a finger, 'but not in the way that people think.'

'What do people think?'

She reached to the worktop for a bowl of sugar and put a spoon in her coffee. 'Sorry, I forgot this if you want some. Mostly, people believe that I'm in denial and torturing myself, because I can't accept that my fiancé deliberately killed himself alongside a fifteen-year-old girl. The implication being that he was having a relationship with a minor. What else would a man in his thirties have been doing with a teenager who none of us had ever heard of?' She sighed. 'The police deem that I'm grieving and distraught and so do my friends. They speak to me as if I'm glass that's about to shatter. I am grieving, of course I am, but the bit of me that's perfectly okay is the bit that doesn't believe that Sam would have been deceiving me, and with a young girl.' She held up a hand as he went to speak. 'It's all right, I haven't asked you to come here to soothe or reassure me.'

'That's just as well, because I often have the opposite effect.'

Toni gazed at him and gnawed the side of a tiny nail. 'Thank you.'

She refilled his cup with paint-smudged fingers, although he didn't want any more of the too mellow coffee. He liked his with a bite.

'I can't find what else to say now. There's so much to say, the words get stuck in a verbal traffic jam, like when the light stays red for ages and you start to believe it'll never turn green. My mind goes blank, too.'

Swift spoke quietly. 'Let me tell you what I know. I read about the deaths after you phoned me. In the early hours of the eleventh of September last year, police retrieved a motorbike and sidecar from the Thames not far from Old Bow Wharf. It had drifted onto a mudbank and was half submerged. The number plate identified the owner as Sam Goddard, your fiancé. The drowned passenger in the sidecar was Naomi Ludlow, aged fifteen. Sam had been thrown clear of the bike and his body was found a couple of hours later, further downstream. Tyre marks and a shard of broken wing mirror indicated that the bike had entered the river from steps at Old Bow Wharf. Sam and Naomi were both heavily sedated when they drowned. A suicide note was found and the coroner's verdict for Sam was suicide.'

Toni said dully, 'Yes. The verdict on Naomi was an open one. She hadn't left an explanation, so there was only Sam's to go on.'

'The police failed to establish how Sam and Naomi knew each other, or any reason why they should have been together, other than that they'd been having a relationship.'

'Neat, isn't it? Tragic and neat.'

'Meaning too neat?'

She twisted in her chair, reached towards the pot of basil on the window ledge, tore off a leaf and chewed it. The scent of a Mediterranean summer filled the kitchen.

'I'm not sure what I mean. I'm just so . . . *angry*. I read somewhere that grief is love that's become homeless. Mine seems to have settled for a home in rage.' She raised her right foot. 'I kicked a door in anger and fractured a toe. Just as well the police weren't here at the time. They'd have recorded it as evidence of my irrationality.' She adopted a solemn tone. '"*Ms Sheringham was noted to be angry and self-harming. Sergeant Delamare advised her to see her GP and gave her a leaflet about bereavement counselling.*" The police got what they wanted from the coroner, so they dusted themselves down and moved on.'

'Do you have any other support? Friends or family?'

'I have amazing friends who are like family. They're kind and consoling, or try to be. Jerome and Chloe — Sam's boss and his wife — Lexie, Conor, Lucy. Lexie's one of my oldest friends. Like my big sister. She sits and advises me to have a good bawl. They're all amazing. They bring me little gifts: tiny savouries, microwaveable soups, creamy porridge, chocolates, wine, vitamin drinks, this amazing posh jam from Fortnum's. I've a fridge full of stuff. See!' Toni got up and opened the fridge door. It was packed with cartons and plastic boxes. She shut it and leaned against it. 'They try to entice me out to films, meals, walks, weekends by the sea. They're lovely to me, everything friends should be. I'm so lucky to have them, but I'm not interested in goodies and outings. All I am interested in is establishing what really happened to Sam.' A little red lamp on a shelf switched on automatically, casting a rosy glow behind her head.

'If you want me to help you with that, I can. I might have to tell you that the police were right. They are most of the time. You'd have to be prepared to hear things that might distress you.'

She switched on the worktop lights and sat down again. 'Fine. I understand. I can handle distress if I *know*.' She tapped her knuckles on the table. 'Have you ever been dumped?'

'In a relationship? Twice.'

'That's awful. I'm sorry.'

'I minded the first time. The second, not so much.'

She ran a hand over the back of the chair beside her. 'My first husband left me. We hadn't been married a year. Sam was so unexpected and amazing. He knew I'd been wounded. He was divorced, but he'd been relieved when his marriage ended.'

'Who was his first wife?'

'Mila Fullbright.'

'Did they have children?'

'No, and they weren't in touch. Sam would never have played away, deceived me. He'd never have been seeing someone else the night before our wedding.'

Swift stared out at the stormy sky. Thin rain was falling. What had happened to Toni Sheringham was terrible, life-changing. People do betray, though. They might not intend to deceive, but they find themselves doing it anyway. Ruth and his recent ex, Nora, had both said similar things to him — *It just happened. I wasn't looking for anyone else.*

He glimpsed Toni's strapped toes and the purple bruise that flowered on the tip of the middle one. Her anger and defiance impressed him, as did her refusal to be soothed, even if her belief turned out to be delusional. It made him want to cheer her on.

'Tell me about the suicide note,' he said.

'Suicide *text*. The police found Sam's phone in his pocket. They say that he and Naomi downed a load of sedatives and he sent a text to himself, saying *FOR TONI*.' She picked up her phone, scrolled and passed it to Swift.

So sorry to do this to you. It's all such a mess. There's no other way out for us. We agreed it's better to end it together, have a long sleep. Tell Naomi's parents we're sorry. Forgive me.

Swift handed the phone back. 'It does seem cut and dried. When was the last time you spoke to Sam?'

'He called me about half five the night he died. He was on his motorbike, heading home from work and he'd stopped for fuel. He planned to get a takeaway and have a quiet evening. He seemed fine. More than fine. Happy.'

'Did he usually travel on his bike for work?'

'No, his bike was for leisure, but his car had an oil leak and it was with the mechanic.'

The doorbell rang and Toni went to see who was calling. Swift heard a faint voice and Toni came in with a petite woman, dressed in layers of grey faded velvet, an earnest expression on her face.

'This is my friend Lucy Wallace,' Toni said. 'She runs the charity shop over the road.'

'Hello, Mr Swift,' Lucy said in low, almost murmuring tones. 'I'm having a coffee break. I just wanted to check that Toni's okay.'

Toni frowned. 'You phoned me this morning.'

'I did. There's no contact quota, is there? I see you're decorating on your day off. Wouldn't it be better to do something nice? Don't forget that pamper voucher we bought you for Christmas. Or you could have a rest, put your feet up.'

'Lucy, I'm not a frail old person. I just work with them.'

'Only saying. It's what friends are for. Isn't that right, Mr Swift?'

'Please, call me Ty.' He was fairly sure that Lucy had dropped in to check him out.

Lucy scanned the table. 'I'm glad you've eaten. I hope it's been more than toast. Did you have that chilli I left for you?'

'I'm having it tonight.'

Lucy glanced at Toni and then addressed Swift. 'What do you make of Toni's idea that she wants a private investigation about Sam's death? Silly question, I suppose. You're hardly going to turn down an offer of work!'

Swift was used to random insults in his line of business, although not usually from whispering women in washed-out fabrics. 'I don't take every case that comes my way. I pick and choose my work. I haven't finished speaking to Toni yet, so it's too early to express an opinion. It's Toni's prerogative to consider a private detective.'

'Well . . .' Lucy seemed nonplussed. Her dull brown hair was escaping from a grip and she tucked a strand in. She hummed under her breath, fossicked in her embroidered cloth bag and gave Toni a purple box. 'Here's that lavender tea I told you about. It's very soothing.'

'Thank you. That's kind of you.'

She put an arm around Toni and fixed anxious eyes on her. 'Would you like to come for supper tomorrow night? Just with Conor and me. We'll put the boys to bed early. A mushroom risotto, the recipe you like, and lots of wine.'

'I'm not sure. I'll get back to you. I need to finish talking to Mr Swift now.'

'Okay. Ring me if you need anything, promise?'

Toni smiled at her. 'I promise.'

'Cross your heart?'

'Cross my heart.'

'Good. I'll let myself out.'

When the door had closed, Toni examined the box of tea bags. 'Do you drink lavender tea?'

'No, just builder's brew.'

'I'm so fond of Lucy and she's very kind. I'm lucky to have such a friend.' Toni opened the bin and dropped the box in from a height. 'But I don't want to be soothed. I want to stay furious.'

'Being angry can be tiring.'

Toni winced. 'It's all that keeps me going. Put my feet up! That's the last thing I want to do.'

'What's your job?' Swift asked.

'I'm an area manager for Solatium Housing. We provide assisted accommodation for older people. I'm responsible for Meadow House across the road, among others.' She sat back down. 'I do hope you'll take the case, but I'd better tell you that I didn't help things by going to the Ludlows' house. Bad move, but it seemed right at the time.'

'When was that?'

'About three weeks after it happened. I couldn't stop thinking about Naomi Ludlow. Who was she? What was she like? Why had she been with Sam? I found out where they lived. Mr Ludlow opened the door but when I told him who I was, he called for his wife. She came to the hallway and she started shaking and crying.' Toni winced at the memory. 'She was so pale, I worried she was going to collapse. I said I just wanted to talk to them, try to understand what had happened. I was pleading. Mr Ludlow shouted at me to go away, so I did. I realised it was impossible and I ran up the road. I had so many questions, but I couldn't ask any of them.'

'Your visit to them was understandable in the circumstances,' Swift said, but he suspected that it might have marred any chance of the Ludlows cooperating with him.

Toni gave him a naked, pleading glance. 'You'll take me on then?'

He couldn't refuse her. She was so raw and bereft and the deaths were unusual, intriguing. 'Yes.'

She slumped with relief. 'Thank you. Thank you from the bottom of my heart. The first thing I'd like you to do is come with me to Docklands, where Sam went into the Thames. I've been wanting to go there and see it with my own eyes, but I haven't had the bottle to go alone. I didn't want to ask my friends, because they'd have tried to talk me out of it and I couldn't bear coping with their anxiety. I don't want to take a wreath or cry, nothing like that. I won't weep all over you or collapse. Will you do that with me?'

'Of course. I need to visit the scene anyway.'

'Thanks. I want to bear witness. Can we go soon?'

CHAPTER 3

Two days later, Swift and Toni took the green-and-blue Docklands Light Railway to East India station, passing blocks of flats and towering offices with hundreds of windows, resembling steel honeycombs. Toni was silent, staring out of the window, her chin tucked down in her scarf. Swift read an abandoned copy of the *Metro*. When they reached East India, a sign on the platform informed them that the station was one of a handful in London that lay on the Greenwich Meridian and invited them to look at the silver line. It ran down the side of the twenty-five-storey Elektron Tower, which overlooked the station. A gleaming sundial flanked it.

'If you stand here,' Swift said, 'you're in the western hemisphere.' He moved away a couple of feet. 'Here, you're in the eastern hemisphere.'

Toni stared at him blankly. 'At the risk of sounding very rude, I don't give a toss about hemispheres. Can we get on with what we came for?'

He pointed towards the exit. They walked towards Old Bow Wharf in a knife-edged wind. It took a good twenty minutes. Toni had a long stride and kept up with him, her knee-high red boots tapping a pacy rhythm on the pavement. Her purple-fringed scarf streamed behind her like a pennant.

Her hair was loose, whipping around her head. Now and again, she'd tuck it into her scarf, but it would escape. Swift had a hood on his jacket and was glad of it. This Docklands area in east London was unfamiliar to him, although his knowledge of waterways indicated that it lay at a confluence of the Rivers Lea and Thames. In the distance, he saw former shipping containers that had been converted to modular housing. They were four storeys high and resembled huge blocks of white, pink, red and orange Lego.

'Did you or Sam have any connection to this area?' Swift asked.

She had her face down against the wind and he strained to hear her.

'No. I'd never heard of this place until the police arrived at my door. I've read up about it since. There's been massive regeneration, with a creative quarter and lots of artists and designers are based here. Sam worked for Spring, an investment management company, and I wondered if he might have been doing business. But Jerome Adcott, his boss, said they didn't have any interests in this part of London. He called in to see me last night. Word has got round that I've hired you.'

'Was he voicing an opinion?'

'He's too oblique for that. He brought me wine and helped me shift some bookshelves. He didn't say much at all. Just that he worried I'd gone back to work too soon.' She grimaced. 'What would I be doing with myself if I wasn't at work?'

Their route took them to a part of the wharf that hadn't yet been redeveloped. They walked past a huge, rusting, orange-brown crane, the broken ground around it pitted with oily puddles, then past a couple of boarded-up sheds and a derelict warehouse, surrounded by mesh gates and *KEEP OUT* notices. Its name was faded but legible — Anderson Spice Merchants Ltd. Someone had sprayed below it: *DOES ANYONE REALLY CARE?* Above the door was an octagonal clock with one hand missing. Once, this place would have been bustling with cargoes of tea, spices, silk and carpets. Now, the only sound was the wind keening.

After about another half-mile they reached the isolated spot where Sam and Naomi had gone into the river. It was at the far end of the wharf area, in a deserted stretch well away from businesses and car parks. One boarded-up shed stood nearby. Swift and Toni paused at the top of some steep stone steps and looked down at the murky, choppy waters. The tide was out and detritus washed against the banks: a hubcap, a leather glove, part of a wooden pallet, plastic bags and containers, a light bulb and scraps of food.

'Such a bleak place to die,' Toni said. 'One of the detectives asked me if Sam had been depressed. When I said he hadn't, quite the opposite, the detective had this dubious expression. He said that Naomi had received treatment for glandular fever and had suffered low moods. He clearly liked the idea of a suicide pact. I told him he was mad.'

Swift's eyes were raw and gritty from the unrelenting, stinging air. The wind was so strong here. Toni wobbled as a gust struck her. She was very near the edge of the steps. Swift put a steadying hand out. She took a pace back and caught at her scarf, tied a tighter knot in it.

'I read that Sam was busy and pressured at work.'

'He was busy, but not in a way that got him down. He liked working hard. One of his colleagues said that he'd been a bit distracted recently, but he was getting married, of course he was!'

'He didn't indicate that he had anything on his mind?'

'Not as such. A couple of weeks before he died, we were finalising the wedding day and honeymoon arrangements. Sam commented that he had just one thing he needed to sort out, and then he could clear the decks for our big day. There was no concern in his voice. I asked if it was anything I could help with and he said no, it was nothing for me to worry about. I presumed he meant something at work.' Toni kicked a scrap of metal away. 'I told the police that apart from not being suicidal, Sam would never have destroyed his motorbike. He didn't own it to pump up his ego or pose as a tearaway or a babe magnet. It had a sedate *sidecar*, for God's sake! He revered the engineering and the beauty of it. It was his joy. He even had a name for it — Bonnie. He loved taking me out for trips to Brighton and far-flung bits of Essex and Surrey at weekends. We pottered and explored. Went to remote woodland and forests, visited junk shops, found out-of-the-way places to eat. He just wouldn't have driven Bonnie into the river with a young girl sitting in my place.' She stopped and raised her face to the wind, eyes closed. Her chin jutted defiantly. 'He said . . . he said that we'd still be jaunting around like that when we were old, with our flask and sandwiches.'

Swift watched two swans land on the river. 'It's hard,' was all he could say.

'Hard doesn't touch it,' she said fiercely. 'It's *savage* and I felt savage, having to listen to the police talk so much *crap*. Sam wasn't a predator who lusted after underage girls. He had everything to live for. He was a mild-tempered, loving man and I won't have him trashed.' She took a bag from her pocket and scattered white crocus flowers from it into the water. 'One of the residents I work with told me the crocus is a symbol of hope. I'm hoping you'll find the truth.'

The wind was at their backs pushing them on as they walked back to the main part of the wharf, passing eye-catching sculptures: a black taxicab with a metal tree growing from the roof, a huge, suspended white fish swinging over a gate, seated and standing metal figures perched on girders attached to brick walls. Swift turned to examine a seated sculpture more closely, but Toni wasn't registering her surroundings and stalked on, head down.

In the café, they sat with a view of Greenwich across the river, drinking coffee. Swift ordered sweet potato soup. The wind had made him ravenous. Toni refused food.

'How did you meet Sam?' he asked.

'Conor and Lucy had a little party. Sam and Conor worked together and they'd invited him. We agreed it was love at first sight for us both.'

Swift knew a bit about that. It had happened with Ruth, the day they'd met in the British Museum café. They'd said they'd be together for ever and now here they were, wrangling over their daughter's care.

'That's like magic, isn't it?' he said.

Toni smiled. 'It's a good memory.' She sipped coffee. 'My friends don't approve of me hiring you. Especially Lexie. They say I'm clutching at straws, resisting the truth, heading down a rabbit hole. Take your pick.'

'They're worried about you.' *Unless one of them has something to hide, of course.* His soup arrived. He buttered a thick slice of granary bread and offered her a piece. She appeared so lanky and cold.

She shook her head and spoke quietly but vehemently. 'I don't want people to worry about me. I want them to *listen* to me. At least you do that. I realise I'm paying you to, but believe me, I'm grateful. When I ask my friends if they really think that Sam was the kind of man to have a relationship with a girl of fifteen, they shift awkwardly, go quiet, change the subject, or say that maybe we'll never know the truth of it. Well, I *am* going to know the truth.'

'I'll do my best, but there's no certainty.'

'I have faith.'

'What's happened to Sam's home in Belsize Park — did he own it?'

Toni nodded. 'Luckily, ever-practical Sam had made a new will just prior to the wedding. He left everything to me, so I inherit the house. I don't want it. I'll sell it as soon as probate's through.'

'Could I take a look around it?'

'Sure. I'll give you the key. I haven't touched anything in there. Can't bear to just yet. Conor went round there with me in November and made sure everything's okay. I gave him a spare key and I haven't been back since. He offered to call in now and again, check that nothing's leaking or misbehaving. I was relieved because it means I don't have to go there. It'd be like taunting myself with the life I should have been having.'

'Can you think of anywhere Sam went, or anything he was involved in, through work or socially, where he might have met Naomi Ludlow?' Swift asked.

'I've racked my brains. I haven't come up with anything.'

They sat silently. Swift ate his soup and ran a crust of bread around the bowl. Toni dabbed at crystals of sugar in her saucer.

'Sorry about being rude to you earlier, at the station,' she said. 'I'm so crabby.'

'That's okay.'

'And thanks for coming here with me. I'll be able to visit on my own now.' She looked through the glass to the slate-grey water. 'I wonder if Sam was terrified. I wonder what was going through his mind. He didn't send that text, I'm sure of it. It was a cold way to say goodbye and he was never cold. He was warm and always cheerful — disgustingly upbeat and happy to the point where it could annoy me.' She rested her face in her hands and slipped into a reverie.

Swift buttered his second slice of bread. Why on earth had Sam Goddard come to these far reaches of Dockland the night before his wedding?

* * *

'You tell me,' Sergeant Arran Delamare said. 'What *was* a man of thirty-five doing out with a fifteen-year-old girl in a deserted area? My money's on a secret relationship and they panicked, couldn't see a way out. Or rather, *he* did and he persuaded Naomi into assisted suicide or drugged her and took her with him. Maybe Goddard worried that she'd spill the beans. He didn't have the guts to tell Toni, especially after her first experience of marriage, and he took Naomi into a vortex with him.'

'You find that believable?' Swift asked. Yet it was the kind of action some desperate men took, opting to end not only their own lives, but those of loved ones.

Delamare sipped his gin and tonic, which he'd ordered with no ice and a slice of lime. He sighed with pleasure and loosened his tie. His face was round and pleasant, with hair brushed straight back from a high forehead. Swift had been relieved to find him approachable and happy to meet over a drink. Some detectives disliked private investigators and refused to speak to them.

'Toni cited her first marriage disaster as a reason why Goddard wouldn't have hurt her,' Delamare replied. 'But it could be that his guilt about that tripped him into killing himself. He didn't say, so it's all supposition. The brief text he left for Toni was all we had to go on, and it indicated that he and Naomi intended to die.'

'I've seen the text,' Swift said. 'What if Sam Goddard didn't send it?'

'I agree it was handy, maybe suspiciously so. But if he didn't send it, who did? There were no one else's fingerprints on his phone. Sometimes, it *is* the way it seems. People back themselves into corners and get despairing, impulsive. Mature men do daft things with young girls. Good luck if you're after a mystery man or woman.' He added more tonic to his gin and watched it fizz. 'That's a beautiful sound after a day's hard slog. Look, I'm terribly sorry for Toni Sheringham, but she's flogging a dead horse with this and so are you. We spent three months chasing up this case. We couldn't find any reason why Goddard was out in Docklands, a long way from Belsize Park, apart from wanting to kill himself and Naomi. They were both full of alprazolam, a sedative and anti-depressant. You can buy it online. It's fast acting, not a bad drug of choice if you wanted to accelerate into the Thames and not be too aware of it. There's no CCTV around that bit of the river. As far as we could tell, they took the sedative and Goddard drove the bike into the high tide. There was no evidence to suggest that anyone else was involved, no prior injuries on the bodies.'

'Toni maintains that Sam wasn't the type to go after a minor.'

'You wouldn't want to believe that of your true love, would you? Leaves a bad taste,' Delamare said. 'Thing is, Naomi Ludlow looked more like late teens or early twenties than fifteen. So many girls do now. Very pretty and mature. Maybe she didn't tell him her real age.'

'Did Naomi have boyfriends?'

'Not according to her parents and no trace of one online.'

'How could Sam have known her?'

'Not a clue. She came from a well-off family in Maida Vale. Mother's a GP, Dad's an accountant. They both work long hours, and it seemed like Naomi and her older brother got on with things on their own a lot. The parents stated that Naomi hadn't mentioned any problems to them, or been upset. Ditto the brother, Dean. He was like a zombie throughout it all. They'd never met Goddard or had any business with him. On the night she died, they thought Naomi was out swimming. She'd been trying to build her strength up after suffering with a debilitating bout of glandular fever. She was supposed to be in by ten.'

'Did she have swimming kit with her when she was found?'

'No, and it was in her bedroom. We checked at the leisure club, but she didn't log in with her member's card that night and no one saw her. She had a shoulder bag with her, with a purse and a make-up bag in. No phone — we've never found it — and it was switched off around five that evening.'

'What about the time she left home — did you establish that?'

Delamare swizzled his slice of lime with his fingertip. 'Naomi was at home on her own that day. Dean got back around half five and she was out. Her father was the last person who saw her, at eight that morning. The parents were distraught, as you can imagine. Mainly very quiet, but now and again the mother wept. Did you hear that Dr Ludlow started shouting at Toni Sheringham after the inquest?'

Swift savoured a mouthful of wine. 'Toni hasn't mentioned that.'

'Probably tried to forget it. Dr Ludlow was yelling about women turning a blind eye to men who are abusers. She couldn't believe that Toni knew nothing about it. It was a bit much, especially as poor Toni was in her wedding dress when she got the death knock. Grief — it makes people unhinged, doesn't it?'

'How did Toni handle it?'

'She walked away.' Delamare drained his glass. 'Whichever way you come at it, Goddard was up to something. He'd lied to Toni, said he was going to be spending that evening on his own at home. The neighbour told us that he arrived home on his bike and then left again soon after, around quarter past six. Maybe the imminent wedding had fried his brain, brought on despair. As for Naomi — plenty of teenagers veer to mental instability and drama at the best of times, and she'd been unwell. A suicide pact can seem romantic.'

'Except Toni Sheringham describes a man who would be unlikely to behave in that way.'

'Well . . . maybe she didn't know him as well as she thought. The way she spoke about him, he didn't have any faults, but everyone's got feet of clay. Isn't that your bread and butter — people deceiving one another and the resulting fallout?'

'A lot of the time,' Swift admitted. 'But I'll assume Goddard's innocence unless I prove otherwise. Isn't it strange that Naomi didn't leave a note for her family?'

'Not necessarily. Suicides often don't.' Delamare yawned and stretched. 'Maybe she didn't care enough about them at that point, or she just wanted Goddard to deal with it, or as I said, she didn't realise she was about to die. He drugged her and she was oblivious to it. Her parents said the illness had made her flat in mood at times, and although she was a lot better, she had bad days.'

'What about Goddard's phone? Was there evidence they'd been seeing each other?'

'Nothing. But they could have used prepaid phones that they got rid of. People having affairs often do and especially groomers, where the sex is illegal.'

'And their social media posts? Were either of them signalling anything concerning?'

'Goddard's were few, boringly normal and all about his wedding. Naomi's social media had a fair bit about her virus, but her comments were getting more upbeat as she recovered. She was back at school, doing half-days for a while. Her parents have closed her Facebook and Instagram accounts now.' Delamare shook his head. 'I realise I'm disappointing you with all this. We asked the questions.'

'I wasn't doubting that. I have to start somewhere.'

'Okay, fair enough.'

'What did the pathologist say about time of death?'

'Difficult, with drowning. Going by body temperatures and the air and water temperature, sometime between 5 p.m. and midnight on the tenth.' Delamare ran a hand through his hair. 'Toni will no doubt tell you that her fiancé would never have driven his beloved motorbike into the river.'

'She already has,' Swift acknowledged.

'Yeah. She seems to forget that maybe in his state of mind, cherishing his Bonnie was the last item on the agenda. Thing is, we investigated up to a reasonable point. We're busy people with much worse crimes on our books. We took it as far as we needed. The coroner put the lid on it.'

Swift understood. Goddard had left a suicide explanation. Why should the police seek extra work when they had daily stabbings and gang-related crimes to resolve?

'Must go,' Delamare said jauntily. 'I've got a date. No offence, but I reckon Toni Sheringham would be better off spending her money on grief counselling and getting on with her life, instead of chasing phantoms through you.'

Swift had a second glass of wine after he'd gone. The trouble with a case like this was that it was easy to argue it both ways. Yet it seemed to him that the police had nothing to go on except a text and an absence of any other evidence. He turned to his phone and the photo of Sam Goddard that Toni had sent him. He was sitting on Bonnie, holding his helmet. A genial face, broad smile, longish, floppy hair, a straggly moustache and oval glasses. Not particularly handsome, and hardly a face that would inspire passion in a teenage girl.

He reached into his pocket for his wallet and found one of Branna's dinosaur-print gloves. He sniffed it, inhaling her malty, biscuit scent. Ruth had told him that they'd be moving to Guernsey after the wedding, in early June. He had just over three months left of regular contact. Then it would be a case of Zoom or Facetime, of making an effort and slotting in chats. Branna's biscuit smell might change and he wouldn't know. He wouldn't be able to nuzzle her neck and swing her onto his shoulders.

His aunt Maura would say, *What cannot be cured must be endured.* He tipped back the last of his wine, swallowing his sadness.

CHAPTER 4

Swift had eaten breakfast and he was in his small, walled back garden, filling the bird feeders with suet pellets and nuts. It was a dank morning of white mists. There was no wind today, but the still air was stealthily cold. He stopped by the tea rose where his friend Cedric's ashes were buried and said good morning. A robin popped out from behind it and peered up at him with tilted head. It cheered him. Mary had bought him a birdbath for Christmas, an oval dish in green stone. As he topped up the water, he heard the front doorbell. It sounded as if someone was keeping their finger on it.

He opened the door and saw a burly, tanned, ginger-haired man with a luxurious tangled beard and a bulging rucksack. He was wearing a thin grey canvas jacket over a T-shirt and jeans. It wasn't surprising that he was shivering.

'Ty, *mi fren*, great to see you! *Mi no lukum yu longtaem.* Thank goodness you're in!'

'Eli, hello! This is a surprise!'

'Yeah, I bet. How've you been?'

'I'm fine. You're dressed for the wrong climate.'

'Tell me about it. I'm freezing my nuts off out here.'

Swift took the hint, albeit reluctantly. He had places to be. 'Come on in.'

'Great, *tangkyu*.'

Eli dumped his rucksack on the living room floor with a reverberating thud and beamed. 'Lovely and warm. This place hasn't changed at all. I love the Art Deco style. Still that Morris wallpaper, the chaise longue by the window and a real fire. You were lucky, inheriting a house in London. Got it from your great-aunt, right?'

Swift got a bit tired of being told how fortunate he was to have been left a property. 'Yep, that's right. Coffee?'

'Great.'

Eli followed him into the galley kitchen and while Swift made fresh coffee, he opened the fridge and studied the contents, taking things out and examining them. He wasn't too clean and he smelled stale and dusty. 'Okay if I make a sandwich? I'm ravenous.'

Eli had never waited to be asked. 'Of course. There's bread just there, plates in the rack.'

Swift grimaced as Eli dug grubby fingers into the bread, slathered slices with butter and stuffed most of a packet of smoked salmon between them.

'Got any gherkins, Ty?'

'No, I don't like them.'

'Pity. They just provide that hit with salmon. I'll make do with this Dijon mustard.' He lifted the sandwich and took a huge bite, catching flakes of fish as they fell. 'Mm! *I tes gud!*'

Swift turned to pour the coffee. He hadn't seen Eli Caldwell for a while, not since they'd worked together in the Met. Eli had been a charismatic, popular man and attractive to women. He'd also been a lousy cop, chaotic and forgetful, tolerated because of his laid-back, genial manner. Eli had decided that Swift was a close friend and would often suggest a drink or a meal after work. Swift hadn't had much in common with him, but his easy company had meant an hour in the pub passed easily. He'd left the force and had taken a job as a travel guide with a global company. Always a strapping man, he'd broadened considerably since they'd last met.

'Here's your coffee. Milk and sugar just there.'

'*Tangkyu.*' Eli heaped three spoons of sugar into his mug and stirred briskly.

At the table, Eli demolished two pears, an apple and an orange. He talked about himself in between yawns. Swift had glimpses of his quivering pink tonsils.

'Long haul flying always makes me ravenous. I have this craving for fresh food.'

'Where have you been?'

'Pacific islands. Vanuatu for the last six months. It's been brilliant, but I lost my job and there was nothing else on the horizon. I could tell you some tales about the scrapes I've been in!'

'I bet, but it'll have to be another time. I have to go out soon. Maybe we can catch up later.'

Eli undid a shirt button and scratched his chest, releasing a waft of rank BO. 'Thing is, Ty, I'm a tad broke and I need a berth for a night or two.'

'Haven't you got a place to live?'

Eli shook his head. 'Plans failed. I had a girlfriend in Shepherd's Bush. I got to Heathrow early this morning and when I arrived at her place expecting a welcome, she announced she'd got another live-in bloke. She got tired of hanging about for me. Understandable, I suppose. I'd have tried to sweet-talk her but the bloke was there, lurking in his dressing gown.'

Swift stared at him. 'She didn't tell you this before you returned?'

'Well . . .' Eli yawned again and rubbed his eyes. 'Communication's been a bit hit-and-miss.'

Swift remembered that useful ambiguity. Eli had always employed it when he'd failed to do something or couldn't be bothered. 'I see. I don't have a spare room, Eli.'

'Oh. But you own the house, right?'

'Yes, but I rent the upstairs flat out to a guy called Chand Malla. He's in the Met.'

'What happened to that old guy who used to live here — Cyril?'

34

'My friend Cedric. He died. I've just one bedroom in this flat.'

'What about the basement?'

'That's my office.'

Eli scratched his chest again. 'How about the sofa? Seems comfy enough. I'm temporarily skint, you see. Tell you about it later. I'm wrecked, to be honest. Just need to crash out. *Plis?* Then I can get myself together.' He stood and moved towards the sofa, swaying with fatigue. He was taller than Swift, with a couple of inches on his six three, and he took up a lot of space.

The sofa was a new one that converted into a bed. Swift had bought it for when Branna stayed. She loved the ceremony of pulling it out and extracting the duvet and pillows from the space beneath. Once, she'd hidden in the cavity, waiting until he was panicking and calling her before she burst out laughing, revealing herself. Swift had only just finished clearing up since her visit, wiping sticky surfaces and crayon marks, removing bits of plasticine from the floor and vacuuming her muddy wellington deposits. He'd been anticipating a return to peace and an orderly home. There was a new case to work on, and the last thing he needed or wanted was Eli's outsized presence in his living room.

Oh, well. The man was grubby and exhausted and white around the eyes, despite his tan. He'd have been flying for around twenty hours. Swift glanced at the cold mist outside. It would have been a shock coming back to it after Pacific sun.

'Okay, you can stay here for a couple of nights.'

'*Tangkyu* so much.'

'What's with the patois?'

Eli managed a smile. 'It's Bislama, the *lingua franca* in Vanuatu. I just slip in and out of it now without realising.'

'I have to go out soon, work to do, but I'll be back sometime this afternoon.'

'*Ale tata.*' Eli kicked his filthy trainers off, releasing a ripe whiff of cheesy socks, lay on the sofa, tucked a cushion under his head, pulled the woven throw from the back and snuggled into it. He was snoring before Swift had finished clearing the table.

* * *

Sleet was falling, insistent and miserable, so Swift had put aside his dislike of the Tube's confines and rode it to Camden Town. He hurried along the slippery pavement, past shop-fronts that still managed a cheerful aspect on a bleak February day: one covered in multicoloured tiles with a bright yellow elephant's head above the door, a tattoo and piercing studio exhibiting eye-catching dragons and mermaids, a massage parlour offering *Treats from the Orient* in flashing red lights and a window featuring 1960s' minidresses in purple, orange and blue geometric designs.

He stopped in a newsagent's doorway when his phone rang. Unknown number, woman's voice.

'Mr Swift?'

'That's right. Who's speaking?'

'It's Lexie Kadis, a friend of Toni's.'

'She's mentioned you.'

'Oh . . . okay. Toni confirmed that she's hired you to investigate Sam's death.'

'That's right.' He moved out of the way of a skinny little girl with a wan face who looked in her early teens. She was wearing an unseasonably thin denim jacket, ripped jeans and slip-on pink pumps, and struggling with a double buggy. Unlike Naomi Ludlow, no one was likely to mistake her age. He wedged his phone under his chin as he held open the shop door for her.

Lexie Kadis' tone was challenging. 'And is that a good idea?'

He wasn't convinced that it was, but that was no one's business but his and his client's. 'It's Toni's wish. That's all that matters.'

'I've seen your website, so I understand you're experienced and above board. But I'm worried about this. Toni's grieving and in a very vulnerable state.'

'Is Toni aware of this call?'

She hesitated. 'No.'

'Perhaps you have to respect her judgement.'

'Her judgement is impaired at present.'

'That's a big statement.'

'I know Toni a lot better than you do,' she said, 'and I was Sam's friend too. The last thing he'd want is for her to take off on this wild goose chase.'

Swift mistrusted people who claimed to interpret a dead person's wishes. There was often self-interest at play. 'I have an appointment to get to, but given that you're a close friend of Toni's, I would like to talk to you. Can I get back to you?'

'Yes, I suppose. As long as Toni doesn't mind.'

That was a sudden volte-face. 'She understands that I'll need to talk to all the significant people in Sam's life, and hers too.'

'Yeah, okay. But I take the view that this is all wrong.'

'Noted. I have to go.'

The girl with the double buggy was straining to manoeuvre it back out of the shop. One of the wheels had snagged on the door, and the full carrier bags swinging from the handles weren't helping her efforts. Swift bent and released it. She thanked him with a muttered 'Ta', while two fat-cheeked toddlers with runny noses gazed solemnly up at him through a spattered rain cover. He smiled at them, but elicited no response. Simone often uttered the mantra that a smile was never wasted, but he wasn't so sure.

He watched the girl navigate a cracked kerb with the buggy. Her dull hair hung in rats' tails around her shoulders, and her legs were stem-like in her skintight jeans. She reminded him of Havana Roscoe, an anorexic teenager who'd run away from home when he'd been investigating her father's murder. Havana had turned up at his house in a distraught state when he was out and Chand, his tenant, had allowed her to sit in his flat and wait. She'd attempted suicide by trying to throw herself from a window. When the ambulance arrived, she'd sped off into the night. Other than a Christmas card to her grandmother, there'd been no trace of her since and Swift often wondered what had become of her. He felt a responsibility towards her, because she'd been in his house, desperate and agitated.

The skinny girl stopped and lit a cigarette. She took two bags of crisps from a carrier bag, tore them open and slid them under the rain cape to the toddlers. Then she trudged on through the icy sleet, puffing away and he continued in the opposite direction.

Spring Investment Management had its offices in a three-storey, end-terrace Victorian house off Camden High Street. Behind the iron railings that set it back from the pavement, a window cleaner was busy wiping the large casement windows. A pet-grooming parlour called Happy Paws occupied the basement. Swift heard frantic barking from below as he climbed the steps to the front door. He shook himself, dog-like, brushed water droplets from his riotous hair, and then smoothed his hands over his head in an effort to appear less wild man, more capable detective.

In reception, he stood dripping in front of a woman with upswept hair, a bony nose and a slash of fuchsia pink lipstick on her narrow mouth. The nameplate on her desk said *Araminta Leadsom*, written in flowery white font on a navy background. She looked him up and down as if he'd trailed in a bad smell.

'I have an appointment with Jerome Adcott,' he said. 'The name's Tyrone Swift.'

'Oh yes, the private detective. I'll tell Mr Adcott, if you'd like to take a seat. Your coat can go on the pegs over there.'

He hung up his battered waxed jacket beside a long herringbone tweed coat and an elegant soft blue cape, which he guessed belonged to Araminta. The way she was watching him, she was clearly praying that his jacket wouldn't touch hers. He pulled his sleeves down, tucking in a fraying strand of wool on the cuff. The red-flecked Aran sweater had come from a shop in Connemara years ago and he'd worn it so much, it was getting thin at the elbows and a button had dropped off the collar.

He caught Araminta's eye. 'Did you know Sam Goddard well?'

She had a cut-glass accent and two jewelled silver pins like tiny daggers stuck in her hair. 'I did, yes. He was a valued colleague. His death was a dreadful shock.'

'What did you make of what happened to him?'

Her nostrils flared. 'I don't indulge in muckraking and gossip.'

'Really? It makes the world go round. I earn my living from it and I'd be lost without it.'

'How fascinating,' she said frostily.

The phone rang and as she answered it, slipping into an unctuous tone, she adjusted the end of one of her hairpins. Her malevolent expression suggested that she'd relish sticking it in him. Swift doubted that she let her friends call her Minty and contemplated, not for the first time, how some status-conscious people attempted to inflate their importance and exercise power through meanness. While he waited he read the wide, colourful banner hanging behind Araminta.

SPRING IS PROUD TO SUPPORT GO KIDS

GIVING KIDS WITH DISABILITIES EQUAL OPPORTUNITY TO FLOURISH

He turned to a brochure for Spring Investment Management. The cover depicted a smug couple standing on a white sandy beach in bright sunshine, holding glasses of wine.

We work with large institutions as well as individuals to manage and develop their wealth. We do this by establishing financial goals and then making judicious investments. Our focus is socially responsible portfolios, enabling you to align your investments with your social and environmental values. Our clients include individuals and families, educational institutions, charities and insurance companies, to name just a few.

The staff list named Jerome Adcott as CEO and Head of Wealth Planning. Sam Goddard was still listed there as his deputy.

Araminta informed him that she'd take him to Mr Adcott, making it sound as if she was bestowing a great honour on him. Swift noticed from the corner of his eye that she moved her cape to a peg further from his jacket as she glided past her desk. She led him up two flights of stairs that had been painted with black-and-white stripes, negotiating the narrow treads carefully in her stilettos. He didn't care for her attitude, but he had to admit that she had very shapely calves.

Jerome Adcott's ebullience made up for his reception-ist's chilliness. He was waiting at his office door.

'Do come in. What a foul day! Coffee?'

'Thanks, yes.'

'Let's sit here by the roof garden. We can be cosy in the warm while we watch the filthy weather.'

Adcott was in his forties, tall, muscular and bald, with a West Country accent. The office was high-ceilinged, light and spacious with blond wood furniture, but Swift's eye was drawn to the roof garden outside. He took a seat by the sliding door and examined the view. It had been created to impress. For that reason, he didn't warm to it, but he had to admire the design. Even in this weather, it was attractive. Around the porcelain-tiled and cedar-decked flooring stood coloured steel planters joined by timber seating. The plants were all ever-greens. A magnificent pyracantha grew up an adjoining brick wall, still clinging on to a few of its orange berries. Chimney pot planters held early daffodils. A glass-topped table and six wicker chairs stood under an awning at the centre of the decking.

Adcott brought the coffee over. 'Handsome, isn't it? We paid a bit for it, but it was worth it. We have meetings and entertain out there in more clement weather. Sometimes, a breath of fresh air while you drink a coffee rejuvenates the day and the brain.' He paused. 'Sam chose the plants. He had an eye for such things. I still can't believe he's gone.' Adcott sat and ran a hand over his face.

'I'm sorry. Toni told me you were close.'

'We were. I started the company nearly twenty years ago, and he was one of the best appointments I made along the way. We've developed an ethos of ethical investing at Spring, focusing on stock market companies that have a positive impact on society and the environment. Sam and I worked hard at growing that over the years and we mixed socially as well, from time to time. He was my right-hand man. My colleagues are my work family and we have strong bonds. I was leaving for the wedding when I heard the news.'

'What did you make of it?'

Adcott rocked back in his chair and took his time. 'I didn't know what to think. I was stunned. Sam was mad about Toni. He was always getting her little gifts and mentioning her. She's a lovely woman, salt of the earth. We all worry about her.'

'Are you concerned because she doesn't believe that Sam killed himself and Naomi Ludlow?'

Adcott stared out at the garden. His bald head gleamed under the reflected light from the windows. There was warmth and sincerity in his tone. 'I get it, believe me. No one wants to contemplate that Sam was messing about with a teenager. It's baffling and heart-rending for Toni. But what other explanation is there? I don't say that to her, mind.'

'Did Sam have any problems here at work? He indicated to Toni that there was something he needed to sort out before the wedding.'

Adcott made an expansive sweep with a hand. 'There are always things to sort out here — take your pick. Sam was brilliant at his job and he'd just taken on a new company. His clients miss him as much as we do. All I can tell you is that Sam was a successful colleague who was relishing the prospect of getting married. That's what I told the police.'

'You'd never have believed he could have been leading a double life.'

'No, but that seems to have been the police conclusion. One detective commented that it happens quite often and with the most unlikely characters. It crops up a lot on those programmes where people trace their ancestors, doesn't it? They discover bigamy and secret families. All sorts. More coffee?'

'I'm fine, thanks.'

Adcott rose and poured himself another mug. Swift examined the large photos on the wall behind his desk, showing Adcott swimming, cycling and running.

'Do you compete in triathlons?' he asked.

'Oh, yes, the photos. I compete for the charity that Spring supports — Go Kids. My wife works for it as a trustee. We spend a fair bit of our time campaigning for it, one way or another. It's dear to our hearts. I did an Ironman challenge last year. I'm booked for another in May, so I'll have to up my training regime soon.' He sighed deeply. 'Sam used to cycle with me sometimes as encouragement.'

'Did Sam ever mention that area of east London where he died?'

'Never. Everything about what happened that night is peculiar, including the location he ended up in with Naomi Ludlow.'

Swift finished his coffee. 'Her father's an accountant. Has this firm ever had any dealings with him?'

'I checked that for the police. None at all. No one here knew the Ludlows. I'm sorry I can't be more help. I expect you'll want to note where I was on the night Sam died, because the police asked. I worked here late, until nine and then I went home to my family. I was last out of the office.'

People didn't usually volunteer alibis so readily to a private detective. Perhaps Adcott wanted to get rid of him and had gauged it the best way.

'What time did Sam leave work?'

'He'd been with a client in the afternoon and went straight home from there.'

'Could I have the name of the client?'

Adcott pursed his lips. 'No, I can't give you that. We have to respect client confidentiality and you're not the police.' He checked his watch and got up. 'Have you spoken to Conor Wallace? He was a close friend of Sam's. He told him about the vacancy here, that's how I recruited him. Conor's in our Pensions team, although he's off to a new job next month.'

Swift got up. 'He's out of the office today. I said I'd visit him at home. I can see myself out.'

Downstairs, Swift discovered that a woman with golden curls, a lively smile, retroussé nose and doe eyes had replaced Araminta. Her name badge said *Hester French*.

'Hi,' he said. 'I've just come for my jacket. I've been with Jerome Adcott.'

Her eyes twinkled. 'Are you the private investigator?'

'That's right. Is my visit common knowledge?'

'Oh yes! Word got round. We've all been Googling "Tyrone Swift".'

'Did you like what you read?'

'You bet! Working for Interpol sounded terrifically intriguing and sexy!'

He recalled long gruelling hours, exhausted, trafficked women and the stabbing that had left a scar on his thigh. Still, he figured it might be worth cultivating a friendly face at this company, so he wouldn't disillusion her. 'It had its moments. I could tell you, but then I'd have to kill you.'

She chuckled. 'I suppose you're sworn to secrecy.' She seemed to find his work a hoot. As if remembering that he was there on a serious matter, she said soberly, 'I was impressed at some of the cases you've dealt with. Not every-one reacted that way, though.'

'Some people don't like the idea of me asking questions?'

'Araminta is underwhelmed by your involvement, but then the way she goes on, you'd reckon she owns the com-pany. Maybe it just seems a tad intrusive after a sad and shocking event and after all, you don't have the right to ask anything, do you?'

She smiled easily, so he wasn't sure if it was a challenge. 'That's true. Speaking of Araminta, what have you done with her? Has she vanished in a puff of self-importance?'

Hester giggled again. 'Lunch break,' she said. 'I'm covering. Do that coat up good and tight, it's bloody cold out there.'

It was as if the good fairy had been substituted for the wicked witch. Swift smiled back at her. 'I've been talking to your boss about Sam Goddard.'

'That's all round the office. It's been a weird time since Sam died. Everyone's sort of off-kilter and grumpy. I'm so sorry for Toni, I can't imagine how awful it must be for her. Some people here say she should move on, try to accept what happened. I think she's brave, getting you to investigate.'

'Kind of you to say so.'

'Well, if I had a fiancé and he'd died like that, I'd want answers.'

He was about to ask Hester if she'd known Sam well, when a man appeared and asked her about a meeting schedule. She fluttered her fingers at Swift and turned to the computer. He admired the turned-up tip of her nose and her peachy complexion, and slipped one of his cards on to the desk as he left.

CHAPTER 5

Outside, it had stopped sleeting. A watery sun was making an effort to cast some warmth through scudding grey cloud. Swift checked the time and took stock. It was almost one. He'd left messages for the Ludlows, but had received no replies. Their home in Maida Vale was a couple of miles away. He could walk there along the towpath to Little Venice and have lunch at Crocker's Folly on the way.

He joined Regent's Canal at Camden Lock and walked through the Cumberland basin, past a red-and-gold pagoda-style Chinese restaurant perched high on the water. The towpath was quiet, the canal sludge brown under the troubled sky. This was turning into a day when his past caught up with him — first the girl who'd reminded him of Havana Roscoe and now a return to Little Venice. He hadn't been back there since he'd been drugged and thrown into the canal. A passer-by had saved him. He'd caught cryptosporidium from the water, a nasty parasite that had affected his health for months. Today, he would stay on the towpath and leave the canal to ducks and moorhens.

He heard the birds calling in the exotic aviary as he neared the stretch that traversed part of London Zoo and walked on fast, following the path along the edge of Regent's

Park, where the gardens of white mansions swept down to the water. Tall weeping willows shaded him and dripped on his head. He passed through a dank tunnel where the smell reminded him of Eli's socks, then crossed the road and approached the splendid Crocker's Folly just as the icy drizzle started again.

Like many London buildings, it had gone through a number of incarnations since it had been constructed in a magnificent Northern Renaissance style in the nineteenth century. Its original use by a publican called Frank Crocker had been as a gin palace and hotel. The ground floor was now a Lebanese restaurant with a blue-and-white facade, with flats above.

Swift sat by a magnificent marble fireplace, beneath an opulent, gilded ceiling. Usually, he preferred a cosy pub but those could lead to introspection and thoughts of Ruth and Branna. This sumptuous space with crystal chandeliers, mahogany panelling and soaring Romanesque pillars offered distraction. He ordered and sat, taking in the intricate patterns in the ceiling, the silverware on the bar and the ornate carving behind it. He ate Mouhamara, warmed by the heat of the green chilli and drank a glass of fresh apple and carrot juice.

What would Frank Crocker have made of his pub now? The poor man had miscalculated when he'd taken it on, expecting that travellers from the new Great Central Railway would flock to him. They'd failed to materialise, because the location of the terminus had been changed. The urban myth was that Crocker had thrown himself from the roof in despair and haunted the building, although the more mundane truth was that he'd died young of natural causes.

Swift loved the myths that abounded about London and had started telling Branna some of the less gory ones, such as that Green Park had no flowerbeds, because Charles II had picked flowers there for his mistresses and his angry Queen had thus banned them. (Although that had involved an explanation of the concept of a mistress, leading to Branna commenting, '*Very naughty!*') He was saving stories about the beast of Hackney Marshes, the killer pool of Epping Forest and the vampire of Highgate Cemetery until she was older.

While he ate, Swift searched online for Naomi Ludlow. A Twitter account was still open with a number of photos. He flicked through her feed.

@nadgad90

I haven't got any old virus, I've got glandular fever, also called 'mono' to those in the know. Well, I'm always special & different!

@nadgad90

I'm kicking this virus out of my life. Loving my medication! Very handsome consultant, too. Maybe I'll be a doctor.

@nadgad90

What about this for a look? Loving my new mascara. #witchyeyes.

@nadgad90

Got highest term grades, even tho hardly been at school! Oxford or Cambridge? They'll be fighting over me!

@nadgad90

Just did a personality test. Scored highly driven and an achiever. No surprises then!

@nadgad90

Playing Board Defenders & smashing it!

She'd been self-absorbed and cloaking uncertainty, but that was teenagers for you. Her photos showed a shapely young woman, dark-haired with thick-lashed eyes and a pouting expression, which she might have believed was sultry. She certainly appeared older than fifteen. There were photos of her grim-faced parents outside the coroner's court — a tall man carrying a briefcase protectively across his chest and a woman in a grey suit, looking daggers at the camera. Swift saw quite a few tabloid stories with headlines such as, *Tragic Naomi Dies in Docklands Mystery* and *Young Girl Dies With Financier — Dramatic Drownings in Thames*.

He read about Epstein–Barr virus and saw that it caused glandular fever. It could be transmitted by kissing or during sex. It would be worth trying to track if Naomi had had a love life, despite what her parents had told the police.

Fortified by wine and spices, he carried on his route and re-joined the towpath. Boats were moored on both sides of this stretch of the canal, many with stacks of firewood, tubs of flowers and herbs on their roofs. The water here had a greenish hue. It was a dismal scene in the drizzle and the cold was making his nose run, but he stopped to listen to someone playing *Chelsea Morning* on the cello. The warm, joyous tones came from a boat called *Happy Highways*. He blew his nose, shoved his hands deeper into his pockets and moved on. Ten minutes later, he left the towpath and entered quiet, wealthy streets of terraced houses.

The Ludlows' house was stucco-fronted, on the small side for the area, with a shallow paved entrance behind a tall gate. Swift rang the bell on the glossy black door. The woman who answered was slim, in her forties, with a long, intelligent face and dark brown hair. He recognised her from the online photos. 'Dr Ludlow?'

'That's correct.'

'I'm sorry to call unannounced. I've left messages for you and your husband. I was in the area, so I thought I'd try in person.'

She took a step forward, her pendant earrings dancing. 'Who are you?'

'My name is Tyrone Swift. I'm a private detective.'

Her jaw clenched. 'You! Go away. We have nothing to say to you.'

'I'm so sorry about your daughter. I won't take up much of your time.'

'We ignored your calls because we didn't want to speak to you. We don't talk to the press or people like you. Go away immediately.' She started to close the door.

He made eye contact. 'Toni Sheringham is deeply troubled. She doesn't believe that her husband was having a relationship with your daughter.'

Dr Ludlow's lip curled. 'I've no interest in Ms Sheringham or what she believes. That woman came here, to our home. I was stunned at her sheer audacity and insensitivity. We told her to leave in no uncertain terms.'

'But surely if she's right, it means that her fiancé and your daughter died for some other reason. Doesn't that bother you?'

She shook as she screeched at him, 'Don't speak that woman's name! I don't want to hear it. The police investigated and we accepted their findings. Now we want to be left in peace to try to get on with our lives. Go away, or I'll call the police.'

Swift heard the gate open behind him. A youth in a tracksuit, carrying a rucksack and a pair of football boots gave him a sideways glance. 'You okay, Mum?'

'Come inside, Dean, hurry up.' She stood back to let the young man in and then pointed at Swift. 'If you're not gone in two minutes, I will dial 999.'

Dean stood behind his mother, mouth open, his boots dangling by their laces from his outstretched hand. Dr Ludlow slammed the door.

Cold-calling was always a gamble. He'd have to try Naomi's school and her friends.

Swift turned away and headed for a bus stop, wet and chilled now. The light was grey and dim. He'd go home, have a hot shower, light a fire. Then he slowed, his heart sinking. He'd forgotten all about Eli, who was probably still snoring loudly on his sofa.

* * *

When he opened the front door, he heard voices and laughter coming from his flat. Elvis was singing 'Don't Be Cruel'. In the living room, the curtains were drawn and the fire was blazing. There were competing smells of drying laundry, food, shampoo and wine. Eli and Chand were sitting on the rug in front of the fire, with a piled plate of buttered toast and anchovy paste between them. Eli had trimmed his beard and was scrubbed, rosy-faced and wielding the toasting fork. An open bottle of Swift's expensive Burgundy stood to one side of the hearth.

Eli turned and beamed at him. 'Ty, *welkam*! The hunter is home from the hill! Come and sit down, you look like a drowned rat. I'm just chewing the fat with Chand here. Have a glass of this lovely red.'

Swift threw his jacket off and sat. 'It is a good red, that one. I was keeping it for a special occasion.'

'Live for the moment, says I!' Eli filled a glass to the brim for him. 'Here, seize the day and all that.' He tilted his own glass to them both. '*Jis*!'

Chand took a gulp of his wine and raised his brows at Swift as if to say, *None of this is my fault.* 'I met Eli in the hall,' he explained. 'He was having trouble working out the heating, so I gave him a hand.'

Eli beamed. 'Then I twigged that Chand isn't just one of the Old Bill, he's also an Elvis fan, so what's not to like?'

Chand hiccupped, giggled and covered his mouth. He got drunk very quickly. Eli was wearing one of Swift's sweaters. It strained over his stomach, riding up at the back.

'How was your day's sleuthing?' Eli asked.

'So-so. Frustrating. Wet.'

'I couldn't stand the idea of going out in it. Suppose I need to acclimatise. I lit the fire and warmed my bones. I've been ravenous, can't stop eating. We need more eggs.'

Swift didn't like that 'we'.

Eli proffered the plate to him. 'Slice of toast, *mi fren*?'

'Thanks.'

Swift took some of the charred toast. It was delicious. Elvis segued into 'Hard Headed Woman' and Eli played an imaginary guitar.

'I saw a girl who reminded me of Havana Roscoe today,' Swift told Chand. 'Still no news of her?'

Chand was a detective in a specialist crimes team. He checked the missing persons records regularly. 'Nothing,' he said. 'No trace at all.'

Swift savoured the wine, sat back and watched Eli's antics. Might as well join in. Eli was relentlessly sociable, particularly when it was at someone else's expense. At least he could head off soon with a full stomach and Swift would consider his duty done.

Eli's next words disabused him of that notion. 'Ty, I've tried a couple of mates, but no one can put me up at the moment. I'm waiting for my final salary to land in my bank, so I'm a cash-free zone for now. It's a bit embarrassing, but I've no savings. I was telling Chand that I was scammed over a property deal in Vanuatu and I lost a shedload of money. Chand said he's got an inflatable mattress he can lend me. I took a peek in the basement. Is it okay if I doss down there for the interim? I don't want to take over your sofa. I'd be out of your hair down there. You won't even know I'm around. *Plis?*'

That word 'interim' sounded ominously open-ended. The traitorous Chand swayed and stared guiltily into the fire.

'It's my office.' Even to his ears, his protest sounded weak.

'I get it. Listen, I'll fold up the bed in the mornings and make myself scarce. I'll be so *kwaet*, you'll forget I've been there.'

Swift gazed at the crumpled sofa, the scatters of toast crumbs, the oozing butter in the packet, the open jar of anchovy paste and Eli's socks and underpants dangling from the mantelpiece. A fierce rain was falling, rattling against the windows. He knew when he was beaten.

'Yes, okay. Not for long, though. I have a business to run.'

'Fantastic! You're a true *fren*,' Eli declared. 'Have some more wine. Chand, pass me another bottle.'

* * *

Next morning, Swift headed for his club, Tamesas, and set out for an early row as the sun was rising. Its pallid yellow light revealed the slow-flowing, cement-coloured Thames. He recognised the river's surly mood. When he pulled his boat down the slipway, curlews were probing the mud with their long bills and oystercatchers were digging for worms.

Ferries and river buses were busily plying up and down. He greeted a dozen other rowers as he travelled as far as Putney and back. The river smelled marshy and the light mist took an hour to clear. At Putney, he spotted a woman mudlarking on the shore. She waved to him and held something up in her hand. He saw a brief glint of amber. She called out, 'Roman glassware!' before bending to her task again.

He reached home in a satisfying, sweaty glow. Before he showered, he removed Eli's underwear and socks from the mantelpiece and noticed a wine stain on a sofa cushion. In the kitchen, he surveyed his plundered fridge and the dirty saucepans in the sink. There'd been no hot water left the night before and he'd had to clean a forest of Eli's hairs from the shower. There was a sink in the basement. Swift suspected that Eli would pee in it. He pictured water splashed around his office.

Swift liked and needed order. He couldn't think straight when there was clutter. He took a breath, showered and then scrubbed the saucepans before he made coffee and toast. It wasn't possible, but he was sure he could hear Eli's snores from the basement below. While he ate, he looked up the Go Kids charity, interested in the link to Spring, and clicked the fundraising page. Dozens of events were listed — marathons, treks, runs, cycling challenges, skydiving and climbing Kilimanjaro. He searched triathlons and saw a number around the UK. Several had photos featuring Jerome Adcott cycling and swimming. In the 'About' section, he read a paragraph headlined 'Chloe Adcott'.

Chloe is a qualified solicitor. She specialised in family law before helping to set up Go Kids. Chloe works hard with our fundraisers as well as being a trustee. Her husband, Jerome Adcott, regularly completes triathlons to help boost our coffers.

Swift studied the 'Corporate Fundraising' link. Go Kids had more than twenty charity partners in the business sector. Spring had a page, with a description of its involvement.

Araminta Leadsom is our champion at Spring Investment Management. She writes:

Go Kids is a great cause and we're all committed to its progress here at Spring. We constantly keep our employees engaged with the charity, and we update them on the work that Go Kids is doing with different families across the UK.

We also have monthly office fundraising activities, including sports challenges, with walking football for the less energetic. We have annual activities such as our quiz night and rounders day, and we support our CEO in his triathlons.

We also promote Go Kids a lot, which keeps people constantly engaged and makes them want to be a part of it.

So there was a pulse lurking beneath Araminta's frost, and the partnership was a laudable fusion of mammon-like greed and charity.

Swift cleared his breakfast away and left Eli a note before he went out.

I'll do a food shop. Can you get the wine stain off the cushion and clean up after yourself?

He took buses through the wintry streets to Holloway, where Conor Wallace had said he'd be working at home this morning. Yesterday's sleet and rain had left deep puddles and the bus wheels sent spray cascading onto pavements.

Wallace was standing in the window of his ground-floor flat and waved when he saw Swift. 'Hi, come on in. I'm working in the kitchen at the moment, keeping an eye on a soup.'

The kitchen was down a narrow, dark hallway cluttered with children's bikes, scooters, a heaped shoe rack and coats. There were wonderful aromas of meat and herbs in the cramped room. Children's paintings adorned the walls and Swift saw two small pairs of wellingtons by the back door that led to a tiny garden. The table was loaded with bowls of fruit, colouring books and crayons, newspapers, playdough, plastic bricks and cardboard files. Wallace's laptop edged up against the chaos with a lamp angled across it.

He poured them some coffee. 'This flat is too small for us, as you can see,' he said. 'The three boys are together in one bedroom and there are numerous squabbles.'

'How old are they?'

'Four, six and eight. Lucy says that she'll go mad if she has to spend another year here. It doesn't help that the people upstairs sound as if they're clog dancing every night. We're viewing houses at the moment.' He was a trim man with thick wavy hair parted at the side. He spoke in a slow-paced monotone and wiped the bottom of the mug before he handed it to Swift.

'Good luck with that — it's a stressful process, especially as you're changing jobs as well,' Swift said. The coffee was welcome, aromatic and strong.

Wallace frowned. 'Who told you I was moving jobs?'

'Jerome Adcott. He mentioned it when I saw him. Is that for a promotion, more money?'

'Naturally.'

'Got to, I suppose, with a growing family.'

Wallace made no comment, but checked a huge lidded pot on the cooker, stirred the contents and turned it off. 'I make soup for the kitchen at the community centre once a fortnight. They'll be here to pick it up soon.' He sat across from Swift, moving the bowl of fruit to one side. 'So, how can I help you? Lucy told me that Toni had decided to engage you. I don't envy you the task, given the circumstances.'

'Tell me about Sam. I'd like to form a picture of him.'

Wallace took a banana from the bowl, peeled it and carefully removed the stringy strands, laying them to one side. Swift watched patiently, wondering why the man was playing for time. He must have expected the question. When he raised his eyes, Swift was taken aback to see that they glistened with tears.

'I find it really hard to talk about Sam. We were as close as brothers. I dream about him.' He took a bite of banana and chewed.

'I'm sorry. I realise this is difficult. Did Sam seem worried about anything?'

'Sam was conscientious about his work and he liked to make sure everything was done properly. Jerome's a fair but exacting boss. He pushes himself and expects his colleagues to do the same. But I wouldn't say that Sam was worried. He was excited about getting married.' Wallace stared at the banana and put it down, half-eaten.

'He had everything to look forward to,' Swift observed. 'Marriage and a life with Toni.'

'Yes, exactly.'

'How long had you known him?'

'About nine years. We both loved motorbikes. He was best man at my wedding.'

'Were you going to be his?'

Wallace folded the skin around the banana and reached behind him to a drawer. 'Sam and Toni didn't want that kind of formality. They'd planned a low-key ceremony, no fuss.' He wrapped the banana tight in cling film, got up and put it in the fridge. 'My children laugh at me for doing things like this, but I tell them what Pope Francis said — "Throwing away food is like stealing from the table of those who are poor and hungry." I'm not sure they understand, but I suppose they will one day and it's important to teach them the lesson. If they bring any food home in their lunchboxes and it's not perishable, they have it again the next day and so on, until it's eaten.'

If Wallace's sons were canny enough, any food they disliked reached the school rubbish bins or was traded. Swift used to do that with his. He'd done a regular deal of his corned beef sandwiches — to him, the meat had smelled like cat food — for another boy's peanut butter. 'Did you and Sam work closely together?'

'No, because I'm in a different section, dealing with pensions. But we'd cross paths regularly at the office and we were close friends outside work. And of course, Lucy and Toni get on well. We're both worried about her. She's not taking care of herself. I've made an extra saucepan of soup for her. I'll drop it round later.'

Swift pictured it sitting untouched in Toni's fridge along with all the other offerings. 'Did you meet Sam's first wife?' He consulted his notes. 'Mila Fullbright?'

The doorbell rang and Wallace leaped up. 'That's the soup collection. Won't be long.' He put the heavy pot in a box and carried it out.

Swift saw that he'd had a text from Eli.

Have you got a tumble dryer? And can you get white sliced bread, I prefer it to brown.

He replied. *Tumble dryer integrated with washing machine. Yes, can do.*

Another text sped back. *Great. Some beers would be good, too. London Particular if you can get it. Tangkyu!*

The cheek of the man. Swift shoved his phone in his pocket.

'Sorry about that.' Wallace sat back down. 'It's a really worthy charity that they run at the centre. We have to watch the pennies, but we're okay compared to some unfortunate folk. We like to give back when we can, do our bit along the way. Of course, Lucy contributes more than me, running the Go Kids shop, but I play my part and I fundraise at Spring for them.'

He sounded aware of his own virtue. Swift disliked it when 'worthy' was attributed to charity. If you were in need, you shouldn't be judged on a scale.

'I was asking about Mila Fullbright.'

'Oh, yes. The marriage was on its last legs when I met Sam. She was okay, but you could tell they'd both checked out of the relationship. He never mentioned her after they split.'

'Did he have many other women friends before Toni?'

'No one serious. There were a few, but just transient.'

'These were women around his age?'

'Yes, of course. Why?'

'He died with a young girl. I want to understand what he was doing with her.'

Wallace's eyes widened. 'Sam didn't go after underage girls. My goodness, he wasn't that kind of man!'

'How would you recognise that kind of man?'

Wallace coloured. 'Well . . . that's like a paedophile, isn't it? No way was Sam like that. There was nothing leery or weird about him. I hope you're not going to start suggesting anything like that to Toni. The police asked those kinds of questions. Things are bad enough for her as it is.'

If paedophiles were so easy to recognise, then parents, schools and the police would have a much easier time. 'I'm asking you, Mr Wallace, because you'd known Sam a lot longer than Toni.'

'Well . . . yes, I see. I've told you my opinion.'

'Yet Sam ended up in the river with a girl of fifteen, apparently in a suicide pact.'

Wallace winced. 'I just don't see what good this is going to do. We'll never understand why, will we? Toni's torment-ing herself.'

'I suppose you have to commend her loyalty and her trust in Sam,' Swift said. 'Unless you believe it to be misplaced.'

Wallace pinched the bridge of his nose. 'Of course not. I admire Toni. I'm amazed that she's able to carry on, go back to work. I'll never forget her face when the police told her about Sam. The whole thing's a nightmare, but what's the point of prolonging it?'

Swift's phone buzzed in his pocket. 'Did you see Sam the day he died?'

'No. I was in Bedford. I rang him that evening, just to have a chat and wish him well for the next day, but I got his voicemail.'

'What time was that?'

'About half eight. I was a bit surprised when he didn't call me back, but I supposed he was chilling out or having an early night. He might have been dead by then.' Wallace cast his eyes downwards. 'I keep recalling that — me leaving him a message he'd never hear.'

'Sudden death is hard to get over. If you come up with anything else that might help, do get in touch.'

Swift checked his phone when Wallace closed the door. Another text from Eli.

How do you get the grill bit of the oven to work? All the lights are flashing.

CHAPTER 6

At one o'clock, Swift was in the Silver Mermaid, his local riverside pub, lunching with Ruth in a quiet corner booth. She was eating slivers of goat's cheese with a green bean and rocket salad and drinking sparkling water — 'I want to fit into my wedding dress.' Rabbit food, as far as Swift was concerned, especially on a cold day. He'd opted for pork and herb sausages, mash, gravy, and a half of Abbot Ale. Ruth reported that Branna had been given positive outcomes at the audiology clinic that morning.

'They adjusted the implant programme settings a little and they said she's doing really well. Branna was busy telling the audiologist about her flower girl dress.' She smiled at him. 'I hope she's not bombarding you with information about my wedding.'

Swift sliced into a sausage. 'I have heard about your dress, the cake and her outfit.' He narrowed his eyes in recollection. 'She's wearing a sequinned, pale blue maxi dress with matching lace knotted headband and cream shoes with a dazzle trim. See, I've been paying attention. I was forced to find them online and admire them.'

'Sorry!'

'I'd rather she talks about it. That's better than her trying to keep it under wraps to spare my feelings. Children shouldn't be saddled with that rubbish.'

'Thank you,' Ruth said. 'That's generous. You're a good man, Ty.'

He wanted to comment, *That wasn't your opinion last year, when you accused me of neglecting Branna,* but he needed this meeting to go well. *Don't rock the boat.* Things had got difficult with Ruth when she'd objected to his ex-partner's lack of patience with Branna, and his own work preoccupations. And to be fair, some of her comments had been justified. In fact, Ruth seemed to be in a mellow, upbeat mood today, so he pressed on with the details he needed to discuss. 'I'd like to talk to Branna regularly when you're in Guernsey, at least three times a week.'

Ruth gazed at him with her clear hazel eyes. 'Fine, of course. And I wondered if you'd like to have her with you for a fortnight in August. She'll have had a couple of months to settle by then.'

'Sounds good. I'll try and visit before then, spend a weekend with her. I can book a place not too far from the airport.'

'Good, she'll enjoy that.'

Was this all going too well to be true? The sun was glinting on Ruth's soft tawny hair, the way it had the day he'd met her. She'd grown it long again. He used to weave it through his fingers. The name of the boat he'd passed on the canal, *Happy Highways,* came back to him, and it brought to mind Houseman's poem, which he'd first read at school.

That is the land of lost content,
I see it shining plain,
The happy highways where I went
And cannot come again.

He took a last mouthful of sausage and mash, determined not to let melancholy infect him.

'I realise that you'll miss her, Ty.' Ruth put a hand briefly on his.

Her touch burned and he moved his away. He had no wish to discuss his inner emotions with Ruth. Those days were long gone. He drank his beer and talked about the river and his boat. When she left, he stayed for a while. He didn't want to go home yet and find Eli spread out, so he sat and watched the world go by. He seemed to be immersed in weddings: Chand and his partner Bella were getting married a fortnight after Ruth and Marcel. Then there was Toni Sheringham's, the wedding that hadn't happened because the bridegroom had drowned.

He sat up straight, drained his glass, rubbed his face and rang Lexie Kadis. She agreed to see him that afternoon.

Toni phoned as he was leaving the pub. 'I don't want to hassle you. Just wondering how you're getting on.'

'I've seen a few people.' He stood watching the river traffic and talked her through the investigation so far. 'I did want to ask you, why were you not going away on honeymoon until October, rather than straight after your wedding?'

'We wanted to be in the Scilly Isles for the autumn, because it's seal-breeding season and you can get fantastic meteor showers in early October.'

'Okay, thanks. I'm seeing Lexie Kadis shortly.'

'Lexie's a bit formidable, but she has a heart of gold,' Toni said. She added glumly, 'She and the others want to come round Thursday night and throw me a birthday party.'

'You're not keen?'

'No. Don't feel like celebrating. They wanted to take me out and when I said no, they insisted that they'll all come here, bring wine and food.'

It occurred to Swift that it would be handy to see Toni's and Sam's circle of friends in one place. He told her so.

'So, it would be helpful to your investigation?'

'Could be. If you want to agree to a party and invite me.'

Her voice lifted. 'Of course. Okay, I'll tell them all it's on. Now I can put up with it, because it's really for Sam.'

* * *

60

Swift met Lexie Kadis in a coffee shop near her office in Fulham, where she was business manager for a hospitality agency. She was tall, big-boned and immaculately turned out in a misty-grey wool suit that exactly matched the vaporous colour of the sky outside. Her Afro hair was tied in a chignon at the nape of her neck. No make-up, but her eyelashes were suspiciously thick. When she put her briefcase on the chair beside her, he saw a small green tattoo of a pine tree peeping out from her shirt cuff, just above her right wrist. It suggested that a more interesting personality lay behind the bland, formal business gear. She drank a chai latte while he had an Americano.

'I've been straight with Toni,' she said. 'I told her I'd called you and that I don't approve of what she's doing, but I said I'd speak to you.'

'Good. It's best to be frank.'

'Well, we agree on that. Not a bad start. I've got just twenty minutes, so fire away.'

It suited him if she wanted to crack the time whip. 'Was Sam having an affair with Naomi Ludlow?'

She pursed her lips and held his gaze. 'Very unlikely. I'd never say impossible, based on my experience of human nature, but highly improbable.'

'Any theories on what he was doing in Docklands when he was supposed to be at home, preparing for his wedding?'

'Not a clue. I couldn't have been more amazed and perplexed if I'd heard he'd been kidnapped by aliens. I'm still baffled.'

'Did you like him?'

'Good question.' Lexie sipped her drink and dabbed her lips with a napkin. 'I didn't *dislike* him. There was nothing to dislike in him. He was decent, affable, polite, good-humoured. A tad dull.'

Swift smiled. 'Sounds like you're damning with faint praise.'

'No, it's not that.' She paused. 'You shoot from the hip, so I'll return the compliment. Toni was nuts to get married again. I told her so. Once bitten, twice shy. I saw the state she was in after Alec, her first husband ran off. Took her ages to piece herself back together. Toni has an affectionate nature. I said to her, why not live with Sam, move in with him if you want, but keep your own flat? I considered that wise counsel.'

'But Toni wanted to make the full commitment.'

'Yes. She wanted the whole package, as did Sam. Fair enough. And Sam was clearly mad about her. Very attentive, always making sure she had a smooth path through life in a caring, supportive way. Toni loved how he treated her, lapped it up. I was happy for her, despite my reservations. You let your friends go their own road. Are you married?'

'No.'

'Me neither. What else do you want to know?'

'How much of Sam did you see in the weeks before the wedding day? Did he seem ill at ease about anything?'

She pushed her empty mug away. 'Toni was my friend, so I tended to see her on her own rather than mix with them as a couple. I did see Sam in a restaurant about a fortnight before he died. He seemed relaxed. He was going on about that motorbike, Bonnie. They were planning to take it on their honeymoon to the Scilly Isles. Sounded like hard work to me — driving hundreds of miles to Penzance and then a ferry. So, he was fine- tuning it, or whatever you do to a motorbike. They looked funny when they were out in it together. Much older than their years. I prefer my sports car.' She smiled. 'Do you honestly believe you'll get anywhere with this investigation?'

'I'm often asked that,' Swift replied. 'I do usually. I always set out with optimism. It strikes me that Toni has very different friends.'

'Meaning?'

'Lucy, for example is a heart-on-sleeve type. You're the opposite.'

'We choose friends to fulfil different roles, I suppose. You're right about touchy-feely Lucy. A tiny amount of her company goes a long way with me.'

'And her husband?'

'Conor's okay. A tad prosaic and humourless. The two of them bang on about the cost of living and how much they have to spend on their boys. Shouldn't have them if you can't afford them. Three is one too many, in my opinion. They're very aware of their altruism, always manage to refer to their charitable work during a conversation, and they make a great virtue out of doing stuff for the charity Lucy works for — Go Kids. Spring's involved in raising money for it as well and of course, Chloe Adcott's a trustee. She's a force of nature and amazing at twisting people's arms for a good cause, gets loads of people to sponsor Jerome's Iron Man challenges.'

'They're all interconnected, then: work, family, charity.'

'That sums it up. I'm on the sidelines and that's where I like to be.'

'You're not involved in any way with Spring or Go Kids?'

'No. I mainly get to hear of stuff through talking to Toni. Anything else?'

'I wondered about your comments — do you find any men interesting?'

She picked up her briefcase. 'Are you hitting on me?'

'No, I'm curious.'

'Sometimes. Rarely. I have impossible standards. Does that satisfy your curiosity?'

'It does. I'll see you on Thursday night, by the way. I'm coming to Toni's birthday party.'

She inclined her head. 'See you then.'

They parted company and Swift walked home under a pale sun. Lexie Kadis had been refreshing. At last, someone hadn't just praised Sam. It was handy to have heard that he could come across as uninteresting, although by her own admission, Lexie would often reach that conclusion about men she met. Still, that assessment, Sam's ordinary appearance and his devotion to Toni made an attraction between him and Naomi even more mystifying.

His phone vibrated and he saw that he'd had a voicemail message. It was from Mr Ludlow and held no surprises.

Mr Swift, my wife told me that you had the temerity to come to our home. We don't want anything to do with you. If you come near us again, or contact us, we'll make a complaint to the police about you. There will be no other warnings.

Swift considered himself told and stopped at the supermarket near home where he bought eggs, bread, cheese, milk and a couple of bottles of London Particular. In the flat, the fire was blazing, the heating was blasting and there was a pungent smell of curry. Eli was in the kitchen, wearing a tropical-print green shirt and matching shorts. He was cooking and listening to folksy music on his iPad with the tumble dryer rumbling in the background. Beside him, surrounded by steam and chopping tomatoes, was Faith Black, Swift's recently discovered Irish cousin.

'*Halo, mi fren,*' Eli beamed. 'I took a chicken from the freezer, so I'm making Tanna chicken, or as near as I can. One of my fave dishes on Vanuatu. No banana leaves, but this is Hammersmith, not Port Vila.'

'Faith, hi! How are you?' Swift put down his carrier bags.

She blew her hair out of her eyes. 'I'm okay. I was out for a cycle, so I called by and met Eli. He roped me into the cooking.'

'She showed me how to work the oven,' Eli explained.

Spice jars and crushed garlic covered the work surfaces. Every pan Swift owned appeared to be in service, and the top of the cooker was spattered with oil and food.

'You don't have to cook,' Swift said faintly.

'Least I can do in return for your hospitality, *mi fren*. You go and put your feet up and chew the fat with Faith. She's staying for dinner. Is that London Particular, or am I dreaming?' He seized a bottle and held it up to Faith. 'I used to fantasise about this on Vanuatu. There's that scene in *Ice Cold in Alex* where they finally cross the desert, get to the bar and watch the lager being poured. This is my *Ice Cold* moment!'

Faith giggled as he uncapped the bottle and lifted it to his lips. She followed Swift into the living room. He was sweating and turned down the thermostat.

'Eli's not really house-trained, is he?' Faith murmured.

'I'm discovering that. He invited himself to stay for a couple of days, because he had nowhere else to go.' *Already seems like a month*, he added silently.

Faith shook her head. 'It's awful, how he was scammed and lost so much money, isn't it? The poor man. He's very cut up about it, embarrassed, too.'

Swift felt like a heel for resenting Eli's presence. Faith was so kind and understanding. He changed the subject. 'How about you? Mary told me you're working.'

'That's right. I'm doing three days a week in an advice centre, managing records. I'm enjoying it and I can pace myself.'

It was good to see that Faith was stronger and her speech was less hesitant, although she still spoke slowly. He'd met her after she and her sister Kelly had been attacked on a ferry crossing from Ireland. Kelly had died and Faith had sustained head injuries that affected her physical and cognitive functioning. She was working with a therapist and she'd stayed with Mary and Simone for a while, but now had a one-bedroom flat in Leyton. Swift had helped her move in and fix it up. She was a pretty woman with long chestnut hair and clear, fine skin. Before the attack, she'd been a keen camogie player with a club called London Harps.

'Do you go to the club these days?'

'Yes, I help with training. I make myself go even if I'm not really up to it. I'm doing much better. Cycling is helping enormously with my fitness.' She scanned the room. 'Where is Eli sleeping?'

'Inflatable mattress in the basement.' Swift hadn't been down there yet and was dreading what he'd find, although, to be fair, Eli had tidied the living room and the stained cushion cover had been removed.

The Tanna chicken was good. While they ate, they listened to Eli's string band music from Oceania, songs about Vanuatu accompanied by guitars, ukuleles and conga drums. Eli regaled them with stories of his exploits on the islands:

scuba diving at coral reefs, peering into an active volcano, jungle treks involving towering waterfalls and deep caves, bungee jumping, swimming and snorkelling, losing tour members on trips, hanging out with a tribe called the Cargo Cult, visiting a cannibal oven . . . After a while, Swift sat back and let it wash over him, but he noted that Faith was hanging on Eli's every word, wide-eyed.

Swift cleared the plates and said he'd make coffee. He surveyed the war zone of the kitchen. Eli had left the oven and one of the hob rings on. He switched them off and stacked the dishwasher. When he returned with the coffee, Eli was teaching Faith some Bislami phrases. She copied him carefully.

'*Gud mitim yu.*'

'*Plis, yu wanem danis witim mi?*'

'*Hapi betdei.*'

'*Man ia i pem evri samting.*'

Swift could guess the meaning of them all except the last one. 'What does that mean?'

Eli winked at Faith. 'This gentleman will pay for everything.'

Swift glanced at the empty bottles of London Particular. 'Speaking of which, Eli, any news of your salary landing?'

'It still wasn't there when I checked online this afternoon. I've sent an email to the company. Don't fret, *mi fren*. Now I'm over my jetlag, I'm going to start searching for work.'

'Not in that outfit, I hope,' Faith said.

'I have my one decent suit — dark blue, suitable for the concrete jungle. It still fits, just about.' He patted his middle. 'I'd better diet and lose some of this. Too much good living in the South Pacific. *Mi laekem* all their food, *i tes gud*. I've hung my suit up to get the creases out. Before I forget — Ty, where do you hide your iron?'

'The iron and ironing board are in the cupboard under the stairs.'

'Gotcha.'

Faith headed home on her bike. Eli stretched out on the rug in front of the fire with his iPad, while Swift spent an hour cleaning the kitchen. When the tumble dryer stopped, he saw that it was stuffed with Eli's bone-dry clothes and his cushion cover, now wrinkled and shrunk to half its former size.

* * *

Eli certainly hadn't started dieting come the morning. He polished off a heap of bacon, eggs, tomatoes and fried bread before heading out, saying that he had to see a man about a dog. Swift opened the kitchen window to let out the blue haze of frying and had just finished his own breakfast when his phone rang. He answered to a hesitant male voice, well-spoken.

'Hi, it's Dean Ludlow, Naomi's brother. Can I see you?'

He fished teabags and eggshell out of the sink. 'Of course. When and where?'

'I looked you up. I'm near your office now. Just round the corner, in fact.'

'Okay, it's down the basement steps. I'll see you there in five minutes.'

He should have given himself longer. His office smelled stale and Eli's clothes were strewn everywhere. The mattress was covered in a crumpled sheet and duvet and surrounded by shoes, wet towels, biscuit wrappers and crisp crumbs. Toothpaste splattered the hand basin, which smelled acrid. Swift tamped down anger, ran hot water in the sink and squirted bleach around it. Dean Ludlow was at the door before he had managed to do anything else.

'Come on in, I'm just clearing up. I have a friend staying and he's left the place in a mess.'

'Wow.' Ludlow stepped in. 'I thought my bedroom was bad.' He was in school uniform, black and grey with a light blue tie and a shield badge on his jacket with an inverted red chevron. He put his bag down. 'I'll give you a hand.'

'You sure?'

'Yeah, I was a boy scout.' He held two fingers to his temple. 'I have to help other people at all times.'

'I won't argue with that. Shove the mattress by the wall and chuck everything on it. I'll deal with the rubbish.'

They restored some order within a few minutes. Swift cranked a window open. He went to the coffee machine he kept for clients, but saw that Eli had used up all the pods.

'My friend has finished the coffee. Glass of water?

'Thanks.'

He invited Ludlow to take a seat and sat in his comfortable office chair, which was deep enough to accommodate his long legs.

Ludlow had an attractive, square face. He was darkhaired, like his sister, with an open expression. He fiddled with the end of his tie, folding it upwards and flipping it back down.

'You wanted to talk to me,' Swift prompted.

'Yeah, about Naomi and what happened. That man who died, Sam Goddard. He was about to get married the next day. His fiancée must be in bits. I'm so ashamed that my mum yelled at her at the inquest. She seemed, like, really honest and grief-stricken. Maybe Mr Goddard was up to no good, but even if he was, even if he was vile, I'm sure it wasn't Toni Sheringham's fault.' Ludlow leaned forward. 'My girlfriend, Yuna, says that women often get condemned for men's misbehaviour, as if it's somehow their fault for not noticing or doing enough for the relationship. There's that Beyoncé song on her album, *Lemonade*. It's all about a woman self-blaming because her partner's had an affair. Yuna says that encapsulates the problem.'

'I get your point. You empathise with Toni Sheringham and I believe you're right to. She's convinced that Sam Goddard wasn't having a relationship with Naomi. Everyone I've spoken to so far has confirmed that he was a decent kind of man.'

'Well, whatever he was like, Toni Sheringham's been on my mind. The whole weird thing has. I can't discuss Naomi with my parents. They're doing that tight-lipped "Must just get on with it" thing. I wouldn't want them to find out that I've come here. They'd be furious.'

'How old are you?'

'Seventeen.'

'Old enough to leave home, get married, start work, so old enough to talk to me if you want to. But that's the technical detail. The emotional fallout of speaking to me might be hard.'

'I realise that. Mum and Dad are off their heads right now. On the rare occasions when they do mention Naomi, they refer to her as if she was some kind of saint.'

'That often happens when people die.'

'Does it? Why?'

Swift paused. 'I'm not sure. Maybe it helps to deal with the pain. And you? You must miss your sister.'

Ludlow sighed. 'Yes, but not as much as people assume. That sounds awful, but it's good to be able to say it out loud. I feel like a traitor, but I have to talk to someone. After you showed up at our house, Mum told me that Toni Sheringham was trying to cause trouble by using you. She said she and Dad had ignored your messages. I decided to contact you.'

Family politics was difficult territory, often the equivalent of stepping through a minefield. 'Don't get me wrong,' Swift said, keeping things light, 'I'd love to hear about Naomi. I'm not going to get anywhere with your parents and I've no idea what she was like, apart from seeing her photo.'

Ludlow tilted his chair forward and spoke in a rush. 'Naomi was a calculating, interfering, manipulative bitch.' His face flushed bright rose.

Swift blinked. He'd needed to get that off his chest. 'Don't mince your words.'

'I wouldn't say it to anyone else. I didn't say it to the police. But I reckon she could have had something to do with that man's death. She loved meddling and causing trouble for people, running rings around them. She got off on it — big time.' He gulped water.

This was more like it. Something to get his teeth into. Dirty laundry was always worth a rummage. 'Tell me what's on your mind.'

Ludlow had dripped water on his trousers. He rubbed it in. 'Naomi was always selfish and spiteful, even when she was little. My mum had really bad postnatal depression after she was born, had no energy. It lasted for ages. It was like Naomi got the upper hand very early on. Mum would just give in to her because she was out of it and so tired all the time.' He played with his tie again, flicking the end. 'Naomi always had to be the centre of attention. She had a callous streak, never cared about other people. She'd hide my stuff, or damage it if I wouldn't do what she wanted, tell lies to get her own way. She never had many friends, because she was the same with them. Mum and Dad couldn't see it, or they chose not to. I'm studying psychology and I believe she had what's called narcissistic personality disorder and my mother's illness just enhanced it.'

'I've heard of it. I'm a bit wary of random diagnoses and labels.' Swift was also reflecting that Dean Ludlow must have felt overlooked as a child, sandwiched between a depressed mother and an attention-grabbing sister.

'Yeah, I get that. Thing is, Naomi was either idle and listless, complaining of being bored, or revving with her foot on the accelerator. Spinning around like a whirlwind. She had no in-between place. It was all or nothing and she cast around for trouble to stave off monotony. That's how I saw it, anyway. I've no idea if that interests you.'

It certainly did. 'Just tell me whatever comes to mind,' Swift told him. 'Then I can sift through it.'

Ludlow grimaced. 'Makes you sound like a rubbish-picker. Anyway, that's what life with Naomi was like. The doldrums, then an eruption. Then she got sick with a virus a while ago. She was ill, but not for as long or as badly as she made out. A lot of it was pretence, and I could tell she was milking it. Laying it on thick with the symptoms. She loved the focus and attention and all the time she got off school.

I heard her dancing around in her room when our parents were at work. She was out and about when she was supposed to be at home in bed. I saw her one day, walking along with a woman near the canal at Little Venice. They were chatting. I was on the bus.'

'Did you recognise the woman?'

'No. In her twenties, I'd say, long fair hair.'

'How does any of that connect to Sam Goddard?'

'I've no idea. But Naomi was up to something in the weeks before she died. I can't be more specific. I could tell from her smug smile. It was the expression she always had when she'd scored over someone, or got her own way. Sorry, it's hazy.'

'It's something. It's more than I knew about Naomi this morning.'

Ludlow rubbed his eyes with his knuckles, like a little boy. 'D'you think I'm awful, saying these things about my own sister?'

'There's no law that says we have to like our families.' Joyce, his stepmother sprang to mind. She was unrelentingly kind, yet he'd never been able to warm to her.

'I wish Naomi was still alive, I really do, but deep down, I can't grieve for her. How's that for a head-twister?'

Ludlow was likeable. He seemed honest and genuine, and his description of his sister fitted the tone of her tweets, but these were his subjective opinions and he might have his own axe to grind about her, particularly as there'd been no love lost.

'When did you last see Naomi and how was she?'

'We had dinner with Mum and Dad the night before she died. She was fairly quiet, said she was tired, but she gave this little smirk now and again.' He swallowed. 'She went to her room after we'd eaten. I didn't see her again.'

'She didn't say anything unusual or seem worried?'

'No.'

'Did Naomi attend the same school as you?'

'No, I'm at Grendon Academy. She went to a girls' only, Moulton Hall.'

'What about friends?'

'Like I said, she didn't have many. They didn't come to the house.'

'Boyfriends? Glandular fever is usually transmitted through intimate contact.'

Ludlow shifted and crossed his legs. 'Naomi never talked about a boyfriend. I'd be surprised if she didn't have one, even if it was as a personal trophy.' He took a deep breath. 'When she was fourteen, she boasted to me that she'd lost her virginity to a "hot" older guy. I couldn't mention that to the police because my parents would have heard about it, and they'd have been terribly shocked and angry with me for not telling them at the time.'

'Did you believe her?' Swift asked.

'Yeah. She was pleased with herself.'

'When was that?'

He scratched the crown of his head. 'She told me last February. It was Valentine's Day, because she said he'd given her a Valentine. That could have been a lie — I didn't see the card.'

'When did Naomi turn fifteen?'

'March. The twelfth of March. Another thing my parents didn't know was that Naomi used to hang around a bar at Camden Lock called the Gadfly. She'd get in there because she looked older than she was, and the staff turn a blind eye anyway.'

'That could be where she met this older guy.'

'I guess. If it's of any help, my girlfriend Yuna Soto goes to Moulton Hall. She didn't mix with Naomi at school, but she said she's okay about talking to you. Do you want her number?'

'Please. Also, if you have a photo of Naomi, that would be helpful.'

'Sure, no problem.' Ludlow gave him Yuna's number and sent a photo of his sister.

Swift skimmed his notes. 'It seems that there were a lot of things your parents didn't understand about Naomi.'

Ludlow sighed. 'Yeah. I love them but I'm not sure they're much good as parents. I mean, they chose excellent schools and they're keen on making sure of opportunities, but they're always so busy. Dad works late most evenings, and Mum's on various medical committees that take up a lot of her time.'

'One last thing,' Swift said. 'Which swimming pool did Naomi use?'

'It's in Montrose, a private club in Maida Vale. You can walk there from our house. I'd bet she was often at the Gadfly or other places when she said she was going there. My parents were easily fooled and Naomi could look you in the eye and lie, no problem.' He checked his watch. 'I'd better get to school. Thanks for listening, anyway.'

Swift locked the office when Ludlow had gone and made coffee in his flat. At least there was some left in the kitchen. He thought with irritation of the mess there'd been downstairs, and realised that he'd have to be stern with Eli, demand that he be more considerate and ask him to move on. It crossed his mind that the man shared some personality traits with Naomi Ludlow in the narcissism stakes. She sounded like a complex and curious young woman who'd run rings around her parents.

He located Moulton Hall's website and saw that it was an independent school, offering '*A happy, fulfilling and dynamic education for girls aged eleven to eighteen*'. When he rang and explained who he was, he was put through to the deputy head. She listened to him repeat himself, and then told him frostily that the school did not speak to private investigators, wished him a good day and ended the call. He rang Yuna Soto and left a message, asking her to phone him. A text arrived from Eli.

Problems with final pay due to admin error. Should be here this week, so if I can just rely on your hospitality a bit longer? Seeing a woman about a job tomorrow.

He was relieved.

CHAPTER 7

Hester French had emailed him to ask if he'd like to meet for a drink. She suggested a bar called Squeeze near Camden Town Tube station. He found her in there at six o'clock that evening, already seated at the curved bar, drinking rhubarb and lime gin and chatting on her phone. She was wearing a silky red shirt tucked into narrow black trousers and pearl earrings shaped like pea pods.

She turned her warm doe eyes on him. 'Hi, I'm starving! Fancy some tapas?'

They ordered Patatas Bravas, Bomba Picante, Olivas Rellenas, Paella Mixta and Bacalao Frito. Swift had a glass of Rioja.

She chinked glasses with him and shook her downy curls. Her scent had coconut tones that summoned suntan lotion and beaches.

'How's the investigation going?' she asked.

'Slowly. People liked Sam Goddard and speak well of him. It's hard to believe that he'd been having a relationship with a teenager.'

'Oh yeah, Sam was one of the good guys. He was always patient and polite, even when he was pressured. Not like Jerome, who can be a bit grumpy and "Jump to it, I want this done by yesterday". But I suppose he's had to be like that to develop his own business.'

'Do you get on with him?'

'Of course,' she said. 'He's the boss. I'm paid to get on with him. Actually, most of the time he's really nice. The fact that there's little staff turnover speaks volumes. Conor Wallace is leaving, and he's the first person to have jumped ship while I've been there. Chloe Adcott is a good egg too.'

'How involved is she with Spring?'

'She helped Jerome establish the company and she's a director. Now and again, she calls in. Chloe knows all the staff and she organises a summer party every year, on the roof garden — it's to relieve us of our money for Go Kids as well as to have a good time. She strikes me as really driven, but she also has an abundance of soft skills. She's a natural at hosting and putting people at their ease.'

'Sounds as if you admire her.'

'I do. I wouldn't want to cross her, though. She's warm, but there's a core of steel. Jerome's success has a lot to do with her, and he says so. It's good when a man recognises his wife in that way, isn't it?'

'Of course. They must make a strong team.'

Hester's glimmering emerald eyeshadow enhanced her natural twinkle. 'I assume you're not part of a team, as you don't wear a wedding ring and you're here, meeting me,' she said.

Swift smiled. 'I fly solo.'

She laughed. 'It's nice when you lighten up and relax. You're serious. Bit intense.'

'Can't help my disposition. Aren't women supposed to like deep and serious?'

'Depends what's lurking in the depths.' She hummed a few bars of the *Jaws* theme music. 'Fancy another drink?'

'Definitely,' Swift said. 'Did you work closely with Sam?'

'On and off. I'm part of an admin team. Araminta manages us, keeps her beady eye on us. We're not allocated to particular staff. Araminta reckons it's better if we take work as it comes, she says it makes our job more interesting.'

'And does it?'

'Probably. I haven't had any other job, so I've nothing to compare it to. I reckon it's also a system that's meant to keep us all on our toes.'

Hester might affect an ingénue style but she was astute enough. They moved to a table when their food was ready.

'How did you find Sam?' Swift asked. 'Was he troubled about anything?'

Hester speared a potato. 'Can't say he was.'

'That's what I'm struggling with. He apparently took part in a double suicide, which is a dramatic act, yet he wasn't exhibiting any distress.'

'It's an awful puzzle, isn't it? Still, I suppose it's the sort of stuff you're expert at.' She wrinkled her tilted nose. 'Some men do go off the rails very quietly. I had a cousin who killed himself just after he'd got a big promotion. He seemed thrilled and full of optimism, but it turned out he couldn't face the pressure and people's expectations. Maybe, despite all evidence to the contrary, Sam was having doubts about his marriage.'

'Maybe. If he'd been having sex with Naomi, that would be one thing, but to commit suicide — that's an extreme outcome to a fling.'

'And if Naomi had threatened to tell, she'd hardly have been willing to top herself with him,' she said.

'Exactly.' From what Dean Ludlow had said about his sister, she didn't seem the suicidal type. And it was hard to see Sam Goddard as a murderer who'd drugged a young woman and driven her into the river.

Hester's eyes sparkled again. 'I asked if you wanted to meet because I liked you but also . . .' She spooned paella onto her plate. 'Mm, this is good, with the chorizo added.'

Swift ate hungrily. The food was terrific. She was teasing him, but he didn't mind. 'But also?'

'I found an envelope on my desk this afternoon. It's addressed to you, but it wasn't sealed, so I read it. Hope you don't mind. I've no idea what it's about. Very cloak-and-dagger.' She dug into her bag and put a small brown envelope on the table. A printed label on the front said, *Give this to T Swift when you see him. It was in Sam's folders.*

Swift opened it and read the scribbled note on lined yellow paper surrounded by doodles.

BN & possibly others. Not sure what it's about, but can't find anything worrying here. Finger seems to point to Patchell Associates.

'Here' presumably referred to Spring. 'Is this Sam's writing?'

'Yep. We use those pads throughout the office. I tried to think like a detective and I anticipated your next questions. We've no member of staff with the initials BN, and there's no client on our records with those initials either. I shouldn't really be telling you that.' She grinned at him.

'Who are Patchell Associates?'

'No idea. They're not on our list of contacts. Is the note important?'

'Hard to say. Thanks for bringing it along. I wonder who placed it on your desk?'

'Could have been anyone. Araminta sits nearest me.'

Swift had experience of how quickly news travelled around offices. 'Whoever put it on your desk was aware that you were meeting me.'

Hester blushed. 'I did mention it in the kitchen.'

He smiled. 'I see.'

They finished their meal and he asked her when she'd joined Spring.

She told him that she'd started a medical degree, but realised she didn't have the stamina for it, so she'd applied to Spring when she was nineteen. She was easy to talk to. The light pink blush of her gin cast a rosy glow on her skin when she sipped from the glass. Soft guitar music played.

'I live near here,' she said when they'd finished their drinks. 'Want to come back to mine?'

He pictured Eli spread out on the rug in his living room like a huge furry animal, and the chaos there would be in the kitchen. Her eyes were so soft and inviting. She was pretty and good company. It was an easy decision.

* * *

His phone rang just before six the next morning. It was Chand Malla.

'Ty, Eli said not to call you, but you ought to know. It's just that there's been a bit of a fire.'

He sat upright. 'Where?'

'In your place. It's okay, all dealt with now. We put it out between us.'

It was dark in the room and for a moment, he couldn't get his bearings. Then a body stirred beside him, he heard a little murmur and remembered where he was.

'What happened?'

'Eli left the iron on in the kitchen. I heard the smoke alarm in the early hours. There's not much damage, more smoke than anything. I opened the window. It's lucky it wasn't worse, though.'

'I'll head back now. Thanks for telling me.'

'Eli said not to fuss, but I guessed you wouldn't just want to walk into it.'

Hester switched on a bedside lamp and sat up. 'What is it?'

'That was my tenant. There's a problem at my house, so I have to head back. Sorry to leave in a rush.'

'Oh, okay. Is it that urgent?'

'A friend who's staying caused a fire.' He got out of bed and searched for his clothes.

'Oh, gosh. Are the fire brigade there?'

'It wasn't that bad.' He shouldn't have stayed out and left Eli to roam the place like a badly behaved bear.

'Want coffee?'

'No, I'll just get going.' He planted a kiss on her forehead. 'I'll call you.'

Outside, it was bone-chillingly cold. Swift needed the quickest way home, so caught a Tube train with the early morning workers. Everyone was hunched and bleary-eyed. Quite a few attempted to continue their interrupted sleep. Swift closed his own eyes and considered Hester. Her flat had been like her — warm and cheery, with colourful rugs and cushions, lots of glass beads hanging from hooks and (not to his taste) white wooden signs on the wall, proclaiming *Faith, Hope, Love*. She'd been very affectionate, but he did hate having his ear nibbled.

He could smell the lingering smoke when he opened his front door. Eli was asleep on the sofa, fully clothed. Swift walked past him into the kitchen, which was freezing with the window open. The wall by the back door was blackened, and he could see the damaged ironing board and iron propped by the fence outside. There were half a dozen empty cans of cheap lager on the worktop. He closed the window and returned to the living room, where he shook Eli awake.

'Eli! What's been going on here?'

He sat up, rubbing his head and breathing out beer fumes. 'Ty, *mi fren*. Whassup?'

'Chand called me. You could have burned the house down.'

Eli blinked and stared at him. 'Yeah, so sorry about that.'

'What happened?'

'I was ironing and having a beer and I got sleepy, so I lay down here. Still a bit jetlagged. Then Chand was banging on the door. Must have forgotten to switch the iron off. Really sorry, just an accident. It's not so bad, *mi fren*. I'll clean that wall for you and repaint it.'

'Don't bother, I'll do it myself. You'll have to move out, Eli. I've had enough. You can stay in the basement tonight, but that's it, so find somewhere today.'

He'd expected wheedling and further references to being skint, but Eli groaned, sank back on the sofa and pulled the throw over his eyes. Swift gave up, returned to the kitchen and spent half an hour cleaning the wall.

* * *

Sam Goddard's house in Belsize Park, which should have been the site of wedded bliss, stood empty. It was mid-terrace in a mews, flat-roofed, and fronted with brick paving. It was unremarkable on the outside, and Swift saw that it was bland and dated when he entered — not that he was one to talk, with his great-aunt's décor mostly still untouched. Cream walls and plain linen curtains, dark brown carpet. The only signs of quirkiness were the ranks of model vintage motorbikes on the hall shelves. There were some letters on the doormat. Swift flicked through. Bills and an invitation to invest in a timeshare. He put them on the kitchen table.

He did a quick tour of the property. The air was cool, with a slight hint of a spicy perfume. The spacious living room had a low ceiling, a fireplace with a brick surround and two plain brown sofas. There were a handful of magazines and newspapers on the coffee table. Swift noted that the top one was *The Times* from earlier that week. Next to them stood a half-empty bottle of red wine and a crumpled prawn cracker bag. Stairs led up from the kitchen to three bedrooms and a bathroom. The main bedroom had an en-suite shower and a huge poster of a Harley Davidson on the wall facing the bed. On the bedside table stood a mug with blue text on the side.

Things I love almost as much as riding my bike
Admiring my bike
Cleaning my bike
Talking about my bike
Watching TV programmes about bikes
Websites about bikes

Next to the mug was a selfie of Goddard and Toni. She was seated in the Norton's sidecar, a hand resting on his thigh. They seemed happy, at ease. Swift sifted through drawers but there was nothing of interest, just the bits and pieces of a life: cufflinks, rolled-up ties, indigestion tablets, old biros, a couple of buttons, reading glasses, another mug with an illustration of an Isle of Man TT race and various coins. There was a birthday card from Toni, showing an illustration of an open country road winding into distant hills.

Happiest of birthdays, husband-to-be. Can't wait for September! Love you so much, T xxx

In the second bedroom there was a double bed and a wardrobe, and the third was empty except for a desk. Swift saw a decked courtyard through the back window. The day had grown mild, with muted sunshine. There was a shed in one corner, marks where planters had once stood and a rear gate, leading on to an alley. There was no garage, so Goddard must have wheeled his Norton through the gate and kept it in the shed. The garden of the house to the right was a small patch of lawn and to the left there was another courtyard, this one stone-paved, where a man was mending a trellis.

Swift started as he heard the front door bang shut and quick footsteps. He went to the top of the stairs and waited. There were noises from the living room, then steps to the kitchen. A cupboard door clicked and a chair was pulled out, followed by a hissing noise. Surely a burglar would have been quieter. He moved carefully downstairs and saw Conor Wallace's reflection in a wall mirror. He was sitting at the dining table, his legs stretched out, a slice of quiche in baking foil and an open can of Coke in front of him. He was wearing a dark suit and was loosening his tie as he went rapidly through the post. His phone rang and he slouched back in the chair as he took the call.

'Yeah, I'll be back in the office in about an hour. Tell her I'll call then to arrange an appointment. Any urgent messages? Okay, see you shortly.'

He rubbed his eyes with the heels of his hands and ate the quiche in gulps. Swift descended the last steps and coughed as he turned the corner of the stairs into the room.

Wallace froze with quiche halfway to his mouth. 'You made me jump! What on earth are you doing here?'

'You startled me too. Toni gave me a key. I wanted to see where Sam lived.'

'Oh, right.' Annoyance shadowed his face, but he forced a smile. 'I call in once a week, make sure the place is shipshape, keep the heating on low. Don't want any burst pipes. I collect the post and give it to Toni. She doesn't want to have to come here for now.'

'She said you're helping her out. I believe she's planning to sell the house.'

Wallace drank from his can. 'That's right. She'll be rich. This is an expensive area.'

Swift wondered how Sam Goddard had afforded it. 'Had Sam owned this a long time?'

'A while. He came into a lot of money when his dad died. Some people have good luck, don't they?'

Swift noted the grudging tone. 'Sam's good luck seems to have run its course in the Thames.'

Wallace reddened. 'I didn't mean . . . That came out wrong. It's just that we could never afford a house like this close to central London. We're having to search in suburbs like Enfield and Bexley. Feels peculiar, hardly like London at all, and we'll have to travel longer to get to work.'

Swift pointed to the courtyard. 'Did Sam keep his Norton in the shed and take it through the back gate?'

'That's right. Why do you ask?'

'Just interested. I believe a neighbour told the police that they heard him return on the evening he died, and then leave again.'

Wallace turned his chair a little sideways. 'Um, there's something on my mind. I should probably tell you. I was debating contacting you, but as you've turned up . . . I didn't mention it to the police, because I was reluctant to cause Toni any more distress and I wasn't convinced it was relevant. Maybe I was wrong, keeping it to myself.'

Swift pulled out a chair opposite him and sat. 'Go on.'

Wallace looked down at the table. 'I had a drink with Sam about a month before his wedding. We were chatting about this and that — motorbikes, mainly — and then he suddenly asked if he could tell me something in total confidence. He expressed some doubts about marrying. I was gobsmacked, I can tell you. It was the last thing I expected to hear from him. It's hard to remember exactly what he said.'

'Were his doubts about his feelings for Toni?'

'Not as such. More that she'd really wanted to remarry, whereas he'd have been happy to cohabit. He wanted above all to make her happy, so he'd agreed. He talked about his divorce and what if it went wrong again — along those lines, anyway.'

'Did it seem to be a wobble or more serious than that?'

Wallace tapped the backs of his knuckles against his chin. 'That's just it, you see. I reckoned it was a case of the jitters and I reassured him. I had some nerves myself before I married Lucy, and I explained that to him. He seemed to find that comforting and said to take no notice of him, he was being ridiculous. But then, when he died like that . . . I wondered if I'd read it all wrong and he'd been struggling far more than I realised. He might have been involved up to his neck with that Naomi and confused. In which case, I can't have been much help, mouthing platitudes about doubts being normal.'

'Did you mention that evening to anyone else? To Lucy?'

He sounded horrified. 'God, no! I wouldn't have wanted it to get back to Toni and I'd assured Sam it was confidential. Please don't tell Toni, because it might have had nothing at all to do with his death.'

'Okay. Thanks for the information.'

'Just don't make me regret that I've told you.' Wallace crumpled the foil and put it in his pocket. Then he drained the Coke and took the can to the bin. He scooped up the post from the table. 'I have to head back to work. Can I rely on you to lock up?'

'Of course. Before you go, does the name "Patchell Associates" mean anything to you?'

'Sorry, no. Must get going now.'

When he'd gone, Swift ran himself a glass of water. Wallace had seemed cagy. Perhaps it was just a reaction to finding someone else in the house. He'd been making himself at home in a way that made Swift curious. Although he'd said he called in once a week, the date on *The Times* in the living room indicated that he visited more frequently. Swift wondered if Wallace might have taken a nap on a sofa if he hadn't been disturbed. He dried the glass and put it away, then headed back to the living room. Sure enough, he found a head-shaped dent on one of the sofa cushions. Maybe this house provided a refuge from three squabbling boys and a cluttered flat.

He sat and Googled "Patchell Associates". There was just one result in London, for a law firm based in Shadwell. The busy home page of its website stated that it dealt with numerous areas of law including debt and insolvency, conveyancing, motoring law, employment, wills and court of protection, personal injury (no win, no fee), property and probate. It looked like a large company and Swift wasn't going to get far with a vague note mentioning BN.

He rang and talked to a sleepy-sounding woman who had a script and was determined to stick to it. He introduced himself and asked if the name Sam Goddard was familiar.

'Are you enquiring if Mr Goddard works for Patchell Associates?'

'No. Mr Goddard is dead. He mentioned Patchell Associates in a note.'

'What kind of legal advice are you seeking?'

'I'm not. I wondered if Sam Goddard was known to you.'

'Do you want me to check if Mr Goddard is a member of our team?'

'No. He didn't work for you. He's dead.'

'I'm sorry, I don't understand your query. Are you with the police?'

'No. As I explained, I'm a private investigator. Sam Goddard might have had links to Patchell Associates. I wondered if he'd contacted anyone at your firm.'

A long pause. He could hear her brain whirring with discomfort. 'I've checked and Mr Sam Goddard doesn't work here. What type of legal query are you interested in discussing? If you can tell me, I'll put you through to a colleague.'

'I don't have a particular legal query. Do you have a manager I can talk to?'

'It's difficult unless you can be more specific about the type of legal problem. Then I can advise which team you need.'

He'd started to wonder if she was a confused chatbot. 'Employment law,' he said, just to get away from her.

'Hold on, please and I'll try to connect you.'

He listened to Handel's *Water Music* for a while and then his tormentor came back.

'I'm sorry, Mr Goddard, our employment department are all busy right now. May I ask someone to call you back?'

'I'm not Mr Goddard.' He spelled out his name and his number very slowly and ended the call with relief.

He locked up and rang next door's bell, where he'd spotted the man in the garden. There was no answer, so he tried the house to the right. It had an air of mild neglect, with grubby window ledges and weeds in the gravel. A woman with a mass of grey curls, full soft lips and an exhausted, tetchy manner opened the door. When Swift explained who he was, she put a hand to her face.

'Oh, Lord! I felt so bad that I'd complained to Sam sometimes. What an awful way to die! It seemed a very tragic and sordid affair.'

'You complained?'

'About that bloody motorbike. He was usually very careful, but there were times when the engine noise annoyed me. He was always apologetic. Seems oddly quiet now. Too quiet.'

'Were you on close terms?'

'Just as neighbours. I saw Toni a couple of times when she stayed over. Nodding terms.'

'Did you see Mr Goddard when he came home that evening?'

He had the impression that she was being polite, but wanted him to go away. 'No, but I was in the kitchen. I heard him taking it round the back and the clang of the gate.'

'What time was that?'

'Around six. I was starting my supper. Was Toni with him?'

Swift pricked up his ears. 'Why do you ask that?'

'My window was open. I heard another voice.'

'Are you sure?'

'Yes, I'm sure,' she said acidly.

'Male or female?'

'Hard to say. I had the radio on and it was just a murmur. Indistinct. But there was someone out the back with him. I assumed it was Toni and they were going on one of their jaunts, because he took the bike out again about five minutes later. But then when I read how Sam died with that girl, I couldn't make it out.'

This woman was brimming with simmering tension. He didn't want to antagonise her, but he had to ask. 'Did you tell the police that?'

She frowned. 'I'm not sure. Maybe not. It's all a bit muddled now.'

'You forgot?'

She bridled. 'I suppose I did. They came to my door and woke me up. I'd spent three nights in Harrow, caring for my mother and I was worn out. It's not any of your business, but I spend hours every week traipsing across London to care for her. Anyway, I'd taken a couple of sleeping pills so I wasn't too on the ball when the police were asking questions. I just wanted them to go away and let me get back to bed. I was about to have a nap right now so if you don't mind . . .'

He handed her his card. 'Thanks for your help. Do contact me if anything else comes to mind.'

She smiled wryly. 'Mr Swift, most of my waking hours are concerned with what my mother might be getting up to while my back's turned, and where she'll have hidden her medication.'

He thanked her again and left her. When he glanced back, she was yanking up a weed from the doorstep.

CHAPTER 8

Sam Goddard appeared to have been a decent and respected man. If he'd had terrible secrets, they'd been well hidden. Everyone said he'd been devoted to Toni, but according to Conor Wallace, he'd had some doubts about his marriage. It was hard to gauge how significant those had been, or whether they'd been triggered because of an association with Naomi Ludlow. He'd mentioned to Toni that he'd had something to sort out before the wedding, but that might have been a run-of-the-mill work issue. Or it might have been very serious, and connected to BN and Patchell Associates.

From what Swift had heard, Naomi Ludlow offered more promising possibilities, and he therefore decided to focus on her for now. Yuna Soto had agreed to come and speak to him, saying that she'd love to visit a private detective's office. Amazingly, Eli had cleared up and folded the mattress away when Swift went to the basement with a fresh supply of coffee. He'd even cleaned the sink. If he hoped it would buy him more time, he was wrong.

Yuna arrived mid-morning, tripping down the steps in spiky-heeled ankle boots, a pair of white headphones around her neck. Her hair was dyed magenta and bobbed. She had a distant manner and she declined coffee or water.

'This is a good space,' she said, gazing around. 'Functional and uncluttered, but comfortable. Simple décor, nothing threatening. No pictures or personal effects. When a client comes, you want them to focus and not get distracted.'

'That's right.'

'I study design. I'm very interested in the effect of colour and shapes on mood, and what a room tells me about people and their intentions, both consciously and subconsciously.'

Swift reflected that if Yuna had visited with Dean Ludlow, she'd have decided he was a disorganised slob. He could see that she was aware of her own intelligence.

'I'm so glad Dean spoke to you,' she continued. 'I told him he should. He's been bottling stuff up and that's never good, is it?'

'Generally speaking, no.'

'The Ludlows are such a dysfunctional family. They don't *communicate*. Both the parents are terribly uptight and emotionally constipated. They're both high achievers. To me, it's like they wanted two kids, one of each, but then they got on with their own ambitions. To say they've been hands-off parents would be putting it politely. I encourage Dean to get things off his chest and he says it's a huge relief.'

'I can't comment on his parents,' Swift said. 'I'm sure their grief is overwhelming. Thanks for coming. Talk to me about Naomi.'

Yuna had a transatlantic accent and a light, chattery voice, like a little bird. 'Ah, the open question,' she said. 'I can see you're skilled.'

It was odd, being patronised by a teenager. He wanted to laugh. 'I hope so.'

She shrugged off her coat. She wore a yellow hoodie underneath with the black logo, *Airplane Mode*. 'Naomi wasn't much liked at school, but she didn't care. She was unemotional, detached. I sort of admired that about her. I was two years above her, so I didn't mix with her but I saw her around. You were always aware of Naomi if she was in a room.'

'What sort of behaviour made people dislike her?'

Yuna took a fruit smoothie from her bag, stuck the straw in and sipped. 'She boasted a lot, often came top in her class and everyone heard about it. She criticised other pupils, showed them up if they made mistakes and she started gossip about people. Didn't care if she hurt their feelings. She never joined in any team events. In my view, she exhibited high-functioning sociopathic tendencies.'

Dean and his girlfriend were keen on labels. So far they'd told him Naomi was narcissistic and a sociopath. 'Sounds as if she must have been unhappy.'

'I expect so. The way she carried on meant that she didn't have any friends.'

'Didn't the school ever worry about her behaviour?'

'Ah, you see she was always polite to teachers, never caused them any trouble and she did well academically. Private schools like ours, where parents are paying £30,000 a year or more in fees, don't want to lose any of their valuable pupils.' Yuna raised an eyebrow at Swift. 'Let's just say it would take an awful lot to get suspended or expelled.'

'I understand. Money talks and protects.'

'Exactly. Naomi could be pure poison to other students. When she heard I was seeing Dean, she made a point of cornering me in the library. She bad-mouthed him, said he was thick, weak and spineless. I was totally shocked at her spitefulness. I told her to shut up and keep her venom to herself. I've never told Dean about that incident. I've no idea why she said those things, except she must have resented her brother. When I pondered it afterwards, I reckon I worked out why.'

'Go on.'

'Dean's a good person. He's kind and honest. Naomi just couldn't cope with that. Maybe she wanted to be like him, wished she had those qualities, so she envied him, carried a grudge.'

Swift weighed that up. It had a ring of truth. 'Was Naomi's illness common knowledge?'

Yuna nodded. 'Naomi made sure it was. She gave vivid descriptions of the aches and pains to anyone who'd listen, and behaved as if she was the only person on the planet who'd ever been ill. Of course, according to her, the medics said her symptoms were fascinating.' She finished her drink and added, 'Naomi was very bright. Maybe her intelligence was a burden.'

'Did you ever hear Naomi refer to a boyfriend?'

'I didn't. She told Dean about losing her virginity. I believe she'd have had sex because she loved attention and admiration.'

'Dean said he saw Naomi with a fair-haired woman in her twenties. Any idea who that might have been?'

'None. Unless it's someone she met when she was news raiding.'

Swift thought he'd misheard. 'Pardon?'

'News raiding. Naomi started doing it a while ago. When I mentioned it to Dean, he hadn't a clue. I expect Naomi was engaged in it at times when she was supposed to be at home with her virus. I heard her boasting about it in the lunch queue one day. It was another thing she got up to that her parents knew nothing about.'

'What is it?'

'You don't know?' Yuna gave him a pitying glance, the kind that made him feel ancient. 'It's a pathetic kind of hobby, I suppose. It's when people deliberately edge behind TV reporters in outside broadcasts, insert themselves into the film. It seems a terrible waste of time to me, but I can see why it appealed to Naomi. She probably hoped that someone would spot her and offer her a modelling or film contract.'

He made a note. 'Thanks for that information. Anything else you can tell me?'

'That's it. She was a piece of work. A puzzling girl.'

He had the impression that there was something else she wanted to say, but she stood and zipped up her coat. 'I'd change those patterned curtains, if I were you. The William Morris print is lovely, but dated. A bit old-ladyish.'

'They belonged to an old lady,' he said. 'My great-aunt Lily. They were there when I inherited the house from her.'

'That doesn't surprise me. I can tell you're not that interested in your surroundings, but you need a more forward-looking design. Put a plain blind up. More business-like. The room could take one bold colour. Something warm and unthreatening.'

'I'll consider your advice,' he replied.

When she'd gone, Swift searched for news raiding and saw that it was a hobby for some. Those involved tended to loiter around Westminster or other parts of central London where events were taking place, and attach themselves to news reports. He could find nothing relating to Naomi. He scanned the day's news and saw that there was going to be an Extinction Rebellion protest in Parliament Square, scheduled to start at one thirty. That was about as central as you could get and should attract plenty of interest. It would be worth a visit.

His phone buzzed with a text from Hester.

Hope your flat's okay, nothing too awful xxx

He replied, *Not too bad. Thank you for a lovely time. I have a big favour to ask. Could you possibly give me the details of the client Sam Goddard saw the afternoon before he died? I'd be very circumspect with the information.*

He was washing up his coffee mug when her reply arrived.

Not sure, Ty. Big ask. I could get into trouble if Jerome found out. He's very hot on confidentiality! xxx

He considered the next step, which required a degree of manipulation and unfair pressure on a kind young woman. Two people had died. His conscience didn't delay him for long.

I understand. It's just that I have no other way of getting the information. But I don't want to put you in an awkward position, so if it's too big an ask, that's okay.

He stood gazing at the patterned curtains. Maybe Yuna was right.

His phone pinged. Hester again.

I'll see what I can do. Call you later xxx

* * *

Swift strolled around Parliament Square in a mild, refreshing breeze. The protest was underway, a couple of thousand people rallying with banners and listening to speakers. There was a heavy police presence. He saw a few broadcasting units, including the BBC and ITV. A woman with the BBC crew was standing by her camera, smoking a cigarette. Swift approached her and introduced himself.

'I'm investigating two deaths. I've been told that the young girl who died used to news raid.'

The woman laughed and coughed. 'We get some of those. Sometimes we have to do retakes, but they still manage to appear on camera. I have to warn the reporter when I spot one. Saddos, with nothing better to do.'

'Is it usually the same people?'

'Depends. Round here it is, because the event has been publicised, but smaller stories attract random passers-by. There's often a guy called Payne, although he's not around today. You get lots of kids doing dance moves or pulling faces, adults mouthing hello or something abusive. Some people want to snag airtime for whatever's on their mind. We've had people yelling about Palestine, Brexit, global warming, Ukraine — there's a varied menu.'

Swift showed her the photo of Naomi on his phone. 'Did you ever see her?'

'Don't think so. But we cover so much stuff . . . Faces blur. I don't recognise her as a regular.'

The ITV crew were near Nelson Mandela's statue, but Swift drew a blank with them and the four others he tried. He asked a number of people who were standing around watching the crews, but none of them recognised Naomi. He wasn't sure what it would have meant if anyone had. He loitered for a while, listening to speeches and then answered a call on his phone. It was from Jake Munro, a paralegal at Patchell Associates.

'How can I help you, Mr Smith? I believe you have an employment issue.'

'It's Swift.'

'Pardon?'

'The name is Swift.'

'Oh, sorry about that.'

'My enquiry isn't related to employment.' He quickly explained who he was and the information he was seeking.

'Oh, I see. Or, that is, I don't quite understand. We don't share confidential information. I really can't help you with that very unclear query.'

'I only want to know if any of your colleagues had contact with Sam Goddard.'

'There are more than forty legal staff working here.'

'You could send them all an email.' He realised that suggestion would get him nowhere fast.

'I'm afraid that's not possible. I honestly can't help you. Hold on please, while I consult.'

Swift was back listening to Handel. He walked around, watching a plane trace across the sky. A woman with a baby in a sling was shaking a placard and shouting, 'We can't eat money!' Swift grinned at the moon-faced infant. It bounced, jerking its legs.

Jake Munro returned. 'Thanks for waiting. It's best if you email or write in, explaining what you want. If you send an email through our contact form on our website, someone will respond to you.'

He gave up and headed home. He needed to check that Eli was making other arrangements.

* * *

Swift was surprised to find Faith in his living room, doing leg stretches with her hands braced against a wall.

'Eli let me in,' she said.

'Of course. How are you?'

'I'm okay.'

'Cup of tea?'

'No, I'm fine.'

He was picking up a chilliness, which was unusual for Faith. 'Where's Eli?'

'In the basement, packing his stuff.'

'Has he got a place to live? That's good.'

Faith spoke slowly and stiffly. 'He's moving into mine. I said he can have my sofa.'

Swift was taken aback. 'But your place is tiny!' It was a shoebox. She hung her bike from hooks in the narrow hall. Eli would struggle to get his bulk past it. He'd dominate the space. This wasn't a good idea.

'So? It's a roof over his head. He can't afford anything at the moment and none of his other friends can help. I'm surprised at you throwing him out, Ty. It's not his fault that he's run into such bad luck. I know a thing or two about that.' She was glaring at him as if he'd evicted children from the orphanage into the snow.

He sat down. Faith was a vulnerable, isolated young woman who was still recovering from a major trauma. She'd rebuilt some social life, but she was often solitary. Eli wasn't ill-intentioned, but he was overwhelming and he took advantage.

'Eli did tell you that he started a fire here?'

'It was an accident, Ty. He didn't do it deliberately.'

'I realise that. Faith, I did explain to Eli that he couldn't stay for long. Branna is here regularly and I need my office for my job. It's difficult to work around the mess that he leaves in his wake.'

She was standing against the wall, arms folded. 'That's okay, Ty, I realise you're very busy.' She made it sound like a shortcoming. 'I'll be glad of Eli's company. I like him. He's interesting. I love his travel stories and he makes me laugh. He's coming back with me now.'

They heard Eli's firm tread. He appeared with his rucksack, a meek expression on his face, like a schoolboy sent to the Head's office. He put his keys on the table.

'I've tidied up and I folded the mattress and left it outside Chand's door,' he said. '*Tangkyu* for the stay, Ty. I'm sorry again about the fire. I gave the wall another clean and as soon as I'm solvent, I'll buy you a new iron and ironing board.'

Swift stood, outmanoeuvred. 'Thanks for that, Eli. You don't need to bother buying stuff, I'll replace them. Good luck with the job hunting. Talk soon.'

He watched them from the front door as they walked to the Tube. Eli put a hand under Faith's elbow when she tripped. Maybe he was just what she needed, if he didn't exhaust her food supplies, or flood or burn her out. Anyway, it was a done deal. He shrugged and checked his phone. Hester had texted.

Sam visited Ms Jenna Beringer that afternoon. She lives in Reigate, Surrey. That's all I can say. Dinner tomorrow night at mine about seven? I don't mind cooking. xxx

He wasn't sure that he wanted Hester to cook for him. It was a step into domesticity, a suggestion that a relationship might develop, but she had taken a risk and done him a huge favour, so he texted back.

Many thanks. Fine, see you tomorrow.

He searched for Jenna Beringer's phone number. When he rang, there was no reply and no answerphone, so he gave up and decided to paint the kitchen wall.

* * *

There were nine guests at Toni's birthday party, including Swift. Jerome and Chloe Adcott were there as well as Lexie and Conor. Swift didn't recognise any of the others. Toni had finished decorating the living room and the golden colour, suited to the evening hours, glowed in the lamplight.

The kitchen table was loaded with food and drink, far too much for the number of guests. Phil Collins was singing 'Another Day in Paradise'. Toni seemed strained, her mouth taut, but she'd made an effort and was wearing a light green jersey dress with a dipping asymmetric hem. Her hair was pushed back with a band. She had the unfocused gaze of a person well on their way to tipsiness.

'I'm several glasses of wine in,' she said to him. 'I'm drinking to make it bearable. Otherwise, I might open my mouth and howl. Conor and Lexie have taken over. I mind and I don't mind at all. That's my life these days. There's enough food to feed an army.'

He took in the guests. 'Where's Lucy?'

'One of the boys has a tummy bug, so she had to stay at home. D'you want me to introduce you to people? They all know who you are.'

'That's okay, I'll work my way around.' He decided he'd better ask her now if Sam had ever mentioned Patchell Associates, before she got too drunk. He took Sam's note from his pocket and showed it to her. She read it aloud, stumbling slightly.

'No idea what this means. Who's BN?'

'I hope to find out.'

'Where'd you get this?'

He'd decided to keep that quiet, in case Toni remarked on it to Adcott. 'It was in a drawer at Sam's house. It might not mean anything.'

'Oh, right. Nothing means anything anymore, to be honest. Never expected to sound like a nihilist. I must need another drink.'

Toni made a beeline for the kitchen and Swift introduced himself to Chloe Adcott. She was a tall, fresh-faced woman with a straightforward manner and a square, firm jaw.

'I understand you work for Go Kids,' he said.

'That's right. I'm a trustee and I also fundraise. I've done four days a week since we had Jed, our little boy.' She glanced across the room, to where Toni had reappeared with a wine bottle. 'This is the first time I've seen Toni since Christmas. She seems to be coping, but maybe it's a brave front for the party. I hope she's not drinking this much every night.'

'I'd say she's a brave woman all the time.'

Chloe smiled and nudged against a bowl of nuts, just catching them before they fell. 'Oops! Jerome admires Toni. He's terribly cut up about Sam. He doesn't say much, but I can tell. Sam was very much his right-hand man.'

'Were you friendly with Sam?'

'Fairly. We met quite a few times over the years. Sam helped raise funds for Go Kids and he attended events, cheered Jerome on at triathlons.'

'And you're friendly with Conor and Lucy?'

'Oh, yes. Lucy manages a shop for Go Kids.'

'So you were all linked through Spring and Go Kids.'

'Exactly.' She had a steady, slightly unnerving gaze.

'I heard that you're a director at Spring as well as being on the board of Go Kids. You must be a busy woman.'

'I like being busy and I believe it's important to commit socially, help build equality and inclusivity. Go Kids is a great organisation and does so much for families. We focus on promoting positive images of disability. You could say that Jerome and I have made it our lives' work.' Unlike Conor Wallace, she stated this with no impression of self-regard.

'When did you last see Sam?' Swift asked.

Her brow puckered. 'Some weeks before he died.'

'How was he?'

'Very well.'

There was a pause while they both sipped their drinks. Chloe smiled and offered him the nuts while casting a keen eye on the other guests. Swift judged her to be the kind of person who could assess a room when she walked in, and determine who she wanted to speak to first.

'Some of Toni's friends believe she's wrong to ask me to investigate,' Swift said.

Chloe rolled her glass rim along her bottom lip. 'Let things lie? Well, I can't say. That's up to Toni.' She pointed at his neck. 'Do you mind? You've got a bit of fluff on your collar.' She picked it off and in doing so, tripped and spilt a few drops of her wine on his sleeve. 'Oh, I'm so sorry! And that's such a lovely velvet jacket. Beautiful rich burgundy colour.'

'Don't worry. It's white wine. It probably needs a clean anyway.' It was the jacket he'd worn to Mary's wedding. There was a matching waistcoat, but he'd have looked over-dressed in that.

'I'm so clumsy.' She laughed. 'Jerome calls me a one-woman wrecking crew.'

She moved away from him, nudging into Conor. He edged over to Jerome Adcott and touched his elbow.

'Quick word?'

'Sure.' Adcott swallowed a tiny pasty and wiped his lips. 'I shouldn't really have eaten that. Trying to stay off carbs, but they're so tempting. Is this about your investigation?'

'Afraid so.'

Adcott shrugged. 'It would be too much to hope to enjoy myself at a party,' he said. 'Fire away.'

'Do the initials "BN" mean anything to you? I wondered if Sam had come to you with concerns about someone.'

Adcott put his head to one side. 'BN. In connection with . . . ?'

'Probably the business.'

'It's not much to go on.'

'I realise that, but thought you might remember.'

'Hm. Well, I don't. I don't recall Sam mentioning those initials or any worries. Where did you come across this information?'

'Just something I saw and it was worth asking you. I assumed that if a problem had come up at Spring that both-ered him, Sam would have spoken to you immediately.'

Adcott gave a slight frown. 'Of course, we shared any difficulties that came our way. Well, I can't shed any light on it. I'm sure Sam would have come straight to me if anything was troubling him at work.'

'How about Patchell Associates? Do you do business with a company of that name?'

'It doesn't sound familiar, I'm afraid.' He signalled that he was closing down the questions with, 'Want another drink? I need a refill. Chloe's driving tonight.'

Swift declined and returned to circulating. He'd just started talking to Stephen Omondi, who worked with Toni, when Conor opened the living room window and a rich soprano voice singing '*O Sole Mio*' drifted across. Everyone moved to that side of the room.

'That's Dora Melides,' Omondi told him. 'She's one of our residents and a retired opera singer. She dresses up and gives a nightly performance. She started when she moved in and she has quite a following, including on YouTube.'

Swift observed the tall, statuesque woman standing on a balcony, one hand resting on the railing. She'd left the doors open behind her and was backlit by the lamps inside. Her long, sequinned black dress was teamed with a wide fur stole. People had gathered on the pavement below her, some filming her on their phones.

O sole
O sole mio
sta 'nfronte a te!
sta 'nfronte a te!

At the end, she gave a deep bow, waved to acknowledge the applause, picked up the flowers that had been thrown onto the balcony and vanished inside.

Swift sat back down with Omondi. As he sipped his sparkling water, he examined Swift with deep mahogany eyes. 'I'm glad Toni has sought your professional help. She's been a little less anxious since she met you.'

'Sharing the burden can ease things. Not all her friends agree with you, though.'

'She told me. I've met most of them before. Lexie is highly interventive and tries to organise her. Lucy is one of those chatter supporters who usually magnify problems.'

'Chatter supporter?' Swift asked, although he could guess what Omondi meant.

'It's a term I read about for people who encourage others to vent their emotions, without awareness that it can heighten anxieties rather than alleviate them. It's hard, when you're troubled, and everyone has an opinion and wants to give it to you. It tires Toni out, but I can already see that your investigation is helping her. It's the sense of *doing* something, having some control. I'm glad Toni's back at work, but she gets distracted, forgetful.'

Swift enjoyed a long draught of Shiraz. 'Did you meet Sam?'

'Oh, yes. I saw him now and again, and of course at times when he was working. Such a good guy. He certainly made Toni happy.'

'How come you saw him at work?'

'He managed investments for Dora, so he visited her occasionally. She's a very rich woman and makes no secret of it.'

'So, Solatium is private sector housing.'

'That's right. Our residents own their flats leasehold. Some of them are wealthy. They like the ease and reassurance of living in a managed scheme. Our accommodation comes with gym, swimming pool, sauna and other leisure facilities on site.'

Jerome Adcott inclined his head at Swift as he and Chloe left half an hour later, saying their babysitter had to get home. Conor turned the music up after they'd gone and came round topping up glasses. He was attentive to Toni, checking in with her and making sure she ate something. Lexie circulated with plates of spring rolls, samosas and cheese muffins. She was wearing a figure-hugging, low-cut dress and high heels. Her impressive cleavage loomed over Swift as he took a spring roll.

She narrowed her eyes at him. 'I believe you nudged Toni into agreeing to the party.'

'That's right.'

'You're not just an ill wind then.'

'I'll take that as a compliment.'

Swift moved around and talked to the other guests. All spoke warmly of Sam. Everyone turned when Toni turned the music down, hushing Donna Summer. She stood, swaying with glass in hand and slurring. Her hipbones jutted against the soft material of her dress and her hair was escaping from its band, spilling over her shoulders.

'Thangs to all for comin'. Sorry if I'm a pain. My last birthday, Sam and me went on Bonnie to Box Hill and hadda picnic. Thought I'd have lots of birthdays with him. Jus' wanna say that I'm glad Ty Swift's here too. He's gonna help me pr-prove that my lovely Sam wasn't cheatin'. Gonna help me get to the truth. Don't care what you all say. Jus' don't care.' She raised her glass. 'My lovely Sam. Miss you, Sam.'

She started to weep, a slow, deep sobbing. The room was hushed, as if holding its breath. Lexie moved quickly, took Toni's glass from her and led her to the kitchen. She mouthed to Conor to turn the music back up. Another friend brought more food round.

It was time to go. Swift asked Conor Wallace to thank Toni for him when she was more composed.

'Maybe this wasn't such a good idea,' Wallace said. 'I hate seeing her so upset.'

'She'd have been upset on this birthday anyway, without Sam. At least she has friends around to help her hold things together. I was hoping to speak to Lucy tonight. Can you tell her I'll ring?'

'Sure, but it's unlikely that she can add anything to what you've already heard.'

'Just covering all the bases,' Swift said.

CHAPTER 9

The evening had turned mild when Swift stepped outside. It was just before nine, not too late to call on an older person. He crossed the road to Meadow House and rang Ms Melides' bell. He explained through the intercom that he'd just come from Toni Sheringham's party. She asked him to show his ID at the camera and then let him in.

When he reached her flat, she was waiting for him at the door, still wearing her sequinned dress. She had a large diamond brooch pinned over her left bosom. Her dark hair was drawn back from her high forehead and fell in ringlets. Below full brows, her eyes shone almost black.

'It's quite late for visitors, but you may come in. I'm having my supper. You can share it if you want.'

She glided before him with an erect carriage as if she was on castors, her ruffled hem sweeping the floor. Her sitting room was long and narrow, with thick cream carpet and a silvery wallpaper, upon which hung framed photos of her singing on stages around the world. She gave him a tour of the pictures, holding his arm as if they were promenading. Her ample right breast pressed warmly against him. He felt underdressed for the occasion, although his black jeans were fairly new and at least he was wearing his stylish jacket.

'This is *Rigoletto* in Montreal. Here, I'm singing Violetta at the Royal Opera House. This was taken at Seattle Opera. In this, I'm performing as Clotilde at the Met in New York. That one is *Der Rosenkavalier* in Sydney and here I was in *Lohengrin* in Milan.' She continued with each photo, adding details of the productions and the length of run. Her manner was grand and had a sniff of haughtiness.

'You've had quite a career,' he said. 'I heard you sing on your balcony this evening.'

'Ah yes, my one public engagement these days. It seems popular and it amuses me.'

'You must have travelled the world.'

'I had an amazing career. Not bad for a farmer's daughter from Chile. Of course, most of it is hours of sheer hard work with the temporary glamour of the performance, but I loved it. Now, you sit down and I'll bring supper through.'

He sank into a deep armchair covered in a peacock print. All the shelves and tabletops held mirrors of many shapes and sizes, bathing them in myriad prisms of light. Plum velvet curtains were drawn across the balcony where Ms Melides had made her earlier appearance. A grandfather clock with a swan neck and inlaid boxwood decorations ticked soothingly. The room was crammed with vases of red roses — presumably the flowers that accompanied the nightly applause.

Ms Melides coasted in silently with a circular wheeled oak trolley. 'Most English people eat so early,' she said. 'This business of having your supper at six or thereabouts. My theory is that it's because you're still frightened of pleasure, despite Europe's influence. Is it the Protestant ethic? Food is something to be got out of the way and everything tidied. I blame Henry the Eighth and his reformation.'

Swift considered the random comment. 'The Tudors used to have their main meal around noon.'

'Did they?'

'I believe so. Maybe an early evening meal is more to do with climate. In hot countries, it's a pleasure to eat in the dusk, when the warmth of the day has gone.'

'Perhaps. Now, we have little rollmops, salmon and cream cheese blinis, chicken wings with peanut sauce and bean salad. Do help yourself. The wine is a Viognier from the Rapel Valley, my home territory.'

Swift put a few bits of food on a small plate but passed on the wine. He'd had enough for the evening and he expected Ms Melides might prove a complicated encounter. It was hard to gauge her age from her strong oval face and smooth skin.

She ate hungrily, rapidly popping blinis into her mouth and appearing to swallow without chewing. Her haste brought on a startling, prolonged coughing fit. She thumped her chest frantically with a fist as her eyes watered. Swift hoped that he wouldn't have to attempt the Heimlich manoeuvre on that ample torso.

'Shall I get water?'

She waved a hand and took a long drink of wine. She sank back for a moment, pressed her napkin to her mouth and then sprang forward and speared another rollmop.

'I'm a greedy woman, always have been.' She coughed deeply again, held a hand up, swallowed and breathed in.

Swift was holding his own breath, distracted by her heaving chest. He decided he'd better let her finish eating before he asked about Sam Goddard.

She cleared her throat. 'Some of my directors were awful bullies. They'd tell me to lose weight. Of course, they were usually skinny men. But I understood that my voice was better when I carried some heft, so I ignored them.'

'I suppose they held a lot of power.'

She dipped a chicken wing in peanut sauce and spoke through a mouthful of food. 'They tried to. But ultimately, they needed the artist more than the artist needed them.'

'How did you come to settle here?'

'I've always had an affinity for London. I retired and I was living in a rented apartment in Finchley. There were always problems with the plumbing, the heating or the gutters. Tedious details. I saw an advertisement for this place. It suited me. Everything is catered for. Anything goes wrong, it's sorted!' She clicked her fingers. 'I can spend my days in museums and galleries. I adore lunchtime concerts. This city has so many, I'm spoiled for choice. I swim in the pool here every morning and there is always someone to talk to if I wish, although I prefer my own company mostly. Toni is a true, dear heart and immensely helpful, although fragile at present after that terrible business with Sam. Life is a rosary of sorrows, I'm afraid, and she has discovered that so young. Her tragedy reminded me of the story of Tristan and Isolde. Have you seen it? I sang Isolde in Dublin.'

'I've only been to one opera — *Tosca*,' he confessed. It had been a school trip. He'd been bored and had played covertly with his Rubik's cube.

She carried on as if he hadn't spoken. 'Isolde is a good, meaty part. She sings "*Liebestod*" over Tristan's body.' Ms Melides straightened, coughed and sang in her rich voice.

'Softly and gently
how he smiles,
how his eyes
fondly open
— do you see, friends?
Do you not see?
How he shines
ever brighter,
star-haloed
rising higher?
Do you not see?'

She gazed through Swift when she finished. He imagined that she saw herself back on a stage. Then she laughed. 'There. I don't suppose you often have a private concert from an internationally acclaimed soprano.'

'Never before. Thank you.'

She yawned. 'I'm weary, I need to retire. I enjoyed your company.' She spoke as if she'd invited him and was now dismissing him.

'Before I go, I'd like to ask you about Sam Goddard. Toni has engaged me to investigate his death.'

Ms Melides dipped her head and poured more wine. 'She believes in him. She will, always.'

'I understand he handled your finances.'

'He invested for me and I had named him as my power of attorney.'

'How did you meet him?'

'A set designer, Jenna Beringer, recommended his firm. When I contacted them, a Mr Adcott spoke to me and handed me over to Mr Goddard. That was before I moved here. He was a sweet soul. Easy company and efficient. Let's say I had no complaints about him or my investments.'

'When did you last see him?'

She closed her eyes for a moment. 'We met annually, to review things, so . . . last summer.'

'How was he?'

'Very well. He and Toni asked me if I would like to attend their wedding party, but I declined. I don't socialise much, and I suspected that they were inviting me because they hoped that I would sing. I don't do that anymore, except once nightly and at my own convenience, as I did just now.'

'Did Sam Goddard ever mention Naomi Ludlow, the girl he died with?'

Ms Melides fluttered her fingers dismissively. 'I saw her photo in the paper. A slutty piece. No, her name never came up.'

'And you say it was Jenna Beringer who recommended Spring to you?' He was wondering if this woman's name cropping up again was more than a coincidence. The connection could be significant.

'Oh yes, I know her well. I met her years ago at Glyndebourne and we stayed in touch. I haven't seen her for ages.'

'I tried to ring her but no luck.'

'I'm not surprised, she's extremely deaf. She's older than me.' Ms Melides yawned and patted her mouth.

He took the hint. 'Just one more thing. Did Sam Goddard mention a company called Patchell Associates to you?'

'Not that I recall.'

She walked him to the door. 'You're a pleasant enough guest,' she said. 'You may call again, if you wish. You have a pleasing appearance and manners. I once had a leading man who you resemble a little, although he was more macho — broader in the chest and much more assertive. *Ciao*.'

Damned with faint praise. He'd have to save that salvo up for Mary, who always enjoyed a laugh at his expense.

* * *

It was a huge relief to reach home and not find Eli. Swift's flat was quiet and orderly. He closed the door, pressed his back to it and heard the lock click with satisfaction. He sat by the fire with his legs stretched out, sipping tea and searching again online under the topic 'news raiding', and came across a blog called *Pop-up Payne*. It was written by Payne Goodyear, a man who devoted a lot of his time to getting into camera shots.

He scrolled through postings. Goodyear concentrated mainly on London, and boasted successful appearances at places like Westminster Abbey, Kensington Palace and Whitehall, where he had appeared behind various government ministers. He'd also popped up at rallies, protests, commemorations, TV shows and once even at a gas explosion. Goodyear always wore his trademark red sweatshirt with black horizontal stripes. Now and again, he referred to fellow news raiders, although he claimed pole position in the field. It made for tedious reading and there was a lot of name-dropping of the famous, but Swift persevered and was rewarded when he saw the name he was looking for.

Met a girl called Naomi again today. She was at the BAFTA awards earlier this year and bumped into her this afternoon at New Scotland Yard. Love that eye patch, Naomi, nice one!

Swift clicked the button for contact.

Hi, I would like to speak to you about Naomi, the young woman you mentioned in your blog. I believe she might have been Naomi

Ludlow. I'm a private detective and I'm investigating her death. Could you ring or email me, please.

He added his details and sent the message. Then he leaned back and listened to the silence. Bliss.

* * *

The ringing phone jerked him from sleep. He heard a sing-song, excited voice.

'Hi, it's Payne here. You messaged me.'

It was 2.15 a.m. 'I did, yes. I was asleep, actually.'

'Oh, sorry. Didn't realise. I've just got back from a police siege in Streatham. All the main networks were there. It was full-on. I got on Sky, Channel Four and the BBC. Took some doing, I can tell you.'

'Well done.'

'Thanks! So, about Naomi. What can I tell you?'

'First, I need to check if we're referring to the same person. I'll send you a photo if you can hold on.'

'No problem. Sounds fascinating.'

The man sounded pumped and agitated. Swift switched on the bedside lamp, sent him Naomi's photo and waited. He could hear Goodyear's rapid breathing.

'Yes, that's her!'

'Were you at the news reports of the drowning or at the inquest?'

'No, I didn't manage that.'

'I expect you were focusing on other stories.'

Goodyear spoke quickly. 'Probably. I'm incredibly busy, as you can imagine. I have such a full schedule, and monitoring news items and broadcasts takes up a lot of time. I have to plan a month in advance for certain events and then there's always the breaking news to check, like this siege tonight. I keep a chart to plot all my movements—'

'It's really good of you to phone me,' Swift interrupted, worried that Goodyear might go on like this all night. 'Could we meet later today and talk properly?'

'Sure, no problem. I'm at home in the morning — unless any stories break, of course. Sometimes, I have to drop everything and race off.'

'I understand. You can contact me if that happens. Shall we say eleven?'

He noted Goodyear's address in Wood Green and ended the call.

Sleep eluded him now. His pillow was hot and he flipped it over. Sofia Weber kept nudging at his thoughts. She was a detective inspector whom he'd met in west Wales during his last case. He was tempted to get in touch with her, but something held him back. Was it the miles between them? It would be difficult to meet up without complex arrangements. If she'd wanted to maintain the contact, she'd no doubt have called by now. Probably, she had someone in her life and barely remembered him. And he had enough on his plate for the immediate future with Branna. She was about to experience a huge upheaval. The next few months would have to be handled carefully, and the last thing she needed was anyone else being introduced into her life. Not forgetting that he'd have to ease away from Hester soon.

There, he'd talked himself out of it. He stood at the window for a while and watched the shadowy full moon. Nigel, next door's plump cat, appeared on the wall and crouched, eyes glinting.

* * *

Payne Goodyear's flat was cramped and didn't smell too good. A MacBook dominated a small table. Empty pizza and kebab boxes littered the floor. Swift avoided treading in the slimy remains of beef kebab and lettuce and sat in a dusty armchair.

Goodyear was small and rotund, with a pasty, chubby face and long, lank hair that curled around his shoulders. His greeting was effusive and he grinned all the time. Swift wondered if he was medicated.

'Come in! Come in! So good to see you. I'm very excited that I can help you. Coffee?' He took a can of espresso from a high stack on the window ledge.

'Thanks,' Swift said. 'You have a good supply.'

'I need the caffeine. Some days are so frantic, I don't get much sleep and I have to stay alert.'

'When did you start attending outside broadcasts?'

'Been doing it about six years now. I fell into it by accident. I was heading to the Tube and ITV was outside, interviewing people about a shooting. I stopped to see what was going on and that night, I saw myself on the report. It gave me a real kick, I can tell you. I was wearing my red-and-black sweatshirt, so I decided I'd have that as my trademark. I've got four of them. I do wash them!' He laughed throatily. 'Lots of the crews know me now. They say hello. One of them always calls, "Hi Payne, you're a pain!" Do you like my chart?'

Swift had been studying the huge whiteboard that spanned one wall. Tiny writing in various colours covered the weekly segments.

'Is that your timetable?'

'Exactly. I keep an online copy, but I like to see it at a glance. Let me talk you through.' Goodyear waddled over and stood by it with his feet turned out. He took a pen and pointed. 'Black is scheduled stuff, like rallies, meetings, protests and public announcements. Red shows showbiz events and celebrity appearances, green means government activity and blue is for royal occasions. Yellow is breaking news — accidents, et cetera. Orange ticks show every job completed. As you can see, this afternoon I'm due at the Emirates Stadium at two thirty. Arsenal are signing a new player. There'll be a real buzz. Neat, isn't it?'

'Very organised.'

'I have to be, otherwise I might miss something important.'

'And is this your work?'

'It's my passion. I pay the bills working part-time on the checkout at Asda.'

He popped open another espresso and sat in his faded armchair, which faced the whiteboard.

'I'm interested in Naomi Ludlow,' Swift said. 'How many times did you meet her?'

'Just a couple or so. Last time was at the Dorchester Hotel. Tom Hardy was there, promoting a film. Naomi was all made up because she said he blew her a kiss, although I didn't see it.' His enthusiastic tone became serious for a moment. 'Some people like to exaggerate their own importance. Naomi was a bit that way inclined.'

'I see. In your blog, you referred to her eye patch.'

'Yeah, that was her "thing", like mine is my sweatshirt. Something distinctive that marks you out on camera. The eye patch was a neat idea.' He sounded as if he wished he'd dreamed it up himself.

'What did you talk about?'

Goodyear was on his third espresso. 'Didn't have much time to chat. You have to keep your eye on the cameras and what's happening. We compared a few notes on broadcasts we'd been to.'

'Did Naomi ever mention a Sam Goddard?'

'No. He's the guy she died with, isn't he? They made quite a splash, literally.' He grinned unnervingly. 'I checked back on why I didn't get to Docklands that morning. A government minister had resigned over a scandal, so I was after a biggie at Westminster.'

'How about the initials BN? Do they mean anything to you?'

Goodyear considered and shook his head. 'Naomi was with another woman once, they were friendly. Naomi said this woman had told her something interesting about one of the TV technicians. Like, if she told the police, he'd be in trouble. But I didn't get the woman's name. She might be BN.'

This was all annoyingly unclear. 'Can you tell me what she looked like?'

'Long light brown hair. Older than Naomi. Funny isn't it — Naomi becoming the news instead of being in it.

When I read about it, it made me think that she'd have been annoyed not to have seen all the publicity.'

'Have you seen this woman who was with Naomi since?'

'Nope.'

'If you do, could you find out her name and ask her to call me?'

'Will do.' Goodyear was distracted and scrutinising his chart. 'I'd best check this afternoon's timetable, if that's all.'

Swift left him to his obsession, fairly sure that out of sight was out of mind with Goodyear. He walked to a bus stop in a surprisingly bright sun. From Goodyear's description of the brown-haired woman, she could be the same one whom Dean had spotted with Naomi in the street. While he waited for the bus, he called Jenna Beringer again and this time she answered in a loud, hectoring voice. 'Yes?'

It took him several attempts to explain who he was, amid Ms Beringer's requests for repetition ('What?', 'Eh?', 'Say again?'), during which time the bus arrived, he boarded, and drew both amused and annoyed glances from other passengers as he yelled at the deaf woman on the phone. He almost ended the call, but decided against it — it might take him days to get hold of her again. Finally, he arranged to visit her the following morning and took her address. One man applauded loudly when he put his phone away and thanked him '*so* much' for sharing. Swift mouthed, *Sorry*, pulled his collar up and stared out of the window at the unlovely, grimy streets.

CHAPTER 10

Hester had gone to a lot of time and trouble to cook roast pork, one of his least favourite foods. He made his way through it, although it was dry. She'd bought expensive red and white wines. There were flowers on her dining table and she was wearing a flowing navy dress. Jamie Cullum was singing. She'd washed her hair and smelled like a garden.

When he complimented her on the meal, she smiled with pleasure. 'It's lovely to cook for someone. I don't get much practice, so I stick to familiar dishes. Araminta was getting very curious about why I was food shopping. She loves to shove her snooty nose in.'

'She wouldn't approve of me as your guest,' he said. The pork was lodged in his throat and he washed it down with wine.

Hester's eyes shone. 'Well, I very much approve and that's all that matters. Did you get hold of Ms Beringer?'

'Just. She's extremely deaf. I'm seeing her tomorrow.'

'I'm glad I could help. It was a bit scary, but I enjoyed it too. I was like a secret agent!'

'I hope you didn't run any risks.'

'I was careful. Do you have to go undercover a lot?'

'Sorry to disappoint, but I'm mostly out there in the open.' He didn't much like talking about his work.

'You don't ever wear a disguise?'

'Afraid not. I do lie sometimes, for the greater good.'

Like I am right now, pretending to be enjoying myself.

Dessert was bread and butter pudding, which was lovely, with plenty of nutmeg.

'Have to confess, I didn't make the pud, it's from Waitrose,' Hester said.

'Terrific choice. Have you always lived in London?'

He listened to her chat about her ordinary middle-class upbringing in Edmonton. She spoke about her medals for gymnastics, her stern piano teacher, her love–hate relationship with her sister and her passion for musicals. She was lightweight, easy company, but he was mildly bored and wished himself at home. Truth was, they didn't share much mental furniture. He could tell that she expected him to stay the night. She'd made a lot of effort and willingly provided information about the case.

He helped her clear up and stack the dishwasher and when she turned to him, with her soft eyes and glinting hair, he showed willing. Debts had to be paid.

* * *

Swift took the train from Victoria to Surrey's suburbia. While he rattled past green fields, he saw that he'd had an email from Patchell Associates.

Dear Mr Swift,

Thank you for your enquiry. As far as we can ascertain, none of our colleagues had contact with Mr Sam Goddard or Spring Investment Management. That is the only information we can share with you.

Kind Regards,

Patchell Associates

Just as he'd expected. He couldn't see how he could make any headway regarding Goddard's note or the firm of solicitors.

Swift walked a mile from the station to Jenna Beringer's house. It was 1920s' built, detached and backed on to heathland. He expected her to be gruff, given their phone conversation, but she was genial when she opened the door.

'You'll have to speak up,' she said loudly, adding in mock-Cockney, 'I'm Mutt and Jeff.'

She offered him coffee in the basic kitchen. The cooker was an antique with an overhead grill and she had a twin tub washing machine, which was churning. Her face resembled a dried apple, the skin scored and dryish. She was wearing red cords, a worn black fleece and orange trainers. The coffee came in chipped mugs and she dumped a packet of fig rolls on the table. It was a far cry from Ms Melides' elegant apartment and supper trolley.

'Help yourself to one of those if you want. They help keep you regular. One of the perils of old age!'

She heard better in person and he could see that she lip-read. She had fluffy white hair, a wistful smile and deeply lined brackets around her mouth. There were at least a dozen bird tables in the huge back garden, so that the area resembled an aviary.

'So,' she said, 'Dora sent you my way. How is she?'

'Very well.'

'Got a posh flat, I believe.'

'It's lovely. She's comfortable there.'

'Been too long since I saw her. We used to have some laughs. I suppose she's sensible, moving into one of those supported places. I love this house, but it's too much for me really, can't keep up with all the wear and tear. Trouble is, I can't imagine moving now. So much upheaval.' She nibbled her fig roll delicately.

'I wanted to talk to you about Sam Goddard.'

Her face clouded. 'Oh, poor, dear Mr Goddard. You'll have to explain who you are again. I only caught half of it on the phone.'

Swift told her about Toni and his investigation.

'Ah, I see. Sam Goddard was my link with Spring for a while. He was reliable. That's why I told Dora about the firm when she wanted to consolidate her money. She'd made a packet over the years, but she liked spending it. I told her she'd better get savvier if she wanted to enjoy her old age.'

'I understand Mr Goddard visited you the afternoon before his death.'

'That's right. We talked about moving some funds.'

'Was he your power of attorney?'

'I don't have one of those,' Ms Beringer said sharply. 'Don't trust my affairs to anyone but myself, thank you very much.'

The coffee was so strong it was making his teeth ache. 'How did Sam Goddard seem?'

'Excited about his wedding, otherwise much the same as usual, I suppose.'

He picked up on the hesitancy. 'You sensed something?'

'Oh, I'm not sure, really.'

'Was he maybe having doubts about his marriage?'

'Oh, not that, no!' She rubbed one of her eyes. They were pale and deep-set with heavy bags beneath. 'Mr Goddard rang me a couple of weeks before that visit, and asked if I'd always been happy with the service from Spring. I said I had. He sounded worried. He wanted to know if I'd recommended anyone else to them over the years, other than Dora.'

'And had you?'

'Probably. To be honest, I couldn't remember. I've invested with the firm for a while, I started with them when I was still working. I expect I've mentioned them to other people along the way.'

'People on the stage?'

'Yes, and working in the theatre generally.'

'Might there have been someone with the initials "BN"?'

'Goodness, quite possibly! I really couldn't say, after so many years. That afternoon when Mr Goddard was here, he asked me if I'd had any financial business with other firms. I told him that Spring handled all my money. I prefer keeping it under one roof, so to speak.'

'Did he ask you about a firm of solicitors called Patchell Associates?'

Ms Beringer knitted her brows, causing deep scores in her forehead. 'Well . . . I don't recall but I suppose it's possible.'

Swift took a fig roll to erase the taste of the coffee. It was old and dusty. 'What time did Mr Goddard leave you that afternoon?'

'About four. I asked if he was having a night out, but he said he was going home to relax and get ready for the wedding.'

'Was he on his motorbike?'

'Yes, he'd parked it on the drive. A rather lovely design, that machine.' She made a little *tsk* sound. 'I tried to give him a china candlestick as a wedding gift, just a little vintage German one I'd bought in an antiques shop, but he said he couldn't take it. Professional boundaries and all that. I understand that's what it's like these days. So much red tape, rules, and regulations. It's a shame. I've been given some lovely gifts from actors and singers over the years, for ensuring flattering lighting and such. If you can't freely give and receive, have a bit of trust between people, life's a poor old business.' She laughed. 'There endeth the third lesson.'

Swift smiled with her. 'If you do recall any of the other people you told about Spring, will you contact me?'

'Will do, but don't hold your breath. Before you go, could you be a darling and replace a curtain pole in the sitting room for me? It's come out of the bracket and I don't trust my balance to reach it.'

Swift stood on a chair in front of French windows in a room that seemed to have been dressed for a Noel Coward comedy: boxy leather armchairs, *eau de nil* walls, Chinese rugs, Art Deco fireplace with speckled blue tiles and glass-fronted display cabinets. The heavy silk curtains were long and patterned with oriental lilies. Swift wondered if Jenna Beringer had got the job lot from a stage production. All the scene was lacking was a man lounging in a smoking jacket or someone dashing through in tennis whites. Ms Beringer hovered below him, holding the back of the chair and managing to rock it as he checked the screws on the bracket and lifted the pole back into place. A filmy cobweb drifted past him, catching on an eyebrow and caressing his face.

'You are an angel,' she said.

'That's okay. If you let go of the chair, I'll get down.'

When he was back on the floor, she seized him by the shoulders and planted a kiss on his forehead. Her lips were rough and firm.

'Couldn't let that opportunity pass me by!' She winked. 'Hope you don't sue me for harassment!'

'You'll be hearing from my solicitor,' he said and her laughter followed him out the door.

Swift stopped at a corner shop on his way back to the station and bought a bottle of water. He took a long draught, reviewing what Ms Beringer had told him. Sam Goddard had had something on his mind when he'd made that note at work, but at that point, it hadn't related to Spring. Sometime between writing the note and his visits to Ms Melides in July and Ms Beringer in September, he'd started to examine his own firm again. What had happened to change his mind?

Swift was distracted by the front of the *Evening Standard* and a photo of a protest outside a tall block of flats. Payne Goodyear was grinning in the centre of the group, making a thumbs-up sign.

* * *

Swift was fascinated by the area around Old Bow Wharf. He'd read about the Channelsea River, a hidden tidal creek which formed a strange dead end off a tributary of the River Lea and Bow Creek. It was a remnant of the Bow Back Rivers, an ancient web of waterways that had been rerouted over centuries. Few people were aware of it or visited it. You could only access it by boat, on high tide. There was a foot-bridge, but it had been blocked. At the centre of the creek was Channelsea Island, a man-made structure, formerly used for chemical works and now a completely overgrown wildlife haven. Swift had read that tidal flows, sheer river walls and mud could pose significant problems for the rower. He had to go there and find out for himself.

He sat with his iPad, studying the tides and planning a trip. He wondered whether to invite Toni. He didn't usually socialise with clients, but he admired her courage and it had occurred to him that exploring more of the area where Sam had died might help her. He emailed her with a link to the information, and she replied within ten minutes to say it was fascinating, she'd like to accompany him and she had the next day off work. He sent a reply with arrangements.

The following morning, he was up at half five. He made sandwiches and a flask of coffee, and placed them with fruit and bottles of water in a waterproof bag. He drove in the dark to Tamesas, secured his boat to the top of his car and collected Toni. She was ready on the doorstep at seven, dressed as he'd advised in warm layers and her pink beanie. Her face was slightly flushed and she had a sparkle of energy about her that was good to see.

She snapped her seat belt and turned to him with a faint smile. 'Is now the time to tell you that I've never been in a rowing boat and I'm a poor swimmer? In case you change your mind about taking me.'

'Time you tried it and I have a buoyancy vest for you in the very unlikely event that you fall in. I've been rowing for more than twenty years and I've never lost a passenger yet.'

'Onwards then, and into the unknown. I've been reading about Channelsea Island online. What an amazing place. You forget that there are abandoned parts of London. The island was probably made to support tidal water mills. Did you see that there might have been secret military experiments on there during the Second World War?'

'I missed that. Anything's possible in a lost backwater.'

The morning was dry and fine with thin drifts of cloud. He parked at the wharf — as near to the café as he could manage — and turned to Toni. 'You're sure about this? It might be upsetting.'

'I'm sure. Upset is my current standby mode. I'm happy to have an adventure. A distraction.'

Getting into the boat was tricky. Swift carried it down the concrete slipway to the high, choppy waters and held it as steady as he could while Toni climbed in. He handed her the supplies bag, which she tucked behind her legs, then gripped the sides with determination.

'Okay?'

She nodded. 'We're very close to the water!'

'As long as we keep the river as our friend, that's fine.'

He rowed gently to start with, letting Toni settle and allowing his muscles to warm through. He steered up winding Bow Creek, past high-rise offices and homes. Tall cranes reached to the blue skies. Construction was ongoing, with the noise of drills and the clang of steel and equipment filling the air.

'There would have been factories, mills and shipyards here not that long ago,' Toni said. 'Now it costs a fortune to have a river view.'

'It doesn't stop the wildlife.' Swift pointed to the reed beds lining the river walls. 'They'll be teeming with insects and birds. Seals and kingfishers have been spotted along here.'

He was excited. He always got an adrenalin rush when he explored a new stretch of water, and this promised to be particularly stimulating. A little further along, he pointed out a flock of sand martins as they hunted insects over the river, snatching them from the surface. Toni had brought binoculars and watched them. Swift picked up speed and the tide carried them along. They passed remnants of nineteenth-century industry and an ornate Victorian footbridge. After a couple more bends, they reached a barge that almost blocked the width of the river.

'We can't get through!' Toni said.

'I checked. There's room to slip by. Breathe in!'

Swift rowed to the right, past overhanging branches and just managed to get past the barge. The riverbank was muddy and overgrown. He had to push them through by levering an oar against the sedge. Then they were in the Channelsea's brown, silty water, rowing in a deserted landscape past the high metal walls that bordered the tributary. The rush of the tide was the only sound as the river flowed past empty warehouses and ruined machinery.

Toni gazed around. 'This is eerie! As if we've gone through the wardrobe into another land entirely.'

'Wonderful, isn't it? And unexpected.'

He slowed as they approached the desolate island, sited between a pumping station and an abandoned chemical plant. It was verdant and teeming with wildlife, a green oasis in the midst of industrial waste. Broken metal structures punctured the trees and the thick vegetation. Patches of soil were stained red from chemical leakage.

'It really is like another planet,' Toni whispered. '*The Land That Time Forgot.* Can we go on the island? I'd love to explore it.'

It was tempting but inadvisable. He liked that she was game, but he couldn't put her at any risk. Lexie would eviscerate him if anything happened to her friend. He'd come back on his own and explore.

'Best not to. It's like a jungle. The ground could be poisoned and it would be easy to injure yourself on broken machinery.'

'Suppose.' She twisted around, taking the island in from all angles. 'Sam would have loved this strangeness. Now that I've seen it, I'm even more certain that he'd never been to this area before. He'd have told me about it. We'd have come as near as we could on Bonnie.'

Swift steered the boat in by tangled blackthorns. He poured coffee and gave her a cup. 'Sandwich?'

'Just this for now,' she said. 'This place smells weird. Not unpleasant, just odd.'

'Who knows what's in the soil, especially if there were military experiments here.' Swift munched on a ham sandwich.

Toni said with an edge of excitement, 'Maybe they played around with nerve gases or new types of bombs. Stuff for dirty tricks on the Nazis.'

'It seems a long way from war and violence here now,' Swift replied. Birds swooped and chattered in the thickets behind them. They'd be busy nest building. 'When I was at your party, Stephen Omondi told me that Sam dealt with Ms Melides' finances.'

'That's right. We used to say that we'd been fated to meet. If Conor hadn't introduced us, we'd probably have come across each other when Sam visited Dora.' She leaned forward, her eyes keen. 'Was Sam's death linked to his job? Is that note you showed me significant?'

'I'm just following up various connections, Toni. I've no idea. Did Sam ever express an interest in news raiding? That's when people attend outside broadcasts and try to get on camera.'

Her brow furrowed. 'You mean so that they appear on TV?'

'Exactly.'

She laughed. 'Hardly! I never heard Sam refer to it. Wouldn't have been his kind of thing at all.'

'Not even before you met?'

'Well . . . all I can say is that he didn't mention it.'

'It was a hobby of Naomi Ludlow's.'

'Oh, I see. Sounds an adolescent, nerdy kind of activity. No, that wouldn't have interested Sam. There's no way he'd have come across her in connection with that. I'll have an apple now.' She took one from the bag, polished it on her sleeve and bit into it. The sun was steady and warming. She raised her face to it and closed her eyes.

'I visited Sam's house,' Swift said. 'Conor called in while I was there. I startled him. He picked up the post and ate his lunch.'

'Oh, that's right, he mentioned it. He did drop off some mail to me. I haven't dealt with it yet.'

'I spoke to the next-door neighbour.' He explained what she'd said about hearing someone with Sam in the garden on the evening he died. 'She assumed it was you.'

'I suppose she would. That neighbour was Delia. She's okay, although she got on to Sam sometimes about the noise of his engine.' She picked at the apple skin. 'Was that Naomi, then? Did she hear Naomi?'

'Possibly.'

She shook her head sadly. 'It's too weird, doesn't make sense. I try to work it out, but my brain gets foggy.'

It was almost two thirty. The tide would start falling soon and Swift didn't want to get stuck on mudflats.

'We'd better head back. Conor mentioned Sam's ex-wife, Mila. I'd like to check her out.'

Toni pulled the stem from the apple. 'Mila Fullbright. Sam said she was an airhead. No idea where she lives. She worked in music promotion.' She readjusted her hat. 'It's peaceful here. I reckon I could take to this rowing lark. Can we come back sometime?'

'I'm sure we can. Maybe you should learn to swim properly. It does give you confidence on the water.'

She was silent on the way back, staring down into the river's flow. Swift concentrated on the falling tide and the chill breeze that suddenly blew in from the east.

CHAPTER 11

Lucy Wallace had told Swift that she could talk to him during her lunch break. He presented himself at the Goodwill Boutique at one o'clock. Lucy took him past racks of clothes and shelves of books and bric-a-brac to the back of the shop. They sat in a poorly lit room filled with bags and boxes of goods. Lucy ate garlicky pasta salad from a lunch box while he drank water.

'It's upsetting everyone that you're going around asking them questions,' she said. 'It stirs it all up for people. What happened to Sam was dreadful. It affected all our lives and it will take ages to recover.'

'I understand that. It's my job to ask difficult questions. None of Toni's circle has seemed that upset.'

'They won't necessarily *say* they are. Doesn't mean it's not terribly difficult. I'm aware of the strong emotions you're whipping up. Conor's up and down at night. He has nightmares about Sam. He tries not to wake me, but I always sense his absence, so then I get up and we're both sleep deprived.' She placed a palm over her heart. 'Sometimes, I'm like a lightning rod for other people's moods. Being an empath is exhausting. You need to tread carefully, especially with Toni.

Her friends are the people she can rely on long-term, rather than someone like you, who's passing through her life.'

He didn't reply. She annoyed him with her low, insinuating voice and solemn manner. He recalled Stephen Omondi's remark about chatter supporters. It summed Lucy up perfectly. With her worn grey jeans and V-neck sweater whose zip had parted from its seam at the top, she appeared to dress exclusively from the second-hand goods in the shop. Nothing wrong with that, of course, and he was partial to a recycled bargain himself, but it was as if she was always making a conscious statement about her virtuous lifestyle. He reminded himself he'd better be careful not to let his dislike of her cloud his judgement.

'I hear you took Toni on the river yesterday,' she continued. 'I called to see her mid-morning because it was her day off. I was a bit worried when she wasn't in and when I tried her mobile, she didn't answer.'

'Why would that worry you?'

'Well . . . she's fragile.'

'That doesn't mean she can't go out. Surely it's good for her, rather than staying at home replaying memories.'

'Sure, but she usually tells me if she has plans to go somewhere.'

Swift was baffled. 'Why should Toni inform you? Are you concerned that she has suicidal ideas? I haven't heard her express any.'

'No, not as such,' she said with great intensity. 'But she does get down and I like to keep an eye on her. She might have a bad day. I'd never forgive myself if I wasn't there for her and something happened.'

This was too much for Swift. 'Toni's not made of porcelain. You sound like an overanxious mother.'

Lucy blushed angrily and put her food down. 'That's pretty rude. She's my dear friend, almost like a sister to me. After what's happened, I like to take care of her. Have you got a problem with that?'

This was a bad direction to go in. Swift needed to dampen down his dislike of the woman and reroute. Sam Goddard was still a one-dimensional character and he had to bring him into focus. He had been hoping this conversation might help with that.

'Sorry, Lucy. I haven't come here to cause any problems with you. Toni enjoyed the time on the river, even if it was just a distraction.'

Lucy eyed him and pursed her mouth. 'She's upset and alone. I hope you're not taking advantage of that.'

They'd got to the real agenda. 'If you're asking me if I'm hoping to have some kind of liaison with Toni, the answer is no. She's my client.'

'Okay. Well then . . . be aware that we're all watching over her.' She picked up her food and carried on eating. The garlic aroma was pungent and slightly unpleasant in the airless room.

'Talk to me about Mila Fullbright and Sam. How was that marriage?'

She paused, a fork loaded with food hovering in mid-air. 'That was a while ago. I met her just a couple of times. She and Sam divorced years back.'

'Toni commented that Sam didn't say much about the relationship.'

'It was over and I got the impression he didn't regret it. Sometimes, people just want to move on. I don't see any point in you asking about Mila.'

'I'm putting a picture together. All information helps enormously.' That wasn't necessarily true, but floating the idea could reassure people.

Lucy wasn't buying it. 'Can't recall anything that would be useful.'

'Where does Mila live?'

'She was in Snaresbrook back then.'

'Why did they split up?'

'The relationship ran out of steam, I suppose. I can't imagine that Mila can help you in any way. She seemed a lightweight kind of person, interested in package holidays, lying on beaches and going to concerts. Nice enough, but just out for fun. She made no secret of the fact that she was bored when Conor and I talked about our charity efforts.'

'Where did she work?'

'Not sure, now.'

Swift sensed that Lucy did know but couldn't be bothered to say. 'Was anything troubling Sam before he died?'

'No way. He was a happy man.'

He could tell from her curt tone that she still hadn't forgiven him for his earlier injudicious remark. He needed a way to get her back onside and gestured at the bags of stock waiting to be sorted. 'You have an amazing amount of stuff here. What sort of things does Go Kids do?'

'We fund sport and exercise opportunities for children with disabilities. Jerome's been a terrific help. He's donated money from his triathlons to us. His son has cerebral palsy, so he takes a great interest in us.'

'And his wife, Chloe, is on the board of your charity.'

'You've been doing your homework.'

'Always. Spring raises money for you too.'

'That's right. Colleagues there get sponsored for charity runs and such.'

Swift picked up a pair of child's dungarees from a box beside him. They were purple with red glittery stars and big pockets. Right up Branna's street. 'If these are for sale, I'd like to buy them for my daughter.'

'Oh, okay. Let's see. I'd probably price those at around a fiver.'

'Let's say ten. It's for a good cause.' He passed a note over.

'Thank you.' She softened a little. 'I don't want to think badly of Sam,' she said. 'He seemed devoted to Toni and deeply protective of her. I used to laugh that if he could, he'd wrap her in cotton wool. It's hard to understand what he was up to with that girl. Such a tragedy and a waste. Our boys miss him. He was godfather to them all. None of our lives will ever be the same again.'

He waited while she wrapped the dungarees and then left her to attend to the shop. Hester rang as he stepped from the doorway into heavy rain. He expected another invitation to meet and was forming an excuse, but her distraught tone stopped him in his tracks.

'Ty, this is awful! I can't believe it. I've just been sacked!'

He stayed under the porch. 'What happened?'

'Jerome called me into his office just now. He challenged me about Jenna Beringer, asked if I'd passed information to you. I didn't even have a chance to bluff.' She burst into tears. 'What am I going to do?'

'Where are you now?'

'On my way home,' she said between sobs. 'He gave me half an hour to clear my things and go. Oh God, I wish I hadn't helped you! It's my own fault. I realised it might lead to trouble, but I really wanted to lend a hand. I can't face that empty flat but where else can I go? I don't want to tell my parents about this yet. It's too embarrassing!'

He took a breath and forced himself to say, 'I'll come round. I'm so sorry.'

'Yeah . . . Thanks, Ty, I appreciate it. See you there.'

He headed reluctantly for Hester's flat. It was the least he could do in the circumstances.

* * *

They sat side by side on the sofa in Hester's gaily patterned living room with mugs of tea. She tucked her hand into his. Her face was wan and tear-stained. Her twinkle had vanished. He felt like a heel.

'How did Jerome find out?'

'Ms Beringer phoned him and said you'd been to see her. He consulted Araminta and she told him she'd seen me accessing the client records. And someone had told her I was meeting you for a drink in Squeeze. It didn't take much for Jerome to put two and two together. I suppose I could have denied it and said I was searching the records for some other reason, but I find it hard to lie. Bloody Araminta. She and Jerome go way back together. She's been with him from the start of the company. She misses nothing and she goes to him with every bit of gossip. I should have waited until she was on her lunch break. I've wondered sometimes if . . .'

'If what?'

'If she and Jerome might be having an affair. They seem very sparky around each other. But that might be my vivid imagination. He and his wife come across as close, with a good marriage. Anyway, I needn't speculate about that anymore.'

'Sorry, Hester.'

'You're not to blame. I didn't have to do it. Jerome went on about loyalty, betrayal and being disappointed in me. He was really nasty when I promised I'd never do anything like it again. He snapped that I certainly wouldn't, because I was heading out the door.' She leaned her head on his shoulder. 'What if he won't give me a reference?'

'Give him time to cool down. I'm sure he will.'

'Are you just saying that to make me feel better?'

'Of course not. See how it pans out. If it might help, I'll contact him and plead your case, say I pressured you.'

She sniffled. 'Thanks. Appreciate it. It's not so bad, with you here. In fact, it's much better with you here.' She took his arm, draped it about her shoulders, cuddled into him and tucked her legs up beside her.

After a little while, he realised that she was dozing. He sat still, listening to her soft breathing and watching the time. Now and again, she gave a muffled sigh. He had to pick Branna up at four thirty. She was staying the night and he mustn't be late. It was important to keep in Ruth's good books.

His phone buzzed in his pocket. Yuna Soto had sent him a photo with a message.

I was in the girls' loos in the sports block at school and saw this behind a door. Might interest you. A Chris Ryman teaches at Dean's school, Grendon Academy. I haven't shown this to Dean yet. Not sure I will, as it would upset him.

The photo was of graffiti in red ink.

NAOMI SHAGS CHRIS RYMAN. BIG SCORE FOR GRENDON — NOT!

Maybe Chris Ryman had been Naomi's sexual adventure when she was fourteen. This was a lead worth pursuing. He replied to Yuna, thanking her, then searched for Grendon Academy and browsed the "Our Team" page.

Ryman was head of Lower Prep. His headshot showed a vigorous man with gelled hair and a wide smile. Swift tapped his phone. That wouldn't be an easy approach and he'd need to give it some consideration.

Hester shifted. He flexed the arm she was leaning against and searched online for Mila Fullbright. She was on LinkedIn, working for a music promoter near Leicester Square called Thornwell Sounds. He sent her an email.

Hester was by now fast asleep. He needed to go, but he didn't want to wake her. That would involve arrangements and commitments. He eased away from her and placed a cushion behind her head. She was so pretty, with her golden halo of hair. Kind, too. He'd text her later.

He let himself out, closing the door gently. He had no reason to feel sneaky, but he did.

* * *

He was in the middle of making peppermint creams with Branna when Chris Ryman rang him. A crisp, sergeant-major voice. Swift could imagine him calling boys to order.

'Mr Swift. I don't believe we've met. What's this about?'

His daughter was sitting on the worktop with a plastic mixing bowl beside her and covered in a light dusting of icing sugar. She'd added green food colouring to the mix and was stirring fiercely.

'I wanted to talk to you about Naomi Ludlow.'

'Who is she?'

'A girl who died. I believe you might have known her.'

'Sorry, never heard of her.'

'She attended Moulton Hall.'

'That's a girls' school. As you left me a message at my school, I assume this is regarding my workplace. We don't teach girls.'

'I realise that.'

'Well then, Mr Swift — Oh, hang on . . . I've heard of a Dean Ludlow.'

'Dean's her brother.'

'I see. Well, I can't help you about the sister.'

'Could I meet with you briefly? It's important.'

'Can't we talk about this now?'

'It's a bit delicate. Better in person.'

Ryman clicked his tongue. 'Very well. Do you have an office?'

'Yes, in Hammersmith.'

'I haven't got time to traipse there. I live in Fortune Green. There's a bar on the main street, the Albatross. I can meet you there tomorrow evening, six thirty.'

'Who that?' Branna asked when he ended the call. She was eating the mixture and had a green tongue.

'Work. You've had enough of that. There won't be any left.'

'It's yummy.' She grinned. 'Simone say just have one taste!'

'If she could see your teeth now, all green and horrible, she'd worry they were rotting away!' He took the bowl from her. She made a face but contented herself with licking her finger.

'Can we make these for Mummy's wedding?'

'If you like. Best check with Mum that it's okay.'

'She won't mind. You can bring them.'

He carried on lining a tray with baking parchment that kept shifting and curling over. Why was this stuff so fiddly? It seemed to have a life of its own.

'I'm not coming to the wedding,' he said gently.

'Why not?'

'It's Mummy's day.'

'And Marcel's.'

'Exactly.'

'But I *want* you to.'

She had her mutinous stare, the one that could presage a meltdown. This was a confusing time for her.

'Tell you what. We could have a party here the weekend after the wedding and make peppermint creams for it. You'll be staying here with me because Mummy and Marcel are going to Rome for a couple of days.'

'Honmoon.'

'Honeymoon, that's right.'

'Why's it honmoon?'

'It's an old expression, about the sweetness of a new marriage. And people used to drink mead at weddings, which is made with honey.'

'Honey's sweet.'

'Exactly.'

'But moon's not made of honey.'

'Definitely not. Some people say it's made of green cheese.'

'That stupid.' She kicked her legs. 'You and Mummy not married.'

'No, we weren't.'

'Why not?'

He was familiar with this relentless mood. He kissed the top of her head. She tasted sugary. 'Just didn't work out that way.' Before she could ask why not, he pressed on. 'So, what about a party? You could wear your wedding outfit. Action replay.'

She raised her eyebrows. 'Who come?'

'Some of your friends. Louis, Simone, and Mary. Nanna Joyce.'

'Nanna Joyce is step-mum.'

'My stepmother, yes.'

'Why she called that?'

'I explained before, remember? My mum died and my dad married Nanna Joyce.'

'Then he died.'

'That's right.'

Her eyes were wide. 'Were you *very* sad?'

'I was. It was a long time ago now.'

'Did you cry?'

'Yes, of course. It's good to have a cry sometimes.'

She gazed at him and then clapped her hands with one of her mercurial mood changes. 'Nanna Joyce makes great cakes!'

'She does. We could ask Faith to our party too.'

'I like Faith. She give me camogie stick.'

'That's right.'

Branna perked up and started rattling off names of friends to invite. He agreed to them all, glad to have defused that particular hand grenade.

CHAPTER 12

The Albatross was a cheerless place with dim lighting, grimy tables and a snitty bartender who gave the impression that he'd rather be anywhere else on this chilly night. They sat on hard chairs with glasses of thin red wine. Chris Ryman had a rugby player's build and sturdy, muscular thighs. His tweed sports jacket strained across his shoulders. He exuded compressed energy and his manner was cool. Swift explained his involvement with Toni Sheringham.

'I spoke to Dean Ludlow's house master,' Ryman said. 'He filled me in on what happened to the sister. Terrible way to die, and so young. Ludlow was very upset, of course and had some time off school, but just a week or so. I only know Ludlow by sight and reputation — he's a fine footballer. That's all I can tell you.'

Swift took a drink to steel himself. The wine was sharp. 'I've been sent a photo of some graffiti. I'd like to show it to you.'

Ryman pulled a face, as if he'd tasted something unpleasant. 'Why would I want to look at graffiti? Where's it from?'

'From the girls' toilets at Moulton Hall, where Naomi Ludlow was a pupil.'

'Charming. Can't imagine a nicer way to spend my evening.'

'Is that a yes?'

'Oh — go on then.'

Swift passed Ryman his phone and waited. The man took his time and then handed it back. He seemed unfazed. 'Nasty little piece of filth. What's your question?'

'If you say you didn't know Naomi, why that graffiti?'

Ryman laughed. 'Are you serious? Why do kids scrawl graffiti? I could offer you boredom, spite, troublemaking for starters. Some girl with constipation sitting for too long on the loo, with nothing better to do. Maybe Naomi Ludlow had pissed someone off. Maybe she wrote it herself for some bizarre motive.'

He'd made reasonable points, yet there was something in his eyes that alerted Swift's bullshit detector. 'Do you know anyone at Moulton Hall?' he asked.

'Not that I'm aware of. Who went to the trouble of taking the photo and sending it to you? I presume you weren't lurking in the girls' toilets there yourself.'

'Just someone being helpful. I wonder how the person who wrote this knew your name.'

Ryman kept his voice low, but his face was flushed with anger. His right hand clenched into a fist on the table. 'Working that out is hardly rocket science. My name's on the school website, for starters. It will have cropped up in the press, connected to rugby games. Maybe whoever scrawled it has a brother at Grendon, like Naomi did. I don't understand why you're giving this muckraking any credence.'

'Naomi told her brother and people at her school that she'd had sex with an older man when she was fourteen.'

Ryman folded his arms. 'Okay. Maybe she did and maybe she didn't. If true, that's a very serious matter. Were her parents informed?'

'I believe not.'

'I see. If that was real, not fantasy, it wasn't me. I've never met the girl. And if I were you, I'd be careful about associating that story with my name. I have a responsible job and a good reputation. If I hear a hint of you spreading idle rumours, you'll find my solicitor contacting you. Do you understand?'

'Yes. I had to ask you, given the circumstances.'

Ryman regarded him with naked hostility. 'Nauseating job you have. I suppose at least you came straight to me. I have to hand you that. Just make sure you don't go anywhere else with this rubbish. The wine in here's crap, so if there's nothing else, I'll head home and open a decent bottle. You can pay the bill as you dragged me here to insult me.'

Overall, that could have gone worse. Swift gauged that Ryman would land a hefty punch if riled enough. There'd been something going on under the surface with him, and it occurred to Swift that there was one obvious fact he needed to check.

He had no desire to linger in the bar. He paid the extortionate bill, but didn't tip. Outside, he watched Ryman kick an empty can as he barrelled along the pavement and then take out his phone and make a call. He aimed another kick at the can when he reached it again. It spun in an arc and landed in the gutter.

* * *

Mila Fullbright was at home in a spacious, beautifully furnished flat in Snaresbrook. They sat on cream leather sofas in the living room. A crystal sculpture of a golden eagle caught Swift's eye. It was delicate and he asked if it was Lalique.

'Yes, that's right. Lovely, isn't it? It was a special present.' She stretched and yawned, then touched her swollen jaw, which she was nursing with a cold pack. 'My own fault,' she said stiffly. 'I was in a nightclub and I tripped on a step. Combination of stilettos and too many cocktails. Went bang into a wall. Am I an awful sight?'

'Sort of. The purple is eye-catching.'

'Ouch! Don't make me laugh.' She shifted the cold pack and flinched. 'I have to go to the office tomorrow. Hope they don't stare too much.'

'At least you were having fun when you did it.'

'Yeah. My dad says I'm too old for nightclubs. He just sighed heavily when he saw me.'

She was slim with ripped jeans slung around her hips and just a red sports bra on top. A diamond-studded belly bar dangled from her navel. She'd tied her fair hair back with a scarf and was wearing a bracelet made from strips of coloured leather on her left wrist. Her pale complexion testified to an indoor life and late nights.

She sat back on the sofa and used a cushion to wedge the cold pack under her chin. Photos of bands, singers and instrumentalists covered the living room walls. Moody jazz played in the background, the kind that brought smoky basement bars to mind.

'I wanted to talk to you about Sam,' Swift said.

'Poor old Sam. I still can't believe he died like that. So bizarre. Sam was so *straight* — in the old-fashioned sense. Straight verging on boring.'

'Is that why your marriage ended?'

'The main reason, yeah. We wanted different things. Sam was a nester. I leave the nest most of the time. My job means I get lots of freebies to gigs and such. Last week I was at a festival in Amsterdam. It was a hoot. A night in with a boxset isn't my thing, but it was very much Sam's. We ended up arguing all the time. He was such a wet blanket, never wanting to stay out late or get rat-arsed. Is the woman he was about to marry the boxset type?'

He picked up her snide tone. 'Toni? She strikes me as a nester. They seem to have been well suited.'

'That's a shame for her then, losing him like that.' Mila didn't sound too overcome. She took the cold pack from her face and rubbed her jaw gently. 'Was Sam really shagging a fifteen-year-old?'

The diamonds in her navel distracted him, winking in the light when she moved. 'Does that seem likely?'

She hooted. 'No way! Sam liked sex in the dark, in the missionary position, and usually only at weekends. He certainly wasn't adventurous. Never wanted me to dress up like a schoolgirl or anything pervy like that. My last fella, a bass guitarist, was heavily into gadgets. I don't mind a bit of experimentation but it got too much for me. Are you into stuff like that?'

Swift kept a straight face. 'Take a guess.'

She gave a dirty snigger. 'No idea. You never can tell until you're between the sheets. Anyway, I can see you're not going to share. Shame.'

'Sorry to disappoint you. Did Sam fall out with anyone during the time you were together?'

'Nah.' She ran a finger under the band of her bra and adjusted the wide straps. 'Oh, hang on — unless you count the row with his brother.'

This was the first Swift had heard of Goddard having a brother. He was sure that Toni had said both Sam's parents were dead and he didn't have any siblings. 'What was the row about?'

'Hold that thought. I just need to get a fresh cold pack. Want a vodka and tonic? I'm having one to kill the face ache.'

Swift refused.

Mila's perfume was aromatic and scented the air as she moved. She had a loping, slouchy walk that suited her feral edge. It must have been a case of opposites attracting where she and Sam had been concerned. Swift considered that she could fit the description of the woman Dean Ludlow had seen with his sister and the one Payne Goodyear had mentioned. He took a quick photograph on his phone of a picture of Mila from her bookshelf and sent it to them both, asking if they recognised her. Then he sat and watched rain dapple the windows.

Mila returned with a new cold pack and a tall glass fizzing with her drink, laden with ice and lemon. 'That's better! Just the cure I need.'

'I wasn't aware that Sam had a brother.'

'Yeah, Jesse. Five years older than him. I never met him. He didn't come to our wedding. No love lost and Sam was always tight-lipped about him.'

'What was the row about?'

Mila rubbed her fingers together. 'Money. Jesse was their dad's executor and after he died, Sam reckoned that Jesse took his time over sorting out the estate, which was worth loads. They had a big bust-up over it. I have to admit, I was keen for Sam to get his share of the money because at that point, we'd agreed to split and he wanted to buy me out of our flat. Far as I'm aware, once the estate was sorted, they never spoke again.' She raised an eyebrow. 'Didn't Toni know about Jesse?'

'Apparently not.'

'Water under the bridge for Sam, I suppose.'

'Do you have any contact details for him?'

'Nope. No clue about him at all, except their dad had lived somewhere in Essex near the coast.'

'Did you ever come across Naomi Ludlow, the girl who drowned with Sam?'

'Nah, I don't mix with teenagers.' She slipped a little mirror from her pocket and held it up, examining her reflection. 'I wonder how long this bruise will take to go.'

'It's quite big. You'll find it will gradually fade to pale green and then jaundice-yellow.'

She pulled a face. 'You sound clued-up.'

'I've had a few bruises along the way. You'll forget about it once it stops hurting. Have another vodka and drown your sorrows.'

'Good advice.' She took a second glance at herself and pocketed the mirror. 'I'll cover it with concealer in the morning. Hey, if you ever want free tickets for gigs, I can get you some.'

'What sort of music?'

'Depends on what we're promoting.'

'This jazz is good.'

'Okay. I'll see what's coming up.'

Swift thought of Chand Malla. 'Do you ever deal with Elvis tribute acts?'

She spluttered on her vodka. 'Really? You wouldn't rather just listen to the King himself?'

'It'd be for a friend — honestly. My lodger loves both Elvis and Elvis impersonators.'

'It's not our kind of thing, but I'll check it out with some mates and get back to you.' She smiled apologetically. 'I need to crash out for a while now. Good luck with your enquiries. I always had a soft spot for Sam. He was a decent guy.'

* * *

Swift was attempting to construct a timeline for Goddard and Naomi on the day they died. Naomi's was frustratingly scant. She'd apparently been at home that day and had left at some point before her brother arrived back. Her parents had thought she was swimming that evening, but bearing in mind Dean Ludlow's comment, she'd often used that as a cover for other activities. Goddard had used his bike for work because his car was being fixed. He'd phoned Toni at half five and had sounded fine, with plans to stay in. At some point between then and when he reached home, he'd decided to set out again on his motorbike. According to what his neighbour had said, someone had been with him at the back of his house. Had that been Naomi or another person?

These two people who appeared to have been uncon-nected had apparently planned their separate evenings. Yet for some reason, their lives had crossed and they'd ended up drugged and drowned. At least his search on social media for Chris Ryman had produced an interesting result on Instagram.

Swift pushed his notes aside and listened to the faint music of Andy Fanning, the trumpeter who lived next door. He could just make out bars of 'The Blue Room' and had opened the window to hear better when Toni Sheringham returned his call.

'That's bizarre,' she said when Swift explained about Jesse Goddard. 'Sam never mentioned a brother. Why wouldn't he have told me?'

She sounded deflated. It was inevitable that she'd now start to wonder if there were other things that Sam had failed to tell her.

'It sounds as if they'd had a major disagreement. People do cut family members out of their lives, and it might have been too painful for Sam to talk about. According to Mila Fullbright, it was something to do with their father's estate.'

She said something, but her voice faded out and he couldn't catch it. 'Are you out somewhere?'

'I'm at the wharf. Just wanted to visit and chat to Sam. What's Mila like?'

'She's okay. Friendly.'

'Pretty?'

What does it matter? 'Yes.'

Toni's voice dropped. 'I hate that she knew important stuff about Sam that I didn't. Doesn't seem right.'

'Stay positive, Toni. I'll try to find Jesse Goddard and we'll have more to talk about when I've spoken to him.'

'Other than that, are you getting anywhere?'

'I have various strands to follow. I'll keep you up to date.'

'Okay. I'm sorry Lucy got on your case. She tends to nag when she's worried and she told me she'd given you a hard time.'

'We parted on good terms — at least I hope so.'

'Yeah. She never stays in a snit for long. I'm going to head to that café we went to before and get a hot drink.'

Icy rain was falling. It was a bleak day to be in Docklands. Swift pictured Toni gazing into the murky waters and doubting her beloved Sam.

CHAPTER 13

The Gadfly was a basement bar, reached by winding iron steps. A long, narrow room of cool chrome, grey wood panelling and green and rose spotlights. The DJ, Python Head, was getting started with dance music when Swift arrived just after eight o'clock. He sat on a stool at the bar and ordered a glass of sauvignon and a halloumi burger. The place was half full, mainly groups of young women who were quaffing cocktails. Some of them might have been underage, but Swift couldn't be sure. The bartender brought his food, placing it down with a flourish.

'Have you worked here for a while?' Swift asked him.

'About four years.'

Swift showed him a photo of Naomi. 'Recognise her?'

'Yeah, that's Naomi. She died last year.'

'Was she a regular here?'

He smoothed his moustache. 'I saw her now and again.'

'Was she friendly with anyone in particular?'

The young man stiffened. 'Who's asking?'

'My name's Swift. I'm a private investigator and I'm looking into Naomi's death.'

The bartender's narrow eyes became saucers. 'Why's that?'

'Someone's asked me to.' Swift showed him a photo of Goddard. 'Was this man ever in here?'

'I don't recognise him. Doesn't mean to say he never came in.'

'So, did Naomi meet up with anyone in particular when she was here?'

The bartender gave him a suspicious scowl. 'Listen, if you're here to cause trouble, you can fuck off. Our customers come here for a relaxed vibe, not for questions about their private lives.'

The DJ turned up the volume on the pumping music. A couple of girls sprang up in front of him and started dancing.

Swift raised his voice. 'So relaxed that you ignore the law on underage drinking.'

The man's eyes flickered around the room. 'That's not true! What makes you say that?'

Swift took a bite of his cooling burger, chewing slowly.

'Why are you saying that?' the bartender repeated.

Swift drank some wine. 'Naomi was fifteen when she died. The police would be interested to hear that she drank here. I expect they'd carry out some unannounced checks on your customers. If you find that you can remember who she mixed with, I'll forget to contact them.'

The bartender grimaced and gripped the edge of the bar. 'She used to be draped around a guy called Chris.'

This was what Swift had been hoping to hear. He showed the bartender the photo he'd found on Instagram. 'This him?'

'Yeah.'

'Expect him tonight?'

'Hard to say. He drops in frequently.'

'I'll have another glass of wine. I'll try an Orvieto this time.'

Swift sat at the bar, nursing his drink. It was hard to concentrate while the music thudded, but he searched for Jesse Goddard. He spent half an hour sifting through the results and at last saw one on LinkedIn, a man in his forties who ran a proofreading business in Walton-on-the-Naze. Right age range and on the Essex coast. He seemed likely. Swift had just messaged him when the bartender appeared.

'Chris is here now, just come in. You'll keep your word about not going to the cops?'

'I will. Thanks.'

Christian Ryman had the same bulk as his father and was taller. He was wearing a knee-length leather coat and silver trainers with red soles. He had a pair of sunglasses perched on his head and stood with one foot on the base of a stool, rocking it back and forth.

Swift waited until he'd bought a cocktail and finished bantering with the woman serving him. He watched Ryman scan the bar. Then he moved up beside him. 'Hi there, Mr Ryman. I assume you're not expecting to see Naomi Ludlow.'

Ryman spun around off-balance, almost knocking the stool over and spilling some of his tangerine-tinted drink. 'Who're you?'

'I'm a private detective. Can we step outside for a couple of minutes? You won't want me to yell what I have to say. It's personal.'

Ryman stuck his chin out as if he was going to refuse, but he picked up his drink and tilted his head. Swift led the way out. They stood to one side of the metal stairs, beside a wall and a couple of straggling shrubs. Ryman put his drink on top of the wall, took out a packet of chewing gum and popped one in his mouth. 'It's bloody cold out here. So what d'you want?'

'I want to hear about you and Naomi.'

Ryman leaned against the wall. 'You're the guy who contacted my dad, nagging him about graffiti.'

'That's right. After I'd spoken to him, I wondered if I had the wrong Ryman and I did. It turned out to be Christian, not Christopher. Your dad didn't mention that he had a son with a similar name. Fair enough. Protective parent. I saw that you were a student at Grendon Academy until last summer. I suppose your dad's been giving you grief.

He was straight on the phone after he left me, and I'd bet you were getting an earbashing. I presume he put two and two together and added up that you were the Ryman who'd been with Naomi. Or maybe he lied to me and he was in on it all along.'

'He knew nothing about it until you opened your big gob,' said Ryman. 'He blew his top, but so what? I'm all grown up and I've left home.' He sounded dismissive and reached for his drink.

'Oh yeah? I'd say your dad's a hard man to ignore. A lick-you-into-shape, jump-to-it type.'

Ryman didn't reply but the glass jerked in his hand.

'Did you know that Naomi died?'

'Saw it on the news. Sounded very strange. Something about suicide.'

'How long were you in a relationship?'

Ryman had small pebbly eyes. Unrelenting. 'That's a grand name for a couple of quick shags.'

Swift assessed Ryman's heft and height and checked the one narrow exit past him. The man signalled a constrained aggression and they were in a small space.

'You realise that you committed an offence, having sex with her.'

Ryman held a hand up. 'You needn't try that. I'd no idea until I saw her age in the press. I was gobsmacked.'

'Her brother, Dean, was at your school. You weren't aware he had a younger sister?'

'Didn't know the guy. It's a big place and she never mentioned him.'

He was very cool. Not at all bothered, except for that tremor in his hand. He spat his gum at Swift's feet.

Swift kicked it aside. 'Even so,' he said, 'she was under-age at the time when you had sex with her. The police might well be interested in you.'

Ryman stepped closer. His breath smelled of spirits and minty gum. 'There's no way I could have known. She hung out in the bar here, made a beeline for me, came on to me big time. Pestered me. I did her a favour. And I wasn't the first guy she had sex with.'

'She told you that?'

'Yeah.'

'Did she say who the man was?'

'Can't remember.'

He might be lying to cover himself. 'When did you last see Naomi?'

'A while ago. She didn't come here so much after we called a halt to things and she had some funny virus.'

'Who called the halt?'

'Who cares? You're boring me now. She's dead, got herself mixed up in something creepy. Nothing to do with me. End of story.'

'Did she ever mention her hobby of news raiding?'

Ryman shrugged, picked up his drink and shouldered open the door to the bar.

Swift stood in the damp, cold air, wondering whether to go back in and annoy Ryman by keeping an eye on him. He wasn't sure he could take much more of the music, which was now deafening. As he hesitated, the woman who'd served Ryman his drink came out, lighting a cigarette.

She smiled when she spotted Swift. 'I saw you talking to Chris. Is he a friend of yours?'

'No. I wouldn't choose him as a friend.'

'Neither would I.'

'What makes you say that?'

The coloured lights in the bar caught the glass behind her, creating a glow around her head. She came nearer. Her manner was steady, quiet. 'My colleague said you were asking about Naomi.'

'That's right.'

'I saw her in here a bit. I'm part-time.'

'I was talking to Chris Ryman because I'm a private investigator. I'm asking about Naomi's death. He was involved with her.'

'Chris gets involved with lots of girls.'

'You sound clued-up.'

She held her cigarette away from her, a hand cupping her elbow. 'I can't stand the man. He's a lech, a hit-and-run type. I've seen too many girls in tears over him, although I'd say he met his match with Naomi. I guessed that she wasn't old enough to come here. She's not the only one. Management take the view that if their parents can't be bothered with where they are . . .'

She stopped speaking as two couples clattered down the steps and entered the bar. One of them saw her and called a greeting. She waved back.

'I have to get back to work,' she told him.

Swift spoke hurriedly. 'Naomi was only fourteen when she had sex with an older man. It might have been Chris Ryman. Any idea when and how it ended?'

The woman stubbed her cigarette out and put the unsmoked butt back in the packet. 'It seemed like Naomi walked away once she'd got what she wanted. Just from watching how she behaved, I'd say she was pretty manipulative even if she was so young. I can't remember exactly, but I reckon she stopped seeing him around last May. Chris was furious, bad-mouthed her to anyone who'd listen. He's not used to women binning him off. He didn't get much sympathy. Most people reckoned he deserved it.' She turned to go, and then paused. 'There was something about Naomi. She was a hunter, reaching beyond herself, reckless.'

Swift handed her a card. 'If anything else comes back to you, can you contact me? And thanks . . . Sorry, I don't know your name.'

'Amy. Amy Sutcliff.'

Swift bought coffee and drank it on the bus back to Hammersmith. Dean Ludlow had replied to his message about Mila Fullbright's photo, saying it was hard to tell if she was the woman who'd been with Naomi. He'd only caught a glimpse. There was no response from Payne Goodyear.

He played around with the scenario that Christian Ryman might have harboured a grudge against Naomi and then discovered that she was seeing Goddard. He could have killed them in a jealous rage. It seemed far-fetched, but he'd sensed a latent violence in Ryman. The question was, had he let it off the leash?

* * *

When he reached home, Faith rang him. She sounded tired, but eager to talk. It was almost eleven and he was aware that she'd usually be in bed by now.

'Ty, Eli's asked me to lend him some money. D'you think I should?'

'I gather that he's not there at the moment?'

'No, he's out at the corner shop.'

'How much has he asked for?'

'£500. He's not had any luck with a job yet and he still hasn't received his final salary.'

Swift wondered if this salary existed. Eli might have been out of work for some time. He had the appearance of a man who'd been living hand-to-mouth.

'Have you got that amount to lend?'

'Yeah, just about.'

'But you're unsure.'

'Yeah.'

'Faith, are you and Eli a couple?'

There was a pause. 'Not as such. We might be in a while.'

'Is that what you're hoping for?'

'Yeah. I really like him.'

Bloody Eli. This was so unfair. 'Faith, all I can say is that you've only known Eli five minutes. I wouldn't lend money to someone I'd only just met. And he shouldn't have asked you.'

'But you're his friend, Ty. He's okay, isn't he? I mean, he was a detective.'

'I wouldn't give Eli a character reference. I've no real idea what he's been up to in the years since he left the Met, apart from what he chooses to tell.'

Her speech was starting to slur. 'But . . . but he told us all about his time in the P-Pacific.'

'There's what he said and then there's what the truth might actually be. With Eli, you have to read between the lines.' Yet that was exactly what Faith would struggle with. Her injury meant that she had difficulty reading situations and people.

It was no good, he couldn't sit on the fence. 'I can hear that you're worried. Don't lend Eli £500. If you want, lend him £100 but with a payback date.'

She sounded relieved. 'Oh, okay, yeah. That's a good idea.'

'Eli can presumably apply for some benefits while he's job-seeking. He doesn't need to rely on you for money.'

'Thanks, Ty. I'm ever so fond of him, you see.'

He gave an exasperated sigh when she rang off. It seemed to him that this situation could well end in tears, and they wouldn't be Eli's.

CHAPTER 14

The following day, Swift was at the Montrose Health Club. He'd had an email from Yuna Soto that morning. It had confirmed his impression that she'd kept something back on their first meeting.

STOP PRESS. I've been turning this over, and I've decided to tell you that I was chatting to a girl in my tutorial group a while back. I'll call her X. (I wanted to divulge this when I saw you, but X has serious emotional issues and is frankly a bag of nerves, evidenced in psoriasis, but that's another story.) So, I was hesitating about passing this on, but I told Dean and he said I should. X told me that she'd seen Naomi around the Montrose club a couple of times with a woman called Demi Holland. Said they were very friendly, hung out in the juice bar together, etc. X — who would collapse into a heap if she knew I'd talked to you — goes to the Montrose now and again for head massages and she said Demi works there. Over to you.

P.S: did you get a blind for your office yet? On reflection, I'd recommend deep orange — a warm colour, energising and positive, so spot on for representing your business.

Yuna would have approved of the Montrose club's understated, sleek foyer with its pale ash floor and silvery tones. The atmosphere was hushed, more like a church than a place of activity and sweat. Membership fees were eye-watering.

The assistant at the desk told Swift that Ms Holland was conducting a class at present, but if he'd like to wait, she'd be available shortly. Swift helped himself to a complimentary coffee and sat by a cascading water feature of five stone pouring pots. The ripples were soothing, but didn't stop him worrying about Faith. He wondered if he should speak to Eli, but that would be intrusive and treading on Faith's toes. It would be the kind of action that Simone or Lucy Wallace might take and that was enough to put him off.

He was lost in thought, a little mesmerised by the flowing water when a woman approached him, hand held out in greeting.

'Hello, I'm Demi Holland. You were asking for me. Are you interested in one of my classes?'

He rose, shook her warm, dry hand and introduced himself. 'Hi, my name's Tyrone Swift. What classes do you take?'

She sat in a chair next to him and crossed her legs. She was in her twenties, slim and supple in a black tracksuit with lime piping. Her cheeks were flushed pink and her long, light brown hair was tied back in a grip. She could fit the scant description of the woman whom Dean Ludlow and Payne Goodyear had seen with Naomi.

'General fitness, body combat and body balance. I also lead meditation groups. Which are you interested in?'

'None. I'm interested in Naomi Ludlow. She used to be a member here.'

Demi Holland looked startled and then focused on the water cascade. 'Naomi? In what sense?'

'I'm a private investigator, asking questions about her death.'

'That was very sad.'

'It was.'

She turned towards him. Her teeth were small and pointy. 'Who's paying you to investigate?'

'I can't tell you that.'

'I don't understand. The police dealt with it, surely.'

'They did. Now I am. There are unanswered questions. I believe you were friendly with Naomi.'

She laid her arms along the side of her chair. Her fingers were long, with neat, square nails. He had the impression that she was keeping her movements controlled.

'No, we weren't friends. Naomi swam here and took some exercise classes. Occasionally I was her group tutor. She came to a few body balance sessions once she started to recover from an illness. She wanted to build herself back up. Body balance is good for core muscle strength.'

He could tell from the light timbre of her voice that she was lying. Or at least, not telling the truth. There were gradations in dishonesty.

'Oh, that's odd,' he said. 'I understand that you spent time together outside classes.'

'Then you understand wrong. Naomi was a group member, that's all.'

'You met in the juice bar, for example.'

'Sorry, you've been misinformed. It's possible that we were in there at the same time, but not as friends. I often drop in there for a break and of course, members use it regularly.'

Usually, someone would ask at this point how he'd come by his information. Demi Holland just gazed at him. He decided to push on and hazard a guess. 'You were seen out and about together, and at an outside news event.'

She cleared her throat softly. 'That's not the case. I only met Naomi here, in the club, on a professional basis. Her viral illness had taken a toll. We discussed her recovery in terms of how classes might best help her. This sounds like mistaken identity.'

Swift leaned forward and ran a finger through the trickling water. 'Did Naomi ever talk to you about her interest in news raiding?'

Her eyes flickered. 'I've no idea what you're referring to.'

'Naomi liked to try to get on the TV news, edging into the picture at outside broadcasts.'

'Whatever floats someone's boat. She never mentioned it, but then we weren't in each other's company. I'm sorry you've wasted your time coming here. Unless, that is, we can interest you in a class.' There was a mocking undertone that riled him.

'If you're aware of anything that can lead to explaining Naomi's death, it would help a number of people who are grieving,' he said.

'If I could help you, I would. The police and the coroner did explain it and it sounded truly tragic. I'm an instructor here and Naomi was in a few of my classes. She was working hard to recover from a debilitating virus. That's all I can say. I've another class soon, so I'll have to leave it there.'

Demi crossed to the desk and spoke to the receptionist, who glanced over her shoulder in his direction. Swift hadn't quite finished, but he didn't want Demi to observe him. He went to the gents' and spent some time attempting to tame his wayward hair with cold water. Why did he bother? As soon as it dried, it would have a mind of its own.

He approached the foyer carefully and was glad that he'd been cautious. Demi and Araminta Leadsom were standing at the bottom of the stairs leading to the fitness suite, heads bent close. Araminta was carrying a sports bag. They started up the stairs, talking intently.

Was this link important, the crossing of a threshold? It was the first hint of a tie, albeit tenuous, between Goddard and Naomi. He waited until the women had disappeared. The receptionist was eyeing him and he pretended to make a phone call. Half a dozen members came through the doors, swiping their passes and he took advantage of the activity to head to the wall display of the club's instructors. He took a photo of Demi Holland and exited sharpish.

* * *

153

Toni Sheringham had asked him if he'd call by as there was something she wanted to run past him. He needed to check a few things out with her too. He arrived early evening and accepted white wine in a green-tinted glass. He'd assumed that she had something to tell him about Sam, but she had a different problem on her mind. She put a hand to her head, where her hair was newly trimmed and coloured with caramel streaks. 'Just a pointless distraction,' she said. 'Like painting this room.'

They sat at dusk by a window in the living room. Toni hadn't closed the curtains. One lamp shone dimly behind them. Bright spotlights illuminated the baskets of fruit and vegetables outside the busy greengrocer. Customers darted in and out of the mini-mart, calling in for after-work shopping. The evening traffic was barely audible, just a distant swish. Swift remarked that it was like having a seat in the circle above a stage.

'I've often thought that,' Toni told him. 'I love sitting here, watching the comings and goings. I'd have missed this if I'd moved to Sam's. It's quiet in that mews, tucked away. That's why I wanted to see you, to discuss the house with you. But first, have you located Sam's brother?'

'I've emailed a Jesse Goddard who lives in Essex. He could be the man I need. I'm waiting to hear back.'

'It's been on my mind. I checked with Conor and Lucy and they were amazed because Sam had never referred to a brother. I suppose he didn't want to tell me about him if there was bitterness. He always wanted to protect me from unpleasantness. If there was an item about starving children on the news, he'd turn it off because of how much it would upset me. Let me know when—' She gasped as a child ran out of the mini-mart towards the kerb. His father dashed after him and caught his arm, pulling him back. 'Life turns on a coin, doesn't it? Another couple of seconds and what might have happened?'

'He's a lucky boy,' Swift agreed, aware that her thoughts were in Docklands.

She was silent and then roused herself. 'I've had an offer on the house. I don't know what to do, but I'm reluctant to discuss it with my friends in case of . . . repercussions, I suppose. That's why I asked to speak to you.'

'I didn't realise it was on the market yet.'

'It's not. I had it valued, that's all.' She pulled an earlobe, frowning.

'What do you mean by repercussions? Why would it impact your friends?'

'Conor and Lucy have made me an offer out of the blue.'

Swift was surprised. 'Conor said they were house hunting, but they could only afford outer London.'

'Yeah. They've offered me considerably under the valuation price. They came round with cake. One minute, we were having coffee and brownies, chatting about Sam's brother and if they could afford a holiday. Then they switched to talking about the house. They've been viewing places and hating the idea of having to move further out. Lucy said all the areas they can afford are soulless. She's been telling me how much it's getting her down.'

'Difficult for them, but plenty of people find themselves in that situation. At least they have the funds to buy.'

'Yeah, I know. They said it would save me a lot of hassle and estate agency fees if we agreed a private deal. Went on about how much they've always loved Sam's place. It would pass into good hands and the area has highly rated schools. It was all a bit full-on. Like an ambush. I was so taken aback, I couldn't get my head round it. I get embarrassed about money, especially where friends are concerned. I said I'd consider it, but I'm horribly confused. I've been losing sleep over it.' She tasted her wine. 'You can see why I don't want to discuss it with any other friends, because everyone's connected. I've wondered if other people might be aware of the situation, if Lucy and Conor have discussed it behind my back. Then I accuse myself of being paranoid. It's so awkward.'

Why were people coming to him with their money problems? Faith and now Toni. He was no financial guru. He was uncomfortable, but his gut reaction was that the Wallaces were being unscrupulous, and that it was unlikely that they'd have spoken to anyone else about their proposal. He recalled how Conor Wallace had seemed at home in Sam Goddard's house. Maybe he called there regularly, trying it on for size and picturing his family in the bigger accommodation. Toni was in a difficult position and Swift considered the irony of Lucy having implied that he might take advantage of Toni's vulnerability, when she and her husband had made this move on their grieving friend.

'I'd be careful about losing out financially, Toni. Entering into complex monetary arrangements with friends is usually a bad idea, and if anything goes wrong with the transaction, there could be a lot of fallout. That property is valuable. Don't do anything you'd regret.'

She gave a sigh of exasperation. 'I wish they hadn't done this. Everything seems even more complicated.'

'You're not in any rush to sell the house, are you? Do you need the money?'

'Not at all. I'm comfortable financially and I'm not planning to move from here.'

'Then I'd suggest at least waiting until I've completed this investigation. One step at a time.' She did need to confide in someone. 'Is Lexie close to the Wallaces?'

'Not as close as me.'

From what Swift had seen of Lexie Kadis, she'd give the idea short shrift and speak plainly. 'Talk to Lexie. She strikes me as a sensible person.'

'She'll think I'm so wet, running to her with yet another problem.'

'I doubt it — but even if that was the case, does it matter, given the circumstances?'

'Suppose not. Sorry to have burdened *you*.'

'I'd say it's the Wallaces who are placing an unfair burden, not you. You don't have to give it another moment's headspace if you don't want to.'

She seemed relieved. 'That's true.'

'Can I ask you something now?'

'Of course, go ahead.'

He showed her the photo of Demi Holland. 'Do you recognise this woman?'

'No. Who is she?'

'She works at an upmarket health club, Montrose. Naomi Ludlow was a member there.'

'I see. Doesn't mean anything to me. Sam never mentioned it.'

'What can you tell me about Araminta Leadsom?'

Toni laughed. 'Sam called her "Snooty Minty". Said she was highly efficient but as hard as her false nails. She's head of the admin at Spring. The people she manages don't much like her, but Jerome always praises her to the skies. In fact, she sent me a beautiful bunch of flowers after Sam died, with a lovely card, so she's not so hard after all.'

'Did Sam ever mention that she and Jerome might have been having an affair?'

Toni sat bolt upright. 'God, no! Where did you hear that?'

'Just an impression someone had.'

'I'm sure that's not true. Jerome and Chloe are inseparable. Their little boy has a disability and Jerome's devoted to him. He'd never do anything to threaten his home life. What have you found out about Araminta?'

'I've no idea. Maybe nothing. I saw her at Montrose. She might be a member.'

Toni's phone buzzed and she grimaced. 'Lucy, asking if I'm okay and if I've thought any more about their offer.'

He was angry that the Wallaces were leaning on her, trying to disguise self-interest as kindness. Some friends. Toni stared down at the street. He could see that he'd lost her for now.

'It's unfair pressure on you, Toni. Don't reply this evening. Ring Lexie.'

'I'll probably do that. Thanks.'

The evening was unseasonably warm. He bought tomatoes, peppers and bananas at the greengrocer. Branna was visiting soon. She consumed bananas at an alarming rate, but they had to be perfectly ripe. He'd told her that she was like Goldilocks with the porridge. When she'd seemed puzzled, he'd discovered that she had heard the fairy tale, but in a revamped version, where Goldilocks gets into trouble with the three bears over her desperation to get likes on social media.

He walked for a while under a dull sky. If the Wallaces were willing to indulge in financial sharp practice, what else might they be capable of under the cover of friendship? Could one, or both of them have killed their friend in order to engineer and take advantage of this situation? It seemed a long shot and if so, how did Naomi fit in the picture?

* * *

'You got here okay, then,' Jesse Goddard said. 'Well done. It's confusing that there are two Woodfield Lanes in this area.'

'It helped that yours is the only thatched house in the street,' Swift said.

'Always worth mentioning that as a landmark, I find. Have you parked at the side?'

'Yes, as you explained.'

Jesse Goddard had given long-winded, precise instructions about where he lived in Walton-on-the-Naze and details about parking. He'd explained that he lived on a narrow lane and he wouldn't want Swift to lose a wing mirror, or worse. Vehicles, including vans and lorries, used the lane as a route to the recycling centre. The issue seemed to exercise him.

He led Swift into a large living room with walls painted deep claret. A huge bressummer beam straddled an inglenook fireplace where a log fire glowed. The floor was oak and floor-length tapestry curtains hung at the bow windows. The room had an atmosphere of solidity and permanence. Swift sat in a tan leather armchair on one side of the fire.

Goddard rubbed his hands together. 'I have a post-lunch whisky and ginger around now. Would you like one?'

'Just a ginger ale would be fine, thanks.'

Goddard opened a sideboard, revealing a drinks cabinet and busied himself with two glasses. 'Ice in your drink?'

'Just as it comes.'

Swift watched the tall man as he poured from a whisky decanter. He had an elegant style — green linen trousers, a navy cashmere sweater and suede moccasins. He bore little resemblance to his brother. Swift had wondered if Goddard would be aware of his brother's death, and had called him beforehand to check. Jesse Goddard said that he'd seen the news at the time. He hadn't expressed any regret. Swift had found this an odd response but hoped that a meeting might explain the man's indifference.

He brought the drinks over with a bowl of smoked nuts, which he placed on a coffee table before sitting on the other side of the fire.

'Help yourself,' he said in his soft voice. 'I have to have something savoury with a whisky. Have you been this way before?'

'No, not to this bit of coast.'

'It's worth exploring, especially the Naze. That means "nose", from the French, *nez*, meaning the way the land noses into the sea.'

Despite the pleasant welcome and the offer of a drink and nibbles, Goddard appeared reserved and watchful. Swift decided an icebreaker would be useful.

'This house is lovely and distinctive. It must be very old.'

Goddard's bottom teeth were crowded in his jaw. All his features were a little odd: nose too small above an expanse of chin, eyes widely spaced but narrow. Yet the overall impression was pleasant.

'It's sixteenth-century,' he said. 'Soused in history. Clients are always surprised to find that I live in an old place. Given my job, sitting at screens all day, they expect me to inhabit somewhere ultra-modern with smart gadgets everywhere. I could entertain you with the potted history I give to customers, but that's not what you've come for. What *have* you come for? If you want me to wash dirty laundry in front of you, you'll be disappointed. Not my style.'

Swift wasn't sure himself why he was there. He explained Toni Sheringham's need to understand what had happened to Sam Goddard. 'She's distressed and can't believe that he'd have been seeing a fifteen-year-old.'

Jesse Goddard nodded. 'I didn't realise that she heard the news on the day they were due to marry.'

'She was in her wedding outfit when the police arrived.'

'That's tough. I'm sorry. I didn't read any details about what happened. I'm not sure I want to hear them now.'

'Then I won't go into them. Toni had no idea that you existed. She was astonished.'

Goddard swirled his drink around. 'That's no surprise. Although — no, doesn't matter.'

'I spoke to Sam's ex-wife, Mila. She said you disagreed about property.'

Goddard said nothing. His silence was expressive.

'I'm sorry to probe,' Swift said. 'I have to ask in case anything in your brother's past contributed to how he died. Toni's a decent young woman who's been thrown into this whirlwind. I won't repeat anything you tell me unless it's crucial to my investigation.'

Goddard put his glass down and crossed his arms. There was a long pause. 'Sam and I never got on. I'm not sure why. That's just how it was. Maybe it was to do with our parents' divorce when we were still very young. Sam was only two when it happened. We spent time between them afterwards and Sam was convinced that both of them favoured me. I could speculate further and I suppose it might interest you, but I'll keep those thoughts private.' He touched two fingers to his neck, looking pensive. 'Mum died first, years ago. Sam was angry when our father died and had appointed me as his sole executor. He seemed to suspect that Dad must have had an ulterior motive, that it was the old favouritism again. He was quick to query how the estate was split. It was fifty-fifty. My view was that our father had just wanted to keep things simple. Also, he was old-fashioned, so he went for the eldest son as executor. Frankly, I could have done without the responsibility. I was going through a difficult patch in my own life at the time and I probably took longer expediting things because of that. Sam kept pestering me about it.'

'According to Sam's ex-wife, he wanted the inheritance to help him buy her out of their flat.'

'He did mention that and I understood that he wanted to draw a line under the marriage. He suggested that I was deliberately dragging my heels, but these legal wheels take time to grind. I couldn't wave a magic wand. I spent hours chasing my bloody solicitor and returning paperwork.' He reached for his glass and took a handful of nuts. 'Never get involved in being an executor, Mr Swift.'

'I was, for a dear friend,' Swift said ruefully. 'I ended up in court with his aggrieved son.' The tussle had taken several years. He'd been relieved when it was over.

'Well then, you'll appreciate how it was when Sam came for me with all guns blazing. I'm sorry it happened and I'm sorry he died, but it was a very difficult relationship.' He gazed into the fire for some time, leaning a little towards it, then took a breath. 'I was amazed when Sam turned up here.'

Swift did a double take. 'He came here? When was that?'

'Late August last year. He was here for about an hour. When he left, I still wasn't sure what the visit had been about. He didn't mention that he was about to marry.'

'What did he say?'

'Not a lot. He had a coffee and walked around the garden. He clearly had something on his mind. Given the long silence there'd been, it was a rather stilted conversation. We discussed propagating geraniums and having a wildflower corner. He referred at one point to doing the right thing, even if it caused pain. He said, "Courage never fails." I'd no idea what he meant.'

'You didn't ask him?'

'No. Frankly, I was put out by him just turning up after all that time. It was so strange. I hadn't forgotten the harsh things he'd said to me. I was relieved when he headed off and baffled as to why he'd come.'

Swift was struggling with the man's detachment. 'You never thought to contact the police and mention any of this to them?'

Goddard shrugged. 'Not my business and it would have brought a load of hassle my way. The way he'd behaved, Sam had burned his bridges with me.'

'And you're sure he didn't mention marriage, or having doubts about it?'

'Quite sure.'

'That was the last time you heard from him?'

'Yes. Next thing, I saw a news item about his death.'

Swift was stumped. Why would Sam Goddard have come all this way to visit his estranged brother, and yet not tell him about a significant and imminent life event? And why hadn't he told Toni? The man must have been troubled about something. Maybe he'd instinctively sought out his older sibling in a time of need, but then he'd been unable to reveal what was bothering him. If the reception had been less than warm, he might have shied away from unburdening himself.

It was agreeable, sitting by the fire in the cosy room, with the savoury nuts and the sharp ginger ale, but Swift wasn't sure where this round trip of almost two hundred miles to the Essex coast was getting him. It had just raised more questions.

'I'll tell Toni Sheringham I've seen you,' he said. 'She might want to contact you. Is it okay if I pass on your details?'

'I suppose so. I don't mind speaking to her on the phone. I'd rather not have to meet. What's the point?'

Swift answered the question with another. 'What's your view of your brother being involved with a teenage girl?'

Goddard cupped a hand around the base of his throat. 'I can't comment. I had no hint of what Sam's interests or proclivities might be. Generally, I find most people unfathomable.'

He could have been speaking about himself. Swift could get little impression of the man behind the polite veneer and wound up the interview.

He needed some sea air. He drove to the central beach and parked opposite a row of splendid Georgian houses. He changed into walking boots and set off along the sand towards the Naze. The sky was clear, the breeze gentle, with a hint of spring. It was good to stride out. He stopped at an ice cream kiosk and bought a strawberry cone while he pondered what to tell Toni Sheringham. No one was ever straightforward, and now it seemed as if Sam Goddard had compartmentalised parts of his life, certainly where Toni was concerned. This latest information certainly painted a more complex man. Perhaps he hadn't wanted to trouble Toni with talk of a brother and old, unresolved problems. People sometimes coped with pain by burying it deep within and maybe that's how Goddard had dealt with his. What had he meant when he'd spoken of doing the right thing and needing courage?

Swift rang Toni and left a message giving her the outline of his meeting with Jesse Goddard, but omitting Sam's visit to him for now. He'd rather inform her of that in person. It would be a blow.

Swift continued walking for a mile or so until he came to the Naze, an expanse of muddy sand that jutted out below crumbling cliffs into the North Sea. He paused to examine an information board that explained how the area was rich in London clay and that there were abundant fossils, including bird and animal bones and sharks' teeth. He caught himself thinking that it would be a good place to bring Branna and do some excavating, but then remembered that such trips would soon be curtailed. Picture-postcard Fermain Bay and other stunning Guernsey beaches would be far more attractive than this remote spit of land facing the cold North Sea.

He wandered the area, finding a couple of tiny bones that might interest her. All the time, he was going over the conundrum that was Sam Goddard and getting nowhere with the unspecified troubles that appeared to have been on his mind before he met his death.

CHAPTER 15

Hail struck sharp against the car windscreen as Swift drove home. He was glad of the rattle, keeping him observant. He worried at the phrase that Sam Goddard had used, 'Courage never fails.' It seemed familiar, but he couldn't place it.

Eli was sitting on his doorstep when he got back at seven thirty. He looked cold and forlorn in the outside light, drinking a can of beer and listening to music on his phone. He held out a wine bottle to Swift. 'Peace offering, *mi fren*. A good red. Not as fine as the one I opened, but hope you find it acceptable.'

Swift wondered if Faith had thrown Eli out and if her money had bought it. 'How long have you been here?'

'Not too long. I tried Chand's bell, but he's out. Cuppa wouldn't go amiss. I promise not to burn anything.'

'Come on, then.'

Swift hadn't eaten and sorted through some of Chand's mother's meals in the freezer. She supplied her son with vast quantities of delicious Punjabi cuisine, some of which he regularly offloaded to his landlord. Swift selected paneer tikka and parathas, set the tikka spinning in the microwave, wrapped the parathas in foil and put them in a low oven. Eli's eyes were glued to the dishes.

Swift could do with talking to him, if only to sound him out about Faith. 'You'll eat with me? Chand's mum made it. Wonderful food, just right for this weather.'

'Sounds great! Shall I set the table?'

'I'll do that.' Swift hesitated. 'You can open a couple of beers and light the fire. It's all set to go.'

'You sure you trust me?'

'Only because I'm here to keep an eye on you.'

Swift put chutney and pickles on the table with a tub of yogurt. They were silent while they ate, the only sound the crackling fire.

'Chand's a lucky man,' Eli said at last, leaning back and patting his stomach. 'My mother's awful in the kitchen. She punishes food, torments the life out of it as if it's her enemy.'

'Depends on your perspective,' Swift said. 'Chand is sometimes plagued by all the dishes his mother presses on him. That's how I benefit.'

'Hand-me-down meals instead of hand-me-down clothes,' Eli said.

'Exactly.' The subject of handouts made him ask, 'Got a job yet?'

Eli shrugged. 'No luck so far and my final pay is still being held up. I've enquired about benefits today. Faith loaned me £100, but I don't want to borrow any more from her.'

But you asked for £500. 'Are you fond of her?'

'Very,' he replied without hesitation. 'She's a great woman, the best. I've stayed out for a while tonight to give her some space.'

Swift studied him. He sounded genuine. 'I'm extremely fond of her,' Swift said pointedly.

Eli finished his beer. 'I get it. Faith told me all about what happened with her sister. She's amazing, to have got through all that. I'd like to . . . well, I'd like to have a proper relationship with her, but I want to be earning some money first. I don't want her to suspect that I'm scrounging. Or you, for that matter, *mi fren*. I can see that you're sceptical.'

Swift sat back. 'You mean that?'

'I do. I'm not as flaky as I seem. I do get how I come across and I admit that I can take advantage of people's goodwill. It's been a difficult time. I'm going to sort myself out. Until I do, I'm on Faith's sofa. And I can tell you, it's bloody uncomfortable.'

Maybe, maybe. We'll see. Swift crossed to the fire and put another log on. He leaned with one arm on the mantelpiece, mulling over an idea and turned to Eli. 'Would you like to earn some cash in hand while you're sorting yourself out?'

Eli brightened. 'I'm all ears.'

'It would be on the understanding that you don't ask Faith for any more money.'

'Okay. *Mi save.* I get it.'

'It's about a guy called Christian Ryman.' Swift sat back down and explained his investigation and his visit to the Gadfly. 'I'd like more on Ryman, but I won't get anything from him now that I've antagonised him. He wasn't as cool about Naomi as he pretended. There's more going on there.'

'He might have committed murder?'

'I'd say he could turn very nasty. Maybe you could hang out at the bar, get talking to him. I'm particularly interested in whether he was telling the truth when he said that Naomi had had sex with someone before him, and if he knows his identity. Chat to him as one of the lads. Revisit your detective skills.'

'Not sure I ever had many, but yeah, I could do that. That'd be great. Great to have something to do. Thanks, *mi fren.*'

'I'm doing it for Faith really,' Swift told him.

'I get it. You're her big cousin. You watch out for her.'

'That's right. Don't forget it.'

* * *

The following morning, Hester rang him while he was trying to get hold of Dean Ludlow. She sounded down.

'It'd be good to see you,' she said.

'I've been busy with this investigation. How are you doing?'

'I envy you, with plenty to do. Mind you, I can't even be bothered to clean the flat. Everything seems too much of an effort.'

He could hear that her twinkle had evaporated and he was partly responsible. Or rather, mostly responsible. 'Have you had any contact from your boss?'

'I rang him. He refused to budge on my dismissal. He agreed to give me a reference, but he warned me it wouldn't be glowing. I'm worried about securing another job. How will I explain having been sacked for breaching confidentiality? Who'll trust me?'

'As long as Adcott doesn't mention it, I don't see why you have to.'

'Really? But how will I explain why I left?'

Swift suggested, 'You could say you wanted time to consider and find new opportunities. Dress it up as your decision, sound as if you seized the initiative.'

'Right. I suppose that might work.'

'Practise it in a mirror. Project confidence.' He sounded like one of those flashy career gurus who preached steps to success, but it seemed to reassure Hester.

'Maybe you could give me a run-through,' she said. 'I could cook us a meal. It'd give me something to keep me busy. How about this evening?'

He didn't want to have to spend a night with her and he told himself that it would do her good to get out. 'Tell you what, let me buy you dinner. It would work better because of my schedule.'

'Oh, okay.'

They agreed on a restaurant near Warren Street and arranged to meet at eight that evening. He left a message for Dean Ludlow while Hester played his mind. A relationship with her wasn't on the cards, but he couldn't leave her in the lurch. A guilty conscience led him to phone Jerome

Adcott. A child answered, speaking indistinctly. Then Adcott was on the line.

'Sorry about that. My son Jed got to it before me.'

'It's Tyrone Swift. Could I see you again?'

'What about? I told you what I could when we met and I'm completely pissed off about you pestering Ms Beringer. That was a real intrusion on a vulnerable client and a pensioner. I had to apologise profusely to her.'

Swift didn't want to mention Hester, expecting a rebuff. Adcott was laying it on thick. Jenna Beringer was no frail old woman and besides, her name had come up when he spoke to Ms Melides too. He'd had to speak to her after that.

'I am investigating murders, Mr Adcott. A bit of inconvenience doesn't seem that awful. Ms Beringer got me to fix her curtains for her and gave me a kiss. She didn't seem traumatised.'

'You can dress it up if you like. I don't see any point in meeting.'

Swift could hear the child talking in the background. 'Even so, it would be very helpful.'

'Yes, okay, Jed, I'll be with you in a minute, don't fiddle with that,' Adcott told his son. 'Oh, if you must, then. I'm at home at present, in Hornsey. I can spare you half an hour, tops, if you get here by mid-morning.'

'Fine, many thanks.'

That suited Swift. He'd rather not visit the man at his office and have Araminta behaving as if he'd dragged in dog poo. He set off for Hornsey through a miserable drizzle and was soaked by the time he walked up Adcott's front path.

When Adcott opened the door, a boy aged around three was holding his hand and flopping against his leg. Adcott introduced him as Jed. The boy smiled shyly, but didn't speak. They went into an airy living room that was full of brightly coloured toys. It was smart but homely. Adcott's laptop was on the sofa. He'd been working while keeping an eye on his son. Swift stepped around a set of plastic building blocks and a half-completed jigsaw of teddy bears picnicking, made of twelve huge pieces. A large foam ball swung from a hook in the ceiling. Jed sat in a hat-shaped seat also moulded from foam, where he rocked and balanced, his torso sagging. Swift remembered that Lucy and Toni had mentioned that Adcott had a child with a disability.

Adcott saw him observing Jed. 'Our childminder is unwell today and Chloe had to pop into work, so I'm on dad duties. You okay there, Jed?'

Jed put a thumb up. He inched his seat over to the jigsaw and inserted a piece.

'Well done!' his father said. 'See if you can finish it while I talk to my visitor.' He swivelled round to Swift. 'Now, what is it you want and make it quick.'

'Make quick!' Jed echoed.

Time for humble pie. 'It's about Hester French. It's entirely my fault that she gave me Ms Beringer's details. I persuaded her.'

'Oh, I get it. You're taking up my time on false pretences. This isn't about Sam at all.'

'It's related to my enquiries.'

Adcott ran a hand around the dome of his bald head, as if polishing it. 'I understand that you and Hester are an item.'

'I wouldn't say that.'

'Not what I've heard,' Adcott said. 'Anyway, that's neither here nor there. Hester didn't have to be persuaded. She should have remembered loyalty to the company, to her work family.'

'Here nor there, here nor there,' Jed said. His father smiled.

'She made a mistake. Does she have to pay such a heavy price?' Swift asked.

'It's no good coming here and pleading her cause. I'm not taking her back, end of. I wouldn't trust her.'

'Then will you give her a good reference? She's young and she means well. She's worried sick about getting another job.'

'Worried, worried, worried.' Jed tried to balance a piece of the puzzle on his nose.

Adcott looked fondly at his son. 'Yes, okay. You can tell her it'll be positive. That all?'

'There is something else.' Swift wanted to see how Adcott would react to a mention of Araminta. The living room was full of photos of him with Chloe and Jed, but that didn't mean he wasn't playing away. What if Sam had found out and posed a threat? Dean Ludlow had said that Naomi was up to something in the weeks before she died. Maybe she'd somehow discovered an affair between Araminta and her boss while hanging out at Montrose, and had become entangled in these adults' lives. 'Is Araminta Leadsom friendly with a woman called Demi Holland? This is Ms Holland's photo.' He showed Adcott his phone.

Adcott smoothed his head again. He didn't seem perturbed. 'I've no idea. I don't recognise the woman. Ask Araminta.'

'Is she at the office today?'

'I certainly hope so. That's why I'm paying her.'

The front door banged and Chloe came in, unwinding her scarf. 'Sorry I was longer than I said darling, there were—' She saw Swift. 'Oh, hello.'

'Mummy!' Jed pointed proudly at his jigsaw.

'Did you do that? Amazing.' Chloe moved across to him, cupped his head in her hands and kissed the top of it.

'Mr Swift called round to ask me to reconsider Hester's sacking,' Adcott told her.

'Not likely,' she said. 'Spring doesn't need people like her. It's a company that fosters reliability and principled behaviour.'

'Fair enough,' Swift said. 'It was worth a try.'

Chloe raised an eyebrow. 'Spring doesn't need people like you, either, causing staff difficulties. Can't you do whatever it is you have to without undermining and disrupting the company?'

'It's okay, Chloe,' Adcott said. 'I've stated our position to Mr Swift. There's nothing more to say.'

'Good. I do wish now that Toni hadn't decided to stir up all this trouble. I'm sure she wouldn't have wanted to precipitate this kind of nastiness.' Chloe added lovingly to her husband, 'You can get off to work now, darling. I'm in for the rest of the day. Did you do Jed's exercises with him?'

'I did, so another ten minutes' worth around two o'clock.'

'Finished!' Jed threw the puzzle up in the air and burst into tears. Swift took it as his cue to leave.

* * *

Dean Ludlow met him after school. Rain had set in, an incessant cold drizzle. Swift waited for him in a café and saw that Payne Goodyear had replied to him regarding Demi Holland's photo.

That's the woman I saw with Naomi. Just the once. Haven't seen her around since.

Hallelujah! He'd proved something at last in this case. Demi Holland was a liar.

When Ludlow arrived, they both opted for coffee. The young man appeared miserable and more withdrawn than at their last meeting.

'Thanks for seeing me,' Swift said. 'You're my only direct family contact.'

'Are you getting anywhere?'

'It can be hard to tell in an investigation.'

'Right. I feel like a bit of a snitch, to be honest, going behind my parents' backs. They don't talk about Naomi at all now. If I mention her, they change the subject or one of them tears up, so it's like I'm a torturer. Seems to be getting worse, not better, as the weeks go on.'

'I'm sorry. Hopefully, I won't need to contact you again and I'll keep this brief. Okay?'

'Okay.'

Swift showed him the photo of Demi Holland. 'Does she seem familiar?'

Ludlow stared at it, biting his lip. 'I reckon she's the woman I saw with Naomi when I was on the bus. How did you find her?'

'She works at the Montrose Health Club. Naomi was in some of her classes.'

'Is she — what is it the police say — "a person of interest"?'

'Not sure. I need to tell you a few things that might be hurtful now.'

'About Naomi?'

'Yes.'

'Go ahead. Nothing would surprise me.'

'Maybe not, but what I have to say will probably be painful. I went to the Gadfly and spoke to someone.'

'Yuna told me yesterday about the graffiti she saw,' Ludlow said. 'Was Naomi really screwing Mr Ryman? That's so yuk. I can't stop worrying about it. If it's true, I want to report him. Except . . . then my parents would have to be told and that'd finish them off.'

'Ryman says it's not true. He has a son, Christian, also called Chris. He met Naomi at the Gadfly. He did have sex with Naomi but he told me he wasn't the first. Do you know him? He's older than you and he's left now, but he went to your school.'

Ludlow crunched the tiny cinnamon biscuit that came with the coffee. 'Not sure. I might have seen him around. We have a house system and if you're not in the same house as someone, you don't mingle all that much. What a bastard.'

'There's nothing you can tell me about him?'

'Sorry, no.' He pushed his cup away. 'You still haven't tracked how Naomi knew Mr Goddard?'

'Not yet.'

'I suppose I was hoping you'd have solved it by now, that you were going to explain what happened.'

'Sorry to disappoint you. These things take time and lucky breaks.'

'That's what Yuna says. She advises me to be patient.'

Swift pitied him, carrying the family's burden, unable to discuss it with his parents and having to deal with his grief alone. He was glad that the sensible Yuna was by his side, and told him so.

'She quoted a Japanese proverb to me. "True patience consists in bearing what is unbearable." Those kinds of sayings always sound meaningful, but I'm not sure they help. Maybe I'm too western to get it.'

'Dean, I understand that this is hard, but I believe you're doing the right thing in talking to me. You're doing the right thing by Naomi.'

'Okay. Better get home. Essays to do.'

It was only five o'clock and Swift wasn't meeting Hester until eight. There was no point in trekking all the way back to Hammersmith in rush hour. He made his way to Soho and spent a comfortable hour in the musty basement of one of his favourite shops, a seller of pulp fiction.

He sat in a threadbare armchair, considering Demi Holland, who'd told Naomi that she knew something detrimental about a broadcast technician. Something that might be of interest to the police. Demi would be a difficult person to challenge with hearsay, but it would be interesting to find out why she'd lied about socialising with Naomi. He put her on the back burner and settled into reading a selection of 1940s mystery magazines while he listened to Sly and the Family Stone.

* * *

He could see that Hester had been crying recently as she picked at the tuna she'd ordered, separating it into flakes and then pushing them aside. She perked up when he told her that Jerome Adcott had promised to supply a positive reference.

'Really? That's amazing! How did you get him to agree?'

'I went to his house. His little boy was there. I reckon that made him more amenable.'

She gazed at him. Her hair was lustrous and her tired eyes pulled at his heartstrings. 'Oh, Ty, thanks so much. I can't tell you how grateful I am.'

She twitched her nose, smiling shyly and he could tell that she wanted to show him her gratitude later on. He changed the subject hurriedly.

'Have you ever heard Araminta Leadsom refer to a woman called Demi Holland? Ms Holland takes classes at Montrose, the health club Araminta attends.'

'Araminta's a member. She hasn't talked about anyone who works there.'

Swift had ordered chicken fillets in a mushroom sauce. They were tasteless. He ground salt and pepper on. The restaurant had changed hands since he'd last been there and the food wasn't a patch on what it used to be.

'You need to start job hunting now,' he said.

'I will. That news about a reference has given me a real boost.' She chewed slowly on a green bean. 'Did Jerome say if he's got a replacement for me yet?'

'No and I didn't ask. Forget about Spring now. Move on.'

'I'll try. I'm not very good like that, though. I'm a nostalgic type. I keep remembering how much I enjoyed working there. I loved going to my job each morning. A lot of people can't say that. It'll be hard to find something as rewarding and satisfying.'

If she wasn't so transparent, he'd have suspected that she was piling on the agony. He ploughed on through his meal and ordered another glass of wine, trying to come up with a safe topic of conversation.

Hester came to his rescue. 'How's your investigation going?'

'Hard to say. Plenty of activity and lots of threads, but I can't tell which one I should pull on.'

'I'm sure you'll win through. Your track record speaks for itself.' She tapped a polished nail on her chin. 'Erm, Ty, I've a friend who owns a flat in Lymington, a little holiday place. It's lovely, just by the harbour. I get that you're really busy right now. Maybe when your investigation ends, you'd like to come away for a weekend?'

He gave up on the food and set his knife and fork down. 'It's a lovely offer, Hester and very kind, but I'm not ready for involvement right now. I don't want to give you the wrong impression, or make plans I can't keep to.'

'Oh.' She recoiled as if he'd slapped her. 'So, what is this, then? A quick fling? If that's the case, you might have said.' Tears sprang in her eyes.

'I've a lot going on. Not just with my work but with my daughter. Her mother's marrying in April and they're moving—'

'You have a daughter?'

'Yes.'

'This is the first time you've mentioned her.'

'Yes, I suppose it is.'

'Oh, you *suppose*.' Hester was staring at him. 'Actually, I know almost nothing about you. You've said so little. You let me chatter on about my life and my troubles. That should have told me you were passing through. You got me to do your dirty work and now you're vanishing.'

'It's not like that.'

She'd become flintier. 'Yeah. So you say. Hang on, did you even have a fire at your place, or was that just an excuse to run away in the middle of the night?'

'Actually, it was sixish in the morning.'

'Don't dodge the question.'

'Of course there was a fire.'

'I really believed you were different. A decent kind of man.'

There was nothing he could do now to retrieve this situation. He'd been in this position with women before and it never turned out well. Anything he said would be turned to ammunition and fired back at him, but Hester deserved her angry scene.

'Hester, I've genuinely enjoyed your company.'

She gave a brittle laugh. 'But not *that* much. How flattering.'

'I'm trying to be decent now. Would you rather I pretended and led you on? Agree to come to Lymington and then let you down at the last minute?'

'You're such a weasel.'

'Hester, I don't—'

'This food's horrible.' She snatched up her bag. 'I'm going. Thanks for seeing Jerome. Although in the circumstances, it was the least you could do.'

She ran away. He stood and watched her, then sat and observed the mess of food on her plate. Conor Wallace would have bagged it up and given it to her to eat tomorrow.

He asked for the bill. The grey-haired waitress who served him had noted Hester's abrupt departure. 'Lovers' tiff?'

'Sort of.'

She held the card reader out to him. 'Never mind. Things have a way of coming right in the end.'

'Oh, yes.' *Not in my experience.*

CHAPTER 16

Swift sat on the sofa, going over his notes. Dean Ludlow was convinced that Naomi had been up to something in the weeks before she died. According to him, she'd been a practised and accomplished liar as well as sexually adventurous. The waitress at the Gadfly had summed her up as a 'hunter'. Naomi had lied about her whereabouts on the night she died and hadn't gone swimming at Montrose.

Ms Beringer believed that Sam Goddard had had something on his mind. He'd asked her about her dealings with Spring and other people she'd recommended the company to. Shortly before his death, he'd visited his brother, apparently troubled. His neighbour had heard someone with him in his garden when he'd reached home on that fateful evening. To date, the only hint of a link between Naomi and Goddard was Swift's sighting of Demi Holland and Araminta Leadsom, and the confirmation that Demi had been friendly with Naomi. There were plenty of dots, but how to join them?

Swift studied Sam Goddard's note again.

BN & possibly others. Not sure what it's about, but can't find anything worrying here. Finger seems to point to Patchell Associates.

He wrote, *Courage never fails.*

He scanned Sam Goddard's immediate network: Jerome and Chloe Adcott, Lucy and Conor Wallace, Lexie Kadis and, of course, Toni. There'd been frequent references to family in this case. Adcott had referred to 'work family' and his closeness to Goddard, Lucy had said that Toni was like a sister and Conor Wallace had seen Goddard as a brother. He'd been godfather to the Wallace children. Toni called Lexie her big sister. Most of them were linked through Spring and Go Kids as well as by friendship. All the people who'd been close to Sam Goddard had lived near him. Perhaps there had been a fracture in this 'family' that had caused Goddard's death and Naomi had been caught up in it randomly. Or perhaps he was heading in entirely the wrong direction and Christian Ryman should be his main suspect. He'd have to wait for Eli's report before he could take a firmer view on that.

He walked restlessly around his flat, made a coffee, took it into the garden and topped up the bird food. Next door, the trumpet was softly playing 'These Foolish Things'.

Swift went over his first interview with Demi Holland. She must have had a reason to lie. He recalled a wine bar a couple of doors down from Montrose. A neutral setting might be best for a meeting. He scribbled a note that should ensure she'd turn up.

You lied about Naomi. I have witnesses. I'll be in the Grape in Glass.

He signed it, sealed it in an envelope, grabbed his coat and set off across London, heading northwest again. At Montrose reception, he asked for Ms Holland and was told that she'd be in class for at least another half-hour. He handed over the note and decamped to the wine bar, where he nursed a small glass of Pinot Noir, ate *Habas Fritas* and read newspapers. It was almost an hour before Demi appeared, wearing jeans and a sweater under a quilted coat and a small rucksack slung over one shoulder. Her hair was damp from a shower and she tucked it behind her ears as she sat down opposite him.

'Drink?' he asked.

'No.'

'Roasted broad bean? They're salty and delicious.'

'No. I'm not stopping. What's with the cryptic note and why are you bothering me with this rubbish?'

'You're here. I'm not sure why you'd have come if it's rubbish.'

She took out a tin of lip salve and smoothed some on her mouth with her little finger. 'I don't like people making up stuff about me.'

'What people?'

'You tell me.'

Swift chewed a broad bean and took a sip of wine. 'This isn't an exhaustive list, but it's a handy one that I find useful: people lie because they're guilty of something, to get out of a difficult situation, because they're covering up for someone, to evade punishment, to avoid embarrassment, to gain approval or admiration, or sometimes they just like lying for the sake of it. I get the impression that Naomi Ludlow might have lied for the last two reasons.'

She half-smiled, showing her pointy teeth. 'Fascinating.'

'I'm not sure why you've lied. You were seen with Naomi in the street and at an outside broadcast. Neither of those activities seem suspicious, so why pretend otherwise?'

Demi pressed her lips together. 'Mistaken identity.'

'By two people? Two people identified your photograph.'

'Who?'

'And when you were at the outside broadcast, where Naomi was popping up as a news raider, you told her — let me retrieve the wording — something interesting about one of the crew technicians. You said that if you told the police, he'd be in trouble.'

Her jaw tightened. 'I've no idea where you're getting this nonsense. That's all it is.'

Swift laughed. 'Hardly. Naomi is dead. The police investigation never came your way. That might change if I take this information to them.'

She glanced towards the door and he wondered if she was going to bolt. She was fit and could probably outrun him. And what would be the point in chasing her?

She pushed her hair back. 'I have to think.'

'Take your time.'

'I need a drink now.'

She crossed to the bar. He watched as she ordered, tapping her nails rapidly on the counter. She came back with a sparkling cider, downed some of it and coughed. 'I didn't want any embarrassment. That's why I said I'd only met Naomi in the club. I regretted hooking up with her. She was a bit too much outside the confines of Montrose. A wild card.'

That could be another lie, but he nodded encouragingly. 'Okay. Go on.'

'I'll tell you, but it's just stupid. I'm sure it's nothing to do with Naomi's death.'

'If that's the case, there's no harm in explaining.'

She took another drink. 'One evening in the juice bar, Naomi told me about her news raiding, how she wore an eye patch to stand out in the crowd. It sounded ridiculous, off the wall, but she made it seem like fun. I agreed to go along with her to a broadcast. Just to see what it was like, I suppose. It was near the Shard. While we were there, I saw Ronnie, a guy I used to go out with. He works as a digital technician with film crews. When we split, it wasn't pleasant. I didn't realise how much I still resented him until I saw him that day. I was caught off guard. I shouldn't have opened my mouth, especially not to someone like Naomi.'

'What exactly did you tell her?'

'Ronnie once told me that he was siphoning money from an aunt. This aunt was wealthy and he said she had so much, she didn't even miss the money. I wasn't sure I believed him at the time. He was a boastful type and a bit of a fantasist. It hadn't crossed my mind until that day when I saw him. I was full of spite. Funny, how emotions like that suddenly grab you from nowhere. Of course, when I mentioned it to Naomi, she wanted details, so that's what I told her.'

'What was her reaction?'

'She laughed and said something like, good for him and maybe he'd cut her in. It was very rowdy there and crowded. Her eye patch was ridiculous and she was elbowing people to get herself noticed. I got really uncomfortable and I wished I hadn't gone along with her. I left soon after. I was worried as well that Naomi's limelight-grabbing might catch Ronnie's eye and he'd see me. I didn't want to acknowledge him, or have him imagining that I was there to contact him.'

It sounded reasonable. Demi looked relieved, as if a weight had lifted.

'What's Ronnie's full name?'

'Ronnie Probert.'

'When Ronnie Probert was telling you about his aunt's money, did he mention her name?'

She threw back her cider, took a broad bean and eyed him. 'No. And I didn't ask. I suppose I closed my ears to it. I'd like to go now. I've nothing else to tell you.'

Swift put a hand on the table. 'Actually, you have. When was this news raiding trip you accompanied Naomi on?'

'A year ago, in January.'

'What's your connection to Araminta Leadsom?'

Demi answered without hesitating. 'She's a club member. She joined a couple of months ago and she's in some of my classes.'

'Araminta worked with Sam Goddard, in a company called Spring.'

'Gosh. I'd no idea. But then, London can be a very small place.'

'Did Araminta join Montrose before or after Naomi died?'

'I'm fairly sure after . . . but I can't be certain.' She picked up her rucksack.

'Hold on. Where can I find Ronnie Probert?'

'I can't tell you. He was on the move last time I saw him. That's it. I never want to meet you again.'

Demi hoisted her rucksack and rushed away, banging the door. It was the second time in days that a woman had run away from him. Outside, she stopped, and he saw her take a shuddering breath and lift her shoulders before she launched into the streets.

Swift was thankful that at last he was edging forwards. Had Naomi challenged Probert that day with what she'd been told? It could have been exactly the kind of thing that would excite her — having the edge on someone, being privy to a secret. Maybe she'd discovered something linked to Spring and had talked to Sam Goddard. But how had she met him? And what was his note about — with the initials BN and the reference to Patchell Associates?

Perhaps BN was Probert's aunt's name. Swift wished that Hester hadn't been sacked, because she could have run Probert's name through the company's records.

Now, he needed to trace how Naomi had met Goddard. It was quarter past five. Araminta might still be at work. He rang Spring, gave his name and asked to speak to Ms Leadsom. There was a long wait, then he heard her chilly voice.

'Yes? How can I help you, Mr Swift?'

'I need to check something. Mr Adcott suggested I do it directly with you.'

She didn't sound surprised. 'Oh yes. Fire away.'

'You're a member of Montrose Health Club.'

'Are you telling me or asking me?'

'I saw you there. When did you join?'

Her tone was brittle. He imagined her pulling a face. 'Why's that anything to do with you?'

'I'm just tracking stuff. Naomi Ludlow was a member there.'

'Naomi? Oh, I see — the woman who died with Sam.'

'It would be helpful if you could tell me when you joined the club.'

'Hold on, I'll check my membership. I have to fetch my bag. It's downstairs.'

He suspected that she was deliberately making him wait. He listened patiently to blank air. A phone rang in the background.

'Okay,' she said, 'here we are. I joined on the fourth of December last year. Is that precise enough for you?'

'Any particular reason why you joined there?'

She cleared her throat. 'Amazingly enough, to improve my fitness and they had a special winter offer. I have other calls to take.'

'You didn't answer when I asked if you met Naomi there.'

'I didn't. Even *you* must be able to work out that would have been difficult, as she was dead by then.'

The call ended. She had a point. It seemed that the link he had hoped for via Araminta didn't hold up after all.

* * *

Eli came round late the following morning, full of beans and pleased with himself. He announced that he was ravenous and made himself a dense cheese and pickle sandwich. He waved half the sandwich in the air, catching escaping pickle in the other hand.

'The wall is fine now, *mi fren*. No sign of any damage. Nice painting job.'

'Thanks.' Swift passed him a coffee and led him to the table. 'Have you got news for me?'

'I have indeed. I hung out in the Gadfly for two evenings. I should charge you for the headache tablets. That bloody awful music! My ears are still ringing. I must be getting old. Give me my gentle Pacific tunes any day.' Eli gulped the last of his sandwich and reached for an orange. He peeled it rapidly and broke it into quarters, tearing the pith off.

Eli liked to regale an audience and Swift could tell he wasn't going to be hurried. He fed him the line he was waiting for. 'Did you meet Ryman?'

'I did, *mi fren*. On the second evening. Chris — we got on first-name terms — does like a supply of beers and a chat. He's well up himself. Full of the old BS.'

Swift pushed the fruit bowl nearer to him. *Takes one to know one.*

'Ta. He's always wanted to travel, so I had a good hook there. Gave him the patter about places I'd been, kept him supplied with drinks. I made up a sob story about a two-timing woman in Vanuatu dumping me. That got him going. I'll tell you something, he's still furious with Naomi, but I dunno . . . I reckon he was in a bad way over her.' Having demolished the orange, Eli seized a cluster of purple grapes. 'Mm. These are gorgeous.'

'Tell me more.'

He wiped grape juice from his chin. 'Ryman went on about how much trouble Naomi could have landed him in because of her age. How she'd come on to him, led him on, et cetera. He sounded bitter. He wouldn't actually say that she'd dumped him, but I'd bet that that's what happened and he's not used to it, so it cut deep and it still rankles. Beats me how anyone can be that angry at a dead person, but there we are. I don't reckon he killed her, though.'

'Why's that?'

'Got any biscuits?'

Swift fetched some chocolate digestives and put the packet in front of him. Eli took four out and balanced them on his plate, then set about dunking one in his coffee.

'I'd say our Chris Ryman is all wind and hiss. He comes across as a bit of a bruiser, but I reckon it's skin-deep. I nudged him into talking about whether Naomi had met anyone else and how she died. He mentioned that she'd died with Goddard in Docklands, but I'm sure he didn't know him. There was no anger around his name. Ryman referred to Naomi as a man-eater and assumed she'd got Goddard in her clutches. Said he was sorry for the guy. But he seemed genuinely clueless about what happened. Way I read it is, he might have killed Naomi because she'd pissed him about, but I can't see that he'd have included Goddard, even if he'd known about him.'

Swift was watching the biscuit, waiting for it to disintegrate. It fell into the coffee mug, creating a mini tsunami. Eli laughed and fished for it with his spoon. 'Coffee-biscuit fusion! Ryman knew that Naomi had been with some guy before him. He alluded to her telling him, and saying that she'd fancied the man because he was stylish and a mover and shaker. Ryman said she was well up to speed with what to do and what she wanted sexually when she, quote, "got her claws into him". Added that she'd taught him a thing or two. I got the impression she'd bragged and divulged plenty of details — but not the guy's name.'

Swift clutched his head. 'That's so frustrating!'

'Tell me about it. According to Ryman, she'd moved on to him soon after her scene with this stylish guy. As he got more and more pissed and sorry for himself, he went on about how she'd made a move on him to practise what she'd learned. He shut down and changed the subject when I probed more. Seemed uncomfortable and . . . I dunno, almost a bit sad.'

'Sad?' That didn't match with the man he'd met. Perhaps Eli had unsuspected talents.

'Yeah. Like it was a painful memory. I left it. Didn't want to push my luck or make him suspicious.'

'Anything else of note?'

'There was one other thing he said. Naomi was Googling "power of attorney" one evening, reading about how it worked. She asked Ryman if it would be easy to fiddle it. He queried if she was involved in dubious dealings and she just laughed and said no, but she might have stuff on someone who was. So, how'd I do, boss?'

'That's great, thanks. Especially that last part. It might tie in with some other information.'

'I kept the bar tab for you. It cost me a bit in beers but hey, whatever it takes. Oh — by the way, Ryman took a phone call and about an hour later, his old man turned up. Very tight-lipped and irritated with Junior. When he clocked me, he tried a smile but it didn't reach his eyes. He told his son he needed to be fit for work and pretty much dragged him out by his collar.'

'How did Ryman Junior react?'

'Like a huge toddler. Bottom lip stuck out and a hang-dog expression. But he did what Daddy told him.'

So much for Christian Ryman's previous attempt to deny his father's authority. The doorbell rang and Swift got up.

'That's probably Faith,' Eli said. 'She said she'd call by for me.' He took two more biscuits.

It was Faith. In the hall, she took Swift's arm and whispered.

'I just wanted to say thanks for giving Eli some work. It made a real difference to him. He's been a lot more positive.'

'That's okay. I was glad to do it.'

'Sorry if I was a bit off with you.'

'Forget it. How are you?'

She appeared happier than he'd ever seen her, her eyes shining. 'I'm okay.' She giggled. 'I'm training Eli in how to be a good house guest. He's turning out to be an attentive student. This morning, we did towels and general bathroom etiquette.'

'I hope you're talking about me!' Eli called.

In the living room, Swift saw that Eli had taken his dishes to the kitchen and wiped the table. He joined them, kissed Faith on the cheek and they stood, holding hands. He puffed his chest out. 'My final bit of news for you both, my *pièce de résistance*, is that I've a job interview this week.'

'Is that for online sales?' Faith asked.

'That's the one. Should be a breeze.' He raised Faith's hand and kissed the back of it.

There was a glow between them. Swift was hopeful for them both. When they'd gone, he refilled his coffee and cleaned up a pool of soggy biscuit from beneath Eli's chair.

The afternoon was mild and bright. He took his coffee out to the swing seat in the garden and searched online for Ronnie Probert. Naomi's comments to Ryman about power of attorney must have been related to him.

Probert's website popped up immediately. A photo of a handsome man with designer stubble, thick, swept-back hair and silver hoop earrings. There were pages with show-reels, portfolio, testimonials and major credits, but Swift just scanned the front and contact pages.

I'm a self-employed digital imaging technician with over ten years' experience in the industry. I've worked for BBC, ITV, CNN, for major corporations and advertising agencies as well as on filmsets. I supply my own kit, but I'm happy to work with a wide range of equipment.

He rang the mobile number. A confident, vibrating voice.

Hi. You've reached Ronnie Probert. I'm away right now, working on a natural history project, but leave a message and I'll get back to you ASAP.

Swift left a general kind of message, just saying that he was interested in a chat. Then he put his head back on the striped cushion. He considered Eli's feedback that Chris Ryman had seemed sad and uneasy when he'd mentioned Naomi's first lover. It sounded as if he'd been more serious about her than he'd admitted, just as the Gadfly waitress had suggested. Jealous too, perhaps.

A jackdaw swooped and tugged at a suet ball, its weight rocking the dangling bird feeder. The sun's rays caught its sleek head as it almost lost its balance and flew away.

* * *

Ronnie Probert hadn't responded to a second message. Toni had called to ask him about progress and he'd had to tell her that it was slow. He took the train back to East India station and walked again to the place where Goddard and Naomi had entered the river. Maybe he'd get inspiration. Not only had he been unable to connect them, but he still had no idea why they'd ended up at Old Bow Wharf.

It was a calm day, although the sky had a murky sepia hue that didn't bode well. Swift sat at the top of the steps and listened to the river wash against them. Someone had been with Goddard after he'd reached home that evening last September. If it wasn't Naomi, and the unknown person had travelled in the sidecar with Goddard, how had Naomi arrived here?

His phone rang. A female voice, indistinct and sounding as if she was in a bath or an echoing room.

'Tyrone Swift? My name's Fizzy Gibson. I'm calling because I spoke to Amy Sutcliff.'

Could someone be called Fizzy? 'I met an Amy Sutcliff recently at the Gadfly.'

'That's right. I got in touch with her to see how things are going. She explained about Naomi Ludlow's death. I'd no idea. I was shocked, especially when she said Mr Goddard had died too and how it happened. Then she told me that you'd been there asking questions.'

The woman sounded as if she was gargling. 'It's hard to hear you. How did you know Sam Goddard?'

She shouted, 'I used to—'

Static crackled in his ear. 'I can't hear you at all now.'

'Bloody phone. Hold — Landline—'

The call died. He waited. The ground was cold and hard beneath him. A soft breeze was blowing off the river, carrying a particular smell that he always categorised as silt and old bones. If he could bottle it, he'd call it *Eau de Thames*. After a couple of minutes, the woman called again.

'Sorry about that. Back to the trusty landline.'

'I can hear you fine now,' Swift told her. 'Did you say your name's Fizzy?'

'That's right, Fizzy Gibson.' She sounded hearty.

'Tell me about Naomi and Sam Goddard.'

'I used to own the Gadfly. I wasn't hands-on, but I chatted now and then with some of the customers. Naomi was very engaging the couple of times I saw her.'

'Did you realise she was underage?'

'Absolutely not,' Fizzy said rather too forcefully. 'She was a mature young woman. Very opinionated and articulate.'

'How come you weren't aware that she and Sam Goddard had died?'

'I sold the bar last summer, moved to Spain.'

'I see. Was Goddard a customer?'

'No, it was a business relationship. I met Mr Goddard when I was making financial arrangements through Spring Investments. I lived in the flat above the bar. That's where he came to see me a couple of times.'

Swift wanted to punch the air and cross his fingers simultaneously. 'Did he meet Naomi?'

'I saw her talking to him once. He stopped for a drink at the bar after one of our meetings. That's all I can tell you.'

'When was that?'

'It must have been late last June. I moved here at the beginning of August.'

'Did you hear any of their conversation?'

'I was passing through the bar, so just a snippet. Naomi was talking about Chris Ryman. They were chatting away, getting along well. I didn't see Mr Goddard again. Amy said that he and Naomi were having a relationship and that they committed suicide.'

'That's the story. What do you make of it?'

She grew hesitant. 'I've no idea. It's all very strange. Mr Goddard told me he was getting married, so it sounds peculiar.'

'You've been an enormous help. Thanks so much for calling me.'

'That's okay. I liked Sam Goddard. Naomi too. She was a cheeky madam and a bit mouthy at times, but engaging.'

'So I've heard.'

He put his phone away. He had a numb bum but he'd been boosted by the conversation. He got up and walked back to the café he'd been to with Toni. He had another, crucial part of the puzzle but he was unsure what to make of it. One interpretation of the snapshot Fizzy had given him could be that Goddard and Naomi had become involved — young girl divulges troubling personal story to older man, who is then both protective and aroused. The verdict from the inquest might have been correct. He hoped for Toni's sake that it wasn't so.

CHAPTER 17

Dora Melides had summoned him with a voicemail.

I've recalled something from my last meeting with Mr Goddard. I'm going to be at a concert at Cadogan Hall between 1 and 2 p.m. If you meet me there, we can have afternoon tea when it finishes.

Swift travelled to Sloane Square. An icy wind whipped around the trees and benches in the centre as he crossed towards Cadogan Hall, making his cheeks smart. He waited in the foyer of the hall at just before two. He could hear resounding applause and saw from a poster that it had been a concert of baroque music, featuring Purcell, Boyce and Vivaldi.

Ms Melides was one of the first out. She sailed towards him, resplendent in a leopard-print coat, alpaca hat and brown ankle boots with a fur trim.

'That was wonderful, although one of the violins seemed a little out of tune,' she told him. 'We'll go just around the corner to a dear little café, run by an Austrian friend. I always have cake there when I'm in this area.' She kissed her gloved fingers in anticipation.

She took his arm and propelled him to a small, chintzy café in a side street. It was painted in dark greens and reds and draped with swagged, floral curtains. The chairs had cushioned seats embroidered with gentians and edelweiss. A couple of dark oak sideboards stood against the walls and two ceiling fans turned gently, whispering above them.

Ms Melides clutched a rotund elderly man wearing a starched white apron to her bosom, and conducted a vigorous sounding conversation in German with him. She introduced him to Swift as Moritz. The old man bowed, and then kissed Ms Melides' hand and took her coat, revealing a matching silk dress with bell sleeves. She ordered tea for two and a selection of pastries.

They sat at a round table covered in a white linen tablecloth with a vase of daffodils in the centre. Moritz brought tea in a rose-pink china pot with a matching tea set and a two-tier gold-rimmed cake stand. He placed them on the table with a degree of ceremony. He and Ms Melides had another chat in German while Swift assessed the artery-clogging array of meringue, chocolate, sponge and cream. Moritz gestured at the cakes, speaking rapidly. Ms Melides translated for Swift.

'Moritz explains that we have *Millirahmstrudel*, *Apfelstrudel*, *Mohnzelten*, *Sachertorte* and *Kardinalschnitte*. I told him it's your first time here and he said he's sure it won't be your last once you've tasted his exquisite pastries!'

Swift smiled and said '*Danke*' to Moritz, who stood, grinning and nodding. He then bowed and scurried away. Ms Melides poured the tea from a height, dipping the spout of the pot up and down. 'Eat, eat!' She urged him.

Swift took a piece of sugar-dusted *Kardinalschnitte*. It was amazingly light and fluffy, with a layer of redcurrant jam. Ms Melides placed three cakes on her plate and seized a fork. She ate in silence for a few minutes, rolling her eyes and emitting little murmurs of pleasure. Swift hoped that she wouldn't choke again.

'Wonderful, isn't it?' she demanded at last.

'Absolutely delicious.'

'Have another!'

'One was fine for me. It was very rich.'

'Oh. You don't have a manly appetite,' she said with disappointment. 'A man should devour food with gusto.'

Swift reflected that he'd been deemed wanting on the masculinity front on their first encounter, but it was refreshing to discover that it could be measured by the ability to down cream cakes. Eli would probably rise to the challenge if he was here, before he tried to borrow money from Ms Melides. He drank his black, fragrant tea.

'Have you visited Austria?' Ms Melides asked.

'No, not been there.'

'I sang in Graz and Salzburg. Wonderful, wonderful audiences. Maybe the best ever. And then the cakes after a performance!'

She was smiling, lost in a sugar-rush reverie. Did she really have anything to tell him, or had she just wanted his company for tea, even if it was unmanly? He stirred his cup briskly to draw her attention. 'You remembered something from the last time you saw Sam Goddard, Ms Melides. Can you tell me what it is?'

She pursed her lips, weighing up what was left on the cake stand, and selected a slice of apple strudel. She forked it into smaller pieces. 'He asked me if I'd heard of someone. I've been trying to recall the name. Something like Potter.'

'How about Probert? Ronnie Probert?'

'Ah, yes, that's it. I said I hadn't. Then he asked me if anyone else from his company had contacted me to discuss my finances. I said no. That was it.'

'You said that Mr Goddard visited you last summer. Can you remember when, exactly?'

She caught a stray drift of snowy cream on her fingertip and popped it in her mouth. 'Let me see. July. The day before Wimbledon ended.'

Moritz approached and she launched into another conversation with him in German. From the glances that came his way, Swift understood that his pastry-eating abilities were being criticised. Moritz brought a cardboard box to the table and carefully placed the remaining cakes in it, tying it with a bow.

'I shall get a cab back, so that these don't get crushed,' Ms Melides said. 'Could you hail one for me, Mr Swift?'

He saw her into a taxi. She was undoing the ribbon on the box as it drove away.

The wind had dropped and the sun was warm in a pale blue sky. Swift sat on a bench in Sloane Square and ordered his ideas and the chronology of events. He made notes, risking some assumptions.

Ronnie Probert. He'd been defrauding an aunt.

Demi Holland told Naomi about Probert last Jan.

Naomi might have got to know Probert around then.

Naomi was interested in power of attorney. That might be how Probert was conducting fraud.

Naomi met Goddard in Gadfly last June. She'd discovered a link between Probert and someone, possibly at Patchell Associates or Spring. Goddard started asking questions. He had professional knowledge of power of attorney.

Goddard asked Dora Melides about Probert in July. Also concerned in case she'd been contacted by someone else at Spring.

Goddard phoned Jenna Beringer in August and asked her if she had any concerns about her dealings with Spring.

Goddard asked Ms Melides and Ms Beringer if they'd had contact with Patchell.

Goddard visited brother Jesse just before wedding, seemed worried. Did he discover something about Spring after he jotted that note?

If Sam Goddard had been concerned about possible irregularities at Spring, he'd surely have gone to his boss. Unless he suspected that Jerome Adcott was involved. But maybe these deaths had nothing to do with Spring and finances. He added to the list.

Christian Ryman. Naomi dumped him April. Sad, angry, bitter. Might have seen her with Goddard in Gadfly.

Maybe this was all about that most obvious and familiar of motives for murder — male jealousy and rage.

* * *

Ronnie Probert called back just as Swift reached his front door. His tone was jaunty and he presumed that Swift's messages involved work.

'I'm uber busy at present. I've just got back to London and I'm straight into a promotional film. I'm pretty booked, unless whatever you have can wait until April or May. Probably best if you email me the gist of it.'

'I'm a private detective. I want to talk to you about Naomi Ludlow.' In case Probert was going to pretend ignorance of her, he added, 'I've spoken to Demi Holland. She told Naomi who you were in January last year. You were working near the Shard on an outside broadcast. I believe that Naomi met you.'

There were voices, clangs and bumps in the background. Probert could still deny having met Naomi, but Swift was counting on the element of surprise and the presence of colleagues to blunt his reactions.

Probert lowered his voice. 'What do you want to discuss?'

'It'd be easier to see you. It sounds as if you're around people.'

'Yeah.'

'I could meet you somewhere.'

'Hang on a minute . . . Yeah, okay. There's a pub round the corner from the studio where I'm working. The Flag and Star on Wrayburn Street. See you in there, eightish tonight.'

When he entered the house, Swift saw a carrier bag of Ms Malla's dishes and a bottle of wine by his door, with a Post-it attached from Chand.

Just to say sorry about letting Eli run riot. He left me a note to say he's moved in with Faith. He's a fast worker. Anyway, bet you're relieved. Catch up soon.

Mary rang while he was eating.

'I was talking to Faith,' she said. 'She sounds very energised. Something about a man you introduced her to. Eli, that's it.'

Swift explained, leaving out his doubts. Not for Mary's sake, but because if Simone got wind of Eli's shortcomings, she'd start interfering and giving Faith her frank opinion.

'I'm glad she's got someone. You've become a bit of a matchmaker on the sly.'

'How do you mean?'

'Faith and Eli, Chand and Bella. You introduced them.'

Bella was an old girlfriend of his from university. He'd met up with her again during an investigation, and she and Chand had fallen for each other. 'True. None of it was deliberate, though.'

'Even so,' Mary teased, 'now we just need to find someone for you.'

'No thanks. I'll do my own groundwork.' He winced, recalling Hester's tearful disappointment.

'What are you eating?'

'Mrs Malla's butter chicken with creamy cashews.'

'Yum. We're having chickpea tagine. Ty, I hope this doesn't give you indigestion, but I wanted to tell you . . . we had a wedding invitation from Ruth today. Seems a tad last minute, given that the marriage is less than eight weeks away. I assume you had no idea she was going to invite us.'

He put his fork down. 'No, I didn't.'

'It's for me, Simone and Louis. Very posh venue in Hampstead. Ruth's put a PS saying that Branna would love Louis to be there as he's one of her best friends. I'm not sure I believed that last part. Does that make me sound horrible?'

Branna had told him recently that Louis was stupid and boring and never wanted to play outdoors. He said diplomatically, 'Branna and Louis get on fine, but that doesn't sound like something she'd come out with.'

'Glad you said that, as it's my impression. What's your reaction?'

'Not sure.' He was nonplussed. Ruth had never expressed any great interest in Mary and they'd never been close. She'd made no mention that she was planning to invite his cousin. He supposed that there was no etiquette about such a situation, although people usually stuck with their tribes once relationships ended. Was Ruth short of people to invite? Marcel had a small family. Surely it wasn't some kind of barb against him.

Mary echoed his thoughts. 'Is Ruth trying to score a point against you?'

'That's unlikely. What would the point be?'

'Oh, maybe that she's the good guy in all of this, so squeaky clean that your family turn up to her next wedding.'

'Ruth and I are ancient history. She's not underhand. The last time I saw her, we had a pleasant conversation and she was fine about me having regular contact with Branna.'

Mary snorted. 'Give me a break. I'd say that having a relationship with Emlyn while she was with you and breaking your heart might be deemed underhand.'

'That's all water under the bridge.'

'Not in my book. Leopards don't change their spots and all that. I'll never forget how shadowy and grim you were after Ruth swanned off. All the weight you lost. Maybe Ruth's annoyed because you've organised a get-together at yours while she's on honeymoon, sees it as one-upmanship.'

That mystified him. 'That doesn't make any sense. I told Ruth that the party is to mollify Branna, and help her through this time when so much is happening. She said it was a lovely idea.'

'Well, I'm stumped. Human behaviour often doesn't make sense. Maybe Ruth's brooded on it and decided you're straying on her turf. I'd rather give her nuptials a miss but Simone's keen to go and spy.'

She would be, Swift thought. And she'd give him a blow-by-blow account afterwards. Perhaps Marcel was behind this latest surprise. He couldn't be bothered with it all. Second-guessing Ruth's motives was a pointless activity. His focus was his daughter and maintaining their bond. Let people do what they liked.

'I don't care either way, Mary.'

'You sure?'

'Yeah. I mean it. Go if you want.'

'I'll consider. Thing is, if Branna's aware that we've been invited and then we don't go, she might be upset.'

'Branna didn't mention it when I saw her last week. Why don't you contact Ruth and ask her? That would be useful, because I need to gauge what to say to Branna as well. I'd rather stay out of it otherwise.'

'I get it. Will do. I'll see which way the wind blows. I can always have an excuse of a pre-arranged engagement on that date.'

'Okay. Must go, I have a call waiting.'

It was Joyce, his stepmother. He rubbed his forehead. Joyce always triggered his guilt because he didn't visit her often enough. She was well-intentioned but overwhelming, and there was a childish nugget of pettiness within him that still resented her for having replaced his mother.

'Ty, my dear, it's been too long,' she said in her fluting tones.

'Yes, sorry about that. I've been busy.'

'As always. How is darling Branna? Still doing well after her implants?'

'She's very well, Joyce, as full-on as ever.'

'She's a brave little trooper. I can't wait to see her at the party you're having in April. Would you like me to bring anything? I could make some of my chocolate and banana muffins. Branna loves those.'

'Her two favourite things combined in one food. That would be great, thanks.'

'I won't keep you and I have a talk on Mesopotamian pottery to attend. I wanted to say that I've received an invitation to Ruth's wedding. Are you going?'

'No.' Who else had Ruth invited? Faith? His aunt in Connemara?

'That's as I expected. It seems odd as I haven't seen Ruth since you split up. I have to admit, I was taken aback when I opened the invite. Of course, I am Branna's Nanna Joyce. Perhaps that's why Ruth wants to include me. In that case, it's a nice gesture.'

'Perhaps. Mary's been invited too.'

'Is she going?'

'She's mulling it over and planning to call Ruth. Why don't you speak to Mary?' He wished they'd all get on with it and leave him out of these snares.

'Yes, maybe that would be best. Oh goodness, this is all so complicated, isn't it? You see, Ty, I don't want to do anything that might upset you. If you'd prefer me not to attend, I won't. I may have forgiven what Ruth did to you, but I'll never forget. I'm always in your corner, my dear.'

He was touched. 'I appreciate that, Joyce, but there's really no need to fret. I told Mary that I don't mind, either way. Up to you. If Branna would like you to be there, that's fine with me.'

'Very well. I'll talk to Mary and see how things stand.'

He put his phone down and prodded his cooling meal. He couldn't be bothered reheating it. Irritability rather than indigestion. Maybe he should go away for the week of Ruth's wedding, turn his phone off. Take his boat to Connemara or the Wye Valley, or maybe even to Lyon, where he enjoyed rowing on the river.

For the first time, he was relieved that Ruth was going to be moving away and putting distance between them, even if it did mean reduced visits with Branna. He'd just have to make sure that the miles didn't become an obstacle.

He put the remainder of the chicken in the fridge, donned his jacket and headed to the Flag and Star.

CHAPTER 18

The Flag and Star was a tiny, cramped place with a well-worn carpet, faded wallpaper, old-fashioned wall lights with fringed shades, and a sign across the bar.

No Internet, No TV, No Games Machines. If you want those, the door's behind you.

Swift admired the management's forthright stance and, judging by the buzz at the bar, so did many others. He bought a pint of Bow Bells Smoke and sat below a classic photo of Muhammad Ali with bare torso, fists raised in boxing gloves. Nothing else suggested that the pub had a link to boxing.

Ronnie Probert arrived late at eight thirty, with no apology. 'What a day! One of those when nothing goes right. I'm getting a whisky sour. Want another of whatever that revolting stuff is?'

'I'm okay.'

Probert sported a dandy style: mustard chinos, a pink jacket over a shirt patterned with lilies and striped braces. His hair was sculpted into a quiff. He could have come from a catwalk rather than a day at work, and fitted Naomi's description of a stylish older man. When he sat down with his drink, Swift saw that his eyelids were blueish with fatigue.

'This place is quaint,' Probert said. 'Distressed verging on neglected.'

'I like it. It's a take-me-as-you-find-me pub.'

Probert ran a finger across the table and grimaced. 'They need to sack the cleaner, if they've got one. Now, let's crack on, bud. I have to get back and finish editing today's work.'

'I'm investigating the deaths of Naomi Ludlow and Sam Goddard, the man she died with. I presume you're aware that she's dead?'

'Saw a bit about it in the news. Suicide or something. Kind of bizarre. I was in LA for a couple of weeks when it happened. It was on the telly when I got back. Poor girl. Why are you asking about it?'

'Sam Goddard's fiancée doesn't accept the suicide verdict.'

Probert tapped the side of his nose. 'Something fishy?'

'Perhaps. I've been trying to determine what Naomi was doing with Goddard.'

'She probably picked him up, like she did with me,' he said ruefully.

What was it with these men who cast themselves as victims of a young girl? 'Tell me about your contact with Naomi. It started in January last year, I believe.'

Probert stretched his arms above his head and cracked his knuckles. 'My shoulders are bloody stiff. That's right. So, one day I'm out with a film crew, doing my job and minding my own business. Trying not to freeze my nuts off in the cold. People presume my work's sexy, but most of the time, it's sheer bloody slog. This girl comes up to me as I finish. She's wearing an eye patch, which is cool. And she's pretty. Vivacious. We go for a drink and hang out for the evening, and we get on like a house on fire. That's how I met Naomi.'

'How old are you?'

'Thirty-four. Why?'

'I'm struggling to understand what a man in his thirties would find to talk about with a girl of fourteen for a whole evening.'

'Maybe you're narrow-minded, bud. Thing is, I'd no idea she was that young, so don't wag your finger at me. She looked at least eighteen. She was stimulating, very bright, interested in my work, some of the celebs I've come across, the locations I've travelled to. She told me about her adventures in news raiding. She was kooky and unusual.'

Swift nodded. 'So, you met up again and had sex.'

'That's right. Tends to be what happens when there's a spark.'

'Where'd you go?'

'None of your beeswax, bud. It was just a couple of times. I decided it wasn't a good idea to continue seeing her.'

'Because?'

Probert savoured a mouthful of his whisky sour. 'Because . . . let's see. Naomi started to drone on about me taking her on jobs and introducing her to people. I suppose she was hoping to meet celebrities or film directors. I explained that I don't generally mix at those levels, but she wasn't paying attention. It disappointed me. She had ideas about modelling, but she wasn't the right shape or height. I couldn't see it going anywhere. And I don't mix business with pleasure — too tricky. She was being really pushy about it. When I got fed up and said she was boring me, she turned nasty and told me that she was mates with an ex of mine, Demi, who'd told her all about me. I went right off her at that point. I don't like being targeted. Manipulated.'

'What had seemed a random encounter with an attractive girl wasn't quite like that,' Swift said.

'Exactly, bud. You've got it. I bailed.' His manner was relaxed, blithe. 'This place could really do with getting an interior decorator.'

'What had Demi Holland told Naomi about you?'

'Tittle-tattle, bud. I was supposed to be bad-tempered and mean. Petty things. I finished with Demi and I suppose she wanted to make trouble for me. Some people get off on that kind of stuff. Not enough to occupy them.'

It sounded evasive. 'Defrauding your aunt is hardly tittle-tattle. It's a serious matter.'

Probert had been downing his whisky, eyes half-closed. They snapped open and he froze for a moment. 'Whoah, bud. No idea what you're on about now.'

Swift leaned forward. 'Demi Holland told me that when she was with you, you were taking large sums of money from an aunt. She'd mentioned it to Naomi, who later told someone that she had something on you. Did Naomi pressure you on that when you didn't want to indulge her whims?'

'No way! You've lost me. I got that Demi was cross with me, but I'd no idea she'd make up crap like that.' He laughed uncomfortably. 'Shit, that's really left field. I'm not even sure I've got any aunts.'

'No aunt with the initials "BN"?'

Probert held his hands out. 'No, bud.'

Swift recalled Naomi's internet search in the Gadfly. 'Do you hold power of attorney for anyone?'

'What the hell's that? Sounds important, but I've never heard of it. Attorney's an American thing, isn't it?'

'It involves taking responsibility for someone's affairs. It seems a strange story to come out with. Why would Demi make it up?'

'Dunno. Ask Demi. Spite? Listen, I love women, but I haven't a clue how their minds work. Some of them get off on hatching plans, laying traps, spinning webs.'

Swift couldn't help recalling Ruth's wedding invitations to his family.

'How did Naomi react to you ending the relationship?'

'She flounced around and cried a bit. That was it.'

'She didn't pursue you?'

'Nah.'

'She was only fourteen. She told her brother she'd lost her virginity with you. I'd have expected her to be more upset if you then dumped her.'

'You didn't know her. She wasn't the kind to bruise easily. Anyway, it would have been hard for her to pursue me, even if she'd wanted to. I was away in Greenland for a month afterwards.'

The pub was getting crowded and noisy. A darts game was starting in one corner and a burly man was calling out team names.

'You didn't contact the police when you saw that Naomi had died?' Swift asked.

'No. It was nothing to do with me.'

'Even so. It might have helped their investigation.'

'Hey, bud, when I saw how old she was in a news report, there's no way I was going to talk to the police. Why should I ask for trouble?'

'Did you ever meet Sam Goddard?'

'Nope.'

'Have you had any dealings with Spring, the financial firm he worked for?'

'No again, bud. Sorry. Got to get back to work.' Probert stood, smoothed his hair and jacket. 'I'm unattached at the moment and after what you've said, I'll stay away from women for now! That goes for this pub, too. I can smell centuries of sweat and grime.'

Swift watched the darts players for a while. There was complete hush as each one took aim. It sounded as if Naomi Ludlow had taken equally careful aim at her targets. He wondered if she'd enjoyed her transient sexual encounters. It was hard to believe she'd have got much joy from them. Excitement and the adrenalin of risk-taking, maybe. Perhaps she'd had a driving need to damage and dislike herself. Whatever had been going on for her, she'd moved on from Probert to Ryman. Something had made her research 'power of attorney' and question financial mismanagement. That must have related to Probert, but Swift had no way of proving it. Then Naomi had encountered Sam Goddard, he'd told her that he worked in finance and she'd divulged what she'd found out.

Swift had the trail as far as there, but still no idea how or why it had snaked from north London to the far reaches of

Old Bow Wharf. He searched Probert's website again, going through the links to recent work and saw that he had indeed been in LA last September.

His phone pinged. An email from Toni Sheringham.

I had a discussion with Lexie about Sam's house. She pretty much said what you advised. I've asked Conor and Lucy to come round and I'll tell them no deal. Lexie will be here for moral support. Hope there won't be too much fallout!

The email took Swift back to Goddard's house in Belsize Park and to the wine bottle, prawn crackers and dented cushion. There was something there that bothered him, but he didn't want Conor Wallace to see him lurking around the place. He decided to put some more work Eli's way. He phoned him and explained what he needed.

'So, you want me to hang around and take photos of anyone going in and out of the property?'

'Correct.'

'How long for?'

'I can't be sure. You don't need to be there all day. Try lunchtime, between twelve and two and after work, say half five until half seven. Call me as soon as you have any sightings.'

* * *

The next morning, Swift was up early. He showered — ah the bliss of having plenty of hot water again — and checked his emails over breakfast. The one that caught his attention was from Amy Sutcliff.

Hi Mr Swift,

I expect Fizzy's been in touch with you. After I chatted to her, I remembered something else about Naomi. Once, when she was in the bar, I asked her how it was going with Chris Ryman. She was fed up and muttered a bit, but I'm sure I heard her say that both of the Rymans were pests. It didn't make any sense to me.

Anyway, just decided to put that your way.

Both of the Rymans. Father and son? Swift looked at the photo that Yuna had sent of the graffiti.

*NAOMI SHAGS CHRIS RYMAN. BIG SCORE FOR
GRENDON — NOT!*

He'd believed that he'd got the right Ryman, but maybe
he'd selected the wrong one, and that scrawl in the toilets
referred to Ryman Senior after all. That would indicate that
Naomi had had sex with the father and then the son. She'd
been a trophy hunter. It might have amused her to sleep
with them both. Another way of staving off the boredom
that afflicted her. Swift recalled what Dean had said about
his sister. *She loved meddling and causing trouble for people, running
rings around them. She got off on it — big time.*

He ate his toast absent-mindedly, then went to make
another slice and top up his coffee. He stopped and smoothed
the loaf packaging. On the side was a green double chevron.
In that moment, Swift remembered where he'd seen the words
Courage Never Fails. They were on Dean Ludlow's school badge.

He hurried to his iPad and browsed Grendon Academy.
There it was, the shield with the motto written below the
inverted chevron. Goddard had repeated that motto when he'd
visited his brother, so he must have been aware of one or both
of the Rymans and their school connection. This was confirmation that Naomi had confided in him. What if she'd regretted
her exploits, got out of her depth and sought his advice? After
all, he'd been a reliable, kindly man, a breath of fresh air after
Probert and one, or possibly both, of the Rymans. Her parents
had been busy and distracted and anyway, she wouldn't have
wanted them to hear about her sexual exploits. Naomi might
have been as tricky and unpleasant as he'd been told, but in the
end, she'd been a young girl taking risks with older men.

The toast popped up and with it, Swift's spirits. Time
to needle Ryman Senior again. He spread marmalade on his
toast and texted him.

*I need to speak to you. You and your son could be in deep trouble
regarding Naomi Ludlow. I'll be outside Grendon Academy in my
orange Mini Cooper at four thirty this afternoon.*

* * *

Ryman came through the school gate at 4.20. Swift liked that he was early. It signalled anxiety. When he got in the passenger seat, he was all bluff and bluster with his sergeant-major tone, but he smelled sweaty.

'What's this about? I have a pile of marking waiting for me.'

'I suppose you're aware that I met your son.'

'He mentioned you.'

Swift showed him a photo of the school badge on his phone. 'Recognise this?'

'Yes, naturally. It's our school badge, it's plastered everywhere.'

'Why would Sam Goddard have known the motto "Courage Never Fails" and why would he have repeated it to someone, indicating that he was worried?'

Ryman snorted. 'It's not an exclusive motto. I'm sure you'll find it's used in lots of places. Actually, it's not that true. Being courageous doesn't always mean you succeed. History's full of brave failures. I led a very plucky rugby team just last week and we lost.' He smiled, pleased with his answer.

'I'll give you that, but coming back to Sam Goddard, it's interesting that he met Naomi Ludlow in a bar called the Gadfly. A bar where your son hangs out and where he also met Naomi. Christian had sex with her and then bad-mouthed her when she dumped him. You turned up at the Gadfly the other night in a bad mood, to haul your son out. I believe I hear your Grendon school motto reverberating around that bar. These are fascinating correlations.'

'I'm pleased for you. I don't share your fascination.' He frowned. 'How do you know I was at the Gadfly?'

'I'm a detective.'

'So you say.' His hand went to the door handle.

'I've a lot more to say,' Swift snapped. 'I have a witness who told me that Naomi Ludlow commented that *both* of the Rymans were pests. Doesn't fit with your claim not to have met her. Both you and your son have been lying to me.'

Ryman stared straight ahead and then turned towards him. His face was puce, his jaw clenched. 'You've got a nerve. Photos of graffiti, shreds of gossip, supposed witnesses, the school motto. It doesn't amount to much.'

Swift opened a window a notch. Time to keep things cool. 'It adds up nicely to me. And try this. Your son has admitted to me — and to someone else, so I have corroboration — that he had sex with Naomi. Other people at the Gadfly knew it too. But I'm sure your son has already told you. Naomi was underage. Your son claimed he didn't realise. Now, that might well be true and so far, I haven't gone to the police with that information. But I could.'

Ryman bristled. 'The girl's dead. What could the police do now without her as a witness?'

'It wouldn't be easy,' Swift acknowledged, 'but a prosecution can proceed without a witness's contribution. The police can rely on other witnesses or sources of evidence. It would be up to the CPS if it passed the threshold, but there's a good chance.' He wasn't at all sure about that last part, but said it with confidence.

Ryman smoothed his trousers at the knees. 'Sounds like baloney to me. I don't believe a word of it. You're not in the police.'

'No, but I used to work in the Met. My cousin's an assistant commissioner.' Truth so far. Now he followed up with a lie — always a good and confusing technique. 'I have lots of friends in the ranks who'd be more than happy to listen to me and come down hard on Christian. Even if he wasn't prosecuted, he'd be dragged over the coals. There's a lot of public contempt for abusers and exploiters these days. The fact that you know about it wouldn't go down well either, especially given your job.'

Ryman was silent, his Adam's apple moving rapidly as he swallowed.

Time to lean in. 'Thing is, Mr Ryman, I'm wondering if you had sex with Naomi too. Hence, she referred to both you and your son being pests. You and your son in court — I can see the juicy tabloid stories now. "*Father and son both slept with vulnerable Naomi. Passed young girl between them like a sex toy.*" You get the idea.'

Ryman slapped a hand hard on the dashboard. 'Absolutely not! That never happened!'

'Then how do you explain her comment?'

Ryman groaned. 'This is a nightmare.'

'I agree. But I don't accept that it compares to the one experienced by Naomi's family. If you don't talk to me now, I will contact the Met. You lied when you told me you'd never heard of Naomi, didn't you?'

Ryman leaned back against the headrest. 'I swear I didn't have sex with Naomi Ludlow. I'd never heard of her until last summer, even though her brother's at Grendon. Why would I have? I wasn't aware that Christian had been involved with her until after the event. He came round one night and told me she wouldn't see him anymore. He was mad about her, couldn't get her out of his mind, but it wasn't mutual.'

He rattled on, not even stopping to breathe. 'He was convinced that he was in love. He kept contacting her and pleading with her to meet him. He waited for her near her house a couple of times and followed her, tried to persuade her to see him again. I was worried that she'd accuse him of stalking. I advised him that he had to let go, but then he told me that Naomi kept teasing him, giving him mixed messages along the lines of maybe she'd get together with him again, he'd have to wait and see. She sounded like a very troubled young woman. I was alarmed at the state Christian was in and what he'd got involved in.' Ryman paused. 'Have you got any water?'

Swift reached into the door well and silently handed him a bottle. He drank and exhaled loudly.

'I contacted Naomi and met her for a coffee. She seemed unwell but she was . . . *fearless* is the word, I suppose. I'm not often out of my depth with young people, but I certainly was with her and I'd never have guessed her real age. Her manner was very assured. She was far more mature than Chris. That young man needs to grow up. I asked her to leave my son alone if she wasn't interested in him. She laughed and said he was a saddo, getting his dad to plead his case. He just needed to get the message, she told me, and stop coming on to her. She wouldn't give me a direct answer.'

'You must have been angry.'

'I was. Mainly because she was enjoying herself, liked watching me squirm. She had a calculating kind of gaze, made me uncomfortable. Naomi Ludlow was one of the most unpleasant teens I've met, and I've come across a fair few over the years.'

'And you're saying that's why she called you a pest?'

'I am. When I met her, she said I was hassling her and she could cause trouble for me if I didn't back off. I took it as a clear threat not to contact her again, so I didn't.'

'And did your chat do any good?'

'I'm not sure. Christian stopped talking about her, so I supposed it had. I was relieved that the matter seemed to have gone away. Then he told me that she'd died and I read the news stories. Chris was terribly upset. I sympathised, but only to a point. I told him he'd had a lucky escape and to learn the lesson, take more care with his drinking and the company he kept.' Ryman had calmed a little, but now he hit the dashboard again. 'I told Chris to stop going to that bloody bar! He drinks too much in there and he meets the wrong kind of people. That's why I went there the other night. I'd called him to have a chat and I could tell he was in there. He was drunk and with some fat ginger chap who seemed pleasant enough. At least he wasn't with a tarty type.'

After what he'd heard, Swift calculated that Ryman Senior had provided a motive for killing Naomi, but not Sam. His son, on the other hand, could have murdered both of them. Or they could have executed it together.

Ryman let out a heavy sigh. 'Are you a father?'

'I have a young daughter.'

'And is she a delight?'

Swift couldn't help smiling. 'Mostly.'

Ryman said morosely, 'Tell you something for nothing, Mr Swift, it's hard bringing up young children, but it's a bloody sight harder when they're adult and behaving stupidly. You can't ground them or stop their pocket money. I could see Chris making a fool of himself and there was little that I could do. I realise now that he was genuinely smitten with Naomi Ludlow, and he was shocked at how deeply he cared for her. He'd never experienced that before.'

'Where were you on the evening of the tenth of September last year?'

Ryman took out his phone and scrolled through his diary. 'At a start-of-term parent-teacher meeting at the school, from 5 until 10 p.m.'

'And your son?'

'I've no idea. He has his own place.'

'Ring him. I want to hear where he was and it's unlikely that he'll respond to me if I call.'

'Hang on — you won't go to the police?'

'Not unless I find out that you or Christian killed Naomi Ludlow and Sam Goddard.'

Ryman's face darkened, but he took out his phone. Swift waited while father and son fenced back and forth, with Ryman growing frustrated and barking away.

'Just speak to him, Chris. He's not unreasonable and he's been doing plenty of digging.'

Angry noises.

'Listen to me . . . I understand, but this guy has contacts in the Met.'

More angry noises.

'*You've* had a shit day? It's not exactly all roses for me. You dragged me into the bloody situation by hooking up with Naomi Ludlow. Maybe you'll learn something from all this. I can only hope so. All you have to do is tell Swift where you were that night—'

Angrier noises.

'Oh, grow up! If you want to create a lot more trouble for yourself, then be my guest. Go ahead. I won't be there to help you out. This is very serious. You could end up in court. That would be good for you. Can't see your employer liking it much. And you might drag me into it. What would that do to your mother and my career?'

More noises, but subdued.

'Yeah. Exactly. Take it on the chin. Man up and speak up.'

Courage never fails, Swift thought.

'Right. I'll hand you over.'

Swift couldn't be bothered with greetings. 'The tenth of September last year. Where were you that evening?'

Christian Ryman sounded sulky. 'Nothing in my calendar, so can't be sure. I'd had a new kitchen fitted, so probably at home, clearing up and stuff.'

'Can anyone verify that?'

'No. I'm on my own. That's the truth, honestly.'

'Give me a break. It's hard to decide who's the biggest liar — you or your father.'

'I'd never have hurt Naomi. I'd hoped that in time, we'd get back together.'

He hadn't got the measure of Naomi Ludlow, despite his apparent prowess with women, but then who had? Swift imagined how it might have been if he'd met Naomi when he was a teenager. He doubted that the encounter would have left him feeling good.

Ryman Junior added, 'I'd really hoped I'd be able to persuade her we had a good thing going.'

There was a rawness in his voice that sounded genuine, but the man had proved himself an accomplished liar, and the emotion might be stemming from fear of being caught out.

Swift handed the phone back to his father. 'Home alone, he says. So that's awkward.'

Ryman told his son he'd call him later. 'What are you going to do?'

'For now, nothing. But I will be keeping an eye on your son.'

'You do believe me, though?'

'Only because I can't see why you'd have murdered Sam Goddard and I can check out your alibi. If I discover anything else that incriminates you, you'll hear from me again.'

Ryman started to say something, then shrugged and got out of the car. This time, as he walked away, his head drooped.

CHAPTER 19

The following morning, Swift saw that he'd had an email from Toni, written at 4.09 a.m.

I woke up and I started fretting about Sam's note, the one you showed me the night of my party. Something's bothering me. Can I see it again? I'm not sure about it, but I suppose if it was in Sam's house, I must be imagining things.

He took a photo of the note and sent it to her. *What do you mean by 'not sure'?*

She rang ten minutes later when he was making coffee, sounding edgy. 'Where exactly did you find the note?'

He might as well come clean with her. Hester couldn't be affected by anything to do with Spring now. Even so, he'd keep her name out of it. She still needed a reference. 'It didn't come from Sam's house. I told you that because I needed to protect the identity of the person who gave it to me. That person found it in the Spring office and also confirmed that it was written by Sam.'

'Well, that person's wrong. That's not Sam's writing. It's very, very like it, so I can see why they were mistaken, but it's not his.'

Swift's heart sank. 'What makes you say that?'

'For a start, it's the way those t's are written. Sam crossed his higher up and with a longer stroke. Also, Sam's writing sloped forward slightly and on the note, it's upright. I'd say the spacing's a bit tighter than Sam's as well. I just compared it to a card I have here that he wrote to me. It's those little details. I thought it was his writing when you first showed it to me. I was already drunk that night. I'm so sorry.'

'Are you sure now, Toni?'

'Absolutely. Sober and in the light of day, it's obvious — well, to me, anyway.'

Swift frowned. 'Can you send me a photo of this card you have?'

'Will do. Do you need it straight away?'

'Please, it's important.'

'Oh God, have I got in the way of your investigation with this mistake?'

The last thing Toni needed was to beat herself up over this detail. 'No, of course not. Don't worry about it.'

'What I don't get is, why would that note have been in Sam's office? I don't understand.'

'I'm not sure. Let me compare the two samples of writing.'

'Okay.' She paused, and then said quickly, 'I told Conor and Lucy I wasn't going to sell to them.'

'How did they react?'

'The air was a tad frosty. Lucy got tearful, Conor was tight-lipped. Said he was sorry that I couldn't see my way to placing the house in their care. He made it sound like a pet, or as if they'd have been doing me a favour. Lexie was great and told them it didn't make financial sense for me. They didn't hang around.' She added sadly, 'I do hope it doesn't sour our friendship.'

I expect it already has. 'Give it time. Is Conor still going to keep an eye on the house for you?' There was no point in paying Eli to watch the place if the arrangement had ended.

'I hope so. He didn't say he wouldn't and he still has a key. I suppose I might have to reconsider that now.'

'Don't do it just yet. I have my reasons for asking you.'

'Righto.' She sounded puzzled, but didn't pursue it. 'I have to be at work soon, so I'd better send you this photo and get a move on. I really hope I haven't messed anything up for you.'

Swift tried to reassure her again and finished the call. He waited for the photo. When it arrived, he examined the message that Sam had written to Toni.

Happy birthday, Toni,
Looking forward to treating you this weekend,
Sam xx

This one was in a looser hand. The subtle differences that Toni had described were there.

Swift sat back and gazed out at the garden. It was glistening after last night's downpour, the leaves heavy with fat raindrops. He'd been played, and cleverly. This was a deliberately vague piece of distraction and he'd fallen for it. He should have been suspicious of how easily it had come his way. He was annoyed with himself, reflecting that he should have checked the note with Toni again when she was sober.

But this discovery was in itself useful. It told him several things, and the first was that he needed to narrow his focus to misconduct at Spring. Someone there had overheard Hester say that she was going to meet him for a drink. They'd been alarmed enough by his investigation to fake the note in the hope that it would misdirect him. They'd only have needed to do that if Goddard had been querying a financial irregularity that was somehow linked to them and the company. It also confirmed that Goddard's death had probably not been suicide. The forger had wanted to take Swift's attention away from Spring and send him off with fictitious initials to Patchell Associates. No wonder no one there had heard of Sam Goddard. Had Hester herself written it? It could have been any staff member.

He could ring Hester and ask her more, but couldn't face the prospect of tears and another guilt trip. He couldn't believe that she was involved in misleading him. If that was the case, she wouldn't have given him Ms Beringer's details and lost her job in the process. No, she'd acted in good faith, taken in by the sudden appearance of the accurate enough forgery. Swift recalled Hester saying that Araminta sat nearest to her, and she'd heard that Hester was meeting him after work. If Araminta and Jerome Adcott were having an affair and/or were engaged in dodgy financial dealings, she might have planted the note under her own steam or on his instructions.

He'd make 'Snooty Minty' his first port of call today.

* * *

The sun was attempting to shine in a washed greyish sky when Swift arrived at the Spring offices. At least he wouldn't be like a drowned rat today when he faced Araminta. She was sitting at the reception desk, looking particularly icy in a white shirt with silver eye shadow and frosted pink lipstick.

'How nice to see you,' she said snidely. 'Mr Adcott's in a meeting all morning.'

'It was you I wanted to talk to.'

'Oh yes?'

Swift placed the note in front of her on the desk. 'Do you recognise this?'

She linked her fingers under her chin. Her nails were also a glittery silver. 'I don't recall seeing it before. It's like Mr Goddard's hand and we use that notepaper.'

'Any idea what it means? I wondered if you might know who BN refers to, or why it mentions Patchell Associates. That firm exists, but I'm unsure about BN.'

She glared up at him, but her gaze didn't flicker. 'No, I haven't a clue. How did you get hold of it?'

'That needn't concern you.'

She pursed her thin lips. 'I hope you haven't removed confidential paperwork from our offices. That would be theft.'

'You have my assurance that I didn't remove it.' He added, 'I have been to Mr Goddard's house, with Ms Sheringham's permission.'

'I see. I can't help you.'

'It's a bit worrying, surely?'

'It's hard to say what it refers to, frankly. Something or nothing, and what's the context? Seems as if you're not getting very far with your enquiry.'

He grinned. 'Would you prefer it if I went away and didn't come back?'

'That would be lovely.'

He was so riled and fed up with her attitude that he bent down and said softly, 'Someone told me that you and Adcott are having an affair.'

He expected anger or confusion. Instead, she started laughing. Her shoulders shook, and she had to put a hand over her mouth.

'Oh dear,' she said at last, smiling at him. 'You're so way off the mark.' She beckoned him to come closer. 'I'm terribly fond of Jerome, but my tastes don't run in that direction. I have a partner at home, a female partner.'

'Office gossip, always a trap,' said Swift, giving himself a mental slap on the wrist.

'And one you walked into,' she said with satisfaction.

Swift rallied. 'I'll allow you that sarcasm, although you do tend to pile it on. Toni Sheringham told me that you sent her flowers and a card after Sam died. She said you're not as hard-hearted as you seem. I reckon you're pretty flinty. I don't mind you being crabby with me, I'm used to stuck-up receptionists, but I'm surprised that you don't want Toni to find out the real reason for Sam's death, if it wasn't suicide. It would bring her such relief and ease her sadness.'

She had the grace to blush and for the first time, he had her at a disadvantage.

'I wish Toni well, always,' she said quietly. 'If I lost my partner in that way, I don't know how I'd survive. I just dislike my colleagues being bothered with all these questions.'

'Even if it's for a good cause? Would you want your partner, the woman you love, to be vilified, her whole life tarnished?'

She stared at him and relented. 'Oh, stop looming over me. Sit down for a minute.' She indicated a chair near her and placed her clasped hands on the desk. 'I've been with this company since day one, watched it grow and become highly successful. We all work so hard to ensure that success continues, not least Mr Adcott, who also has the huge worry and responsibility of a disabled child. We raise lots of funds for Go Kids. I have a great loyalty and commitment to Spring, unlike Hester French. I don't approve of the way you manipulated her. She had a crush on you and you took advantage. I liked Hester and rated her work, although Mr Adcott was right to sack her. I expect you've dumped her, now you got her to snoop for you.' She sat back a little, her face relaxing. 'The day you came through the door, you disrupted the atmosphere, made staff anxious. You must see that we'd had the police here, coming and going at all hours. After the coroner's verdict, it seemed as if we could grieve for Sam and get on with the job. I don't dislike you; I dislike what you do.'

At last, a more human, honest exchange. 'Fair enough, I can understand that.'

Araminta said, mystified, 'You can?'

'Yes. My job can be tacky. I appreciate your forthrightness. I prefer that to caustic comments and hostility. Given your allegiance to Spring, let me just ask you, have you ever had doubts about the integrity of anyone who works here?'

'Absolutely not,' she snapped back. 'The only person who turned out to be untrustworthy was Hester, and we know who was behind her behaviour.'

'Touché. I'll leave it there. Just remember that all I want to do is find out if Sam Goddard has been wrongly discredited. If anything does occur to you about the note, maybe you could contact me.'

The stare she gave him as she turned to answer the phone indicated that hell would freeze over first.

Outside the offices, he remembered that he'd skipped breakfast and decided to get a hot dog from a nearby stall. He placed his order and waited, turning his collar up against the brisk breeze. Despite her criticism — some of it valid — the conversation with Araminta had been surprisingly refreshing and helpful. She was indeed snooty, but in her own way driven and, he reflected, candid. There did seem to be a heart beating beneath the glacial exterior. Her remarks about her commitment to the company had the ring of truth. Unless that had been an Oscar-winning turn, he doubted that she'd get involved in malpractice, or tolerate her boss doing so. But that left him grasping for another lead and he'd no idea where he might find it.

Despite the savoury, mustard-drenched hot dog, his spirits sank further when he received a text from Eli, who was loitering near Goddard's house.

Nothing happening here, no sign of any activity. Bored to tears and eating too much chocolate.

* * *

That afternoon, he took his boat back to Old Bow Wharf and set off towards Channelsea Island, hoping that fresh air and exercise might give him inspiration. Clouds had gathered, but it remained dry and the river flowed quietly.

This forlorn backwater fascinated him. It had a timeless quality. He was the only person on the river and the solitude was a balm. He wasn't sure how accessible the island would be, having read that others had given up their attempts to explore it. Apart from the poisons in the soil, there were risks from damaged structures and giant hogweed, which could cause angry blisters if it caught your skin.

As he rowed, he cast his mind over the people involved in this case and the way their paths crossed and interconnected. He could picture them all clearly, yet somehow they stayed elusive. Most elusive of all were Sam and Naomi, heading into the swirling river, already drugged into a sleep they'd never wake from.

Swift navigated around the shoreline, until he saw a small inlet with white-plumed egrets fishing in the water. He put on gloves and wellingtons before he stepped ashore and pulled his boat up on the dense mass of vegetation.

For a moment, he stood still. All he could hear was birdsong. He pushed through ivy, wild columbine, tall ferns, and tangled hawthorn and hazel bushes for a couple of metres, aware of rustling around him. Suddenly, in front of him and almost covered by encroaching nature, was a large derelict brick building. He stepped forward carefully, noting hogweed to his left. All the windows were shattered, the roof caved in, and buddleia covered one side completely. He peered through the gap where there had once been a window into the dark interior, and saw a huge glistening rat crossing a floor scattered with debris.

He was contemplating trying to skirt the side of the building when his phone rang. It was Ronnie Probert.

'Hi, bud. Listen, I was remembering Naomi last night. Daft kid. I did like her, even if she was a pain in the arse. I've been reading some of the news coverage about her. I didn't see much because I was leaving for the States last September. I hadn't twigged that she'd died at Old Bow Wharf.'

It sounded as if Probert's conscience had nagged him. 'That's right. She was in the sidecar of Sam Goddard's motorbike when she drowned.'

'Yeah. That wouldn't have been Naomi's style at all. A Ferrari or a Porsche would have been her thing. But you see, she came to Docklands with me one time, around that bit of the river.'

Swift leaned against the cold, jagged brick, but he was warm, his blood flowing with exertion and this welcome news. 'You mean Old Bow Wharf? I'm in the area right now.'

'Yeah. I was doing some work there. Naomi tagged along with me. it was the one time I gave in, and said she could come as long as she wasn't a nuisance.'

'When was that?'

'Beginning of February last year, before I told her I'd had enough. I suppose it was a kind of parting gift to her.'

How generous of you. 'What work were you doing?'

'Not sure. A private commission. I can check my diary if you hold on.'

'Thanks.'

Swift waited. The silence was as dense and rich as the vegetation. A blackbird flitted silently and vanished into a blackthorn thicket. He imagined scores of eyes observing him.

Probert came back. 'Hi. I was advising on some promo material for a charity that was setting up a base along the wharf. A soft play area for kids, a climbing wall, adventure corner, stuff like that.'

'What's the charity called?' He was expecting to hear Go Kids.

'Hang on . . . its name is ACT — Active Children's Trust. It was still half-finished at the time. Naomi was fed up, because they said she couldn't actually come into the building. They were very strict about access. Suppose they have to be these days where kids are concerned. So, she was at a loose end. I sent her off to have a walk and buy a snack so that I could get on. On the way back in the car, she said the wharf was a "skanky dump".' He gave an embarrassed laugh. 'In fact — and this sounds awful, given what happened — I'm sure she said that she wouldn't be caught dead there again.'

Swift thanked him and ended the call. He stood motionless, turning this information over. Probert had willingly revealed that he was familiar with Old Bow Wharf and this was the first link between Naomi, Goddard and the location where they'd died. Surely it must be significant. Goddard's friends were connected with a children's charity, as was Spring. As for Probert, he might have dealt in fraud and boasted about it, but he had an alibi for the time of the murders.

It was almost four o'clock. If he rowed fast, he might be able to speak to someone at ACT before they closed.

CHAPTER 20

Swift secured his boat to the car roof and Googled "ACT". It wasn't far from the café where he'd been with Toni. Perhaps Naomi had visited it, might even have sat at the same table as they had when Probert had sent her off to get her out of his hair.

He drove along the quay and parked outside the octagonal, timber-frame building that housed the charity. The huge front windows faced the river and were fitted with one-way privacy glass, rendering them opaque from the outside. The grounds were surrounded by a tall, solid cedar fence that was attractive but shielded the premises. The entrance was locked, so Swift pressed an intercom and explained who he was. The door clicked open.

He crossed a spacious foyer with a café to one side and presented himself at the reception, showing his ID. A young man in a bright pink T-shirt greeted him.

'Would it be possible to speak to the manager? I'm investigating two deaths that happened nearby.'

The receptionist clutched the desk. 'Goodness! Let me see if Ms Hollerton is available.'

Swift stood and read about the centre while he waited. It provided services for children with visual and hearing impairments, Autistic Spectrum Disorder, developmental delay, learning disabilities, emotional and behavioural difficulties, ADHD and cerebral palsy. Swift pictured Jed Adcott, but this centre would surely be too far from his home. There were lots of activities on offer, including sensory rooms, climbing frames, soft play, zip wires, nest swings, tree houses, bikes and scooters. Swift could smell coffee, but he saw that the café was closing. Ah, well.

A woman wearing a pink T-shirt and jeans appeared. Her black hair was neatly bobbed and she turned grave, chestnut brown eyes on Swift. 'I'm Binda Hollerton. Would you like to come to my office?'

Swift followed her to a small room at the back of reception and sat on a plastic chair. He explained his investigation and his contact with Ronnie Probert.

'I've been trying to find a reason why Naomi Ludlow and Sam Goddard would have been at Old Bow Wharf. No one has been able to understand what brought them here to die. Now, at least, I've confirmed that Naomi came here early last year. This is her photo.'

Ms Hollerton had a piercing gaze. She examined the picture of Naomi. 'I don't recall her, but then if she didn't enter the building, I wouldn't. You see, Mr Swift, this centre didn't open until May last year and we were still very much a work in progress. I did meet Mr Probert with some of our development team. I read that there'd been deaths in the river near here, but I'd no idea that this young woman was involved.'

'This is Sam Goddard. Do you recognise him?'

She shook her head. 'No, sorry.'

'Have you had any involvement with a financial company called Spring? They're based in Camden.'

'We have a number of funding streams. That name isn't familiar.'

Swift realised that the woman hardly blinked, hence her slightly robotic appearance. 'There's a children's charity called Go Kids. Do you liaise with them at all?'

'I'm aware of them because they're in the same line of work. They have a national presence, whereas we're very much a local venture. We don't conduct any joint working.'

'I see.' He wondered about Jed Adcott again. 'Would children come here from outside this area?'

'No. We only offer services to families from this borough. Just as well, as we have a waiting list.'

He seemed to have hit a wall again. He gave Ms Hollerton his card and took his leave. He could now place Naomi at Old Bow Wharf on one day last February, but that was months before she met Sam Goddard, so what good did it do him?

* * *

Eli rang as he was driving through grinding traffic back to Hammersmith.

'Bloody hell, *mi fren*, I'd forgotten how cold and numb you can get doing obs. At last, someone went into the house. A woman, at about quarter to six. I'm sending you a photo.'

'Is she still in there?'

'Yep.'

'Okay, stay there for now. No sign of anyone else?'

'Just her.'

Swift pulled over as soon as he could, speculating that he was about to see a photo of Toni. She might have decided to visit the house and check it for herself, now that Conor was disgruntled. He opened the image of a woman sideways on, with a key in the door. He was astonished. He called Eli back.

'That's Mila Fullbright. Sam Goddard's ex-wife. Is she still there?'

'Yep, but on her own.'

'Can you stay until she leaves and grab another photo? It would take me ages to get to Belsize Park in this traffic.'

'No problem. What's going on, then?'

'I have absolutely no idea. I'll have to ask her.' He ran through possibilities. 'In fact, I'm going to call her now, see what she says.'

Eli chuckled. 'That'll startle her. *Ale tata.*'

Swift called Mila. She picked up after a few rings, sounding irritable.

'Yes?'

'Mila, this is Tyrone Swift.'

'Oh, yeah. How're you?'

'Fine. How's your jaw?'

'Much better now.'

Reel her in gently. 'Great. Have you managed to get me any tickets?'

'Tickets — Oh yeah, sorry, not yet. Been a bit busy, one thing and another. I am now, actually. Can I call you back?'

'No problem. Why are you in Sam's house?'

There was a stunned pause. 'Sam's house? Why would I be in Sam's house?'

'That's my question. You're in there right now.'

'How — Don't be daft.'

'Mila, don't piss me about. You're in the house. I have proof. What are you doing in there and how come you have a key?'

She gave a nervous laugh. 'Have you got a drone spying on me or something?'

It sounded as if she was moving around. She'd have gone to a window.

'Just answer the question.'

'Why should I?'

'Because although you didn't break in, you've no right to access that house. It could be a criminal matter.' He heard a door creak. She was probably looking outside. He hoped that Eli was well concealed.

'No need to make a drama out of it,' she said with bravado. 'There's no mystery. Sam gave me a key back in the day.'

'Why would he have done that? You'd divorced when he bought the house.'

'I was between flats at one point. I stayed over a couple of nights. Purely platonic, you understand.'

It was plausible, but convenient. 'But why would you be using the key now?'

She switched to a sweeter, reasonable tone. 'I shouldn't have, but I realised that Toni Sheringham might sell the place soon. That time I stayed, I left a bracelet here that I really liked. Sam was going to return it but I dunno, it just never happened. I'd forgotten I had the key until your visit reminded me. I decided on the spur of the moment to come over and see if I could find the bracelet. I didn't want to bother Toni after all she's been through. Awkward.'

'And have you found it?'

'No. Maybe Sam got rid of it.'

Best to play along for now. 'Oh dear. You had a wasted trip then.'

'Yeah, seems like it.'

'It's not a good idea for you to have a key. Could cause problems for you and Toni would be upset. Leave it on the kitchen table when you go. I have a key, so I can pick it up and return it to Toni. I won't tell her about your visit or your bracelet.'

'Right, thanks. But hang on, how did you know I was here?'

'Best to leave now, Mila, just so that there can't be any misunderstandings about you being in the property without permission. Key on the kitchen table, and shall we agree that you'll be out the door in the next five minutes?'

'Sure,' she said. 'Whatever you say.'

Swift called Eli and gave him the gist of the conversation. 'If she's not out of there in a few minutes, ring me.'

'Okay, *mi fren*. Oh — I have eyes on her now. She's closed the door and she's looking around.' He laughed. 'You should see her — she's got a face like a dried lemon. Now she's making a phone call and heading up the road. Okay if I stand down now, boss?'

'Fine.' Swift couldn't see the point in paying Eli to loiter there any longer. 'In fact, you can leave the monitoring now.'

'Great. By the way, I got that job. Start next week. Faith's delighted.'

'Me too. Thanks a lot.'

Swift sat in the car, tapping the wheel. Everything Mila had said could be true, but he had an uneasy sense about it. If her story concerning the key was a lie, he had to hand it to her for thinking on the spot, and there was only one person she could have got it from. He was pretty sure that the phone call Eli had seen Mila making was to Conor Wallace. Perhaps she'd been expecting him.

Why would they be meeting in the house? An affair or something more sinister? He deliberated whether or not to contact Wallace and see what he had to say, but decided against it. If Mila had already spoken to him, Wallace would back up her story and he'd be at another dead end. Wallace might have had more keys cut, but if not, he now had no way to get into the house and would have to sweet-talk Toni into parting with another key.

There was a solution to that. Frustration might well lead to activity that would offer a break in this investigation. Swift phoned Toni.

'Hi, have you heard from Conor and Lucy?'

'No,' she said. 'Radio silence.'

'To be expected for now, really. Listen, you should get the locks changed on Sam's house, front and back doors.'

'Oh, why's that?'

'It's always advisable when someone's died, because keys might have gone astray.'

'I suppose. But I don't want to offend Conor and Lucy, make them worry that I don't trust them now.'

This woman was much too nice for her own good. 'Toni, I don't see why they should take it that way. It's your property. If you want, you can tell them that I advised it. And from now on, you should keep all the keys to the house in your possession. If you don't want to go there, I can arrange for the lock change. Just send me a signed permission. I can do check calls at the house for you as well, until you're ready to take it on yourself.'

'Is it really necessary?'

'Yes, and at this stage, after what's happened with them, it's best to remove the issue of the house from your friendship with Conor and Lucy. Make things simpler.'

'I understand. Would you . . . Can I take you up on your offer on both counts?'

'Certainly. I'll sort the locks tomorrow, first thing.'

Swift drove slowly home, stopping by Tamesas to unload his boat. He wished he could make out what was going on here and what these alliances were about.

* * *

Early the next morning, the locks at Goddard's house had been changed and Swift was in possession of two sets of keys. He walked around the house when the locksmith had finished. In the living room, he saw new signs of activity: a crumpled crisp packet, a half-empty can of gin and tonic and yesterday's *Evening Standard*. That drift of spicy perfume was in the air again. It reminded him of cloves and he suddenly recalled where he'd smelled it before. Mila had been wearing it when he visited her flat.

She'd been conning him. She'd come here more than once. It was worth putting pressure on her now. He sat on the sofa and phoned her.

'Not you again,' she said. 'I left the key in the kitchen, like we agreed.'

'You did. I'm in the house now and I can smell your distinctive scent. I smelled it here before, and you were wearing it when I came to your flat. Last night wasn't your first recent visit to this house.'

She giggled, a high, forced sound. 'Please, give me a break! I wear Cinnabar by Estée Lauder. Loads of women must use it.'

'You've been up to something, Mila, and I'll find out what it is. I hope it didn't involve murder.'

228

'What? Don't be ridiculous.' She sounded scared. 'Are you saying I did that to Sam? No way!'

'You'd been married to him. Conor Wallace has a key to the house. He's been keeping an eye on it for Toni. Wallace worked with Sam and you knew Wallace through him. It all points to the conclusion that you've been meeting Wallace at the house. The question is why?'

'It's not what you think—'

'What do I think?'

'Honestly, it's none of your business and nothing to do with what happened to Sam.'

'Obviously, I'll have to get in contact with the Wallaces, see what they say. I'll be in touch again.'

'Hold on, wait!' she screeched.

'What now?'

'Oh, for God's sake! Why are two adults usually meeting in a borrowed house? I've been seeing Conor for a while.'

'You're having an affair with him?'

'Yes. The house was a handy bolt-hole, bit of a gift really.'

'So you lied to me about having a key that Sam had given you.'

'Yes. I had to, didn't I? I was trying to cover for me and Conor.'

'How long have you been seeing each other?'

'What's that got to do with you? You going to snitch to his wife?'

'Just wondered.'

She made a noise like a growl. 'I'd always liked him when I was married to Sam. I got in touch with him last summer when I was at a loose end. Life was suddenly a man-free zone. My place is a bit out of the way for meeting up, so after Sam died, his house was handy. Satisfied?'

'Maybe.'

'Don't tell Lucy. It wouldn't do anyone any good.'

'I won't unless my investigation requires it,' he said curtly. 'We'll talk again.'

She started to speak, but he ended the call. Did he believe her? He was unsure. Everything she said was credible.

He could imagine her getting bored and contacting a man she'd once fancied. Maybe Wallace had been tired of his wife nagging him about finding a bigger place to live, and Mila had offered novelty and distraction. Now she and Wallace would be agitated. He'd leave that mixture simmering. He didn't have to wait long. Conor Wallace rang him as he was ensuring that the back door was locked.

'I wondered if I might hear from you,' Swift said. 'I assume you've been in touch with Mila.'

Wallace sounded as though he was speaking through gritted teeth. 'I realise that this doesn't look good, and I should never have used Sam's house for such a sordid activity. You have to believe me, we had nothing to do with Sam's death. Obviously, I'll end the affair now. It was a fading fling anyway. Please, please don't tell Lucy or Toni.'

'A bit tacky, definitely, but I'm not your conscience. The locks on Sam's house have been changed now, so you can't be tempted.'

'Toni has just texted to tell me. I expect you were behind that decision.'

'Sorry. You'll have to find another love nest.'

'I won't need one,' he said. 'I'm so ashamed. I don't understand why I've been putting my marriage at risk. Mila got in touch with me and I was flattered by the attention. I'm glad that you found out, despite the embarrassment. This has been a wake-up call.'

'If you say so. Some might find your offer to Toni for the house somewhat crude as well, considering what you've been up to in there.'

'That was ill-judged on all fronts, I realise that now. To be frank, Lucy came up with the idea and I went along with it. I should have quashed it.'

'I don't care which of you dreamed it up. You upset Toni.'

Wallace cleared his throat. 'Well . . . I'll . . . We'll apologise to her for that. I'll just have to trust in your compassion over this affair with Mila. I promise, I'm ending the relationship. I do believe that you're a genuine man. You wouldn't want to distress Lucy for no good reason.'

'You're right, I wouldn't do it without good reason, so as long as you're being honest with me now, it won't go any further.'

'Thank you. I can't begin to tell you what a relief that is. Believe me, I've learned my lesson.'

Swift stood, turning his phone over when the call ended. Was it all a bit too managed and glib? Someone at Spring had taken him for a ride with that forged note. If it had been Conor, he might be doing it again, but how did it involve Mila?

He checked that the windows were secure and was leaving the house when Jenna Beringer called him. He stepped back into the hallway to listen to her yelling.

'Mr Swift, how are you?'

'I'm fine. I hope you're well?'

'Creeping along. I'll cut to the chase as this phone lark is hard work. You asked me if I'd recommended anyone else to Spring.'

'That's right. Sam Goddard had asked you as well.'

'Oh, yes, he did. Well, last night I was watching a film on the telly and up popped Reece Redman. He's a middling kind of actor, but not bad at all. Always plays the sidekick and he can do menace well. I told him about Spring. It was when we were doing a Chekov season in Northampton. He was keen as mustard to sort his money. Acting's such an unreliable profession for many. Feast to famine in the blink of an eye.'

'Are you still in touch with Mr Redman?'

'Not for a while. I do have a phone number.'

She bellowed a London landline number to him. He massaged his ear when she rang off and then called it.

Reece Redman answered and proved to be very chatty, albeit vague. Maybe his phone didn't ring often these days. He said that he'd had dealings with Spring in the past, but not any longer. He agreed to see Swift that afternoon, at his home in Chiswick.

CHAPTER 21

Swift sat in the living room of Reece Redman's pretty terraced house. Unlike Dora Melides, he hadn't decorated the
walls with pictures from his career. Instead, he had a number
of paintings, mostly abstract contemporary art. He was in his
late sixties, medium build with pure white hair, handsome
but not strikingly so. Swift couldn't recall seeing him in anything. It was the remarkable voice that would stay with you,
resonant and musical.

Redman had shaved patchily and had a large plaster on
his right hand. The room was dusty and untidy, with a couple of drooping houseplants. A smoky-grey cat was sleeping
on the sofa and judging by the marks on the wood, it used
one of the legs as a scratching post. Things were crumbling
at the edges.

Swift explained his investigation but after a few minutes'
conversation, he realised that although Redman had a bright
smile and a good social front, his memory was poor. He'd
offered coffee and then forgotten to make it.

'Jenna Beringer told me that she'd advised you about a
financial company called Spring,' Swift said.

'Jenna, goodness me. She was a laugh. Quite naughty,
too.' He smiled. 'I bet she flirted with you.'

'She tried her best. So, when I phoned, you said you'd had dealings with Spring?'

'That's right. A few years ago.'

'Who was your financial adviser?'

Redman ran a hand through his hair. 'Now, that's a bit tricky. A nice chap.'

'Jerome Adcott? Sam Goddard?'

'Sorry, name's gone now. I parted company with them, you see.'

'Do you mind me asking why?'

'I read a thing in the financial pages, said collectibles were better value, so I moved my money. I buy porcelain, whisky, art.' He gestured at the walls.

'I see. So it wasn't because you were unhappy with Spring?'

Redman's eyes were distant. 'Unhappy? No. I do like my adviser now. How amazing to hear about dear Jenna. So talented and I did enjoy her company. I suppose she's retired?'

'She is, yes. She lives in Surrey.' Swift wished he was better at handling this kind of memory lapse. He didn't want to knock too hard on Redman's fragile facade and upset him. 'Are you retired?'

Redman struggled with the question. Finally he said, 'Let's see. My agent never calls, although we still have lunch now and again.' He half-rose from his chair. 'I have a food delivery coming at four. What's the time now?'

'It's only twenty to three.'

'Ah. That's good.' He sank back down.

Swift smiled reassuringly. 'I expect you have family who help out.'

'Not as such. I'm here on my own. My agent might ring soon, arrange lunch.'

'It might happen. I hope he or she pays.'

Redman chuckled. 'Oh he does, even though I don't really make him any money these days.'

Swift smiled. 'Speaking of money, you said you have a financial adviser now.'

'Indeed, yes. Lovely woman. Keeps everything shipshape for me, takes care of the bank and whatnot.'

'That's good. How did you find her?'

A shadow crossed Redman's face. 'Oh dear, that's a tricky one. Anyway, she's terribly helpful and manages all the bits and bobs for me. Internet stuff, buying and selling. I don't understand that at all. Have you met her?'

'I'm not sure.' Swift plucked a name at random from his friends. 'Is she called Bella?'

'Oh no — at least, I don't . . . It *is* a short name.' He narrowed his eyes. 'Mila, that's it!'

Here we go. 'Mila Fullbright?'

'That's right. Don't know what I'd do without her.'

'I can imagine.' *And I bet I know exactly what she's doing with you.* 'Does Mila have power of attorney for your affairs?'

'Let's see . . . That's a bit of a poser. Best to ask her, really. I haven't seen her for a while. Expect she'll call by soon. She's going to raise money for me on this house . . . I can get a lump sum, she says. That'll be handy.'

'It's called equity release,' Swift said.

'Is it? I expect so. I leave it to Mila, you see.'

'Does she ever come with a man called Conor Wallace?'

'Oh, now I can't recall . . . She comes here on her own,' Redman said and then, less confidently, 'I do believe there was a friend who came with her once. Very natty man. Wore braces and his hair was sort of—' he made a shape above his head — 'I mean, it was in a kind of wave.'

'Do you mean like a quiff?'

'That's it!'

Ronnie Probert. Intriguing that he'd popped up again. 'Has this friend of Mila's ever been back here?'

'I believe not,' Redman said. 'I would recognise him, because of that . . . wave thing. Very striking.'

Swift was seething with anger. 'Mr Redman, do you have a solicitor?'

He made a vague gesture. 'I do need to make a will. Mila said she'll organise it . . . Coffee! I never made you any.' He tapped his forehead and made to get up. 'What must you make of me?'

Swift put a hand out. 'Please, don't bother, I should be on my way.'

'Oh, I see. Well . . . it's been lovely. Do call again and give Jenna my best.'

Swift walked from Redman's house to the nearby Thames and sat on a bench. He huddled into his jacket, incensed and disgusted. Reece Redman offered such easy pickings and there must undoubtedly be other victims. No wonder Mila could afford a large flat and Lalique crystal.

How did Ronnie Probert fit into this picture? Had he upgraded from swindling his aunt to a wider group of victims? Maybe he was working a three-way scam with Mila and Wallace.

Swift took out his phone and called Demi Holland.

'I won't take more than a minute of your time,' he said. 'Did Ronnie Probert ever mention a woman called Mila Fullbright?'

'Mila? Yeah. They had an on-off thing before I met him. They hooked up at some music gig they were both working at. He said she was quirky and demanding.'

'That's all I wanted, thanks.'

'That's all you're getting,' she said drily.

That had established a firm connection between the two, and Probert might well have boasted to Mila about his easy money from his aunt, in the same way as he had with Demi. Reece Redman had previously been a Spring client, giving a link to Wallace. If Mila was in cahoots with Wallace, finding vulnerable people to defraud, that might explain why they needed to meet. Of course, they could be having an affair as well as being partners in crime, with theft causing a lovely warm glow that bonded them in more ways than one.

Wallace could easily have planted the fake note on Hester's desk. If Sam had discovered what they were up to, how had that come about? Naomi had talked to him, but her information about a swindler was related to Probert.

Someone else at Spring, other than Wallace, might have been involved. Once again, Swift wished that Hester hadn't been sacked.

He mulled over this situation and had an idea about how Wallace and Mila might have selected their victims. Time to take a gamble. Adversity makes strange bedfellows, as his great-aunt Lily had been fond of saying. He rang Araminta.

'I've just stepped out to a café for a sandwich,' she said.

'Are you on your own?'

'Yes.'

He tried for the right mix of appeasing and forthright. 'I appreciate that you dislike what I do, but I'm turning to you now because I have to. I've a favour to ask.'

'Why should I do you any favours?'

'You have no reason to. But you see, I trust you. You're a good egg, despite your snappiness.'

'I'm truly flattered. Go on.'

'Also, you're proud of what you do and the company you work for. It has integrity and helps a charity. You wouldn't want to see its reputation dragged through the mud. I respect that.'

'I don't understand.'

He had to be careful now. Wallace and Mila were possibly linked in crime. They might or might not be killers. He didn't want to put Araminta in jeopardy. 'I've learned something that's potentially very serious about one of your colleagues. It might be connected to Sam Goddard's death. I can't tell you that person's identity, or the information I have, because I don't have proof yet and I don't want to alarm them.'

'Hang on, are you saying that someone at Spring might have killed Sam and that girl?'

'Possibly.'

'Oh God. Let me sit down a minute. I need my coffee.'

He waited, heard a chair scraping. 'You okay?'

'Yeah. It's not . . . It can't be Jerome. Please tell me it's not him. I wouldn't believe you if you said it was. He's a good man.'

236

'The person I've identified isn't Jerome. I'm sorry to do this. I need information and I have no other way of getting it. I'm not even sure if you can.'

'Hold on. You're sure that this discovery about a colleague is reliable?'

'Yes. My suspicions are strong enough to seek verification.'

She took a long breath. 'Tell me what you need.'

'I need information about older people who have previously been clients of Spring, who live alone and probably have no close family. Going back say, ten years. Names and contact details. Can you get that from your system?'

'Yes. It will take a bit of collating if they're not active records. I presume you're going to contact these clients?'

'I have to. I'll try to be as discreet as possible. I need evidence, Ms Leadsom, details that I can take to the police.'

'I'll see what I can do, but I sincerely hope that you don't find anything.'

'Thank you so much. I realise that it's a huge ask. If I find the proof I'm after, at least Spring might manage damage limitation. And please, it's important that you don't mention this to anyone at work. I caused enough trouble for Hester. I don't want you put at risk.'

'I'll keep it to myself. I can run the search when the team's gone home.'

'Thanks. I owe you.'

'I'm doing it for Spring,' she said primly, 'not for you.'

'Of course. Thanks anyway.'

Swift walked to Hammersmith, following the river. Lights gleamed along the path in the falling dusk as he went over everything again. He hoped that the trail of radiance was leading him to the right conclusions as well as home.

* * *

Swift was making a toasted sandwich for supper and doing his accounts. The toaster had been glued together with burnt cheese and he remembered that Eli had made himself a late-night snack. After ten minutes of scraping off the debris, it was fit for use. Now his ham, cheese and tomato sandwich was bubbling and browning nicely while he checked columns of figures. His phone rang and he saw Araminta's name.

'Hi, Ms Leadsom, have you got something for me?'

'Mr Swift, I'm a bit worried,' she whispered.

'What's the matter?'

'I'm in the office. I've compiled a list of clients within those parameters you mentioned. Work's been full-on, so it took me quite a while. I went to get a cup of tea and I heard someone on the stairs. They were moving about in my office and now they've gone up to the next floor.'

He checked his watch. 7.45. 'Are you sure everyone had gone home?'

'Positive. I checked before I progressed with my search. The front door was locked. I just ran down and made sure, so it must be someone who works here.'

'Maybe one of your colleagues forgot something, or Jerome has popped back.'

'That's what I thought,' she hissed. 'But I went into the corridor and called out loudly several times. No one answered. I heard the floor creak up there. I'm not sure what to do.'

'If you're worried that there's an intruder, you should leave the building and call the police. I can do it for you if you like.'

'Maybe that would be — Oh, hold on, I can hear some-one calling me.'

He heard her quick footsteps and guessed she was climb-ing the stairs. He heard her say with surprise, 'Oh, hi, I did call out and I wasn't sure if anyone—'

There was a thud and her voice vanished.

'Hello! Hello! Ms Leadsom, are you there? Araminta?' The line was dead.

He called her number. It went to voicemail. He tried again. Same message.

Swift tasted fear. He rang 999 and reported an intruder, giving the address. Then he ran to his car.

* * *

He made it to Camden Town in just over forty minutes, thankful for the rain that meant the roads were fairly quiet. He ran towards the Spring offices and saw uniformed police outside, drawing blue tape around the front of the building and across the road to the side of it, where an ambulance stood. A small group of people were standing on the opposite pavement, watching, some of them pointing.

A constable stepped forward, holding up her hand. 'Sorry, sir, you can't come any closer.'

'I reported this incident to the police. Can you tell me if Ms Leadsom is okay?'

'I can't tell you anything. My colleague will take your details.' She beckoned to another constable who drew him to one side and asked for his name and address.

Swift told him and explained that he was a private investigator. 'I called the police. You can check. I was on the phone to Ms Leadsom when she said she'd heard someone in the office.'

The constable regarded him blankly.

'Can you tell me what's happened here?' Swift asked. 'It's important.'

'Not just now, sir. Come with me, please, and wait until an officer can speak to you.' He took Swift to a police car parked across the road and asked him to sit in the back. As he was getting in, Swift heard some voices from the pavement.

'Heard an awful scream . . .'

'Have to hand it to the emergency services, they were here really fast . . .'

'Something happening in that side road . . .'

Swift sat, his mind racing. Araminta had been climbing the stairs and the ambulance was in the road adjacent to Spring's offices. The roof garden overlooked that road. He pictured the side of the garden, recalling a wall topped by a trellis and climbers. It must be six feet in height, so it would take some effort to topple over it. Unless you were pushed. An 'awful scream'. He clenched his hands.

Long minutes ticked by. The ambulance sped away, its siren blaring. He considered what he should tell the police, and what he'd omit for now. He was edging towards a resolution in this case and he didn't want them closing him down.

Finally, a man got in beside him. 'I'm Sergeant Mark Latimer. I'd just like to check your details, sir.' He ran through them. 'Talk me through what's happened tonight.'

Swift wanted to ask about Araminta, but he realised that this stony sergeant wouldn't part with any information until he'd got what he wanted. Swift briefly explained his investigation. He decided not to mention what Araminta was doing for him. It would only complicate matters, for him and her.

'Ms Leadsom called me. She was worried because she was working late and she'd heard someone moving around the offices.' He carried on describing the rest of the conversation and repeated the last words he'd heard Araminta say.

'And Ms Leadsom gave no indication about the identity of this person?'

'She didn't get a chance before the call was cut off.'

Latimer scribbled notes. 'Why did Ms Leadsom phone you, rather than the police or her boss?'

'I'm not sure. We'd spoken earlier in the day, about my investigation. Maybe it was because of that and she was aware that I was previously a detective in the Met.'

Latimer sounded unimpressed. 'What exactly is your relationship to Ms Leadsom?'

'I've spoken to her several times during my contacts with Spring. Is she okay?'

Latimer's phone rang. He took a call, saying little except, 'Tyrone Swift, yeah.' The sergeant was checking out his background. He pocketed his phone and turned back to Swift, scrutinising him. 'Ms Leadsom was lucky to survive.

She fell from a roof garden and landed on the pavement. She has broken limbs and other injuries, possibly.'

Swift exhaled. 'Thank goodness. Which hospital is she going to?'

'Probably the Royal Free. Do you have next-of-kin details?'

'No, but I have a contact for Jerome Adcott, Ms Leadsom's employer. He might know, or have access to the information.' Swift gave Adcott's number.

'Thank you, Mr Swift. You can go now. Someone will be in touch about a formal statement.'

The keys were shaking in his hand as he walked back to his car. Whoever had pushed Araminta from the roof must have got wind of the information she was checking for him. He'd asked her not to discuss it with anyone, but perhaps she'd let something slip. When her attacker heard that she was still alive, they'd be panicky.

He drank water and splashed some on his face. Then he checked his emails, holding his breath and hoping. *Yes!* There was one from Araminta, sent at 7.40, just before she'd phoned him.

Eight people match your criteria. See attached, AL.

He opened the document and scanned the list. Reece Redman was there, surely proving that Wallace was Mila's partner in crime. Four others lived in London, two in Kent and one in Buckingham. From their dates of birth, most were in their seventies or older.

He'd make an early start tomorrow and work his way through. He'd been determined to solve this case for Toni, but now he'd do it for Araminta, too.

CHAPTER 22

At seven the next morning, Swift rang the Royal Free hospital and enquired about Araminta. They wouldn't give him any information, so he called Jerome Adcott.

'I'm terribly sorry about what's happened to Ms Leadsom. Do you have any news of her? I contacted the hospital but had no luck.'

Adcott was snappy. 'Her partner informed me that she's had surgery on her legs and pelvis and it went well. So far, so good, and she's expected to recover.'

'Thank goodness. I'm glad to hear that.'

'Yes, it's a huge relief. She's being kept under sedation at present. It'll probably be a couple of days before she'll be alert enough to talk to the police. I haven't slept. I can't believe this has happened. Sam and now Araminta. It's as if the company is jinxed.'

'It's very bad luck,' Swift agreed.

'Not sure I believe in luck. What's this all about, Swift? The police said Araminta was working late. I've no idea why, I hadn't asked her to.'

'She rang me unexpectedly, saying someone was in the building. That's why I called the police.'

Swift was expecting him to ask, as Sergeant Latimer had done, why Araminta had rung him rather than 999, but he heard a bang and Jed shouting. Adcott barked that he had to go.

He made coffee and set about contacting the London clients on Araminta's list. The first he tried was no longer at that number or address, the second had died and there was no reply from the third. He struck lucky with Coralie Spark, who lived in Petersham and had been a Spring client for five years until 2015. She was a softly spoken woman with a trembling voice. She accepted his request to visit that morning with no questions about who he was or what he wanted. That told him a great deal before he'd even met her.

He took the train to Richmond, buying an egg and mushroom breakfast roll to eat on the way. He was glad that his carriage was almost empty, as not everyone delighted in a whiff of egg. Mushroom juice trickled steadily down his chin.

Ms Spark lived a thirty-minute walk from the station. Her detached house stood on the east side of Ham Common, opposite oak woodland. It was well maintained, with neat flower beds to the front, blooming with hellebores, narcissi and snowdrops. It took her a while to answer the door. She was small and slight, balancing on a tripod walking aid and with pink scalp showing through wispy grey hair.

He held out his ID. 'Good morning. I phoned you earlier. I'm Tyrone Swift.'

She peered at the card through thick-lensed glasses that almost covered her tiny face. 'Well, I'll have to take your word for it. I have such poor sight. Come in, come in.'

He followed her as she shuffled slowly and led him to an enormous room with doors opening into a wide conservatory. A gleaming black piano occupied one corner, with four cellos of varying sizes ranked to one side of it. She put a hand out when she reached an armchair, patted the arm and then lowered herself carefully down, never letting go of her tripod. She gave a sigh of relief. The walk to and from the front door had exhausted her.

Swift waited until she'd settled herself, pulling her heather-coloured cardigan around her. 'Thank you for agreeing to see me, Ms Spark. Would it be okay if I ask you a few questions? Some of them might seem intrusive.'

She took a hanky from the pocket of her cardigan, raised her glasses and dabbed her watery right eye. 'Do go ahead. Did you say you're from the tax people?'

'No. I'm a private investigator.'

'Oh, I see,' she said, clearly not understanding. 'Well, fire away.'

'I believe that you live on your own.'

'That's correct. Just me. My husband died eight years ago.'

'A company called Spring managed your finances at one time.'

She peered at him. 'Yes, for a while. A very nice chap called Jerome. I remember him because I told him his name means "sacred" or "holy".' She gave a little sniff and dabbed at her sore, weeping eye again.

'You decided to leave them, move your money elsewhere?'

'After my husband died, I needed some cash so I wanted to keep the funds in an accessible account. Then I found an adviser who told me I could do much better with a more personal involvement. She manages everything for me now. It's hard, you see, with my poor sight.'

'Would your adviser be Mila Fullbright?'

Her seamed face brightened. 'Yes, that's right. She's lovely and so helpful. I honestly haven't a clue what I'd do without her.'

'How did you meet her?'

Ms Spark blew her nose. 'I believe she called and introduced herself. Yes, that's it. We had a good chat. I was impressed with her financial acumen and it was handy that she could visit me every month. I don't get out since my sight deteriorated. Mila takes care of everything, pays all the bills. She got a gardener for me, someone to paint the front of the house. All of these things become such a burden. When she took over, a great weight was lifted from my shoulders. Oh, this dratted eye!'

Swift watched her pressing her eye with her hanky. He wanted to weep himself, wondering how much money this trusting woman had lost over the years. If only she'd tucked herself away in a secure flat like the one Ms Melides lived in, she might not have been such an easy target.

'Has a man ever visited you with Mila?'

'Yes, a chap came with her, quite a while ago, some kind of associate of Mila's, I believe. Anyway, he was helping her and he very kindly sorted out my TV for me. I could watch it then. I rarely turn it on these days. It's a blur. I listen to the radio.' She wiped a tear from her cheek.

'Do you remember his name?'

'Oh, I'm not sure. It was some years ago now. He had an Irish kind of name.'

An Irish kind of name. It had to be. Swift sat forward in anticipation. 'Would he have been called Conor?'

Ms Spark beamed. 'That's it! Conor. I worked with a flautist called Conor at one time.'

'Did he come here just the once?'

'Yes, that's right. Another lady — well a girl, really, came here more recently and asked me if I knew Mila. She said she was from the same financial firm. Long dark hair. I can't recall her name at all.'

Swift's scalp tingled. 'Ms Spark, I understand that your sight is bad, but I'd like to show you a photo on my phone.' He enlarged the photo of Naomi and showed it to her.

She took her glasses off and held the phone in front of her nose. 'Yes, that is like her, the hair and the build. She was a bonny girl. She had one of those T-shirts on that showed quite a bit of cleavage. Rather a lot on display.'

Ms Spark was the gift that kept on giving. 'Can you remember when she visited you?'

'Not as such. Last summer sometime. It was a hot day, anyway. She said she was just checking that I was satisfied with the financial help I was getting. I told her I was more than happy. She was very pleasant and made me a cup of tea.'

'Did you mention her visit to Mila?'

'No, it went out of my mind. Should I have?'

'I wouldn't worry about it.' A huge shock was going to land on this fragile woman soon. Swift couldn't bear to think of it. 'Do you have any family you can rely on?'

'I do have a cousin, but he's in Hamburg. We're in touch, but he has his own health problems. I'm rather tired now, if that's all you need. Can you see yourself out?'

Swift crossed the road to Ham Common and walked along primrose-lined paths through oak trees interspersed with yew, beech and hornbeam. He barely noticed his surroundings, his mind busy with the latest revelations. The cowardly nature of these crimes sickened him. Wallace and Mila were like carrion crows, picking at the bones of the vulnerable.

This must be how it had played out. Mila Fullbright had met Ronnie Probert along this tangled route and had learned about his financial misdeeds with his aunt. That had sparked an idea that she'd then baited Conor Wallace with, aware that he dealt with people's money. Wallace had a reputation for moaning about the expense of raising a family. His and Lucy's behaviour over their offer to buy Sam's house had proved they were money-grabbing.

Wallace had found a group of ex-clients at Spring who ticked the necessary boxes: elderly, rich or comfortably off, with property, alone, isolated and vulnerable. Mila had then wormed her way into their homes and their trust. How many more were there? It wouldn't have to have been many to provide a nice extra income for Mila and Wallace.

Swift stopped for a moment, hands in pockets. Was Lucy Wallace in on it? Perhaps not, and that explained why her husband had to be careful not to splash the cash and still plead lack of funds. Naomi had visited Ms Sparks last summer — how had she located the woman? Sam Goddard must have been prompted by something Naomi had told him, and he'd run a search similar to the one Araminta had carried out. He'd then asked Naomi to check the situation with Ms Sparks. That had to be it. Naomi had returned to him with the confirmation that his close friend had been using Spring's data to assist Goddard's own ex-wife in fraud.

Rain started falling, a light shower. Swift stayed under the tree and rang two more of the clients on the list, both elderly women. They confirmed that Mila Fullbright was their financial adviser. As with Mr Redman and Ms Spark, neither questioned his reason for enquiring. These people were such easy prey.

He had enough now in terms of evidence to take to the police. But before he did that, he was hungry to ascertain if Wallace and Mila were murderers as well as thieves.

He phoned Sergeant Arran Delamare and asked if he remembered Conor Wallace's alibi for the night of the deaths last September.

Delamare asked him to hang on.

'Right,' he said at last, 'Wallace and his wife were at home with the kids all evening. Why, have you got something on him? Surely not — the best man?'

'Something, maybe a lot. You'll be the first to hear.'

Delamare laughed. 'Promises, promises!'

Swift walked back to the station. The Wallaces had alibied each other. That was always a difficult one. He needed to go home and consider his next move.

On the train back into London, he drank coffee and checked his emails. There was one from Binda Hollerton, the manager at ACT.

Dear Mr Swift,

I mentioned your enquiries to some of my staff. One of them, Mike Neary, informed me that he worked for Go Kids at one time, in their charity shop in north London. The manager, Lucy Wallace, gave him a reference when he applied here. Mike said that she was very interested in our work and asked him about the development.

Swift gazed out of the window at the tatty backs of houses. They looked exposed, naked. A man stood at a door, blowing up a balloon, with a toddler bouncing at his knees, trying to touch it. Lucy Wallace was aware of Old Bow Wharf, even if she'd never been there. She hadn't mentioned that knowledge after Goddard's death. Given the information Swift now had about his activities with Mila, Conor Wallace had to be a major suspect for the attack on Araminta.

Swift cancelled his plan to go home. Instead, he headed for King's Cross. From there, he hastened to the grimy depths of the Tube and rode the Northern line to Archway.

* * *

The Go Kids Boutique was quiet, with a couple of customers leaving as Swift arrived. He approached a woman who was tidying a stand of greetings cards. 'Hello, my name's Ty Swift. I'd like to speak to Lucy Wallace.'

Her name badge said *Nuala*. She replied, with a generous smile, 'Lucy's just popped out to bank some money. She shouldn't be long.'

'Mind if I wait?'

'Of course not. Something might take your eye while you're here. We've just had a load of books in. Unless . . . are you from head office?'

Swift returned her smile, amused that he might be taken for a manager in his old jeans and waxed jacket. 'No, I'm a private investigator, here about Sam Goddard's death. He was a friend of Lucy's. I've met her before and I just wanted a chat.'

Nuala put a hand to her throat. 'Oh goodness, yes. That was so shocking and sad. Lucy was distraught. And Toni, of course . . . I saw her in the street last week. I said hello but she didn't hear me. In a world of her own, I suppose.'

'Did you meet Sam?'

'Now and again. He came in a couple of times and I served him when he bought a waistcoat for his wedding. Such a pleasant man.'

'I suppose you knew Mike Neary, who worked here. He went to another charity called ACT last year.'

Nuala pulled a face and laughed. 'Mike! He had big ideas but he wasn't much good at selling stuff. I was glad he got that job, it sounded much better suited to him. Lucy said the same. She told me Mike went on at great length to her about it being a new project. It sounded fascinating and she was a bit envious!'

'I wonder if she ever visited it?'

'I can't say. She's a busy lady, what with this job and three young children.' Nuala was settling nicely into a chin-wag. She picked up a bag of donated items and took out a green shirt. 'Funny, this reminds me of Sam Goddard. It's a colour he wore sometimes. I told him we had a couple of things he might like last time he was here, but he was in a hurry. Wedding plans on his mind, I expect.'

'I can imagine. When was that?'

'Must have been shortly before he died. He popped in to see Lucy and they had a chat in the back. They were in there quite a while. I did wonder if there was anything wrong because they were both a bit tense afterwards, and Lucy was tearful. When I asked Lucy she said she was fine, she had a slight head cold. She told me Sam had been keen to go over the wedding schedule. He had a lot on his plate and he wanted everything to be just so. My son was the same when he got married. He was a bag of nerves on the day. Mind you, Lucy was as pale as if she'd seen a ghost, but then she takes things to heart and worries so about other people. She's been a bit jumpy for a while, actually, not been herself since Mr Goddard died. Probably not getting enough sleep.' Nuala gave herself a little shake. 'Listen to me rattling on when I have sorting to do! Lucy will accuse me of slacking. Will you be okay browsing until she gets back?'

'Leave me to it.'

Swift pretended interest in a rack of men's clothes. He took out a long black wool coat and admired it, but put it back. It would attract every floating scrap of fluff. He leaned against the rack, working through this latest information. So much in this case revolved around the members of this extended "family" with Spring at its centre. Why would Lucy have looked tearful and shocked if she and Sam Goddard had simply been discussing the wedding? He must have come here to divulge his suspicions about her husband and Mila. And why was Lucy agitated now? Swift had plenty of details at his fingertips, but he still didn't have the frame that it all fitted into. He needed to approach Lucy skilfully, goad and trap her, otherwise she'd insist that she'd only been talking to Goddard about his wedding.

She stopped in her tracks when she bustled in and saw him.

He waved cheerfully. 'Hi, Lucy. Have you got a minute for a chat?'

'Not really. Can't this wait until I finish work?'

'Not really,' he echoed. 'I have things I need to discuss, about Sam and also your interest in a charity called ACT. Well, mainly its *location*.'

Her eyes widened and she became aware of Nuala listening in.

'Okay, we'll go in the back. Nuala, can you mind the shop for a bit longer?'

Swift followed her to the back room, where they sat on the same chairs they'd occupied last time. Lucy was wearing a cross-over dress in swirling pastels, lavender wool tights dotted with pilling and scuffed, buckled shoes. She fiddled with her dress, straightening and smoothing it.

Swift waited until she'd finished fussing. 'Why have you never mentioned that you know of the Old Bow Wharf area in Docklands?'

'Because it didn't occur to me,' she said simply. 'I'd only heard of it.'

'That was through Mike Neary, who left here to work at a charity called ACT.'

'That's right. I've never been there.'

'You discussed the project in detail with Neary. Seems odd that you wouldn't remark on having heard of it when Sam died there. People were mystified and wondering how

Sam and Naomi Ludlow had ended up in that location. The police must have asked you about it.'

She was tense. Fidgety. 'It just didn't seem important.'

The lie was so obvious. Swift stretched his legs and pointed at hers. 'I'm surprised that you have to wear tatty tights and old shoes, given your extra income streams.'

'Pardon?'

'You heard me.' Straight for the jugular now. 'What do you make of the fact that your husband's been swindling vulnerable old people? Doesn't seem to align with your philanthropic take on life.'

She licked her lips. 'Don't be ridiculous. Conor would never do something like that.'

'You wish. And he's doing it with his girlfriend, Mila Fullbright. They've had a nice little scam going for quite a while.'

Silence. Lucy squinted down at her shoes. She wasn't a quick thinker and was struggling to respond, but he wasn't sure which bit of information was confounding her.

'Oh, sorry, Lucy. Did you not realise that they've been having an affair as well as thieving?'

'You're lying.'

'What about? The stealing or the affair?' Time to present the facts. 'I have reliable information pointing to Mila and your husband. Conor provides the victims by using Spring's client data. Mila's the front woman. She visits and very caringly relieves them of money. It's clever. Maybe you already knew. If you didn't, you've been benefiting from fraud. I'm about to go to the police. I'm being generous, coming and talking to you first.'

Her cheeks flushed. 'This is just nonsense.'

'You wish. Sam came to see you here before he died. He had confirmation that Conor and Mila were stealing. He'd met Naomi Ludlow, as I'm sure he told you. Something that Naomi said put him on the track to them. Sam must have been alarmed and conflicted, because his best friend was involved. Instead of going to Jerome Adcott, he came to you to talk it through. I expect that you pleaded with him to give you a chance to speak to Conor, and that was his inclination. Sam had a good heart. Once he went to the police with what he had, all hell would break loose. You persuaded him to hang fire until after his wedding. Maybe you promised that straight afterwards, Conor would come clean.'

Lucy was breathing rapidly. 'This is just stuff you've dreamed up. You can't prove any of it.'

'I don't need to, it's all part of the picture, and the police can go into the details of your meeting and Sam's discoveries. They can talk to the victims and the witnesses. Thing is, Lucy, what did you do with that time you bought with Sam? Did you go home to Conor, and the two of you decide to kill Sam and Naomi, get rid of the threat of exposure?'

'No!' She pressed her hands together.

'I've been wondering about you. Lucy the empath. Terribly upset about Sam's death, unable to sleep. Pestering Toni with kindness — stalking her almost, checking up on her whereabouts. That puzzled me, but not anymore. The guilt's been weighing on you, although it didn't stop you trying to get Sam's house at a bargain price.' She was so pale, Swift worried she might faint, but he pressed on. 'Your husband will go to jail for what he's been doing. It'd be a shame if your children were deprived of both parents. If Conor killed Sam and Naomi, it'll be more than a sentence for fraud.'

'He didn't kill them! He didn't have . . .' Her voice trailed away.

Swift needed her to stay upright. He handed her a bottle of water from a shelf, but she pushed it away.

'He didn't have anything to do with it?' he supplied. 'If you're so sure that it wasn't Conor, that suggests that you know or suspect who it was. Were you involved?'

She put her hands over her ears. 'Stop it! I won't listen to you.'

Swift continued, hoping that he'd shock her into revealing more. 'If you're protecting Conor and Mila, you might like to consider the fact that they've been meeting in Sam's house, until the last few days.'

Lucy dropped her hands and raised misery-filled eyes, staring at him in disbelief. Good. That was unexpected, nasty news.

'Conor gave Mila a key to the house. I saw her go in there and I've photos. They both admitted to me that they've been having an affair and the empty house was just too handy to resist. Conor accepted how tacky it was, using a dead friend's home like that. He begged me not to tell you. "*I'll end it now, honestly,*" and all that.'

'But he said that Mila . . . he said it was purely . . .'

'Let me guess how the conversation went. When you challenged Conor after Sam's bombshell, he said it was just a business partnership with Mila.' That could well have been true, and he'd concocted the story of the affair to put Swift off the scent, but what the hell, he had no reason to spare Lucy's feelings. 'That's not what they've both told me. You've been tricked, Lucy, taken for a fool. I expect that Conor admitted that what Sam told you was true, and he promised that he'd stop the frauds immediately, never be naughty again. Am I right?'

She nodded.

'Hasn't happened. All these months later, they're still meeting, and Conor's playing away behind your back — or rather, right under your nose. He and Mila have been laughing at you.' Swift saw that she was shaking and moved his chair closer to her. 'Whatever you've done — and I'm sure you did play some part in what happened to Sam and Naomi — was all for nothing. Conor and Mila have carried on anyway. And I haven't touched on Araminta yet. Did you push her off the roof?'

'No!' Tears spilled down her cheeks.

'Then your husband must be in the frame.'

Swift left a long silence while she cried. Finally, he said, 'Your poor kids. So much for charity beginning at home.'

Lucy licked tears away. 'When Sam came here and told me, I was so stunned. He showed me a list of clients who Conor and Mila had been stealing from. Then he went on about a girl called Naomi Ludlow and how she'd given him information. He explained that she'd been snooping and seen a text on someone's phone. Some man she was going around with. It was from Mila, saying that she and Conor were doing well, following his example and raking it in from crazy old people. Naomi had forwarded the text to herself and kept it. Then she met Sam and they got talking . . .'

That was a crucial piece of the jigsaw, right there, the trail that led from Probert, through Mila to Wallace. *Oh, Naomi, if only you hadn't been so keen on manipulating people and so bored and meddlesome, you'd still be alive.* 'Naomi realised that Sam worked in finance. I expect she asked him about power of attorney and how easy it would be to misuse it. Then she'd have shown him the text and he'd have been astonished when he read the names.'

'I can't remember everything he said, but it was like that. I didn't want anything bad to happen to Sam. It's not my fault,' Lucy whispered.

'Did Conor tell Mila they'd been rumbled?'

'No. I wanted him to, but he was in a state and couldn't face it. He was going to after the wedding.'

If Mila didn't know, she wasn't a suspect for the murders. 'You're sure you didn't contact her, have a rant?'

'Absolutely not! I wouldn't have gone anywhere near that bitch and I was relishing the shock she'd get when the police arrived at her door.'

'What about a man called Ronnie Probert? Was he involved with Conor and Mila?'

She rubbed her forehead. 'No . . . I'm fairly sure he's the man who Mila got the idea from. Oh, I was so distraught . . . I had to talk to someone after Sam came here, and then it all got out of control.' She drew her hands across her eyes and made an effort to stop weeping. 'That's all I did.'

'Who did you talk to?'

Lucy carried on, spilling out her story now. 'You have to understand, Conor was in bits when I went home and told him. He admitted that he and Mila had been siphoning money from old people for about five years. When I asked how much, he said he'd made about £80,000. Most if it was invested for our future. Our future — that's a laugh now!' She choked, threaded her fingers tightly. 'He tried to speak to Sam, but Sam didn't want to discuss it. Sam told Conor that for Toni's sake, he'd wait until after the wedding but then Conor and Mila had to confess, or he'd go to Jerome and the police. I didn't know what to do. I had to share the burden, so I turned to someone. None of it was *my fault*!'

The door opened and Nuala stood there, her eyes darting between them and then resting on Lucy's reddened face. 'Is everything okay?'

Lucy swallowed. 'Yes, thanks, Nuala. I'm just a bit upset still about Sam.'

'Oh, I am sorry. Can I get you a cuppa?'

'No, that's okay. If you can mind the shop.'

'Righto. Just say if I can help.'

'Thanks, Nuala,' Swift said. He waited a while. Lucy grabbed the water and gulped it down. 'Lucy, it's over now. Tell me who you talked to and what happened.'

'I'm such a fool. I wanted to believe Conor. Life's so frantic, with my work and the boys . . . I never have a minute to myself. Our flat is so cluttered and hard to keep tidy and the boys are always squabbling. I didn't mean anything bad to happen. They can't blame me. Oh God, I'll go to prison.'

'Depends on what you've done. The police sometimes do deals with witnesses. Salvage what you can. Think of your kids.'

She pressed hard against her eyes. Swift hoped that she was about to unburden herself.

Lucy shuddered. 'I don't know the details. I can't tell you those. All I did was discuss the situation.'

'Then tell me what you can.'

She started talking, pausing now and again to blow her nose. He was astounded but it all made sense now. He felt only repugnance for her and Conor. She'd sat back, let her husband keep the stolen money and allowed someone else to make the problem disappear. And she'd watched Toni suffer, smothering her with gifts and food while people believed that Sam had been exploiting a young girl. With a friend like her, you wouldn't need an enemy.

She finally ran out of words.

'No wonder you and Conor didn't like it when Toni got me to investigate,' Swift said coldly. 'That's why you were always flitting around her, keeping a close eye. And then you came on strong to her about selling you Sam's house. How could you do that?'

'We couldn't bear the idea of moving out to the suburbs and Conor didn't want us to touch the money he'd . . . saved—'

'*Stolen*,' Swift interrupted.

Lucy flinched. 'Toni's comfortably off financially, it wasn't going to make that much difference to her if she sold to us at a lower price.' She added pleadingly, 'It wasn't just for our own sakes, either. It meant we could stay nearer to her, help her out.'

Swift thought of Toni on that first afternoon he'd met her, the way her sadness had filled every space. What was it she'd said? '*Grief is love that's become homeless.*' He stood, glaring down at Lucy. 'Help her! Your self-delusion amazes me.'

She burst into tears again and sank forward, head almost in her lap. Swift went to the door and signalled to Nuala.

'Could you make Lucy a cup of tea? She's very upset.'

'Oh dear. I'll get her one now. Would you like a hot drink?'

'Strong black coffee, please.'

Nuala quickly brought the drinks. Swift could see that she wanted to linger, but some customers were waiting in the shop. He put the tea in Lucy's shaking hands and sipped his coffee. His field of suspects had narrowed in the last half-hour. Probert and Mila were out of the frame, and Lucy's information had told him where he had to go.

He glanced down. *So much stolen money, and the sole's parting from her shoe.*

CHAPTER 23

It had just gone four when Swift approached the Adcotts' house in Hornsey under a darkening sky. Before he rang the bell, he stepped along the path to the front window. The curtains were still open, the lights on. The bottom glass was opaque but if he stood on tiptoe he could see into the living room. Chloe was curled on a sofa with Jed, reading him a story, a woollen throw across their legs. His head lay on her breast as he sucked his thumb. The gas fire glowed with orange flames. Many a time, he'd lain on his sofa with Branna in the same fashion. Part of Swift wanted to turn and walk away, but just a small part. He only had to recall Toni's gnawing grief to brace himself.

He rang the bell. Chloe came to the door, carrying Jed, who turned his face into her neck. She'd pushed her reading glasses on top of her head.

'Mr Swift, this is unexpected. Do you want to speak to Jerome?'

'No, you. May I come in?'

Something in his voice or his face made her step back. Her grip on Jed tightened. 'Of course.'

In the living room, she offered tea or coffee. Swift declined. Chloe closed the curtains and sat back on the sofa

257

with Jed on her lap. Swift wished that the child wasn't there. It was going to be hard to have this conversation with him present. The room was warm and snug with familial comfort that he was about to destroy.

'Story,' Jed demanded, yawning and flopping against his mother.

'Let me talk to Mr Swift, darling. You look at the pictures and then I'll finish your story.'

She opened the book, the kind with thick card pages and handed it to the boy. From where he sat, Swift could see bright illustrations of jungle animals.

Chloe fixed her gaze on him. 'So, how can I help you?'

'I've just come from Lucy Wallace. She told me all about the fraud carried out by Conor and Mila Fullbright. I have the list of Spring clients they targeted. She also told me that she turned to you after Sam Goddard exposed their racket to her.'

The corner of her mouth twitched. 'Interesting. What exactly did she say?'

Jed giggled and pointed. 'Monkey!'

'That's right,' his mother said. 'A striped monkey.' She smoothed his hair and turned to Swift. 'What did Lucy say?'

'That she visited you the day after Sam told her what he'd uncovered. She had no one else to confide in. Usually, it would have been Toni, but in the circumstances, that was impossible. Lucy said you've always been solid and reliable, very active in the charity. She was in turmoil, desperate to get advice and she could bank on you being steady, a good listener.'

'Kind comments,' Chloe said.

'Lucy didn't tell Conor she was seeing you. You were shocked but calm. You took Lucy for a long walk and got all the details about Naomi and Sam. Then you instructed Lucy not to tell anyone else that she'd spoken to you, not even Conor, and you didn't want any hint of it getting to Jerome. Lucy said that you're proud of him and what he's done with the company. You always protect him and Spring.

I've heard similar comments from other people during this investigation.'

Chloe winced. 'That's true.'

Jed threw his book down. 'Thirsty, Mummy.'

Chloe reached beside the sofa for a lidded plastic cup with a spout. Jed lay propped up in the crook of her arm and drank from it. 'Good boy,' she whispered.

'Shall I continue?'

'Please. You clearly want to, having bothered to come here.'

'You calmed Lucy and told her to leave it with you, you'd contact Sam and see what you could sort out to repair any damage. You insisted that the police mustn't be involved, because Spring and Go Kids would be tarnished. Lucy asked if Conor should give the money back and try to get Mila to do the same, but you said that wasn't a priority as far as you were concerned. Lucy was surprised by that, but she wasn't going to argue.'

Jed coughed, a liquid sound. His mother sat him up, rubbed his back and wiped his chin with her sleeve. He settled back down, his eyes drooping.

'I wasn't surprised that you told Lucy the money wasn't important to you,' Swift said. 'After all, it wasn't Spring's money. You would concentrate on protecting what was close to home.'

Jed's cup slid to the floor. He was asleep now, breathing gently, his hair flopping on to his forehead. Chloe pulled the throw around him, tucking it under his legs. 'It's true that I always look after my own. It's what most people do. I'm sure you do too, with your family.'

Was that a coded appeal? 'It didn't stop there, though, did it?'

She said with only the tiniest hesitation, 'You'll have to explain what you mean. Most of this is news to me.'

She was good, choosing her responses carefully, admitting nothing.

'The next thing was that Sam and Naomi were dead. It was dreadful, but of course Lucy was thankful in a way, because it meant Conor was safe. He was stunned, but she could tell that he was relieved too. Two days after they died, you rang her and asked her to go for a coffee. You said that Conor was lucky that Sam and Naomi had drowned, and you gave Lucy an ultimatum. Conor had six months to find another job and he had to be squeaky clean from then on, no more theft. He had to make sure that Mila Fullbright stopped her activities too. Lucy said she'd make sure of it. You commented that she'd better, because you'd saved the Wallaces' skins. When she asked what you meant, you replied never mind, you'd done it for your family, no one else, but Lucy needed to make sure that Conor behaved himself in future and that Mila Fullbright got the same message. You stressed again that Jerome must never hear anything about it. Lucy went home and told Conor. He promised faithfully that he'd stop the fraud and cut his connection with Mila.'

Chloe shifted Jed's weight a little. 'Have you come here to tell me a long story? I've plenty of those on my bookshelves.'

'What did you mean by saying you'd saved the Wallaces' skins?'

She stared straight at him, her colour high. 'There are a few true things in that farrago you've spouted. Lucy came to me in bits about her feckless husband and his friend Mila. I wasn't going to tell Jerome or the police. I didn't see why Conor's behaviour should impact on everything we've built up — the business and Go Kids. I was planning to discuss the situation with Sam and this Naomi who he'd been speaking to. I believed that if I got Conor and Mila to stop their activities, Sam would agree not to involve the police and help me limit the damage. After all, he had a big personal investment in Spring and its reputation.'

'And Naomi Ludlow?' Swift asked. 'How were you planning to deal with her, the wild card?'

'Frankly, I was planning to buy her silence. She was a teenager. They can always use some money.'

'But then you didn't have to go to all that trouble with Sam and Naomi. Handy.'

Chloe wriggled, tugging at the throw. 'It's true that their deaths cleared a path. When I told Lucy that I'd saved her and her pathetic husband's skins, I meant that I'd decided to manage it by putting a stop to him and easing him out of the company. I let them off the hook to save a scandal for us all. I'm sure you don't approve, and it's true that I failed to report a crime, but I had good reasons.'

'And I suppose Sam's and Naomi's deaths were a coincidence.'

Chloe rubbed her lips along the top of her son's head. 'Yes. Terribly sad, but in the end fortuitous for some of us. That's the cruel way of the world sometimes.'

Swift had to hand it to her, she was quick and brave, albeit callous. Maybe she believed that courage never fails. He wished that this investigation had led to one of the Rymans, Probert or Mila Fullbright. It was hard to accuse a mother with her sleeping child in her arms, but in her own words, that was the cruel way of the world sometimes.

'No,' he said, 'that doesn't add up. Those deaths were no coincidence and they clearly weren't suicide. There are only a small number of people who could have been responsible for the murders. At that point last September, Mila Fullbright wasn't aware that Sam had found out, Conor and Lucy were at home and your husband was at work. The finger is pointing to you. And frankly, I can see you having had the bottle to do it.'

'Strange kind of compliment,' she said.

Swift carried on. 'You should have been more circumspect in what you said to Lucy at that second meeting. She has just as much to lose as you and she's not going down quietly, I can assure you. I believe that you killed Sam and Naomi. You're not the type to leave loose ends, and it was the only sure way of resolving the situation. Sam had given Conor until after his marriage, then he had to fess up. From what I've learned of him, Sam was a principled, honest man. He wouldn't have accepted a whitewashing proposal from you, and you'd have realised that. You had to kill him and

Naomi, otherwise Sam would have gone to the police and your attempts at protection would have been meaningless. I don't know how you managed to get them to Old Bow Wharf, but I am aware that you're a resourceful woman. The police will find out, unless you want to tell me now.'

Her shoulders went up. 'This is all absurd. I certainly didn't kill them. Do I really seem like the kind of person who goes around committing murder?'

'If it wasn't you, who did? Your husband? Perhaps you did tell him the story in the end, and he despatched them.'

'No!' She straightened and Jed whimpered. 'Shh, shh,' she said, rocking him gently.

They waited for the child to settle. Soon enough, his world would turn upside down. Chloe took her glasses from her head, folded them and placed them on the wide sofa arm. 'I've never liked Conor and Lucy. I've pretended to, for the sake of the business and the charity, but they're needy and dreadful grumblers. One has to get along with people, but with them it was a real effort. They're bloody lucky that I stepped up and sorted out their disaster. You wouldn't think it, from the way Lucy is now denigrating me. She's telling you what you want to hear. You do realise that? You'll have an awful lot of egg on your face if you go on spreading this nonsense around.'

'I agree with you about Conor and Lucy,' Swift said. 'They're takers and I can't stand them. I can see why you'd have been infuriated when Lucy came to you with her tale of woe. You're worth ten of her. I've read and heard about the tireless work you do for Go Kids. Everyone speaks highly of you.'

Chloe gave him a puzzled glance. 'Thank you.'

'I wouldn't bother with thanks, because that aside, I still believe you're a murderer. I'm sorry, because I admire you and the work you've done.' It was hard to dislike her, despite the blood on her hands, whereas he despised Lucy and Conor. 'It's no good, Chloe. It will come out.'

'You only have Lucy's word for all this,' she said. 'Some of what she's told you is true, some of it made up. Lucy's not the most reliable of witnesses. You'll have noticed her emotional style. She was out of her mind about Conor. What woman wouldn't be, finding out that her husband had been stealing and probably having an affair, too? Her distress swamped her.'

'That's true, I'm sure, and you must have had to act quickly to deal with the situation. There'll be forensic evidence, gaps and holes that you can't account for,' Swift said. 'You won't realise it, but there will be, and you'll fall through one. Months have gone by and you've been feeling safe, but you never are truly safe when you've committed murder.' He saw in her eyes that he'd hit a mark. 'Was it worth it, Chloe?'

She cradled Jed closer. Swift could barely hear her say, 'Worth it?'

Moments passed. If someone had glanced through the window, they might have assumed that they were witnessing domestic harmony with the man, woman and child sitting quietly by the fire while evening sidled in. Soon, they'd probably stir themselves, wake the boy so that he'd sleep that night, prepare a meal, maybe open a bottle of wine.

'The police will be here soon,' Swift said. 'I called them before I walked up the path. They'll interview you and Jerome. You'll be bombarded with questions. If you tell them straight away, it will save your husband, your friends and Go Kids a degree of heartache and stress. And Jed — he'll need his dad's focus and energy. You can string this out, but if you do, he'll suffer even more.'

Chloe pushed her hair back and was silent, her gaze fixed on Jed. After a long pause she said, 'I understand what you're saying.' She went to speak, stopped, then made a little sound. 'I suppose I'd better protect my loved ones.'

'Isn't that what you've always done?'

Her voice trembled. 'I've tried to.' She touched Jed's cheek. 'I was devastated and furious in equal measure when I heard about Conor and Mila. If it went public, Go Kids and Spring would be dragged through the mud and our lives exposed to the gawpers and gossips. I contacted Naomi

Ludlow. She was self-important and easy to fool. I told her she was needed for an important meeting about the fraud, and she was eager to be part of it. I drove her to the wharf and sedated her. Then I made up a story to get Sam there and gave him a sedative. It wasn't too hard, pushing the bike into the river. I'll give the police the details. I thought I'd managed a neat, inventive solution to our problems. They were going to drift away on the tide.' She glanced at him with a degree of respect. 'They had, until you came along.'

Hester had said that she wouldn't like to cross Chloe. Now he could see why.

The fire burned steadily and Chloe stared into it. Hearth and home. He recalled how she'd spilled wine on him at Toni's party and wondered if that had been deliberate aggression. She remained unaware, but Swift heard car doors and footsteps. The doorbell pealed. Jed woke with a start and a small cry.

'I'll get it,' Swift said. 'It will be the police. I phoned Jerome, too. After all, someone will need to be with Jed.'

CHAPTER 24

Three days later, Swift and Toni were sitting at the top of the steps at Old Bow Wharf. The river was choppy under a crisp blue sky and the breeze was fresh. Swift had bought them both hot chocolate. Toni was calm but washed-out.

'I find myself wishing that Sam had been killed by a stranger, rather than this,' she said. 'Someone I've known for years and trusted. The way he was led here — a lamb to the slaughter. It's hard.'

Chloe Adcott had confessed and Naomi Ludlow's DNA had been detected in her car. She'd been remanded on two counts of murder. Conor and Lucy Wallace and Mila Fullbright were in custody until Araminta was brought out of sedation. The police could hold them for ninety-six hours, so Swift hoped she regained consciousness soon. Ronnie Probert was still being questioned, but Swift was sure that he'd been a bit player in Mila's swindle. He'd planted the seed of accessing easy money in her mind and she'd gone on to cultivate it with Wallace's help. Mila had probably taken him on a visit to Reece Redman to show off her prowess. Hopefully, though, Probert would be charged as an accessory and on account of his own criminal activities.

'Finding out the truth is sometimes horribly painful,' Swift agreed.

'I'm glad though, because the truth honours Sam's memory. No one can speak ill of him now. I understand a lot, but I still don't get why Sam didn't tell me. He must have been so worried. I get flashes of anger towards him for keeping all this from me.'

'He was chivalrous, protecting you. He wanted you to be able to get married and enjoy the day. You were all such a close-knit group, with work and personal boundaries over-lapping, the ramifications were going to be enormous. Maybe he also wanted everyone to have a good day, with laughter and happiness before the storm broke. It was bad enough that it would all be out in the open by the time you went on honeymoon.'

Toni pushed her hair from her eyes. 'That sounds like Sam, considering other people, finding a way through. But his generosity cost him his life.' She swallowed hard. 'Explain to me again how it all happened. The police told me, but my recall isn't too clear. Take it slowly. I find it hard to process.'

At her request, Swift had sat with Toni and Sergeant Delamare while he took them through a summary of interviews the police had conducted. Swift had no difficulty remembering the detail. Much of it he'd already detected or guessed.

'It started with Mila Fullbright's fling with Ronnie Probert after she and Sam divorced. Probert boasted to her that he'd conned a frail aunt out of more than £10,000 by offering to help manage her finances, and he said it had been easy. Mila tucked this information away and gave it some consideration. She didn't have any family members vulner-able or rich enough to prey on, but Conor came to mind as someone who might have such people on a database. He'd often spoken about how he and Lucy had to economise, so he might well be open to a proposal.'

'How can anyone even think like that!' Toni protested.

'More easily than you might imagine. Conor was inter-ested when he'd mulled it over. They agreed that it would be safest to select previous clients of Spring. That way, nobody at the company would notice. In all, he chose eight clients. He and Mila also agreed that she would be the one to pose as a financial adviser, visiting on her own so that there was no link to Spring, and that they'd take it steady and remove regular, small amounts.'

'Once she'd scoped each person's finances, Conor steered Mila about methods of doing that.'

'Exactly,' Swift said. 'Their big mistake was when Conor visited Ms Spark with Mila. Maybe her finances were particularly complex and he needed to see for himself. He went there just once, but that was enough for me to tie him in. He and Mila had a very successful joint career for more than five years. Mila upgraded to a much bigger flat. Conor had to be more careful about spending the money, because he didn't want Lucy to become suspicious. He'd buy stuff for their children now and again, but he was salting most of it away for the future. Seems that his plan was to retire early and have a home in France.' Swift remembered Wallace placing his uneaten banana in the fridge, scrimping and saving when he had money saved. He'd done a good line in delayed gratification.

'Bastard,' Toni said. 'And he was trying to get me to sell Sam's house cheap. His friend who'd trusted him completely.'

'Sam had no reason not to until he came across Naomi Ludlow in the Gadfly. Fizzy Gibson said that Naomi needed a shoulder to cry on. She spoke to Sam about her problems with Christian Ryman. Maybe that's when she mentioned her brother's school motto, "Courage Never Fails", and Sam used that to strengthen his resolve, because Jesse heard him say it. I'm sure he must have had to summon all his determination. When he told what he'd uncovered, lives were going to splinter.

'Anyway, I digress. I expect Sam was deeply concerned about Naomi's sexual exploits and advised her to report Ryman, but Naomi wouldn't have wanted to do that, because then a lot of her own shenanigans would have been exposed.

When Naomi heard about Sam's line of work, she disclosed Ronnie Probert's fraud to him, and explained that she'd seen a text on his phone, from a Mila Fullbright, concerning her fraud scam with Conor Wallace. She'd kept the text message and she showed it to Sam.'

'He must have been so stunned,' Toni said. 'His ex and his best friend up to no good.'

'And Mila crowing about it to Probert. Sam would have been reeling,' Swift added. 'He had the idea of examining Spring's client records and saw a Ms Sparks who was very wealthy, had parted company with the firm, lived alone and had poor sight. He didn't want to involve Spring in any way at that point, so he asked Naomi to visit Ms Sparks and of course, Naomi reported that Mila was now handling her finances. Sam's fears were confirmed.'

Toni took a sip of chocolate. 'Sam went to Essex to see his brother. Pity he couldn't bring himself to offload.'

'I agree, although I'm not sure that Jesse would have been much help. Sam must have realised that his brother didn't really want him there, so he left without saying anything about what was on his mind. Your wedding was fast approaching and Sam didn't want it ruined. He probably took the view that Conor's and Mila's activities were shameful, but there wasn't any need for urgent action. He then decided to speak to Lucy, put her and Conor on a warning and give Conor a chance to come clean. He didn't bother contacting Mila. I expect as far as he was concerned, she could fend for herself and the police would take care of her.'

Swift rubbed the scar on his thigh, his legacy from working with Interpol. It was aching today. 'Lucy turned to Chloe and told her everything. Chloe realised that Spring was going to be in deep trouble once the police got involved. Its reputation would take a terrible blow, and Go Kids would be caught up in the flak. She worried about what it would mean for her husband, their family's future and the charity so dear to her heart.'

'She helped Jerome a lot at the beginning with Spring, including financing him,' Toni said sadly. 'Chloe was so proud of their success and their ethical approach. She lived and breathed Go Kids, too.'

'That's right. Chloe was desperate and angry — with Conor, but also with Sam for talking to an interfering teenager, collaborating with her over the visit to Ms Sparks and causing this crisis. If it had just been Sam who knew, Chloe hoped there might have been some chance of keeping it quiet and resolving the issue within the company, but Naomi's involvement made that impossible. Chloe's a clever woman with a backbone of steel and devoted to her husband and son.' Swift thought of her resolute expression and the determination that had led her to such a grim decision. 'She decided that the only solution was to get rid of both Sam and Naomi, but it had to be in a way that would steer the focus of any investigation away from Spring. The idea of an affair and suicide came to her as a way of causing huge confusion. Chloe ordered liquid alprazolam online, and saw Naomi's photo and mobile number on social media.

'Chloe called her the day before the murders, explained that she was a director of Spring and thanked Naomi for bringing this fraud into the open, adding that the management of Spring would like Naomi to attend a top-level meeting with them, to ensure that they could go to the police after Sam's wedding with the full story. She emphasised that Naomi had a valuable contribution to make to justice being done.' Swift imagined Naomi's smugness and her ideas about how she'd publicise her role on social media afterwards. 'Chloe advised her that they didn't want to burden Sam any more at this stage, so they weren't inviting him to the meeting. They wanted him to be able to put this worry aside and enjoy his wedding. But Naomi's attendance would be invaluable. Naomi agreed not to contact Sam so that he could enjoy his marriage preparations.'

'Heady stuff for a fifteen-year-old girl who liked attention and a fair dose of drama,' Toni said.

'Naomi would have lapped it up,' Swift agreed. 'Lucy had told Chloe all about the ACT development at Old

Bow Wharf earlier that year. Chloe had driven by to see it, because Go Kids were considering a similar enterprise at some point, and she wondered if Docklands would offer the right kind of space. She'd noted that part of that area was deserted, and decided it would offer a remote location to carry out her plan. Chloe told Naomi that she'd pick her up at her house the following afternoon and drive her to the meeting.'

A launch sped up the river, its engine chugging noisily. Swift waited until the noise had faded. 'They reached Old Bow Wharf late afternoon — Chloe must have got a surprise when Naomi said she'd been there once before. She'd bought them both coffees before she parked at this far end, and she put enough alprazolam in Naomi's to ensure she'd sleep for hours. When the drug had taken effect, she took Naomi's phone and put her on the back seat of the car, covered with a blanket. She tucked the car in beside that deserted shed across the way, then she threw Naomi's phone into the river and caught a cab back to Belsize Park.'

Toni caught his arm. 'Wait a minute. Let me make sure I've got all that and steel myself again for the next bit.'

He sat watching the river with her. A couple of gulls screamed and wheeled overhead, probably waiting to see if they had food. The sun slid between high arcs of cloud, warming them in between puffs of breeze.

'Okay, go on.'

'Jerome had mentioned that Sam's car was out of action and he was using his bike. That suited Chloe — the bike would be quicker if traffic was bad and easier than a car to push into the river. She was waiting for Sam by the back gate when he got home, and she told him that Conor was in a bad way. He'd gone to somewhere in Docklands in great distress and he'd called Jerome and was pleading for he and Sam to go and talk to him. Jerome was on his way there. Chloe urged Sam to go with her immediately and they left straight away.' He checked Toni. 'You okay?'

'Yes.'

'When they reached the wharf, Chloe directed Sam here, near the steps. They couldn't see the others and Chloe said she'd ring Jerome. She gave Sam coffee from a flask in her bag, saying she'd brought some with a drop of whisky. It contained sedative and she pretended to ring Jerome while Sam drank it. He soon slumped over the handlebars. She took his phone and sent that suicide text, then put it back in his pocket. Then she brought her car over here by the steps. Naomi was still deeply asleep. Chloe pulled her into the side-car and then pushed the bike down the steps into the river. She was lucky that nobody saw her, but this is a deserted area. It'd be quiet in the evening. She drove home before Jerome came back from work. He thought she'd been in all evening, but in fact she'd hired a sitter from an agency for Jed.'

Toni pulled her collar up. 'It's hard to believe that a respectable family woman like Chloe could kill two people. She was like a pillar of society.'

'Fear tends to override respectability. And the way Chloe saw it, her and Jerome's social status and lives' work were going to be seriously threatened if one of Spring's employees was prosecuted for theft from people who'd been the firm's clients.'

Toni's phone rang. She answered and listened intently. 'Do you mind if I put you on speaker? I'm with Ty Swift and I'd like him to hear this too. Okay, great.' She mouthed to Swift, *It's Sergeant Delamare.* She switched to speaker and held the phone between them. 'We can both hear you now.'

'Right, yep,' came Delamare's voice. 'So, as I was starting to explain, Araminta Leadsom came out of sedation last night. She named Conor Wallace as her attacker. We've interviewed him again and he's now been charged with attempted murder.'

'How did he find out what Araminta was doing?' asked Toni.

'He'd stopped at Ms Leadsom's desk to check some appointments late that afternoon, after her conversation with Mr Swift. She'd already started searching previous clients on her computer. Wallace noticed that she'd highlighted several of the names targeted by him and Mila Fullbright. When he asked about the information on screen, Ms Leadsom unwisely commented that someone had phoned and queried an investment.'

Swift groaned. 'I thought I'd primed her not to reveal anything.'

'He caught her unawares,' Delamare said. 'Wallace went off to his desk and worried. He decided that it couldn't be a coincidence and suspected that you, Mr Swift, were probably the "someone". He got angry because the forged note he'd put on Ms French's desk for you hadn't worked. He left, waited in a pub nearby and returned to the building around quarter past seven. He observed Ms Leadsom at her computer and made sure that no one else was working late. While Ms Leadsom made tea in the kitchen, he checked her computer and saw that she'd compiled the exact same list as Sam had handed to Lucy Wallace. He quickly deleted it, not aware that Ms Leadsom had already emailed it to Mr Swift, and then went to the top floor. When Ms Leadsom responded to his calling her name, he dragged her to the edge of the roof garden and pushed her over.'

'Did he say why he and Mila Fullbright were still meeting in Sam's house?' Swift asked.

'They're both saying there was no affair, it was a money-based partnership. Mila didn't want to stop the fraud, couldn't see any reason to now that no one was going to ask questions. Wallace could back off if he wanted and it would leave more for her. So he was meeting her at the house now and again, trying to persuade her to give it up. He was worried in case she'd make errors working solo and arouse suspicion. The trail might eventually lead to him.'

'I'm glad that he was suffering. I hope he didn't get a wink's sleep,' Toni said fiercely.

'He certainly isn't now,' Delamare assured her. 'Wallace fretted as well that Chloe Adcott might somehow find out and go after him because he'd broken their agreement. Once a private investigator was involved, Wallace was even keener for Ms Fullbright to stop. Mr Goddard's house was a handy place to meet and Wallace felt safe there. He'd lied to his wife and assured her that all the fraudulent activity was over. He assumed she'd never get wind of him meeting Ms Fullbright in Belsize Park.'

'Lucy must have known about Chloe, mustn't she?' said Toni. 'When she heard where Sam and Naomi had died, she'd have remembered that she'd discussed this area with her.'

'She'll be charged with being an accessory after the fact where the fraud's concerned,' Delamare said. 'It's trickier with the murders. She's said that she didn't remember conversations about the Docklands area after the deaths. Regarding Chloe's comment that she'd saved the Wallaces' skin, Lucy insists that she took that to mean that Chloe was keeping the fraud quiet, and ensuring Conor stopped his activity and left Spring. It'd be hard to prove otherwise, frankly.'

Swift asked, 'How is Ms Leadsom?'

'She's doing okay. On the mend, but I'd guess she has a hill to climb.'

When Delamare rang off, Toni stood and swung her arms.

Swift finished his almost cold drink. 'Ready to go back?'

'In a minute. I had a note from the Ludlows this morning. Brief and formal. A thank you for what I'd done.'

Swift got up, shaking his head. 'They'll have been hearing astonishing things about their daughter. I suppose one less liaison with an older man is some relief.' He hoped that Dean would be able to weather his parents' turmoil. He'd have Yuna's support. She'd no doubt counsel him that it was best that it was all out in the open, with his parents expressing their emotions.

'I guess. Poor family. Poor Jerome and Jed. How will they cope?'

'People do manage somehow.'

'As I've been finding out. Lexie's asked me to stay with her for a couple of days. I'll say yes. It's all been a bit full-on.' She turned to him. 'Thanks, Ty. Thanks for letting Sam rest in peace.'

'I'm just sorry that you lost him and the life you should have had together, motoring on Bonnie with your flask and sandwiches.'

'Yes. All the joy that should have been.' Toni blew a kiss at the water. 'Bye, Sam.'

They turned their backs to the river and walked to the station.

* * *

Swift waited outside the doors of the high-dependency ward in the hospital. Araminta was only allowed one visitor at a time and Jerome Adcott was with her. While he sat on the bench, he reflected on the events of the last weeks, tying up loose ends. Wallace had been clever at misdirection. Apart from the forged note, he'd added confusion with his lie that Sam Goddard had expressed doubts about marrying again. And his wife almost matched him in betrayal. How could Lucy have joined him in pressuring Toni over the house, given what she must have suspected about Chloe Adcott? What a pair they were. When Toni had time to fully digest all of this and her anger abated, she'd undoubtedly suffer all over again. Luckily, she had Lexie to rely on. Lexie had turned the air blue when she'd heard about the Wallaces, and had spoken of strangling them both with her bare hands.

Swift stood as Jerome Adcott came out. There was no sign of the fit man who did triathlons. His shoulders slumped and his face sagged. When he saw Swift, he winced, but stopped and said hello.

'I'm sorry,' Swift said simply.

'How could this happen? How could Chloe do such a thing?'

'Only Chloe can say, really.'

'Yes. I realise that you did what you had to do. But I never want to see you again.'

'Understood.'

Adcott stepped away, then hesitated. 'I've offered Hester her job back. Least I could do. She accepted.' He walked to the lift as if lead weights were attached to his feet.

That was one guilt item off Swift's list. Now for the next one.

The door buzzed and a nurse peered through. 'Ms Leadsom says you can come in. No more than ten minutes.'

Swift approached the bed where Araminta was propped up on pillows, attached to a drip. She smiled weakly. With no shield of make-up and loose hair, she appeared softer, much younger.

'I expected that you'd refuse to see me,' Swift said. 'I didn't bring flowers in case you'd throw them at me.'

There was a flicker of the bossy Araminta. 'Sit down.'

He did as he was told. She took a sip of water through a straw.

'I am so sorry,' Swift told her.

She shifted her head slightly. 'No need. Glad you did it. Did the right thing.'

'That's generous, Araminta. I appreciate it. Jerome's going to need you.'

'Yep. Got to get back on my feet, back at Spring.' Her eyes flashed. 'Want to be at the trials. Watch justice.'

'Good to have goals to work towards,' Swift smiled. 'Jerome told me he's reinstating Hester.'

'Right thing. Excellent worker until you turned up.' She sipped more water, moving her arm carefully. 'How's Toni?'

'Shocked. Sad. Relieved.'

'Tell her she can visit if she wants. Like to see her.'

'I will.' Araminta's eyes were growing dull. 'I'll go now. I won't come back, bothering you.'

She raised a finger and beckoned him. He leaned forward. Part of him still expected a chilly rebuff.

'My friends call me Ama,' she said, and closed her eyes.

His guilt load lifted, Swift's stomach was telling him that he needed lunch. He stopped at a Portuguese café near the hospital and ordered *Sopa da Pedra*. He drank a beer while he waited and read an email from Mary.

After intense, behind-the-scenes diplomatic discussions, Joyce is going to attend Ruth's wedding and she'll take Louis. Simone and I pleaded prior engagement. This solution has gone down well on all fronts. Minefield successfully negotiated. Phew.

He replied, thanking her. He just wanted Ruth to marry and have it all done and dusted. Then he could navigate the future with Branna as best he could.

The soup was thick, meaty and delicious. It would keep him going until tonight, when Faith and Eli had invited him for a meal at her flat. That would be an interesting, if cramped experience. Eli was going to cook. Swift was glad he was now wreaking havoc in someone else's kitchen. He hoped those two would work out. They'd both experienced tough, challenging times. Order and harmony from chaos. It did happen sometimes.

When he'd finished his meal, he ordered coffee. The sun was warming his face through the window and he leaned back, enjoying its rays. Despite the food and sunshine, he felt exhausted, bleak. The investigation had been particularly nasty, exposing so much betrayal and viciousness in a group of supposed friends. Four children had been left in a terrible limbo, facing the legacy of criminal parents. The scars would last for years, maybe even generations. Then there was Naomi, who had certainly been confused and tricky, but she'd been just a young girl whose future had been snatched away. If she'd had a chance to mature, maybe she'd have harnessed that wayward intelligence and turned into someone extraordinary.

The smooth, strong coffee boosted him, shook him from his depressing notions. The wonders and comfort of caffeine.

He had no immediate commitments and Branna wasn't staying with him for another week. His mind turned to Wales. He could take his boat and explore the River Nevern in Pembrokeshire. A scruffy detective with an endearing habit of wriggling her eyebrows lived not far from it. The worst-case scenario was that she'd ignore him or turn him down. If so, he could handle that and continue rowing.

He sent a text to Sofia Weber's number.

Hello and hope all is well. I'll be taking a break on the Nevern with my boat in the next few days. Would you like to have lunch somewhere near you this weekend?

All the best, Ty.

He put his phone beside his saucer and drank his coffee, pretending that he wasn't waiting for a reply.

THE END

ALSO BY GRETTA MULROONEY

THE TYRONE SWIFT DETECTIVE SERIES
Book 1: THE LADY VANISHED
Book 2: BLOOD SECRETS
Book 3: TWO LOVERS, SIX DEATHS
Book 4: WATCHING YOU
Book 5: LOW LAKE
Book 6: YOUR LAST LIE
Book 7: HER LOST SISTER
Book 8: MURDER IN PEMBROKESHIRE
Book 9: DEATH BY THE THAMES

**DETECTIVE INSPECTOR SIV DRUMMOND
SERIES**
Book 1: THESE LITTLE LIES
Book 2: NEVER CAME HOME
Book 3: MURDER IN MALLOW COTTAGE

STANDALONE NOVELS
OUT OF THE BLUE
LOST CHILD
COMING OF AGE

Thank you for reading this book.

If you enjoyed it please leave feedback on Amazon or Goodreads, and if there is anything we missed or you have a question about, then please get in touch. We appreciate you choosing our book.

Founded in 2014 in Shoreditch, London, we at Joffe Books pride ourselves on our history of innovative publishing. We were thrilled to be shortlisted for Independent Publisher of the Year at the British Book Awards.

www.joffebooks.com

We're very grateful to eagle-eyed readers who take the time to contact us. Please send any errors you find to corrections@joffebooks.com. We'll get them fixed ASAP.

Made in the USA
Las Vegas, NV
18 March 2022

45917093R00166